THE JAGGED LINE

CAROLYN MAHONY

To my family, friends and beta-readers – you know who you are!
Your support and feedback have been invaluable. I'd have given up
years ago if it hadn't been for all of you!

PROLOGUE

The vehicle ploughing into the back of his van seemed to come from nowhere – the impact of it shooting him forward, causing the engine to splutter and stall. For a moment, he sat there shocked, clutching ribs that were already painful.

Before he had time to take stock of what was happening, the door was flung open, his seat belt unclipped, and he found himself being dragged out into the cold night air.

He fought as hard as his bruised ribs would allow, his eyes fixing desperately on the illuminated police station up ahead of him. But when he felt the sharp edge of a knife pressing tightly into his neck, his struggles came to an abrupt stop.

'You need to calm down, mate, or this is gonna get messy.'

The words breathed into his ear sent a chill through his veins. He had no doubt the man meant what he said, as he found himself being dragged towards the dark car behind them.

He had just enough time to cast a last, frantic look in the direction of the police station, before he was tossed head first into the back of the car, and felt the lurch as it sped off.

'Hello, Paul.'

He froze at the sound of that voice. The dark shape was turned away from him, staring out of the window, but he knew exactly who it was.

His eyes widened in terror. *He needed to get out of there.*

He heaved himself up to a sitting position and swung towards the rear passenger door, but found his assailant was blocking his escape.

'It seems you didn't learn your lesson from earlier on,' the voice continued smoothly.

Sweat trickled down the back of his neck.

'And when I saw you heading for the police station ... well, we can't have that, can we? You're going to wish you hadn't done that tonight. You really are...'

CHAPTER ONE

Kirsty Cartwright packed her lunch box away and stood up on the sandy beach, flicking the sand off her dress. She gazed out to sea just one more time, enjoying the feel of the cool October breeze as it blew wisps of fair hair across her cheeks. It was a daily indulgence that the weather would soon be putting an end to, but she'd come to value this hour to herself every day. It was a chance to sit back and take stock if she wanted to, or simply drink in the rather indulgent ambience of La Rochelle.

Today, though, her expression was tense and her thoughts were more focused than usual. The day of her return to the UK was drawing ever nearer, and it wasn't a trip she looked forward to. In fact she was even debating making her excuses and ducking out of it. Would she even be missed? She hadn't seen her family in nearly a year – admittedly her choice not theirs – and she wasn't sure she was ready for this enforced visit. The inevitable questions from her mother and brother – the uneasy truce with her father. How much simpler life was without the mixed emotions their presence induced. Already the negative feelings she'd managed to put behind her these last few months were wheedling their way back into her consciousness.

But it was her cousin Rachael's wedding and they'd all be expecting her. And how could she let Rachael down? Rachael – who, unwittingly, was the reason for Kirsty's self-imposed banishment?

'Ah, it is only for a few days, chérie,' Jean-Pierre had said last night in his thick French accent. 'It is not so long – and you will have me there to hold your hand if you need it.'

She'd smiled at him, wondering if he realised how much he'd saved her from going into a complete decline these past months.

'I know that and you're a star, Jean-Pierre. I don't think I'd have managed without you.'

He'd given his typical Gallic shrug. 'Of course you would. I have done nothing except give you a job and some space in which to heal. Are you worried about seeing Luke at the wedding?'

Kirsty shook her head, suppressing her guilt that she hadn't given him the full story. But it was far simpler that everyone thought she was nurturing a broken heart – which she was.

'Luke and I are over,' she said. 'I've accepted that because I know that what I did is the one thing he can never forgive. It's my own fault.'

'I think I will not find it easy keeping my opinions to myself when I meet him at this wedding,' Jean-Pierre had responded severely. 'Everyone deserves a second chance, but …' He'd forestalled her interruption with a grin. 'For you I will do my best.'

Now, as she stared out over the water, her mind took one of those wayward turns she'd banned herself from taking, as she allowed herself to dwell briefly on Luke. Of course they were over. She'd seen to that. But it would be hard seeing him again. Had he met anyone else?

She sighed, remembering that memories hurt, which was why she'd banned them. But it was too late now. Luke's thick, dark hair, his easy smile and deep brown eyes, that could be both sharply intelligent and so heart-meltingly tender, were etched indelibly in her mind – the memory of his occasional uninhibited roar of laughter almost bouncing off the waves that lapped gently at the shore. She smiled, remembering when they'd first hitched up in the sixth form. They'd been the best of friends throughout their school years … sharing, laughing, talking into the early hours as you did at that age – but when the sexual attraction had kicked in, it had blown them away. The sheer intensity of it. They'd grabbed those precious moments together whenever they could, the depth of their feelings given freedom to soar because of the implicit trust they already had in each other.

A trust she had completely destroyed.

She sighed. She had no right to be angry with him, she knew that, but that didn't mean she understood how he could cut himself off from her so completely when they'd managed to defy all the odds of separate universities and enforced separations. Had he suffered half the heartache she had? Though it probably wasn't very charitable to think it, she hoped so … surely the destruction of their relationship merited at least a *bit* of heartache on his side.

She turned away from the shoreline and started to make her way slowly back up the beach. She'd go back for the wedding … of course she would. But her return could unleash a host of events that might gather speed at an alarming rate.

And where that would end was anyone's guess.

CHAPTER TWO

Detective Sergeant Harry Briscombe walked rapidly through the drab entrance to police HQ and thought, not for the first time, that this building was beginning to feel more like home to him these days than his own flat did. It was hardly surprising, bearing in mind the hours he put in, but it didn't take a therapist to tell him that it probably wasn't a good thing.

'Morning, Amy,' he called to the duty officer on the reception desk. 'Anything interesting come in overnight?'

She shook her head. 'Nothing you'd want to bother yourself with, but I think Geoff put something on your desk after you'd gone last night that you might want to take a look at. You're in early.'

'Yeah … impressive if anyone was around to see it.'

She grinned. 'You're right. You're first in. You need to get a life, Harry.'

'Tell me about it. Catch you later.'

Up in the whitewashed, open-plan office, where he was lucky enough to have been given a prime position by one of the windows overlooking the car park, he poured himself a coffee, determined to make the most of the peace and quiet he knew wouldn't last.

In the next half-hour the room would fill up with all the different members of their team, and it would be transformed from the blissful refuge it was at the moment into the driving thrum of the Beds & Herts Major Crime Unit.

He flicked through a couple of reports on his desk, but his mind wasn't on the job.

He sighed, running an irritable hand through his thick, sandy-coloured hair. Life's path was made up of many forks along the way, everyone knew that. So the fact that he was facing one now didn't make him unique – but it *was* costing him sleepless nights. He needed to make his decision – he was only putting off the inevitable. So what was he dithering for?

He knew the answer to that of course, because once he made his decision, he'd be locked into it – and then he'd be faced with a stand-off he wasn't sure he could handle.

He turned his attention back to the report in his hand and read the brief, the title spiking his interest. *Possible Kidnapping.*

Some woman claimed to have witnessed a man being dragged out of his van and thrown into a car. Someone else had then apparently jumped into the van and driven off in it. And it had happened last night on the road outside this very building. Murray wouldn't be happy about that.

No registration number of course and no descriptions worthy of merit – nothing to get his teeth into. He tossed the form into his Thinking About It basket. What the hell were they supposed to do with that, other than wait and see if a missing persons report came in?

He looked up as the newest and youngest member of their team, Detective Constable Bethany Macaskill, approached his desk.

She wasn't your typical DC and he couldn't help wondering

what DCI Murray would make of the razor-short, auburn hair that stuck up in vibrant, gelled spikes.

What she lacked in stylish hair, though, she more than made up for in enthusiasm and, although she'd only been with them a week, he was already impressed by her attitude and the attention she paid to detail. Those were qualities you were either born with or you weren't, and they were an absolute necessity in this job. He had no doubt she was going to be a good addition to the team.

'Morning, Beth. You're as sad as I am coming in this early – or maybe you never got to bed last night after meeting up with your friends?'

She grinned. 'I wish. Even I'm too old for all that now. I need my sleep.'

There was an air of suppressed excitement about her as she waved a piece of paper in the air. 'We've just had a call from a member of the public... There's been a body found at a place called …' she scanned her handwritten note … 'Gobions, in Brookmans Park?'

Harry briefly scanned her notes, then jumped up from his desk. Related to the kidnapping maybe? Was that too easy? Experience taught him it probably was.

'I know it. Want to come with me?'

'You bet. I'll just go fetch my jacket: it's freezing out.'

He liked the soft lilt of her Northumberland accent – not quite English, not quite Scottish – and he smiled at the thought that again it was somehow at odds with the spiky hair.

She headed towards the row of pegs on the far wall and Harry grabbed his own well-worn, brown leather jacket from the back of his chair. 'I'd have thought you'd be used to the cold, coming from Northumberland?'

She laughed. 'Yeah, well, that was a while back now. I've gone soft over the years.'

When they arrived at Gobions Park, the car park had

already been sealed off and apart from police and a couple of other vehicles, it was pretty empty. In the distance, across the heavily dewed grassed, he could see signs of activity.

'Looks like it's all happening over there,' Beth said, following the direction of his gaze.

'By the lake, then. I know this area like the back of my hand. My mates and I used to hang out here all the time when I was younger.'

Beth looked around at the large, detached houses surrounding the open space and raised an eyebrow. 'You're one of the posh boys, then, living round here…'

Harry shook his head. 'Oh no. I didn't live round here. I lived in Enfield.'

'You sound posh, though.'

He shrugged. 'That's what boarding school does for you. My father's an archaeologist, so my parents spent a lot of time travelling around. That's why I lived in Enfield – with my grandparents.'

She looked surprised. 'Do you still live with them?'

'No … although that could be about to change. My grandfather died several years back so my gran's alone now – and not well. I might need to move back in for a while.'

The thought of his grandmother reminded him of his current dilemma and he knew he couldn't put things off much longer.

He unclipped his seat belt and opened the door. 'Come on … you ready for this? Let's go see what they've got.'

The area by the lake had been sealed off and SOCO were already there.

'Alright if we take a look?' Harry asked one of the duty policemen, as he approached.

'Yup. Forensics are already here.'

He handed them a couple of white cover-ups for their

clothes and shoes and waited until they'd donned them before lifting the tape.

It was Edwards who was painstakingly examining the remains and Harry was glad. He was one of the more cooperative pathologists they dealt with, and knew his stuff. With a bit of luck he'd give them something to start on while they were waiting for the full results to come back.

'Give me a couple more minutes, Harry, will you?' the pathologist said.

'Sure.'

Harry watched as Edwards removed what looked like a couple of twigs from a gruesome stomach wound, and slipped them into sample bags. While he was waiting he made his own observations. The man was probably a year or two older than him, mid-thirties maybe, and shorter than Harry's six feet, with a sizeable beer gut on him – he clearly hadn't seen the inside of a gym in a while. His hair was receding at the front, but what hair he did have was brown and wispy. His face, which was bruised and swollen, was covered in muck, as were his clothes, indicating that he'd probably been lying face-down in the mud before being turned over. There was a large patch of red that had seeped through his pale grey T-shirt, indicative of the stomach wound that was clearly visible. Harry could see no evidence of any weapon. It looked like the man had been beaten before being stabbed and left here.

He looked at Beth. 'You okay?'

She nodded. 'Yeah, I'm just not looking too closely.'

'You'll get used to it. You have to if you want to be any good. No room for squeamishness in this job.'

He smiled at her, knowing she'd take his words on-board.

'Right,' Edwards said, straightening up. 'I've still got a way to go before I let the body be moved, but what I can tell you is that he's a male Caucasian, early to mid-thirties probably, who's been badly beaten, stabbed and dumped here within the last four to five hours, I'd guess. I suspect that cause of death was the stab wound to the stomach, but I'll confirm that after I've done the PM. No ID or wallet.'

'So that would be some time after four o'clock this morning he was brought here. How can you be so sure?'

'Because his clothes and hair are dry. And up until about four o'clock this morning it was chucking it down.'

'No personal effects at all on him? Mobile phone?'

'No.'

'And when you say 'dumped' – was he killed here do you reckon, or brought here afterwards?'

'I'll have to check a few things out to be sure but my guess is the latter. For a start there aren't any signs of a fight in the surrounding area, and his shoes aren't muddy, indicating that he didn't walk here. And if my calculations are right about the amount of time he's been lying here, then that wouldn't fit with my provisional estimation of time of death, which I'd put at somewhere between eight and eleven o'clock last night. That'll need confirming of course.'

He turned to another smaller area near the body that had been marked off with tape. 'One benefit of the ground being so wet … we've recovered a couple of partial footprints here, which could be relevant. We may be able to match them up if you get a suspect. Trainers I'd guess, by the look of them.'

'That could come in useful. Anything else?'

The pathologist looked back down at the body. 'Only that he was given a bloody good pasting before they killed him, poor bugger, and he'd have been in a lot of pain from that. Someone's used him as a real punchbag.'

'Right.' Harry looked around, taking in the relatively undamaged scene around the body. Edwards was right. It didn't look like a fight had taken place here – though SOCO would do a thorough search of the surrounding area to confirm that – and the man had literally been dumped in the middle of a pathway where someone was bound to have found him sooner rather than later. Was that symbolic … some sort of warning to others, perhaps?

He snapped his notebook shut and pulled out his phone. 'Mind if I take a couple of photos with this? It'll give me something to start the incident board off with when I get back.'

'Be my guest.'

'Thanks. Murray's off at the moment, due back tomorrow, so if you've got anything for us before then, send it through to me, will you?'

'Sure.'

Harry took the photos then looked about him. 'Is the person who found him still here?'

'Talking to the WPC over there.'

Harry wandered over through the group of SOCOs to where a middle-aged woman was being comforted by the WPC.

'Hi, Jo.'

'Harry.' Jo gave him a thin smile, confirming what he already knew, that she still blamed him for pushing her into ending their relationship six months back because of his commitment issues.

'Your trouble is, Harry, you keep everyone at a distance. You don't let anyone get too close and that doesn't work in a relationship. You need to give as well as take.'

He guessed it was true because she wasn't the first to have said it or the first to end their relationship because of it. But he didn't understand it any more than they did and sometimes he wondered if, as a theory, it wasn't somewhat overblown. Maybe he just hadn't met the right woman yet?

Either way, the end result was the same. Each time it happened it tended to put him off taking those first steps into a new relationship again.

'This is Mrs Engel,' Jo said now. 'She came across the body this morning, when she was walking her dog.'

'Did you know the man?' Harry asked the middle-aged woman, noting her pallor.

She shook her head.

'Is his face familiar at all? Could he have been one of the regular dog walkers round here, for example?'

Another shake of the head. 'I'd know if he was.'

She dabbed at her eyes with a tissue. 'I was just walking the dog like I always do and saw him lying there right in front of me. Twinkie ran over and wouldn't come away. I had to go right up close to get her back. It was horrible.'

'I'm sorry you were put through that,' Harry said, glancing at the tiny, rat-like dog at her feet. He instantly dismissed the theory that the person who found the body should be high on the list of suspects. Anyone who could call their dog Twinkie …

He turned to Jo. 'Have we got a statement from Mrs Engel?'

She nodded, and he turned back to the woman. 'Is there someone at home? Or someone you can call?'

'I'm a widow but I'll call my friend when I get back. She'll come over.'

'Good. Then I don't think we need to keep you any longer. Are you okay to drive home?'

'I can walk back. I only live over there. My back gate opens onto the park.'

'Well, I'm sure DC Evans here will see you home. We'll be in touch if we need to talk to you again.'

Turning around, he made his way back to where a thorough search of the undergrowth near the body was already underway.

'Found anything?' he asked one of the SOCOs.

'Nothing so far. Whoever did it was a pro if you ask me. But we'll keep looking.'

'Let me know if you find anything.'

Harry and Beth trudged back across the wet grass to their car and removed their temporary clothing.

'If he was killed somewhere else and then dumped here, why leave him where he's so easily going to be found?' Beth asked. 'It doesn't look like they even tried to conceal the body, does it?'

Harry shook his head, impressed that she'd picked up on the same thought he had.

'Good question. See if you can come up with an answer to it. Are you ready for some door-to-doors? Everyone whose garden backs onto here will need to be questioned to see if they saw or heard anything suspicious during the early hours. I'll come back tomorrow morning, too – see if any of the regular dog walkers saw anything.'

Beth looked around. 'That's quite a few houses.'

'Yeah, but look at the style of them – you'll get to see how the other half live. Just be aware that any one of them could hold the murderer, though, so anything suspicious, you let me know straight away.'

She shot him a look. 'You're making me nervous now.'

Harry's lip curved. 'Don't worry. It's unlikely anyone's going to do you in when the place is crawling with cops. We'll do the first house together and after that you're on your own. I'll phone Geoff Peterson, get him down here to give you a hand while I get things rolling back at the station.'

It wasn't much of an incident board, he was forced to acknowledge a couple of hours later, once he'd pinned his pictures and what few bits of information he had onto the wallchart – but it was a start. And that was what really fired him about the work he did. It started off as a few scrappy pieces of paper that grew in front of your eyes, to a shitload of photos, information, clues and leads – each one going off on its own tangent, each one needing to be followed up with precision and care in case you missed something crucial. He'd always been a bit nerdy at school – probably not totally unrelated to the fact that his father was an archaeologist – and he thrived on the minutiae of a case, watching as the information built, sifting through the debris to find the pearls. He'd known from the age of ten that this was what he wanted to do. His parents had had reservations about his choice of career when he'd informed them, but not his gran. He smiled to himself as he remembered how fiercely she'd supported him. But then she'd brought him up and his decision had come as no surprise to her.

He studied the rather harrowing pictures of the unknown man on the information board. Had he woken up yesterday morning knowing he was in danger, or had his life started perfectly normally and then been snatched away from him on a quirk of fate? It was a question that always intrigued him, but he supposed it didn't really matter as far as the victim was concerned. Dead was dead – a life cut brutally short whichever way you looked at it. It never failed to strike Harry how tenuous life was, and somewhere out there, there were people who cared about this man. It was a visit he never relished making.

His phone rang as he was still studying the picture.

'Ah, Harry. Great.' It was Amy, on duty on the front desk. 'There's a lady here wants to report a dodgy bloke who she reckons was following her last night after she left the pub. She says he tried to get her to go for a drink with him and was aggressive when she said no. Can you come down and deal with her? Geoff's not around – he's still doing the door-to-doors.'

'On my way,' Harry said, hanging up his phone and heading for the door. He wondered what separated aggressive from pissed off. Most men probably had tendencies towards being pissed off if they felt they'd plucked up their courage to make a move on a girl and she subsequently turned them down. But true aggression was a different kettle of fish, as he'd seen only too often – and there'd been a couple of attacks on women in the last year that were still on file. Couldn't afford to be complacent.

CHAPTER THREE

At seven o'clock sharp the next morning, Harry swung into the Gobions car park and parked his car. He'd come better prepared this morning, donning a thick scarf and solid walking boots, before heading off across the wet grass to meet the local dog walkers. He wasn't really surprised to find that none of them had seen anything unusual the previous day, though several of them looked alarmed at the thought of a possible murderer stalking their well-trodden paths.

'I hope you're putting someone on watch out here to protect the public,' one coiffed, white-haired lady said, looking somewhat incongruous in her Barbour jacket and thick wellington boots. 'One doesn't feel safe knowing there are criminals like that wandering around. I mean, it could be anyone, couldn't it? Even someone I see here every day.'

Glancing around at the rather motley selection of people walking their dogs, Harry thought that was unlikely, but he knew better than to ridicule the woman's fears.

'We don't believe that's necessary at this point in time, but don't worry, we're keeping an eye on things. I'm sure you're quite safe.'

'Well, I hope for your sake you're right, young man,' the woman sniffed.

Traffic was light going into the station, so despite hanging around for a few of the later park frequenters, it still wasn't late when Harry got into work. He glanced into DCI Murray's office as he removed his jacket, and saw that his boss was back from leave and, true to form, already stuck into wads of paperwork.

He beckoned Harry through the glass partition. Beth was in there looking terrified.

'Our new DC here's been filling me in on what's gone on in my absence,' Murray said briskly, as Harry entered the office. 'She also happens to make a very good cup of coffee. Your job could be under threat, Harry.'

Harry grinned, his eyes flashing to Beth. Thank God she didn't seem to be the sort to take offence easily over women's lib issues. Her expression was relieved as their eyes met.

'I was just telling DCI Murray that we might have a possible ID on the body found at Gobions yesterday,' she said. 'A woman phoned in this morning reporting her boyfriend missing since Monday. She says they had a bit of a row, so when he didn't come home that night and yesterday, she thought he was still sulking. But when she still didn't hear from him last night, she began to get worried.'

'Where does she live?' Murray asked.

'Barnet. She said she'll be there if we want to go over. She's not going into work today. She's too worried.'

'You'd better get over there, Harry. See if she can ID him.'

Harry looked at him in surprise. 'You not coming?'

DCI Murray shook his head. 'No. It's always the same after a break. Nice to have it for the fact it earns me a few Brownie points at home ... but then I come back to this lot and wonder if it was worth it.' He waved his hand at the overspilling in-tray. 'Take PC Macaskill with you instead – what's your name, by the way?'

'Beth.'

'Right. Take Beth. If it is him, the girlfriend might need a bit of TLC.'

Harry pulled up outside the rather dilapidated house in Myton Road, Barnet, and looked around him. The road was typical of its kind – large, semi-detached dwellings built quite close to each other with small front gardens. Most of them had been renovated and converted into upmarket flats, but No. 28, though it may well have been converted, clearly didn't fit into the renovated category if its exterior appearance was anything to go by. There was a large 'Let By' board in the corner of the front garden.

He and Beth exited the car.

'Her name's Susan Porter,' she whispered as he rang the doorbell.

The door was answered by a pretty, dark-haired young woman, who surveyed them anxiously as they showed her their cards.

'Have you got some news?'

'Is it alright if we come in for a minute? Talk to you inside?'

In the house Harry wasted no time pulling out the photo of the man in the morgue.

'I'm sorry, Miss Porter, but from the physical description you gave of your boyfriend, I'm afraid it's possible we may have some bad news for you. Would you like to sit down?'

'Just tell me.'

'A man's body was found in Brookmans Park early yesterday morning, but we had no means of identifying him. He had no wallet or papers on him to help us with that.'

He hesitated, but she was already holding her hand out for the photo in his hand. 'Show me,' she said abruptly.

He passed it to her. 'It's not a very nice picture but it's all we've got, I'm afraid.'

She looked at it, then gasped, her hand flying to her mouth. 'Oh my God. Yeah, that's him, but … his face … What happened to him?'

'I'm afraid he was beaten up. We're still waiting for Forensics to confirm exactly what happened.'

She looked as if she was about to pass out and Beth stepped forward, placing an arm around her shoulder and guiding her gently to one of the armchairs.

'You're alright. Just you sit yourself down here. Can I make you a cup of tea or coffee?'

The woman shook her head, turning frightened eyes to Harry. 'What happened? Was it a fight? Who'd wanna hurt him? I can't believe it.'

'He didn't have any enemies that you knew of?'

'No.'

'What work did he do?'

'Decorating, odd jobs – anything he could get his hands on. Money's short at the moment, especially now social's cut our benefits. He took whatever he could.'

'And what about you?'

'I do shift work at the Pizza Bar. Should've been in today – but I knew summat was wrong. I just did.'

'When did you last see your boyfriend?'

'Monday morning.'

'I understand you had words?'

She shrugged and went quiet for a moment. 'It weren't nothing serious – just a silly row, and when he didn't come home Monday night I thought he was still pissed off and had stayed at his mum's. But when he didn't ring me all day yesterday and didn't come back last night … I began to worry, you know? We've never gone that long without being in touch, not even when we rowed. So I phoned his mum and she said she hadn't seen him either. That's when I phoned your lot.'

'Do you mind telling me what your argument was about?'

Tears welled up in her eyes. 'I hardly even remember now. It was to do with the flat. He was bangin' on about buying somewhere and I said who did he think he was kidding – we didn't have that sort of money. He got arsey about it – told me I didn't know everything, and stomped out.'

'And you have no idea where he might have gone?'

She seemed to give it some thought and when after a few moments she still hadn't said anything, Harry looked at her keenly.

'If there's anything you can tell me, Susan, that you think might help us find whoever did this to him?'

She shook her head. 'He told me he was meeting someone that morning, but I don't know who and I don't know where he went after that. He hasn't got any jobs on at the moment, see, so I don't always know where he is. Do you mind…?' She pulled a pack of cigarettes out of her bag and lit one with shaky fingers. She took a deep drag and exhaled, staring at the cigarette in her fingers almost resentfully. 'No need for me to give these up now, I suppose – I were only doing it for him.'

Harry pulled out a card and scribbled something onto it. He'd done enough interviews to know they wouldn't be getting any more mileage out of Susan Porter at this point in time. Better to give her some space to come to terms with everything and see her again when she'd had a bit more time to think. 'This is my card, and I've written my colleague's name on it as well. If you remember anything or want to talk to us, just call and one of us will get back to you. I'm sorry about your boyfriend but we'll do our best to find whoever did this. Do you have anyone you'd like us to call for you?'

She shook her head and reached for a tissue on the table

with a shaky hand. 'My bruvver'll come. But I'll call him when I'm ready. Don't want to talk to no one at the moment.'

Harry stood. 'Who lives in the upstairs flat? Is anyone there for us to have a quick word with?'

He waited while she blew her nose fiercely.

'They went out about half an hour ago,' she said, her voice more composed. 'You'd know if they was in. Bloody noisy lot. That was part of the reason why Paul and me wanted to move. What with them and the grumpy old bugger next door.'

'Did they know Paul? Might they have seen him on Monday, do you think?'

'Dunno – doubt it, we don't really know 'em. It's a friend of our landlord what lives there. We only ever said 'ello – not our sort.'

'Well, if you do see them, can you tell them the police will be round to interview them? We'll be questioning everyone in the road.'

'Yeah, alright.'

She looked suddenly crestfallen again and Harry exchanged a look with Beth.

'You sure you'll be alright until your brother gets here?' he asked.

She nodded and stood up, crushing her cigarette out in an ashtray. 'I'll be fine. I'll see you out then.'

Back in the car, Harry looked at Beth.

'What did you think?'

'She was genuinely shocked, wasn't she? It must be awful when the police turn up on your doorstep with news like that.'

'Yes. Did you get the impression she was holding back on anything?'

'Don't think so. Did you?'

'Not sure. People don't always give all the information on those first interviews until they've had time to assimilate everything. It's probably worth a second visit at some point.'

He pulled out his notebook and jotted down the phone number on the letting board in the front garden, handing it to Beth.

'Cartwrights. They're in the High Street. Give them a call and tell them we're heading over there, will you? Bit of a long shot but you never know, we might pick up something useful from them.'

Then again they might not, he thought fifteen minutes later, as Dominic Cartwright stared at Harry from across his desk. He was a tall man in his late-fifties, and as he listened to what Harry had to say, it was clear that he was visibly shaken.

'Murdered? Good God.'

'How well did you know him?'

'Not well. He paid his rent on time, didn't give us any aggravation. We only heard from him if there was a problem with the flat or occasionally when he did a bit of decorating work for us.' He shook his head. 'I can't believe it.'

'When did you last see him?'

'He was here a couple of days ago. My son Robert saw him. He said he was thinking of giving notice on the flat.'

Harry looked through the glass partition to the other office, where a younger man was busy talking on the phone. 'Is that your son?'

'Yes. Do you want to talk to him?'

'If he can spare us a couple of minutes?'

Dominic Cartwright moved over to the partition and knocked on the glass, making a beckoning sign to his son. Within a couple of minutes Robert Cartwright was looking as shocked as his father.

'Jesus – that's terrible. When did it happen? I only saw him Monday morning.'

'We reckon that was probably the day he was killed. How was he when you saw him?'

'Fine – apart from the fact he looked like he'd been in a bit of a fight.'

'Oh? His girlfriend didn't mention that when we saw her.'

'Well, it could have been an accident of some sort, I suppose. He had a black eye and a split lip from what I remember. I assumed someone had taken a pop at him.'

'Why did he come to see you?'

'Said they might be looking to move – either another rental or possibly even to buy – asked if we'd do a reference for him. I said yes and told him the terms of his contract for giving notice.'

'Did he seem agitated in any way?'

'Not that I remember. He asked me to let him know if any cheap flats came up. I told him I would and that was it.'

'How well did you know him?'

'I used him a couple of times for the odd bit of decorating when we were pushed, but apart from that I had very little to do with him.'

'What about his girlfriend, Susan?'

'I've met her a couple of times. She seems nice enough, although I remember him once saying she was like a pit bull when she got her teeth into something – usually him.'

He gave a shaky smile. 'But we all say things like that, don't we? He was only kidding around.'

'So no reason you know of why someone might want to hurt him?'

'God, no. He seemed an ordinary chap, a bit rough, but one of our better tenants as far as paying his rent went.'

Harry sighed and stood up to go. 'Well, thanks for your time. We might need to see you again, but in the meantime.' He pulled out another of his cards and passed it over. 'This is my number if anything else comes to mind. Don't hesitate to call me.'

Robert took the card from him. 'I guess I'll need to go and

see his girlfriend. See what she wants to do about the flat. That's not going to be an easy conversation, is it?'

'Might be better if you leave it a day or two, but if she says anything you think might be useful to us…?'

'Sure, I'll let you know.'

He saw Harry and Beth to the door and they took their leave unaware of the man standing watching them on the other side of the street. Once they'd driven off he sauntered across the road and made a study of the houses for sale in the window before walking, as any prospective buyer might, into Cartwrights Estate Agents.

CHAPTER FOUR

K irsty was just leaving Raoul's Boulangerie with a bag full of goodies, when she felt her mobile phone vibrating. She managed to hook it out of her pocket and looked at the caller display. Robbie, her brother. She sighed. When she'd split with Luke he hadn't been there for her as much as she'd have been there for him, and it hurt.

'I'd have thought you, of anyone, would completely get where Luke's coming from,' he'd said, in one of their early conversations.

'I do. I just don't get how he can be so rigid about it.'

'Kirsty, coming from you …'

'I know.'

'You're the worst for seeing things in black and white, you know you are. But we can't all be saints a hundred percent of the time, as you're finding out. Life isn't like that.'

It had infuriated her, mostly because she knew that what he said was true. She *did* have very clear-cut lines on what was acceptable or not – it was those same principles that were responsible for her self-imposed banishment now. But only her father knew the real reason for that, and these days, the fact that she occupied the moral high ground was proving very little consolation.

She put the phone to her ear. 'Hey, Rob ...' she said brightly.

'Kirsty?'

From that one word she could hear the distress in her brother's voice.

'What's up?'

'Jesus. I don't know how to tell you this – there's no easy way. Dad's been involved in an accident. He was hit by a car today.'

Kirsty gasped, stopping dead in her tracks.

'Is he –?'

'It's not looking brilliant. He's in intensive care at Barnet Hospital. He's in a coma.'

'Oh, God ... I must come back.'

'Can you change your flight, do you think?'

'I'm sure I can. But ... what happened?'

'We don't really know. It looks like it was a hit-and-run.'

'No! Is Mum alright?'

'Bearing up. Just get back as soon as you can, will you?'

'I'll get onto it and call you back.'

She was already running towards the office as she snapped the phone off, a desperate prayer tumbling from her lips.

'Please let him be alright. Please don't let him die before I see him ...'

The bounce of the wheels was followed by a squeal of brakes and the roar of the reverse engine thrust as the plane landed smoothly on the runway at Stansted Airport.

Kirsty was up from her seat the minute the plane had stopped, grabbing her carry-on bag from the overhead compartment, making sure she was one of the first passengers off the plane. A relatively short wait at the baggage reclaim, during which she phoned Robbie to let him know she was ready for picking up, and she was heading briskly out to the pick-up area where she knew her brother would be waiting for her.

Outside, the evening was setting in and she wrapped her jacket around her as her eyes scanned the waiting cars.

'Kirsty!'

She followed the sound of the voice along the line of parked cars until she made out the familiar outline of her brother hurrying towards her.

'How is he?' she asked, as they hugged.

'Not good. He's still in intensive care.'

'Oh Rob.'

He relieved her of her suitcase and swung back towards his car. 'Come on. I'll take you straight there.' Kirsty had to half-run to keep up with him. 'What have they said? Is he going to be alright?'

'They don't know. They say it's a waiting game now.'

At the hospital they went straight to the intensive care unit. Their mother was already there and she lifted a tear-stained cheek for Kirsty's embrace, clutching at her hand briefly, before letting it go and returning her gaze to the still form of Dominic Cartwright, lying lifelessly on the bed.

Kirsty's eyes followed the direction of her gaze, absorbing the solid frame, the familiar features … and all the animosity, all the shame, simply dissipated into nothing. This was her father, Dominic Cartwright – a man who, despite what he'd done, had only ever acted out of love for his family. That's what he'd told her and deep down she knew he believed it. It was just that somewhere along the line his scruples had become a little blurred, as had his definition of 'family' – and he hadn't liked it that she'd questioned the moral fabric of what he'd done.

'Running your own company isn't a piece of cake, Kirsty,' he'd admonished severely. 'Sometimes the lines are grey rather than black and white, and you have to make tough decisions. You'll find that out yourself when you come into the business. I've never claimed to be perfect, but I'm telling you now that every decision I make has you, your mother and brother at the heart of it. Remember that before you judge me.'

And when it came to it, after endless soul-searching, she had remembered it – and she'd despised herself for letting him organise a temporary job for her with a friend in France. An opportunity to give her some space, he'd called it.

Running away was how it felt.

But her breakup with Luke had clinched the matter. It was a timely escape from everything.

'I'm glad you're here, Kirsty.'

Her mother didn't even look up as she spoke, but any encouragement Kirsty might have taken from her words was dispelled with her next. 'I just wish you'd come back sooner.'

'Not now, Mum. We just all need to get through this.' It was Robbie who stepped in and Kirsty felt his hand squeeze her shoulder reassuringly. On the way to the hospital he'd told her what little he knew. Their father had carried out a valuation on a house that morning and had then been the victim of a hit-and-run in the road outside.

'Surely someone must have seen something?' Kirsty had said, and her brother had shaken his head.

'Apparently not. The car was a dark colour. That's all they've got. It won't be easy tracking the driver down unless someone comes forward.'

Kirsty looked down at her father. He'd always been so vital, such a forceful, larger-than-life character. It just wasn't conceivable that he might …

They all turned as a doctor approached. 'No signs of returning consciousness yet?'

'No.'

It was her mother who spoke.

The doctor picked up the chart at the foot of the bed and studied it, before replacing it quietly. 'Well, we've made him as comfortable as we can. He has marked swelling to the brain, which we hope will reduce over the next few days, several broken ribs, a broken leg – and a ruptured spleen. We've operated on that but I'm afraid we can't rule out the possibility of further internal bleeding, so we'll need to keep a close eye on him.'

He saw the horror on their faces and was quick to try to reassure them. 'He's in good hands and we'll do our best for him. The most immediate issue we're facing is the brain trauma. It's very difficult to assess how severe that is or how long it might be before he regains consciousness.'

'And what if he doesn't?'

Again it was her mother who asked the question neither Kirsty – nor, she was sure, her brother – could bring themselves to ask.

The doctor's voice was gentle. 'We'll cross that bridge if and when we come to it, shall we? For now, all we can do is watch and wait – and hope that he'll come round fine.'

He looked at his watch. 'Why don't you folk head off home for the night? We'll call you if anything changes. You can come back in the morning anytime you like after eight-thirty.'

They were a sorry bunch, Kirsty thought, as they picked up their bags and headed for the lifts. Outside the intensive care unit, a man and his son sat quietly weeping. Hating herself for even thinking it, she couldn't help wondering if that could be them in the not-too-distant future.

'You go on, I'd like to stay with Dad a bit longer,' she said impulsively to her mother and brother.

'We'll stay with you,' Robbie said.

'No. I'd rather have some time with him alone, if you don't mind?'

'Then we'll wait for you in the canteen,' her mother said in a tired voice. 'I could do with a strong coffee.'

Back in the room, she sat by her father's bedside, took his hand in hers and gently squeezed it.

'Hey, Dad, it's Kirsty. If you can hear me, I'm sorry I've stayed away. I've missed you all.' She hesitated. 'None of what we argued about seems important now. Just get better, that's all that matters. I love you.'

There was no response – no returning pressure of fingers, no flickering of eyelids to reveal the twinkling blue eyes that captivated everyone who stared into them. He could have been a marble statue lying there so still, if it hadn't been for the ugly abrasions and bruising showing through the bandages on his head.

She sat there for another half-hour, memories bombarding her of what she'd always considered to be an idyllic childhood … nice house, lots of friends, a family life she was proud of and had totally taken for granted – until the day she'd been forced to realise that her beloved father wasn't quite the man she'd so unquestioningly thought him to be.

She frowned. There'd be questions, she knew, from her mother and possibly even her brother, over what exactly had gone on and she didn't know how she was going to answer them.

She was still none the wiser when she finally left his bedside to rejoin them in the cafeteria.

CHAPTER FIVE

Harry walked into the police canteen that evening and was surprised to see Beth Macaskill sitting at a table, sipping a drink and poring over some notes. Her spiky, auburn head would be recognisable anywhere, he thought, and whilst it wasn't an unattractive style, the thought popped into his mind that with longer, softer hair, she'd be stunning. It shouted rebellion at him and he was aware of an unexpected stab of envy. He'd never done the rebellion bit himself when he was younger and, ridiculously, had always felt a shaft of regret about that. If he'd been living with his parents like most kids did, he liked to think he might have been a bit more challenging as a teenager, a bit more *interesting* – but somehow it hadn't felt fair putting all that crap on his grandparents when they'd done so much for him. So he'd been boringly conformist – an image that probably hadn't harmed him when it came to applying to join the police.

He bought himself a mug of hot chocolate and walked over to join Beth.

'Haven't you got a home to go to?'

She looked up and grinned. 'Aye, but not one I'm in any hurry to get back to,' she drawled in her soft accent.

'Why not?'

She shrugged. 'Put it this way. I'm twenty-six years old and living in a flat share – with four women I don't know from Adam. The place is a mess and full of people I have nothing in common with.'

'Ah right, I see.'

She threw him a cheery look. 'I doubt you do somehow, Harry, but never mind.'

'Have you got a boyfriend?'

She blinked, as if he'd caught her on the hop, then said cautiously, 'No … there was someone a few years back, but he died.'

'God, I'm sorry. Don't talk about it if you don't want to.'

Beth shook her head. 'It was a while back now – he died trying to save someone else.'

'That's awful.'

'Yeah, it was. I won't go into details, but I will say this. He turned my life around. I wouldn't be here doing this job if it wasn't for him.'

'Wow, that's some legacy to leave behind. Has there been anyone since?'

'Nope.' She grinned suddenly, her manner relaxing again. 'Why? Are you offering?'

He looked shocked. 'No – not at all.'

'Well, *that's* flattering.'

Taking her cue, Harry smiled back. 'I never mix business with pleasure,' he said. 'I found that out to my cost a couple of times – once when I was working on a case. It was a lesson well learnt.'

She shrugged. 'I'm sure you're right. But sometimes it's nice to open the door and let someone in for a while, don't you think? It blunts the crap of everyday life.'

Harry looked at her a little closer. He was beginning to suspect that still waters ran deep with Beth Macaskill.

'That sounds cynical for one so young.'

She laughed. 'I feel like I'm fifty sometimes. How old are you?'

'Thirty-three.'

'Not that old, then. I wouldn't feel *too* embarrassed being seen out with you.'

'Well, I'd feel like a cradle-snatcher being seen with you. What made you move down here – away from your friends and family in Northumberland?'

She tapped her nose and even while she grinned, he sensed her withdrawal. 'Too many questions. Now … want to see what I've got here that's quite interesting?'

He took the change of subject without comment and watched as she withdrew a piece of paper from a plastic wallet. 'I've been looking into our victim's background, and it seems he had a bit of a past.'

'Oh?'

'Yup – served two years in prison for dangerous driving and only came out in June this year. He put a woman in a wheel-chair. A Mrs Lazard.'

'Really? That is interesting. And your thinking is?'

A light came into her eye. 'Well, the woman's husband's got to be worth questioning, hasn't he? He kicked up a real stink with the local media when Paul Copeland was only jailed for two years and then released after fourteen months. It wouldn't be that surprising if the guy decided to take matters into his own hands, would it? Apparently Copeland refused to apologise – said she'd brought it on herself, crossing the road where there wasn't a crossing.'

Harry read the brief report she passed him, then handed it back. 'Good work. I'd say definitely interview him – and I've had an interesting development, too. You remember the estate agent we went to see, Dominic Cartwright?'

'Yeah.'

'Well, he was the victim of a hit-and-run accident earlier today. It could be just an unlucky coincidence that both he and one of his tenants came to grief in the same week, but again, I think it warrants following up.'

He drained the contents of his mug and stood up. 'Are you happy to interview the Lazards on your own?'

'Sure.'

'Good. Well, you do them in the morning and I'll do the Cartwrights. We can compare notes when we get back and see what we've got. Good work on the door-to-doors, by the way.'

'Well, it's a shame we didn't come up with anything more useful but the trouble is, the gardens are so bloody long most people can't even hear what's happening on the other side of the fence – let alone see it. Some of them weren't happy, I can tell you, at the thought of a random murderer wandering around at the bottom of their gardens – wanted to know if we were going to put some sort of security patrol out there to protect them.' She rolled her eyes. 'As if we'd get approval for that. They have no idea, do they?'

'No, and it's probably just as well.'

'Will the DCI be okay about me interviewing the Lazards on my own?'

'Murray? He'll be fine. He's not as scary as he looks, and as long as you do a good job you'll get a pretty free rein. He's great for delegating and letting his team follow their noses. That's not common these days.'

'Great, I'll see you in the morning, then.' She glanced at her watch. 'Best be off. I'm meeting a couple of my gym mates in the pub tonight. Want to join us?'

'I think I'd feel a bit old next to your friends.'

She grinned. 'We're a pretty mixed bunch, as it happens – one of them's nearly thirty, if that suits you better?'

'Thanks … maybe another time. I promised I'd visit my gran tonight.'

And life didn't get much more exciting than that, he thought, as the two of them went their separate ways.

Out in the car park, he climbed into his car and headed out onto the road. Ahead of him, cars were pulling out of Hatfield University, some of their occupants heading home after a day's work, others heading in the direction of the Galleria to catch a film or a bite to eat. He eased himself into the slow-moving traffic, his head full of the conversation to come and turned on the radio as a distraction.

Half an hour later he was pouring his grandmother a cup of tea as she sat in her winged chair in the sitting room.

'I've stopped the last of the pills,' she said, watching as he made room for the cup on the table next to her. 'Dr Roe said it was alright.'

'Good. You gave them a try but there's no point taking them if they just make you feel sick all the time. And you've felt better since you stopped the other ones.'

She was looking worse, though, he thought. More frail by the day. He couldn't help wondering how much longer she could go on living in her own house, but she was such a stubborn one.

'If I have to, I'll go to the Hospice,' she'd said a week or so back. 'But I don't want to. I want to die here in my own home. Is that too much to ask when we all know I haven't got long now?'

She'd looked at him with those clear blue eyes. She was still so damned lucid.

'Of course it isn't and if that's what you want then I'll do my best to try and make sure it happens.'

But he'd known what she was really asking and the time for his decision had come.

Now, as she sat huddled in her chair, sipping tea through her straw – a picnic rug draped over her legs for extra warmth – he took the first step forward in what he vowed would not be the slow road to ruin.

'I was thinking about our conversation last week,' he said carefully, not meeting her gaze. 'I can't agree with all of what you said, but if you'd like me to move in with you for a while … just to see you through the winter months?'

She drew back from her straw and gave a little cackle as she looked up at him.

'Well, you may have taken your time about it, lad … but your old room's already made up. I asked Claire if she'd mind doing that a few days ago.'

He did return her look then, shaking his head at the triumphant gleam in her eyes.

'You're a devil, you know that? And who's Claire, anyway?'

'You know … the carer that comes in. I told her I was hoping you'd come to stay for a bit.'

The old lady paused, and there was just the tiniest suspicion of moisture in the corner of her eye as she looked at her grandson.

'I know I can rely on you, Harry, and out of everyone – my own daughter included – there's no one I'd rather have with me at the end. But I'll only let you stay on one condition.'

He stared at her suspiciously, knowing he wasn't going to like it.

'And what's that?'

'That you won't go against my wishes when the time comes. I know there are things we don't agree on, but I don't want to be forced into treatment I don't want. I'm ready to go. I want to go. And you need to know that.'

'Gran–'

'Is it a deal?'

She gave him that smile that had twisted him around her little finger so many times in the past, and he sighed, knowing he couldn't fight her.

'You're enough to try the patience of a saint – you know that? I'll move my stuff in over the weekend.'

CHAPTER SIX

The following morning, Beth Macaskill stood on the doorstep of the neatly kept semi-detached council house in Potters Bar and looked around her. Most of the houses on the estate were well maintained, in total contrast to the inner-city estates she'd been exposed to during her last stint in Leeds. There, she'd got used to seeing houses in a semi-derelict condition and local churches with barricaded windows and razor wire on their walls.

Outwardly, it was all so very different to the rural life she'd grown up with and yet she, more than most, knew that the underbelly of crime slithered insidiously into all walks of life and communities, sucking its victims into ever-deeper water until it became impossible for them to swim free. And from then on, for most of them, it was game over.

But not her.

She took a breath, focused her thoughts and rang the bell.

'Who is it?' The voice coming from the intercom was female and made her jump.

'Detective Constable Macaskill,' she said into the mouthpiece. 'We spoke earlier?'

'Just push the door.'

The buzz of the intercom was followed by a click and Beth entered the small hallway.

'I'm through here.'

Beth made her way into what was a reasonably sized lounge, warmed by a brightly glowing wood-burner.

She shouldn't have been surprised really to see the woman sitting in the wheelchair, but she was – though more by the fact that she was quite striking to look at with curly dark hair and bright blue eyes, than by the fact that she was disabled.

'Mrs Lazard?'

Beth held out her ID but the woman waved it away.

'Don't need to see that. I recognise your voice from when we spoke. Where's the accent from?'

Beth smiled, used to the question. 'Northumberland.'

'Ah, I guessed as much. I've got a sister who lives in Hexham. Now, what did you want to talk to me about? If it's to tell us that Paul Copeland's out of jail, then you're a bit late. The victim support people already told us when he first came out. Though what they thought we were going to do about it, I don't know.'

'No … I haven't come to say that, though it is about Paul Copeland.' She hesitated. 'You may not have heard … that he's dead?'

That got the other woman's attention. '*No.* You're kidding. How?'

'He was murdered on Monday night.'

'Bloody hell.'

She was silent for a moment. Then she looked at Beth and shrugged. 'Well, I'm not going to say I'm sorry because I'm not – the bastard didn't give a shit about what he'd done to me. All he worried about was the fact he might have to go to prison. I can still hear him bleating on about it while we were waiting for the ambulance. Look at me now – there's more than one type of prison, I can tell you.'

She reached for a glass of water on the table beside her and sipped from it. Beth waited until she'd put the glass back down on the table before saying, 'I'm sorry to have to ask you this, Mrs Lazard, but we need to eliminate you and your husband from our enquiry. Do you mind telling me where your husband was last Monday night?'

The other woman's look became guarded. 'Not out killing Paul Copeland, if that's what you're suggesting.'

'As I say, it's just for elimination purposes.'

She seemed to give it some thought. 'I'm not sure exactly – my memory's not as good as it used to be since the accident – but he was here for the early part of the evening and then I think he nipped down to the pub for a pint a bit later on. Probably The Crown in Barnet. We used to live in Barnet: it's where all his mates are.'

'Do you remember what time he got in?'

'Well … I was watching Newsnight, I remember – more rubbish about post-Brexit Britain – and it was coming to an end when he came in. So about twenty past eleven, I'd say.'

'What time will he be home today?'

'Probably around six. You can catch him at work if you want to speak to him before then.'

Beth thought about it. It would be good to tick the box and go back with a complete dossier.

'Where's that?'

'He runs the Carefree Day Centre in Welwyn, for his sins – as if he doesn't have enough of that with me. It's just off the square not far from John Lewis.'

'Thanks. I'll maybe do that – get it out of the way so we can concentrate on other stuff. Is there anything I can get you before I leave?'

'No thanks, love. I've got all I need.' She gave a rueful smile. 'It's been good to chat – God, how pathetic does that sound? Must be desperate if I enjoy being interviewed by the police – but you've brightened up my day, no doubt about it. That's what I miss most being stuck in this thing, you know – the company. It's true what they say about finding out who your friends are in these situations.' She looked reflective, as if there were several things she could add to that. Beth couldn't begin to imagine how awful it must be to have your life snatched away from you in an instant. The thought struck her that if Andy had survived he could well have ended up in a wheelchair, too, with her as his carer. She'd have been happy doing that if it meant he was still in her life, but she couldn't imagine feeling that way about any other man.

She smiled. 'Well, it makes a change for me, too – not often a visit from me is the highlight of someone's day.'

'Don't believe that for one minute, pretty thing like you. You don't look like a normal copper, though, if you don't mind me saying.'

Beth laughed. 'Are you referring to my hair, by any chance?'

'It's certainly different – not that it doesn't suit you,' the other woman added quickly.

Beth smiled self-consciously. 'I've had it like this ever since my best friend died. We were eighteen and thought we looked so cool. I guess I've just not been able to ditch it.'

'You'll do it when you're ready, don't worry about that. Life moves on at its own pace – you can take that from me. Just be sure you move on with it when the time comes, if you don't want to be left stuck in a rut.'

Beth didn't answer. The truth was she didn't want life to move on. It was her fault Andy had died – if she hadn't called him, telling him what Briony was about to do – at least one of them would still be alive today.

A photograph on the mantelpiece caught her eye and she

moved over to pick it up, changing the subject. 'Are these your kids? They look smart in their school uniforms.'

'Yeah, James and Emma. They're great. So's Ken – I don't know what we'd do without him.'

There was a trace of fear in that throwaway remark, and as their eyes met, Beth understood it.

She could see that without her husband, life for Maggie Lazard would be very difficult indeed.

'Dead? You kidding me?'

There was no doubt Ken Lazard looked shocked when Beth told him, but she found herself eyeing him carefully, trying to assess how genuine that shock was.

They were sitting in a back office at the day centre sipping coffee, although Ken Lazard had made it plain he didn't have much time to spare. 'I've got to help with the mid-morning snacks in ten minutes. We're short-staffed.'

Now he was looking at her directly. 'That bastard ruined our lives the day his car ran into my wife and not a word of apology or sympathy out of him. As far as I'm concerned he deserved whatever he got. I'm not going to pretend I'm sorry …'

'Could you tell me where you were on Monday night, Mr Lazard?'

'Me?' He looked taken aback. 'Well, uh … I dunno … at home, I think.'

'Only, your wife thought you'd maybe gone out to the pub that night?'

'Oh yeah, I think I did. I remember now, I went a bit later than usual because Maggie and I got locked into a particularly long game of Trivial Pursuit.'

He smiled, and there was pride in his eyes. 'She beats me

hands down every time. I'm thinking of switching to Scrabble. I might have a chance then.'

'So you left home at what time?'

His expression changed to one of irritability. 'God, if I'd known I was going to be questioned I'd have made a note. I don't know, probably around eight?'

'And what time did you get back?'

'Elevenish, I'd guess – that's as late as I'd ever normally be. If I go earlier, I'm usually home by ten-thirty.'

Beth took out her notebook. 'What pub was it and can anyone vouch for you?'

He hesitated. 'The Black Boar in Potters Bar, I think. They might remember me, but it's not my usual haunt. I fancied a change.'

Something in the way he said it made Beth look at him closely, but she didn't say anything.

'Okay, thanks for that. Obviously we'll head over there at some point and see if anyone can remember you. Did you talk to anyone? Meet up with friends?'

'No. I was alone, and as I say, I'm not a regular there. But someone might have noticed me.'

Beth stood up to go. 'That's a nasty cut you've got on your lip.'

'Yeah.' Ken touched the corner of his mouth gingerly with his finger and he didn't look at her directly as he responded. 'I caught it on the corner of the kitchen cupboard. Stupid.'

'Well, thanks for seeing me – that's all I need at the moment. We'll get back to you if we've got any more questions.'

She looked through the internal window to where staff were beginning to assist patients to their places at the tables. 'How long have you worked here?' she asked curiously.

'Five years. Ironic, isn't it? I never thought I'd be bringing my work home to the extent I am now. Not that I'd have it any other way. Magz didn't deserve what happened to her and she's been so strong – so have the kids. I have to be strong in a different way. I'm not perfect at it, but it works – we work. We're doing alright.'

She wasn't sure if he was trying to convince himself or her, as he stood up to show her out.

CHAPTER SEVEN

K irsty looked at her mother's drained features over the lunch table and couldn't help feeling that she'd never understand Sylvia Cartwright in a million years. Here she was, completely shell-shocked by all that was happening, yet all that seemed to be bothering her at the moment was the fact she'd had to cancel her hair appointment for the following day because she didn't feel up to talking about what was going on with Ramon, her hairdresser.

'Of course you don't,' she said gently. 'Not when Dad's so poorly. Your hair looks fine anyway, and a few more days isn't going to make any difference.'

'I know it seems stupid worrying about my hair, but I don't know if I'm coming or going at the moment.'

'I feel the same. It's natural, Mum. Look … why don't I visit Dad on my own this afternoon? You need a break. Have a lie-down and catch up on some sleep – then Robbie can bring you in later.'

'I don't know … what time's he going?'

'He said his last appointment's at five and he'd be along after that. He'll be happy to pick you up.'

'I'm not sure …'

'There's nothing you can do at the moment. It'll be the same as it was this morning. If anything changes I'll call you straight away, I promise. You need to keep your strength up.'

'I just can't get over how awful he looks.'

'People always look terrible when they're in hospitals.'

'I suppose I could call that policeman back – the one who wanted to come this morning – tell him I'll be here now if he wants to come.'

'Good idea. I'd forgotten about that.'

'What did you and Dad argue about?'

The question caught Kirsty off guard. Now wasn't the time to be going into it.

'It doesn't matter now.'

'It does to me. You were always such a daddy's girl and then suddenly you're not talking to him. What can he have done to you that was so bad?'

'He didn't do anything … not to me anyway.'

'Then who?'

'Mum, let it drop. Now isn't the time.'

Her mother scraped back the chair and stood up. 'Fine. I can't force you to tell me. You must be protecting someone – probably me. Is he having an affair or something?'

'*No.*'

'Well, that's the sort of thing that's been running through my head these last nine months – and God knows what else. So just think on that. It's not just *your* relationship with him that's been affected.' She sighed. 'You better get off to the hospital now. I'll call Robbie – see if he can pick me up later.'

Kirsty watched her mother leave the room. She felt wretched. She hadn't realised how deep the backlash of her argument with her father would run, but how could she tell her mother the truth now?

Her thoughts were preoccupied all the way to the hospital.

As she stepped out of the lift into the intensive care unit she took a breath and headed for her father's room. But at the door she came to an abrupt halt.

It was empty.

Her first terrifying thought that he was dead was quickly crushed. They'd have rung if that was the case. *Maybe he's regained consciousness.*

She spun round on her feet just as the doctor they'd spoken to the previous day reached her.

'Miss Cartwright–'

'Where's my father?'

'I'm so sorry. We phoned your mother and she said she'd call you.' He hesitated. 'I'm afraid your father passed away very suddenly, quarter of an hour ago.'

'*No…*'

The ground seemed to shift beneath her feet. She was hardly aware of the hand on her arm, leading her gently into a side room.

'Come through into here and sit down. It's a shock, I know.'

In the room, Kirsty turned to him in bemusement. 'But you said he was *fine* this morning. What happened? We'd have stayed with him if we'd thought there was any chance of …'

'We don't know for sure. There'll be a post-mortem to find out, but more than likely it was related to his brain injury. I'm afraid it happened so quickly there was no time to call you in. I'm sorry.'

Kirsty sank down into a chair and buried her head in her hands, hot tears springing to her eyes. She was never going to see him again – never get the chance to tell him how much she loved him.

'Ah, here's Emma,' the doctor said, looking up as the door opened to reveal the duty nurse.

'I'm sorry to interrupt, Doctor, but Mr Hayes in bed 3 is having breathing difficulties.'

'I'll see to it. Can you stay with Miss Cartwright? Maybe see if she'd like a cup of tea or something?'

He turned back to Kirsty. 'I'm sorry to dash off, but do feel free to give me a call at anytime if there's anything you want to ask.'

She nodded.

'I'll leave you in Emma's safe hands now.'

She watched as he swiftly exited the room and couldn't help wondering if Mr Hayes was about to end up the same way as her father.

'I'm so sorry for your loss, my love,' Emma said, breaking into her thoughts. 'Please do accept our condolences. Can I get you anything?'

Kirsty shook her head. All she wanted was to see her father and go home.

'It's come as a shock, I know,' the nurse said gently, 'but do at least take some comfort from the fact that your dad didn't suffer. It was very quick.'

'That's what the doctor said.'

'Well, it's true. And I know it doesn't make it easier for the ones left behind, but for the person involved…'

Kirsty couldn't reply. It was too soon to be able to take comfort from that. She sat in a state of numbed shock for several minutes, unable to process the fact that her father was gone. But gradually the reality sank in, and as it did, she found herself rising shakily from her seat.

'Can I see him?'

'Of course. We've moved him to another room.'

'Did my mum say if she was coming in?'

'She said she'd rather not.'

Kirsty followed the nurse slowly into a room across the

corridor, not sure what to expect, but knowing she needed to do this.

She sat down on the hard-backed visitors' chair and braced herself to look at him. He was lying on his back, eyes closed, with a sheet drawn up to just below his chin. It was a strange sensation, knowing that he looked exactly as he had that morning, yet realising that the essence of him had gone. But he looked peaceful, and for that she was grateful.

She covered his hand with hers. It felt cold in her grasp but she squeezed it tightly as if she could instil some warmth into it, knowing it would be the last physical contact she'd ever have with her beloved father. 'I'll make sure they catch the person who did this, Dad,' she vowed fiercely. 'I promise.'

She sat there for what felt like an age, wishing she'd never found out what she had, so that her memories of him could be the simple, untainted ones of a man much loved and now missed enormously by his family. But the reality was he hadn't been quite as straightforward and untainted as she'd believed, and now, somehow, she needed to unravel that and come to terms with it. What he'd done hadn't stopped her loving him, but it had rocked her faith in him.

She stood up and deliberately didn't look around her. This wasn't how she wanted to remember him, not in this stark, clinical room with a cotton sheet draped up to his chin.

She left the room and found the nurse waiting for her outside.

'Thanks for everything. I know you did your best by him. I think I'll get back to my mum now. What happens next? Do we need to do anything?'

'We've already spoken to your brother about the post-mortem and that will go ahead possibly Monday or Tuesday next week. After that, once the release papers have been issued, the funeral directors that you've chosen will come and collect your father and take him back to their chapel of rest while the funeral arrangements are sorted. Someone will also need to come up in the next day or so to collect his belongings.'

'Okay. Thank you.'

'I'm sorry for your loss. We did everything we could to revive him, but…'

Kirsty nodded. 'Thank you.'

Twenty-five minutes later she swung into her parents' drive in Brookmans Park. There was another car parked next to her mother's that she didn't recognise. She let herself in and followed the sound of voices. In the lounge she found her mother, her brother and a man she'd never seen before.

Her distraught eyes met her mother's, and the next thing they were in each other's arms, clinging to each other tightly.

'I tried to call you – to stop you.'

'I know. It must have gone straight to answerphone. I only picked up your message as I was leaving the hospital.'

Her mother drew back. 'Did you see him?'

'Yes.'

'How … did he look?'

'The same as he looked this morning. And peaceful.'

Her mother drew a shuddering breath and nodded. Then she turned to the man in the room.

'This is Detective Sergeant Briscombe. He's come to ask us a few questions about the accident yesterday.'

'It's obviously not a good time. I can come back,' Harry said.

'No.' Sylvia Cartwright's voice was unusually firm. 'Let's do this now and get it out of the way. We're going to be tied up the next couple of weeks. There'll be a lot to do.'

'Well, I'm afraid it's not very good news. No one's come forward admitting to the accident and there was only one witness, who didn't see anything in detail. We've put up an

Accident board, though, and may get a response to that, and we have a team carrying out door-to-door investigations.'

'Someone must have seen something, surely?' Kirsty said. 'How can an accident like that happen and no one see it?'

'People don't always realise the value of being a witness and it was in a relatively quiet road. There's a good chance when they see the Accident board that someone will come forward, but until they do it's difficult for us to get hard facts. It was a residential area so we'll be continuing our door-to-door next week and checking for any CCTV nearby – that could also be a valuable source of information if we can pick up images of a car that fits the bill.'

He turned to Robbie. 'This is probably a bit of a long shot but is there any chance at all that there could be a link between your father's death and that of Paul Copeland, do you think?'

Her brother looked shocked. 'No. I'm sure not.'

'Who's Paul Copeland?' Kirsty asked.

Robbie looked at her. 'One of our tenants who died earlier this week.'

'He was murdered,' Harry corrected.

'*Oh my God,*' Kirsty's mother gasped, her fingers flying to her mouth.

'Mum, I'm sure there's no link,' Robbie said quickly. 'The guy was just a tenant – he had nothing to do with Dad.'

'Well, obviously it's a line of enquiry we'll need to bear in mind until we can exclude it,' Harry said cautiously, closing his notebook. 'The fact that the driver of the car that hit your father didn't stop makes it more complicated than a straightfor-ward road accident unfortunately.'

He looked at Sylvia Cartwright. 'I'll take myself off now, Mrs Cartwright. I'm sorry for your loss. We'll do our best to catch whoever did this.'

'I'll see you out,' Kirsty said.

On the doorstep she looked at him. 'What are your chances of finding the person responsible?'

Harry shook his head. 'That's not an easy one. It depends if anyone comes forward to say they saw something. But we'll give it our best shot, I promise you that.'

She watched as he made his way to his car and climbed in. There was a reassuring air about him that she found herself clinging onto. She couldn't bear to even consider the possibility that they might never find out who killed her father, or the exact details of what had happened.

Harry parked his car and walked briskly into the police station, taking the steps two at a time to the second floor. When he got to DCI Murray's office it was empty.

'They're all in the incident room,' someone volunteered. 'He said to join them when you got back.'

The room had most of the team in it and as Harry slipped quietly in and sat on a desk at the back, he studied the evidence and pictures on the board.

'So ... two incidents on our patch which may or may not be connected,' Murray was saying. 'One is definitely murder, the other at the very least unlawful hit-and-run. At this moment in time there doesn't appear to be any link connecting the two incidents, apart from the fact that the two victims knew each other.'

'Also that Paul Copeland did some work for Cartwrights,' Beth interjected.

'Quite right. Good point. Speak to Cartwrights and get a list of the jobs he's done for them over the last year, can you?'

Murray added another connecting line to the two names and wrote the word *decorating* on it, then studied what they'd got.

'Now you know me, I don't do coincidence unless the facts

are irrefutable – so I think we need to keep an open mind, but certainly don't – at this stage – indicate to the press that we think there's even a possibility the two cases might be related. I think the Cartwrights could do without the extra interest that line of enquiry would attract. Anything you can add, Harry, from your interview with Mrs Cartwright?'

'Only that Dominic Cartwright died a couple of hours ago, so we're looking at a second death now. No CCTV on the residential road where it happened – but we're checking the cameras on the main road to see if they picked up any dark cars turning onto it from that road around the same time.'

'So, in summary, we've got Paul Copeland murdered some time Monday night, kept somewhere for a few hours – possibly the boot of a car or a building – and then dumped in a very visible location in the early hours of Tuesday morning. That could have been deliberate – as a warning to others, maybe – or it could have been because the person who killed him was in a hurry and didn't have time to dispose of the body properly. He'd recently been released from prison after serving a sentence for dangerous driving. His victim's husband's alibi has yet to be checked out. What's happening about that?'

'He said he was at the Black Boar in Potters Bar. I thought I'd check the pub out tonight, see if the landlord remembers him,' Beth volunteered.

'I'll come with you if like,' Harry said. 'Two heads and all that.'

Murray tapped the other photo. 'Here we have Dominic Cartwright, respectable businessman, hit by a car yesterday after meeting a client for a house viewing in Hadley Wood. We have one witness who was walking down the other side of the road, a Mrs Taylor, but she says it all happened so quickly she didn't really see it. The only thing she could say with any certainty was that it was a dark-coloured car, possibly black or blue. Have we interviewed the client Cartwright was seeing yet?'

'Officers on the scene conducted an initial interview,' Harry said. 'I'll probably go and see them myself on Monday. I've arranged to visit Cartwrights office tomorrow morning to look at Dominic Cartwright's appointments diary – see if there's anything useful in there.'

'Okay, well I'll leave that lot with you. Geoff, I'd like you to carry on with the door-to-doors in Myton Road – make sure you speak to anyone who was out that we've missed. Find out if anyone saw Paul Copeland leaving his flat Monday morning, and if so, what time. Also, if he returned to his flat at any point. We need to establish his exact movements on Monday before whoever it was got to him.'

He tapped one of the photos showing Paul Copeland's body lying on the ground. 'Forensics have shown that he died from a single stab wound to the stomach, but he'd also been beaten up pretty badly – probably on two separate occasions. There was evidence of older bruising as well as the more recent extensive damage that had been done. No trace of the knife yet, but there's a picture here of the type of weapon that was used, and they picked up footprints of two different sets of shoes around the immediate area where the body was found. Obviously, if we can find the knife or a match to the shoes, that would be significant. Right … that's all for now. If anyone digs up anything new, let me know. Harry and Beth, come to my office and fill me in on what you've found out this morning.'

Harry waited for Beth to join him before they exited the room together. 'Anything significant your end?' he asked, as they headed in the direction of Murray's office.

'Not really. The wife seemed nice – and brave. It must be awful being stuck in your house in a wheelchair every day. Makes you appreciate what you've got. The husband was pleasant enough as well. They both seemed shocked to hear

Paul Copeland was dead and not surprisingly, neither of them were that upset about it.' She shrugged. 'Can't really blame them. What about you? How did you get on with the Cartwrights?'

'It wasn't the best of times to call – they'd literally just heard he hadn't made it. But I met the whole family, which was useful, and if anyone suspected the two deaths might be linked, they weren't letting on.'

'What were they like?'

'Well, you met the son Robbie. His sister Kirsty's younger than him – mid-twenties probably? She's just come back from a stint in France and was out of the country at the time of both incidents. They're obviously close as a family and the son seemed very protective of the mother when I first got there, as did Kirsty when she arrived. But I didn't get anything useful out of any of them.'

They'd arrived outside Murray's office and, with a brief tap, Harry opened the door. Inside, Murray fiddled with some papers on his desk while Harry and Beth filled him in.

'I've got an appointment with upstairs in half an hour to update them,' he said when they'd finished. 'So nothing new to offer them, then?'

Harry shrugged. 'You know what it's like. It takes time.'

'Try telling that to the Super. Still, I've more or less caught up with the backlog here, so I can give you more of a hand now hopefully. When are you planning on checking the pub out?'

Beth checked her watch. 'I thought I'd do it on my way home. Are you still up for it?' she asked, turning to Harry.

'Sure thing. The sooner we can get some of these alibis tied up, the better.'

CHAPTER EIGHT

'What'll you have?' Harry asked Beth, casting a quick glance around the inside of the pub as he did so. What it lacked in aesthetic charm it made up for in warmth, as the large coal fire burned merrily away in the hearth. Yet there was hardly anyone there, considering it was a Friday night.

'Doesn't normally pick up until about half-eight or nine,' the landlord said, handing Beth her Diet Coke and Harry his half-pint. 'If you come back then you won't recognise the place.'

'Do you remember this man from Monday night?' Harry asked, pulling out the photo of Ken Lazard. 'Probably on his own. Would have come in about half-eight?'

The man studied the photo and shook his head. 'Nah. Can't say I do, but, as I say, things pick up around that time so I'd be hard pushed to notice him. What's he done?'

'Nothing that we're aware of. We just want to ask him a couple of questions. If we leave the photo with you – any chance you can ask around with your regulars? Just in case any of them remember seeing him?'

'Sure.' The man tucked the photo in his pocket. 'I'll see what I can do.'

'That's a pity,' Beth said, as they headed for a table by the fire.

'What's he like, this Ken Lazard?' Harry asked.

'Seemed okay. Works in a care home. You've got to be quite a nice sort of guy to do that, right? Not the sort of job I could do, that's for sure.'

'Horses for courses – a lot of people would say that about our job.'

Beth grinned. 'You're into all that, aren't you?'

'What?'

'Sayings. Horses for courses, two heads are better than one … dah dah dah. I like it. I see it as part of you and your little ways now.'

Harry looked horrified. 'God forbid.' He smiled ruefully. 'That's what comes of being brought up by your grandparents, I guess. It's inevitable I'm going to sound like an oldie sometimes.'

'Anyway … going back to Ken Lazard. He seemed alright. And I feel he genuinely loves his wife.'

'Which would give him a strong reason to avenge the person who put her in a wheelchair.'

'Yup.' Beth sat thoughtfully for a while. 'Come on, drink up. I've got an idea. I think we should give something else a try.'

'What?'

'Maggie Lazard mentioned another pub, The Crown, in Barnet. She said that was Ken's regular, because it's where they used to live and all his mates hang out there. Maybe we should have a word with the landlord there? You don't have to come, I'm happy to do it on my own.'

Harry thought about the packing he needed to do for moving into his grandmother's tomorrow and found it wasn't a difficult decision to make at all.

'No, that's fine. I'm with you…'

'Yeah, I remember seeing Ken Monday,' the landlord said, handing him back the photo. 'He comes in most Mondays and stays for an hour or two. I'm sure several people would have seen him. He's a regular.'

Harry and Beth exchanged glances.

'It's Monday this week we're talking about. Are you sure he was here? And if so, what time did he leave?' Harry asked.

The man gave it some thought. 'Yeah, he was here. Can't say I remember what time he left, though. One day rolls into another in this job.'

'Can I have your name?'

'Derek Mason.'

Harry wrote it down. 'Anyone else here at the moment who might have seen him on Monday?'

The landlord looked around the room. 'Ginger over there might. The guy with the red hair,' he clarified unnecessarily.

Harry and Beth made their way over to a table by the window where a man was sitting talking quietly to a woman.

'Mind if I ask you a couple of questions?' Harry asked, pulling out his card.

'Depends what it's about,' the man said, making a show of studying the card.

'I understand you know Ken Lazard?'

'Yeah. Good guy.'

'Were you here Monday night?'

The man looked at his wife.

'I think so. We were, weren't we, Mary?'

His wife nodded.

'Do you remember if Ken came in that night?'

'I think he did. Why?'

'Do you remember what time he came and what time he left?'

Again a quick glance at his wife. 'Can't say for sure – it was four days ago now. I remember seeing him briefly but I can't remember when exactly, and we left before he did.'

'Anyone else see him, do you think?'

'You'd have to ask around. Sorry, not much help, I know. Drink up, Mary, we need to get back for that film.'

'Do you mind giving me your name and address, sir, for my notes?'

'Sure.'

Beth frowned at Harry as they sat down at a table. 'Why would Ken Lazard lie about where he was? Especially if people here can give him an alibi?'

'I don't know. Maybe they *can't* give him an alibi – not a full one anyway. Edwards said Copeland had been killed between eight and eleven. If Ken didn't get here until, say, eight-forty-five and we don't know what time he left, but he didn't get home until nearly eleven-thirty, then theoretically that gives him a whole window of opportunity to kill Copeland, both before he arrived and after he left. We need precise confirmation on the alibi and maybe he knew that was going to leave him with time unaccounted for.'

Beth shook her head. 'I'm not sure he strikes me as being the kind of guy who'd kill someone like that. With a knife, I mean. I'd have him down as more a fisticuffs type.'

'You speak from experience, do you?' Harry's voice was amused.

She looked him straight in the eye. 'Aye, Harry, I do. I'll bet I've experienced more of that sort of stuff than you have – even if you do have seven years on me.'

Something in her tone warned him from making a joke of her statement. He could imagine not many people would mess with Beth.

'You could be right,' he conceded mildly. He looked around. 'The place is filling up. I think we should split and do the rounds and compare notes later.'

Twenty minutes later they were standing outside Harry's car preparing to head home.

'I don't know about you,' Beth said, 'but I got the impression there was some sort of cover-up going on in there. Several people knew Ken – said they'd talked to him – but no one could remember exact timings, although one bloke did say he thought he'd left about ten-thirty or maybe a bit before that.'

'In which case what was he doing for the next hour or so before he got home? I agree there was something odd going on in there. A couple of people suggested I pop back another night and in the meantime they'd try to think back to Monday and see if they could remember in more detail.'

'After they've spoken to Ken, do you think?'

'Wouldn't surprise me. I think I'll pay him a visit myself on Monday, see what he's got to say now he's had a bit of time to think about things.'

He watched as Beth flicked the key fob at her car and opened the door.

'What are you up to this weekend?' he asked. 'Anything exciting?'

'Nah. You?'

He tried to think of some way of sexing it up, and failed. 'Moving in with my grandmother for a couple of months. I think I mentioned she's not well.'

'You must be fond of her.'

'Yes, I am.'

'I never knew my grandparents. My dad's parents are dead and my mum's parents disowned her when she married him. They haven't spoken to each other since. My grandparents live somewhere in the East End, I think, but I've never met them.'

'That's sad. Don't you ever feel tempted to get in touch?'

'What's the point? They're a rum lot, my family. I'd probably only be disappointed. Need a hand moving in tomorrow?'

Harry shook his head. 'Nice of you to offer, but I haven't got much to pack. It's not as if I live miles away. Hop in. I'll drop you back at the station to get your car.'

'No worries. I can get a cab. There was quite a nice guy I got talking to in there. Offered me a drink if I was going off duty. I might just take him up on it. See if he's turned on by a woman in uniform.'

'Er … you don't wear one.'

'Soon remedy that if I need to.'

'Is that how you usually grab a guy's interest, then?'

She grinned. 'No … it's a new approach – I'll let you know how it works. See ya, good luck with the move.'

'Take care,' Harry couldn't help saying.

'Don't do anything you wouldn't do, you mean?'

Beth's expression was openly taking the mickey out of him.

'Just look out for yourself,' Harry said. 'What was his name?'

'Harry …?'

'Yeah?'

'Piss off, eh? I'll see you Monday.'

The man walked into the new nightclub in Hatfield and looked around him. It was the same as any other club, really, although he had to admit the newness of the place gave it a classier feel than most. It was gone midnight and the dance floor heaved with drug-and alcohol-infused bodies gyrating to the heavy beat of music that blared from the speakers.

He could do it now. The thought excited him as he imagined his strategy. Approaching a girl of his choice, making eye contact, moving in …

It hadn't failed him yet, and there was no reason to think it would now. But no ... he had an established routine and it hadn't let him down. He'd be patient, do what he always did. Case the joint (he loved that expression), watch how the bouncers worked – whether they were on it the minute something happened, or more laid-back – and last, but not least, work out his escape strategy in case anything went wrong.

Taking his time, he sauntered over to the bar and ordered himself a beer.

CHAPTER NINE

H arry rolled over in his bed and clicked the alarm off with an irritable groan. He'd forgotten to unset it last night, which put paid to any thoughts of a weekend lie-in this last morning in his flat. From now on, he'd be waking up in his old room in his grandmother's house.

He lay back on the pillows and gave it some thought. It was fine, but it was something he'd have to get used to again – having someone else to factor into his way of life. He'd lived alone for a number of years – had undoubtedly become a bit stuck in his ways. But it was a comfortable rut he'd carved for himself and he liked living like that.

Then he remembered why he was doing it. They'd known two years ago when his grandmother's cancer had been diagnosed that the prognosis wasn't good, but now her demise was imminent, it was dawning on him what a void she'd leave in his life.

He didn't want to think about it. Throwing the duvet back he got out of bed. He looked at the suitcase lying open and empty on the floor, and decided it could stay that way for the time being. Plenty of time for packing later.

Two hours later, he was pulling up in a side road near Cartwrights Estate Agents and crossing the road to their office. Robert Cartwright was already there, talking sombrely on the phone, and he acknowledged Harry's presence as he walked in.

'I'll be with you in a moment,' he mouthed, covering the handset with his hand. 'Dad's diary's on his desk and so is Paul Copeland's file if you want to take a look while you're waiting for me.'

Harry sat down in Dominic Cartwright's chair and picked up his diary. It was pristinely kept and fairly concise. There were only two appointments for the Thursday he died, one to go and see Paul Copeland's girlfriend, Susan Porter, and the other the viewing in Hadley Wood with a Mr and Mrs De Souza, for eleven-forty-five. It was the same road where he'd been killed. He reached for the file on Paul Copeland and flicked through it. Everything seemed to be straightforward and in order. Even his references, despite the fact he'd been in prison. There was one from a long-standing friend and another from a firm of accountants in Cockfosters. He made a note of the names and resolved to give them a call.

'Found what you're looking for?' Robbie walked into the office looking harassed.

'Not much to go on. No entries in his diary for Thursday, apart from the valuation in Hadley Wood and a visit to Susan Porter.'

Robbie shrugged. 'His visit to Susan was an impulse decision – I'm surprised it's in there at all. I was going to go but he thought it should be him as he was the senior partner.'

'I was just going through Paul Copeland's tenancy stuff. It all seems in order, although there's no copy of his actual contract?'

'Isn't there?' Robbie took a step forward so he could flick through the file himself. Then he shrugged. 'It's probably in the backlog of filing that's waiting to be done. I'll get Sharon to dig it out on Monday.'

'Thanks. And the owner is …' Harry glanced down at the paperwork. 'Simon Jordan, is that right?'

'Yes, he's a solicitor in Whetstone. His details will be in the file even if the actual contract isn't there, but I can give you his number if you like? He's an old family friend.'

'That's fine as long as it's here. Is it okay if I take the file and diary with me to the station so we can go through it properly?'

'Sure. But I haven't gone through his diary properly myself yet, which I'll need to do.'

'I can photocopy it all here if you'd rather?'

'That might be better, if you don't mind. Or again, I can ask Sharon to do it on Monday. I'd offer to do it for you myself but I'm up to my ears at the moment. I was in at half past six this morning trying to get a handle on what's urgent out of Dad's work, plus having to deal with my own.'

'No worries. I think I can manage to work out how a photocopier works. If you come across anything you think might be significant while you're sorting through his stuff–?'

'I'll let you know straight away.' He looked at Harry sharply. 'Are you thinking Dad's accident might not have been an accident?'

'Not at all,' Harry responded smoothly. 'The chances are it was exactly that, but obviously we need to cover every angle until we find out what happened.'

The phone in Robbie's office rang and he sighed. 'Excuse me. If it's a long one, can you see yourself out once you've finished your photocopying?'

Ten minutes later, Harry sat in his car and perused the notes he'd made from Dominic Cartwright's diary and Paul Copeland's file. It made a sorry apology for evidence of any kind. The only things of any significance were the address in

Hadley Wood where he'd carried out the valuation, and his visit to Susan Porter first thing that morning. Could anything have happened at either of those meetings that might have put him in danger?

There was only one way of finding out. He'd start with Susan Porter first as she was the nearest.

As soon as he arrived at Susan Porter's flat she told him she had to go out.

'Sorry, I've got a lot on today,' she said, leading him through to the lounge. 'And I'm working this afternoon.'

'I won't keep you long. I just need to ask you a couple of questions about Dominic Cartwright, the estate agent who manages this flat. Were you aware he'd been killed?'

She stopped dead in her tracks, swinging round in shock. '*No*. When? Bloody hell.' She sank down onto a chair.

'Hit-and-run on Thursday. We're trying to establish if there could possibly be a connection between his death and your boyfriend's, or whether it's just an unfortunate coincidence. I understand he came to see you Thursday morning – do you mind telling me why that was?'

She was looking stunned, and for a moment she didn't say anything. Then pulling herself together with an obvious effort, she said, 'To say he was sorry about Paul and that there was no rush for me to move out. He was kind – told me if I couldn't afford to stay here they'd try to help me find somewhere cheaper.'

'Did you talk about anything else – anything to do with Paul's death, for example?'

'No.'

'It seems odd that you wouldn't have talked about Paul at all?'

'It's private. I don't like talking about it. He just asked when the funeral was and I told him I didn't know yet. Paul's parents were fixing it.' She looked as if she was about to say more, then clamped her lips together.

'What?' Harry asked, picking up on her indecision.

She shook her head. 'Nothing.'

'Susan, if there's something you're not telling me – it could stop us finding out who did this to Paul. Don't you want justice for him?'

''Course I do.'

She chewed on her thumbnail, considering for a moment, then blurted out, 'There was something going on. I don't know what, 'cos Paul wouldn't tell me, but he thought he could make money out of it – enough for us to move out of here and get a better place, he said. I told him if it was illegal I didn't want to know – I didn't want him going back into jail again. But he said it weren't him what was likely to end up in jail. Then, when he came in that night before he was killed, he'd been in a fight. I asked him what it was all about, but he just told me to stop banging on. That's why we argued, 'cos I told him we shouldn't have secrets like that from each other.'

'Did he say who it was he was suspicious of? Or who the fight was with?'

She grabbed her handbag off the back of the chair.

'No.'

'Susan–'

'I don't know and that's all I'm saying. It's your job to find out what happened – I don't want to end up like Paul.'

She pushed past him into the hall and took her coat off the peg. 'You'll have to go. I'm running late.'

'Have you still got my card?'

'Yeah.'

She opened the front door and waited.

Harry had one last go. 'If you change your mind and want to talk more, call me. I'll meet you wherever you want. I know it's a difficult time for you – and frightening – but don't you think you owe it to Paul to help us as much as you can? If we feel that puts you in danger, we'll take steps to protect you. Think on it, okay?'

Her gaze met his briefly and he saw the fear in it. She nodded. 'Will you be at his funeral? I know the police some-times do that on the telly, when there's been a murder.'

'Someone will probably be there, if you let us know when it is. I'll make it if I can. And if you want to talk afterwards, just say, okay?'

Another nod.

And that was all he could do, he thought, as they both exited the house and he watched her hurry off down the street. She was clearly frightened of something, but unless she chose to tell him what, there wasn't much he could about it.

He climbed into his car and looked at his watch. Still only ten-thirty, plenty of time to interview the De Souzas in Hadley Wood if he wanted to, before heading home to pack.

Pulling out his mobile, he checked his notes and dialled their number.

'Come in, come in.'

Mrs De Souza spoke in a heavily accented voice as she ushered Harry through the marble-floored entrance hall into the luxurious living room. 'My husband he will be down in a minute. Can I get you something to drink?'

'No thanks.'

'You have come about poor Mr Cartwright, yes? It was terrible, terrible. He'd only been gone a few minutes when our neighbour knocked on our door and said what had happened.

She'd seen Dominic leave the house and thought he might be a friend of ours.'

'And was he? I notice you call him by his first name?'

'Not a close friend – he was of course younger than us. But we knew him through the golf club – it is why we asked him to come and do the valuation. So good to feel you can trust someone these days.'

'And neither you nor your neighbours saw anything at all of the accident?'

'We saw nothing. I wish we had. Denise – our neighbour – said it happened so quickly, she didn't get the chance to note any details. I know she has spoken to the police about it.'

She gave a little shudder. 'Such a shock. As you can imagine, everybody is talking about it since.'

'And I keep telling you, you need to try and put it out of your mind now,' another voice said from the doorway.

Mr De Souza, like his wife, was probably in his late-sixties. Grey-haired and spritely, he was the sort of chap you might expect to see out on the common with the regular exercise brigade.

'Do you mind my asking how long ago you made your appointment with Mr Cartwright?' Harry asked.

'Last Sunday,' De Souza responded. 'We were playing golf and I mentioned we were wishing to downsize and he offered to come and do a valuation.' He spread his hands and smiled. 'No pressure, he said, it didn't mean we had to use him.'

So it hadn't been a last-minute arrangement.

'And when he was here, did you notice anything unusual about him or did he seem quite normal?'

Mr De Souza stroked his chin thoughtfully. 'Well, now you say this, he did seem a little … preoccupied. We kept having to bring him back into the conversation, if you understand what I mean. He apologised most profusely after about the third time I had to do it – said it had been a difficult morning. Then his phone rang and he went outside to take the call, which seemed a little strange. I saw him through the window and he looked quite agitated. He said he could do with a drink when he came back in, so I poured him one of my special malt whiskies, which he seemed to enjoy very much.' He looked around the opulent living room with pride. 'He considered our little pile here is worth nearly two million pounds. Not bad for a Portuguese chef, eh?'

'Not bad at all. Did he have just the one drink?'

'Yes. He wasn't drunk if that's what you are wondering. I offered him another one but he said no, he was driving and was meeting someone for lunch, so he'd have another one then.'

'Did he happen to mention who that was?'

The man shook his head. 'I'm sorry we can't be more helpful. We are still quite shocked. Nothing like this has ever happened around here before and I know it is stupid, but we can't help feeling just a little responsible, you know? If he hadn't come here for the appointment ...'

'It's not your fault.'

'I know. You must come to our restaurant,' he said on a new note. 'It is in Whetstone – or we have another one in Swiss Cottage. De Souza's Eatery. Bring a friend if you like, we will feed you very well.'

Harry smiled. 'Thanks,' he said, standing up to go. 'I'll remember that. If you should hear anything that you think might be useful...'

'I will let you know straight away. It is not good that people get away with those sorts of crimes. To knock someone down like that and drive off ...' He sighed.

'Well, we'll try to see that they *don't* get away with it,' Harry said.

Out on the doorstep, he took stock of the time. There was no putting it off any longer ... he needed to pack his stuff and take it round to his grandmother's. The thought of it was causing a permanent knot in his stomach because he knew what would happen once she got her claws into him. Determination was a family trait, and she had it in spades.

But then so had he, he thought. So bring it on. Come what may, he'd stand strong and wouldn't let her manipulate him.

CHAPTER TEN

'How did you and Mum get on at the undertakers this morning?'

Kirsty looked up as her brother walked into the kitchen and sat down opposite her. Fatherhood hadn't been kind to him, she thought. He looked tired and strained – and no wonder, with sixteen-month-old twins and a busy office to run on his own now.

'It was overwhelming to be honest,' she sighed, helping herself to another biscuit from the tin. 'We've come back with stacks of info. Mum's been amazing. I can't believe how strong she's being. She said she wants it done as quickly as possible – before Rachael's wedding if possible – so she's provisionally taken a cancellation for next Thursday. Can you believe there are cancellations of funerals? Anyway, the memorial service is at St. John's and then there'll be a small service at the crematorium for family and close friends afterwards. I phoned the golf club to see if we could have a room there for people to go back to, and that's booked. So it's just the finer details, like notifications, that need sorting now.'

'Well done.'

'I didn't do much. Mum's been really proactive – not her usual dithery self at all.'

'That's a bit harsh.'

Kirsty smiled ruefully. 'Sorry … but you know what I mean. I worry how she'll cope without Dad, don't you? He did everything.'

'Yeah, I know what you mean.'

'How are Lizzie and the twins?'

'Fine, but it's exhausting. The girls are teething at the moment and every night it's the same … as one goes off, the other wakes up. We've put them in separate rooms now and they don't like it. I can't remember the last time we had a decent night's sleep.'

'Poor you. Maybe when things settle down a bit, Mum and I can come over and stay the night – or they can come here – give you both a night off?'

'Maybe but they only seem to want Lizzie or me at the moment. No one warned us it would be this hard.'

'Oh, Rob, it'll get easier.'

'I hope so.'

He looked so down about it that it upset her. She didn't like to think he might be regretting anything. These were meant to be the happiest years of his life, weren't they?

'It's still really early days. Everyone says once they hit two–'

'We'll have the terrible twos to look forward to?'

He flashed her a rueful smile and she grinned, feeling her world balance again. 'Maybe … but at least they'll hopefully be back to sleeping by then.'

She changed the subject. 'How did it go with the police this morning?'

'Fine. They copied Dad's diary and stuff from Paul Copeland's file and took it away with them. It's just surreal.'

'*Could* there be a connection between their deaths, do you think?'

'I doubt it, but I suppose they have to cover every angle. Aunty Anne rang me at the office, by the way. She and Rachael are coming over later.'

'Oh God no. Are they?'

The words were out before she could stop them and he looked at her curiously. 'I thought you and Rach were always so close?'

'We are … it's just …'

It took her a nanosecond to realise that she was fed up hugging her secret knowledge to herself, especially now her father was dead. What was the point? Now more than ever, she needed to know that Rob was onside with her.

She paused for a moment before saying, 'Did Dad ever talk to you about what we fell out over?'

'Kirsty, I don't want to talk about your problems with Dad right now. Sorry, but I haven't got the energy. It was between the two of you and should probably stay that way.'

He got up and moved over to the worktop to pour himself a cup of tea from the pot, the droop of his shoulder revealing the strain he was under.

'Weren't you even curious?'

'I figured if you wanted to tell me you would. And it could have put me in an awkward position with Mum if I knew the details and she didn't.'

Was he another one who thought their father had had an affair? It hadn't even occurred to her that they might think that.

She watched him add sugar to his cup, considered his words, then took the plunge anyway. 'You worked with Dad. Did he ever do stuff that was … dodgy?'

'Do we have to do this now?'

It was typical of her brother to try and shelve things in the hope that the matter would be go away, but for once she wasn't going to be fobbed off. She hesitated, mourning the loss of the close relationship they'd shared. It was all part and parcel of him getting married and having his own responsibilities, she knew, but she still wished she could talk to him like she used to.

She took a breath and ploughed on. 'Yes, I think we do.'

He sat back down opposite her and sighed. 'What do you mean, dodgy?'

'Oh, I don't know. Cash deals, backhanders, stuff like that?'

'There's always an element of that sort of thing that goes on in our business, Kirsty. Dad built up a lot of relationships over the years – I'd be lying if I said they didn't sometimes work to mutual advantage. It happens all the time.'

'It doesn't happen out in Jean-Pierre's office.'

'Of course it does. He's just careful not to let you see it.'

She frowned. 'And you condone it?'

Her brother shrugged and she could sense him choosing his words with care. 'It's inevitable, I'd say. We all help each other out in this business and yeah, quite a lot of cash changes hand one way or another. Maybe someone comes to us because they want a tenant out early so they can develop their property before flogging it. We slip the tenant a sweetener to leave, help the owner organise the works, maybe take a bit of a backhander from the builders they use for the introduction – and everyone's happy. The owner makes a bundle when he sells it, the tenant's happy because we've paid him off … and we've pocketed a bit of cash, a fee for overseeing the works and an agent's fee when the property's sold on. That sort of thing's always happened. It's nothing new.'

Kirsty stared at him. 'Did you know about the deal Dad did on Grandma's land? About him swindling Aunty Anne out of her money?'

For the first time Robbie looked uncomfortable. 'Yes, I did. And I didn't like it. But you know what Dad was like – he didn't see it that way. As far as he was concerned, she made fifty grand out of her share which, as he pointed out, she only got because she'd been married to his brother – and she was happy with that. Is that why you've distanced yourself from Rachael?'

'Of course it is. Are you surprised? I feel guilty every time I speak to her. It was when I was doing the work experience at Jordan's. I came across a second contract for the sale of Grandma's land dated six months after the first, and realised it was being turned for a massive profit with planning permission. And not only that, it had been bought first time round by a development company owned by Dad and Tony Jordan that I didn't even know existed. I suppose you knew all about that?'

'No need to say it like that. They formed it years ago, way before I came onto the scene, so that they had a company for buying properties they could renovate and sell on afterwards.'

'Do you know how much Grandma's land sold for second time around?'

'Kirsty, you have to realise that Dad saw that land as our family land – not Anne's. It was a punt. We know the guys in the planning department for sure, and sometimes we slip them a sweetener ... But he didn't know for certain he'd get planning permission on it.'

'But when he did, he should have given Aunty Anne her fair share. He made another two hundred and fifty grand on it, Rob. Rachael's our cousin – she and Anne were as entitled to that money as us. I feel terrible about it.'

'Look ... I'm not saying I disagree with you. I'm just saying that Dad, being Dad, I wasn't going to fall out with him over it. I had to carry on working with him.'

His words were met with a stony silence.

'What time are Anne and Rachael coming?' Kirsty finally asked.

'About four, they thought. You should be here. They'll want to see you.'

She was sure they would – she was just dreading seeing *them*.

But when it came to it, it wasn't as bad as she feared.

'Oh Kirsty, I'm so sorry,' her cousin said, giving her a fierce hug. 'I can't believe it. First, Dad last year with his heart attack – and now Uncle Dom. It's just not right. Are you okay?'

Kirsty nodded, hugging her cousin tightly back, realising how much she'd missed her. The same height as Kirsty's five foot six, with the same coloured fair hair, they'd always been more like sisters than cousins – and as children had often pretended they were. 'But I'm the big sister,' Rachael had always said, ''cos I'm three months older than you.'

Now, as she drew slowly back from Kirsty, her eyes were compassionate. 'Mum said you and Aunty Sylvia went to see the funeral directors today? That's quick.'

'She wants it done before your wedding so it's not hanging over us all.'

'That's thoughtful of her. I must admit, I feel bad about celebrating my day with all this going on.'

'You mustn't. You know Dad wouldn't want that.'

'I know. And maybe it's best for you, too, that it's done quickly. Once you've had the funeral, it's still awful but that's the worst bit over with.' She hesitated, then added simply, 'I've missed you. If there's anything I can do to help?'

'Thanks, Rachael.'

As Kirsty smiled her gratitude at her cousin, she resolved there and then not to touch a penny of any inheritance she might receive in the future until she'd worked out a fair division of the land monies. That decision made, her sense of conflict eased just a little.

'I've missed you, too. I'm sorry I've been crap at keeping in touch. I just needed to get away for a while.'

'I know. Have you heard from him?'

She feigned ignorance. 'Who?'

Rachael gave her a look and she felt the colour warm her cheeks.

'No and I don't expect to.'

'He'd like to come to the funeral. He asked me to ask you if it was okay. But he said he won't if you don't want him to.'

She could hardly bear to think of Luke at the moment with everything else that was going on, let alone see him. But she knew that was impossible. He'd been a part of her life for so long – knew everyone she knew – it was inevitable they were going to run into each other. She needed to see him and get it over with.

She shrugged. 'It's fine. He can come if he wants. I don't mind.'

'I'll tell him. He's not seeing anyone else, by the way, just so you know. No one serious, anyway.'

'He can see who he likes. We're not engaged anymore.' Kirsty looked at her cousin and held her eye. 'Too much went on, Rach. You know how he felt about his mum's affair. He's never going to forgive me.'

'Do you want him to?'

'It would be nice to think we could at least be friends.'

But even as she spouted the words, she knew she was kidding herself. She could never be just friends with him – the mere thought of seeing him with someone else…

She could tell from her cousin's answering smile that she wasn't fooled. 'The heart's a funny thing,' she said. 'Time can be a great healer – maybe he–'

'No. I know you're trying to make me feel better, but I messed up. Plain and simple.'

And that had to be the understatement of the year, she thought. So much had been left out in those few words – the self-recrimination, the hurt, the shame. But the end result was the same. She'd lost the love of her life, and there was no going back.

'How's Ben?' she asked, changing the subject.

'He's cool. Working all the hours God sends at the moment so we can hopefully save enough money to buy our own place in a year or two. I know it has to be done but we hardly seem to see each other at the moment … and he's so stressed. Not ideal. The honeymoon can't come a day too soon as far as I'm concerned.'

Kirsty didn't need to hear that, knowing that if her father had been more honest it might have freed up a bit of extra cash for them. She couldn't imagine her aunt pocketing a sizeable amount of money without giving at least some of it to her only daughter. Later, as she prepared for bed, it firmed her resolve. She'd sit down with her mother and Rob and sort out the land issue sooner rather than later.

'What have you got there, boy? It feels like you've been locked away in here all weekend.'

Harry looked up from his seat at his grandmother's dining table, as she limped into the room leaning heavily on her stick. Despite the fact she'd aged these last few months, and putting aside the walking stick and physical frailty, she was still the same gran she'd always been, her inquisitive expression as sharp and all-seeing as ever.

'Oh, just some papers for a case I'm working on. Trying to sort out my priorities for tomorrow.'

'Is it the murder of that man they found in Brookmans Park?'

'How did you guess?'

'Not that difficult when your grandson's one of the best detectives the police force has got. Who else are they going to get to look into it?'

There was real pride in her voice and Harry smiled wryly.

'Thanks, Gran. Good to know someone's got confidence in me, but I can't say I'm getting very far at the moment.'

'You'll get there. You always were a bright boy. Never stopped talking when you were little – like you'd been injected with a gramophone needle, your grandfather used to say. Don't know what the equivalent of that would be these days with all the newfangled technology that's around.'

The sound of the doorbell had her tutting. 'Can't be that time already.'

'What time?'

'Eight o'clock. The time Claire comes to help me get ready for bed. It's far too early for me, but I suppose the girl has to have some sort of private life. And at least she tries to make me her last call of the night. Let her in for me, will you? Then I'll leave you in peace, I promise.'

Harry got up from his seat and went to the door. The woman who stood on the doorstep was about the same age as him, with shoulder-length, chestnut-coloured hair swept neatly up into a ponytail. Her collar was pulled high up to her chin in an effort to keep the cold air at bay, and the smile she flashed at Harry was coolly professional.

'You must be Harry,' she said, as he stood aside to let her in. 'I'm Claire, your grandmother's carer – not that I'd dare use that word to her. It's good to meet you finally.'

She took her coat off and hitched it on the base of the banister in a calm, efficient manner that reflected familiarity. 'Where is Jean? Is she in the lounge?'

'Er, no. Dining room.'

'Right. I'll just get on then, shall I?'

'Yes, sure. Anything I can do? What's the routine?'

He watched as she picked up a black document bag and tucked it under her arm.

'Well, usually I help her wash and undress before getting her into bed, but if you're here I could probably do the first two, and then – I don't know how you're placed as a general rule – but I know it bugs her no end that she has to go to bed so early.'

'Of course,' Harry jumped in. 'No problem. I can help her up the stairs last thing at night. I might not be able to do it every night because sometimes I work late, but I can always ring and let her know on those occasions.'

She flashed him a wide smile and it lit her whole face, catching him by surprise.

'I'm glad you've moved in,' she said simply. 'She's such a trooper but she's quite poorly, as you know, and she was getting fidgety about being here on her own if anything happened. It was worrying her.'

Harry shrugged. 'Yeah, well … She knew she was going to get her way on that one eventually. I couldn't go on stalling forever.'

He didn't mean it to come out quite the way it did, and wasn't really surprised when she looked at him disapprovingly. 'Old age and infirmity come to us all,' she returned mildly. 'You might want to remember that.'

'I stand reprimanded,' he murmured back, and she flashed him a sharp look before turning away and heading for the dining room.

'Hello, Jean,' he heard her say, 'and how are you on this freezing cold night? It's lovely and warm in here, I must say.'

Harry waited until they'd disappeared upstairs before heading back to his work in the dining room, but he found his mind wasn't quite as focused as it had been – the image of a pair of disdainful blue eyes somehow managing to come between him and the jumble of words written down on the pad in front of him.

CHAPTER ELEVEN

God, that had been a grim night.

Kirsty threw back the bedclothes and padded to the bathroom, trying to shake off the image she'd woken up to – her father's body lying in the morgue, as she'd seen it yesterday. She'd only viewed it because her mother hadn't wanted to go alone – and now she wished she hadn't.

She splashed water on her face and stared at her reflection. She looked a mess but really, who cared? It was hardly surprising, and there were more important things in life than the image you presented to the outside world. It had been a long time coming, that realisation – she'd been brought up in a material world where things like appearances mattered – and when Luke used to say that she could wear a sackcloth for all he cared or noticed, she'd been affronted rather than flattered, not seeing the statement for what it was – an affirmation of his unconditional acceptance of her.

In the bedroom her phone rang and she walked back in to answer it. It was as if thinking about him had conjured him up as she viewed the caller display. *Luke Mob*. About to hit the Reject button, she hesitated, and on impulse hit the Accept.

'Hey,' he said.

'Hey.'

A pause.

'How are you?'

'Not brilliant.'

'Sorry to hear about your dad.'

'Thanks.'

Another pause.

'Thanks for saying I could come to the funeral. I liked Dom, as you know – even if he did threaten to string me up and hang me out to dry when we broke up.'

'He did?'

'Oh, yeah – told me I was lucky there were mitigating circumstances.'

She couldn't help smiling at that deliberate understatement on her father's part – not at all in keeping with the way he'd ripped into her about it. The words *reckless* and *foolhardy* sprung to mind – not to mention *not appreciating what she had*. He'd made no bones about the fact he thought she'd been an idiot. As if she *needed* telling that.

She thought about all the letters – pages of them, still sitting on her computer – telling Luke how sorry she was, desperate ramblings in her darkest moments about how she couldn't envisage her life without him. But they were letters that would never be sent. Even in that state of mind she'd known that. The truth of it was, she'd betrayed him and there was no coming back from that.

Luke was still talking, saying how he'd met up with Rachael last night and that she'd passed on the message that Kirsty was okay with him going to the funeral. The deep timbre of his voice stirred memories she was better off forgetting. She still remembered the physical piercing pain in her heart when she'd realised they were finished. She'd hoped having nine months away from him might make things easier, help her move on –

but it was as if he was here in the room with her, the familiarity of him everywhere. Overwhelming her.

'I'd better go, Luke,' she said, frightened she was about to disgrace herself.

'Oh, right. Sure. I'll see you Thursday, then ... look after yourself.'

'You, too.'

She ended the call and grabbed a tissue off the dresser, blowing her nose hard. Her gaze drifted to the picture of her parents on the windowsill – her father beaming out at her as if he didn't have a care in the world. She moved over to pick it up. *Had* he been a good man? She felt she didn't know him anymore – found it difficult reconciling the man who'd always loved her, been there for her – with the one who could swindle his own sister-in-law and niece out of a significant amount of money. It had rocked her faith in him. She couldn't help wondering what else he might have done.

And it made another anxiety gnaw at her. Could the police be right in wondering if his death might be linked to that tenant's? Could he have been mixed up in something illegal that had gone wrong?

A year ago she wouldn't have countenanced the thought, but now that she knew he sometimes walked a fine line in his business dealings…

What if someone *had* killed him? If there was even the slightest possibility of that, could she bury her head in the sand and not want to see justice done? Even if it meant embarrassment to them as a family?

Let it go, she told herself. Leave it to the police to sort out.

But *would* they, with their overstretched resources? How could she be sure they'd do a proper job? Guilt plucked at her – at how she'd refused to talk to her father these last few months, punishing him. Now she felt she needed to make it up to him. If she did a little delving herself – going through the office files, for example, to see if there was anything untoward that might have led to someone wanting him out of the way ... what harm could it do?

The answer of course was none, as long as she didn't discover anything bad. But if she did discover something...

Trepidation plucked at her stomach as she realised the possible ramifications of that. After all, if someone had killed once...

She put the photo back down on the windowsill. Yup, she should definitely let it go.

But she knew she wouldn't.

An hour and a half later, she was walking into Cartwrights office where Robbie was sitting at his desk. Sharon, the secretary, was busy at the photocopier, but she was quick to offer her sympathies as Kirsty walked in.

'I'm so sorry about your dad. I can't believe it. It must have been a dreadful weekend for you all. If there's anything I can do.'

'Thanks,' Kirsty said. 'We're still reeling from the shock of it, but there's not much I can do at home, so I thought I'd come in here and give Rob a hand.'

She walked through to her brother's office and closed the door behind her.

'You okay?' she asked, sitting down in the visitors' chair.

He nodded.

'I thought you could probably do with some help?'

'Thanks. I don't know if I'm coming or going at the moment. I'll need to think about employing someone to help out, that's for sure.'

'I can do it.'

'You've got a job.'

'No I haven't, not really. We both know Dad conjured that

job out of nowhere to give me some space. And he was right, I needed space back then – but I don't need it now. Coming home's made me realise that this is where I want to be. Jean-Pierre's been great but he doesn't really need me. Whereas you, I suspect, do.'

'I haven't even given a thought to the business and how it's going to work.'

'Well, I have and I'm sure we can work together if you're prepared to spend a bit of time filling me in.'

She was annoyed to see that her brother didn't look particularly enthused at that prospect.

'You know it's what Dad always intended, Rob. That's why he asked Jean-Pierre to give me a job. I've learnt a lot these last nine months.'

'You're not experienced enough.'

'Yes, I am. I've worked at Jordan's to see how the conveyancing side works, I've spent the last nine months working in sales for Jean-Pierre and I've done Saturday and holiday jobs here since I was sixteen.'

'It's a big responsibility, Kirsty. Mum still needs an income–'

'Dad will have provided for her, you know that – and the business does well, doesn't it? I wouldn't expect to be paid a fortune.'

'I don't know…'

'Well, I do,' Kirsty said firmly, standing up. 'I'm going to familiarise myself with Dad's files and get on with it. Trust me – I won't let you down.'

She flashed him a quick grin to diffuse the situation, trying to hide her annoyance that he obviously *didn't* trust her.

At the door, she turned. 'By the way, where did Paul Copeland live? What was his address?'

'Why do you want to know that?'

'I thought I'd call in on his girlfriend. Offer my condolences.'

'Dad already did that – there's no need.'

'All the same, I'd like to. She was one of the last people to see Dad alive. Aren't you even curious about that? That there could be a connection between the two deaths?'

'Kirsty, don't start meddling. The man was murdered, for God's sake. You don't know what you might be getting into if you start poking around.'

'I'm not going to do anything stupid.'

'I hope not. Mum couldn't take it if anything happened to you as well.'

'So you think there *could* be a connection?'

'No … I'm not saying that. I'm just saying we don't know what Paul Copeland was into and you might be putting yourself at risk if you start interfering.'

The memory of her father's body lying on that slab surfaced in her head, and she knew she couldn't let it rest. Not yet … not until she had at least seen the woman to get a sense of the situation if she could.

But she wouldn't add to Robbie's stress. She'd get the address from the files.

CHAPTER TWELVE

'Morning! Good weekend?'

DCI Murray breezed up to Harry's desk and chucked a packet of chocolate biscuits at him before heaving himself into the spare seat. 'Don't say I never think of you.'

'Thanks, sir.'

'What's on the agenda for today?'

'Well, I had planned on calling on the couple where Dominic Cartwright did the house viewing the day he died, but I ended up doing that on Saturday.'

'Learn anything?'

'Nothing new, except that Cartwright had apparently arranged to meet up with someone for a bite to eat after the viewing. They didn't know who of course – that would be asking too much, but they did mention that he seemed quite stressed. Beth's visiting Copeland's parents to have a chat with them and then we're both going to talk to the Lazards again – Ken Lazard lied to us about where he was the night of Copeland's murder, so I'd like to try to get to the bottom of that.'

'So he has no alibi?'

'Not sure. Beth remembered his wife mentioning another pub that he frequented, so we gave that a try and several people confirmed that he'd been there Monday night, but they were all noticeably cagey about timings.'

'Trying to help their friend?'

'That's what it felt like.'

'I take it you informed them they weren't helping their own causes by withholding evidence from the police?'

'For all the good it did us.'

Murray reached for the biscuits he'd bought, helping himself to three, and Harry suppressed a smile. He liked it that his boss was a bit of a maverick who openly stuck two fingers up at the accepted norms of what he should and shouldn't be doing.

'Afraid I'm not going to be much use to you on this one,' Murray said. He frowned irritably. 'The powers that be, in their wisdom, have got nervous with all the media hype that's going on at the moment, and want me to look into our historic handling of rape accusations over the last ten years. They want to be seen to be giving it high priority and high seniority, which means I'm going to be tied to my desk for a while.'

That wasn't good news: Harry suspected that his boss would be like a bear with a sore head within a very short space of time, not being in on the action.

'Our record's not bad, is it?'

'Historically we haven't done too badly, I don't think, but I won't know exact figures until I go through all the case files. There have been a couple of local attacks in more recent months – plus a couple in Barnet I seem to remember that came under the Met.'

'You saw the report I left on your desk last week? The woman who had the incident with the 'dodgy' chap?'

'Yes, she sounded a bit of a nutcase if you ask me – don't look at me like that – there wasn't much to go on, was there?

Apart from the fact she didn't like his tone. Probably some drunken yob trying his luck, rather than anything more sinister.'

As Harry had come to the same conclusion, there wasn't much he could say to that. The woman had admitted to drinking 'maybe a bottle of wine' to herself, and after filing the complaint had gone off on one about how all men were shits and after only one thing.

'Well, I'll give you regular updates on the Copeland case, no worries there,' Harry said.

'And obviously I'll still have my finger on the pulse if you need me. How's DC Macaskill doing?'

'Keen as mustard and very capable is my impression.'

'That's something at least. You don't need me to tell you that you need to keep pressing on this case, Harry – don't let the grass grow under your feet, or what few clues you have may rapidly disappear.'

Harry was only too aware of that.

Murray rose to go. 'Keep me in the loop and if you need any input from me just ask. I'm one of that rare breed of men who can multitask – I just don't like to broadcast the fact.'

Two hours later, Harry was in the incident room going over what they'd got, when his mobile rang.

'Hi, Beth, where are you?'

'Just leaving Paul Copeland's parents in Whetstone. They're heartbroken. He was their only child, but even they admit he was a bit wayward.'

'Anything useful?'

'No. They hadn't seen him in three months. Do you want me back at the station now?'

'I'm heading over to the Lazards. You can join me there if you want. The husband's not due into work until twelve-thirty today because his wife had a hospital appointment. I thought it might be useful seeing the both of them together.'

'Cool, I'll see you there in about half an hour.'

Ken Lazard looked nervous, Harry thought, as he sat down in their lounge – as well he might. He was an average-looking guy – early forties, medium height, brown hair and eyes – and his manner as he sat close to his wife in her wheelchair, clutching her hand tightly, was one of protectiveness.

'It's about your alibi,' Harry said, coming straight to the point.

'Oh, yeah?'

'Well, it seems you gave us the wrong pub. I was just wondering why you'd do that?'

'Did I?' He made a show of furrowing his brow. 'Could've sworn it was the Black Boar I went to.'

'No one remembered you there, but several people remembered you in your usual – The Crown.'

Ken shrugged. 'Must've got the days mixed up. Maybe it was the Tuesday I went to the Black Boar. In fact, now I think about it, yeah … I think it was. Sorry about that.'

'I wouldn't like to think you're messing us around, Mr Lazard, and I'm not sure you appreciate the seriousness of this situation. A man was murdered last Monday – a man you had a motive for wanting to harm. Unless you want to find yourself down at the police station for formal questioning, I need some straight answers.'

The front door buzzer went and Ken jumped at the chance of answering it.

'That'll probably be my colleague, DC Macaskill.' Harry said.

As Ken went to answer it, Harry turned to his wife. She was looking anxious, clearly unsettled by what was going on.

'I don't know why you're picking on Ken – there must be a queue of people out there who have got it in for Paul Copeland. He was scum.'

'I'm not picking on him; I'm trying to establish the truth of where he was so we can eliminate him,' Harry said. 'And Paul Copeland may have been scum, but he didn't deserve to be murdered.'

'My Ken wouldn't murder anyone. You tell him, love,' she said, as he walked back in with Beth.

'I already have,' Ken said. 'Maybe I did get it wrong about the name of the pub, but you caught me on the hop, and I don't know about you but I don't keep a diary of which pub I go to every night. How did you find out I'd been at The Crown?'

'I remembered your wife saying that was your usual haunt,' Beth said. 'We thought we'd have a chat with them.'

'And what did they say?'

'What do you think they said?' Harry asked.

A shrug of the shoulders.

'Well, several people said that you'd been there Monday night – but here's the strange thing – no one could give any definite information on times.'

Harry noted the small smirk that came into play around Ken's mouth. 'So now you've got your memory back, perhaps you could enlighten us on that?' he added.

Another shrug. 'It's pretty much as I said before. I probably got there between eight-thirty and nine, and was back here by eleven.'

'Your wife told DC Macaskill here that it was nearer eleven-thirty.'

'Did she? Could've been, I suppose. I'm not good at detail.'

'It's a shame that, Mr Lazard, because I have to tell you that unless someone can confirm the exact times, it doesn't put you in a very good place as far as your alibi's concerned. Paul Copeland was killed pretty much within that window.'

'*No.*'

It was Maggie Lazard who gasped the word, her eyes flying in fear to her husband's. '*Ken–*'

'There's nothing for you to worry about, Magz – I'm sure there are people at the pub who'll be able to back me up when they've had a bit of time to think back to last Monday. They can't pin it on me when I didn't do it, can they?'

The look he threw at Harry was hostile. 'Is that all?'

'One other thing. Do you know a man called Dominic Cartwright? He owns Cartwright Estate Agents in Barnet and was the managing agent for Paul Copeland's flat.'

'Never heard of him. Are you going to accuse me of killing him, too?'

'So you know he's dead, then?'

For the first time, the other man looked rattled. 'No, I didn't – I was being sarcastic.'

'It's not a good idea to play games in these situations. I generally find plain talking and the truth work much better.'

'I'll try and remember that.'

'Is there anything you want to add to your statement before we go – something you may have forgotten?'

'No.'

'Then that's all for now,' Harry said, standing up. 'But please don't leave the area without informing us – we don't want to be chasing around looking for you if we need to question you again. You know where we are if you want to talk to us.'

'He's hiding something, isn't he?' Beth said as they walked down the path to their respective cars.

'Yeah, I'm pretty sure of it. But not much we can do at the moment apart from hope that something more comes to light at some point. I might go back to the pub tonight seeing as it's Monday. See if anyone's there who was there last Monday. It can't do any harm to jog people's memories.'

'So what's next?'

He pulled out the handwritten notes he'd made from Paul Copeland's tenancy file and leafed through them. 'Ah, here it is.

Next is Simon Jordan, of Jordan's Solicitors – Paul Copeland's landlord. They're in Whetstone. I'm not holding out much hope they'll have anything interesting to add, but we need to tick the box. Are you happy to come with me?'

'Sure, I'll follow you.'

'Here it is, Jordan & Son, Solicitors,' Beth read out loud, as they stood outside the swish, modern premises on Whetstone High Street. She pushed open the door and they walked in.

Inside, the attractive brunette sitting at the reception counter smiled as they approached.

'We'd like to see Simon Jordan?' Harry said.

'Do you have an appointment?'

He pulled out his ID. 'No, but hopefully he'll see us.'

The receptionist studied the ID and gave it back to him. Then she picked up her phone and dialled a number.

'There are two police officers to see Simon,' she said into the mouthpiece. 'Okay.'

She smiled at Harry and got up from her chair, escorting them to a large office to the left of the reception area. There, an older man half-rose from his chair and stepped forward to greet them, indicating a couple of seats as Harry and Beth were shown in.

'Hi, Tony Jordan. I'm afraid my son's out visiting a client. Can I help at all?'

'We're investigating the murder of Paul Copeland,' Harry said. 'I understand he was a tenant of your son's at his property in Barnet?'

'Yes. Terrible business. In fact, it's been a shocking week one way and another.' He looked haggard as he said it, shaking his head as he sat back down in his chair.

'Did you or your son know Mr Copeland personally?'

'No. Cartwrights manage a couple of properties for us and that includes finding tenants as and when necessary. We don't usually have any input into the process, apart from accepting their recommendation when they find someone suitable.'

'So you never met him?' Harry asked.

'No.'

'Was your son aware Paul Copeland had just come out of prison when he took up the tenancy?'

'Yes, I believe so. Robbie told him he'd been done for dangerous driving or something – he wasn't exactly a criminal – and the fact was the flat had been empty for three months. His references stacked up and Robbie reckoned he'd be a safe enough bet. Which he was, until this happened.'

Harry changed tack. 'What about Dominic Cartwright? You obviously knew him quite well?'

The older man looked shattered. 'We went to school together. Our families are very close.' He shook his head. 'It hasn't sunk in yet – I can't believe it.'

'When was the last time you saw him?'

'He dropped by Thursday of last week – the day he died. I think he wanted to talk to us in person about the Paul Copeland thing. It had obviously upset him.'

Harry's ears pricked up. 'You saw him last Thursday? What time was that?'

'Well ... as I say, it was a spur of the moment thing, so I didn't make a note of the time, but I reckon it was probably around ten-thirty to ten-forty-five? He'd just been to see the chap's girlfriend and was clearly upset. He was hoping to see Simon, as it was his tenant, but Simon was out so we had a coffee together and he told me about it instead. I reckon he was here about twenty minutes.'

'He didn't say anything that you think might be relevant regarding Paul Copeland's death?'

'I don't think so. He said he'd been to see the girlfriend and wanted to talk to Simon.'

'He didn't say what about?'

'I presumed it was to do with the tenancy and how they'd handle things.'

'Did he say where he was going after that?'

'Another appointment, I think. I told him I'd get Simon to ring him when he got back and that was it.'

'And did he?'

'I'm not sure. Simon hasn't mentioned it if he did, and Dom went on to his next appointment which I believe is where he had the accident, so there wouldn't have been much time between leaving here and that happening.'

Harry rose from his chair, Murray's comment about not letting the grass grow under his feet beginning to sound like an ominous foreboding.

'Okay, thanks. Maybe you could ask your son to give me a call?' He pulled out yet another card and handed it over.

'Of course. I'm sorry I couldn't be of more use.' Tony Jordan looked suddenly anxious and much older than his age, as he said, 'Dom's death *was* an accident? You're not thinking it might be linked to Paul Copeland's?'

'We can't say for sure. At the moment we're pursuing the two lines of enquiry separately, but we can't rule out that they might be connected. I'd rather you didn't share that with the press, though.'

'No, of course not. Jesus…' The other man looked devastated. 'I can't believe it … Poor Sylvia. If there's anything more I can help you with?'

He looked up suddenly as the street door to their offices opened.

'Oh, looks like you're in luck. Here's Simon now if you want to talk to him.'

Harry's eyes followed his gaze to the man who had just walked in. Simon Jordan was early thirties, pristinely dressed in suit and tie, and had the air about him of a man in a hurry. But when Harry explained to him who they were and why they were there, his manner changed instantly to one of concern as he led them into his office and sat down at his desk.

'God, it's a dreadful business. What do you want to know?'

'Well, I understand Dominic Cartwright wanted to talk to you about the death of your tenant, but you were out when he called?'

'Yes. Dad said he was quite upset about it.'

'Did you call him back? Speak to him?'

'No – I tried, but it went to answerphone. We learnt later that the accident had already happened. We couldn't believe it.'

'Is there anything you can tell us about Dominic Cartwright or Paul Copeland that you feel may be relevant to our investigations?'

'I wish there was. Dom was a lifelong friend of my parents' – he was like a second father to me, and I've known Kirsty and Rob all my life … but I hardly knew Paul Copeland – apart from to say hello to when I was living upstairs. But there was never any trouble with him that I was aware of.'

'Okay.' Harry didn't even bother getting his notebook out again. 'Thanks for your time. No … don't get up, we can see ourselves out.'

'Do you think he was telling the truth?' Beth asked as they walked back to the cars.

Harry sighed. 'Who knows? He sounded genuine enough, but at this stage we need to keep an open mind on everything.'

CHAPTER THIRTEEN

Kirsty stood outside number 28 Myton Road that evening, and wondered what the hell she was doing there. The memories associated with this house, when Simon had lived upstairs, were ones she was desperate to put behind her, impossible though she knew that was. She shoved them resolutely to one side and concentrated on the task in hand.

She hadn't a clue what she was going to say to Paul Copeland's girlfriend. She'd been fretting about it all day.

She took a breath and rang the bell.

The girl who came to the door was only a year or two older than herself, and she looked exhausted – and anxious – her eyes darting beyond Kirsty along the road, before coming back to settle on her face.

'Yeah?'

'Susan Porter?'

'Yeah.'

'I'm sorry to bother you. I know it's a difficult time, but my name's Kirsty Cartwright, Dominic Cartwright's daughter? I wondered if I might have a quick word with you?'

The girl's look became more edgy. 'What about? I've already seen your brother this afternoon. He gave me the money and I'm off.'

'I'm sorry? Money?'

The girl sighed impatiently. 'The two grand.'

'*Two*–?' Kirsty stared at her stunned. 'Look, can I come in – just for a moment?'

'I'm in the middle of packing.'

'I won't keep you long, I promise. I just want to ask you a couple of questions about my father.'

The girl's expression relaxed, almost reluctantly. 'He was nice, your dad. I'm sorry about what happened to him.' She opened the door wider. 'Okay, just for a minute.'

The flat was almost identical in layout to the flat Simon had occupied upstairs, but mercifully the décor was very different, which made it easier for Kirsty.

Closing the door behind them, Susan headed straight for the bedroom, her manner brisk. 'I need to carry on with my packing. My brother's coming soon to pick me up. What did you want to talk about?'

Kirsty followed her through, marshalling her thoughts. 'I'm trying to piece together what happened to Dad – you know it was a hit-and-run accident? The police don't seem to have ruled out the possibility that it could be linked to your boyfriend's death, and I can't get my head around that.'

The other girl peered at her sharply before turning away to open a drawer. 'I'm sorry, but I can't help you with that. The police were here again on Saturday asking more questions, and I'll tell you what I told them. Your dad came to offer his sympathy, we talked a bit about Paul and what I was going to do now, and then he left.'

'You mentioned about my brother giving you some money. What was that for?'

Susan hesitated. 'It was kind of him. He came here on Saturday after the police had been, and asked what I wanted to do about the flat. There's still eight months to run on the contract, see, and I couldn't afford it on my own, but he said as how the landlord was thinking of doing the place up and selling it, and was prepared to give me two grand to go. I couldn't believe it.'

'And you say he came up today and paid you the money?'

'Yeah. In cash. He told me not to tell anyone 'cos it's not really the done thing – and I won't. I thought as you're family you probably already knew.'

Kirsty stared at her. It made her wonder what else Rob might be getting up to on the quiet.

She stopped her mind from thinking about that now and concentrated instead on the issue in hand. This would probably be the only chance she got to talk to Susan.

'Was there any link between Paul and my dad, do you think – no matter how small – that might have made them a danger or threat to someone else?'

The girl shook her head but her eyes dipped away from Kirsty's. She wasn't being straight – Kirsty sensed it straight away.

'Susan, please–'

'There's nothing.' She turned her back on Kirsty and pulled some articles of clothing out of the drawer.

'There was something – I can tell. Why aren't you telling me? It may be relevant to why Dad was killed – why Paul was killed.'

The girl swung round, her expression one of defiance mixed with pure terror. 'You don't get it, do you? Maybe it was – and maybe that's why I'm not saying! Jeez, I'm scared out my wits if you want the truth. I don't wanna end up like them – that's why my bruvver's coming to get me.'

'So you do think their deaths are connected?'

'I don't know.'

She glared at Kirsty as if it was all her fault, then shrugged, returning to her task of ramming more clothes into the suitcase. 'It's possible, isn't it? Seems too much of a coincidence to me.'

'I just want to find out what happened to my dad, Susan. Like you probably feel about Paul.'

She could sense the girl weighing it up in her mind. Finally, with another little shrug, she shook her head. 'Paul was suspicious about something, that's all I know. He thought he could make money out of it, but he wouldn't tell me what it was – and I stopped asking. Knowing him, it were probably nothing anyway. I just want out of here. I'm sorry, but you must go now.'

'Did you tell my father that? You must tell me.' Kirsty could hear the desperation in her own voice. 'Please ...'

'Yeah, I told him. But I ain't got nothing else to say. I mean that.' She slammed the lid of the suitcase shut and led the way out into the hall. 'You best go now.'

Kirsty followed her, searching for something ... anything ... that might yet change Susan's mind, but she'd run out of ideas. At the last minute, she pulled a Cartwrights card out of her bag and scribbled on it, then thrust it at the girl. 'That's my mobile number. If you change your mind and want to help me find out what happened to Paul and my father, just call me. I'll keep anything you tell me confidential, I promise. I'm not the police, but I've got friends in influential places who might be able to help us without drawing attention to anything. Please call.'

It was all bollocks, but what did she have to lose? She heard the front door close behind her as she walked down the path, feeling more worried than she could ever have imagined, and trying to make some sense it all.

What was going on? What the hell was going on?

She needed to talk to Rob.

But when she rang his mobile, and told him where she was, he cut her off.

'Sorry, Kirsty, but I'm nearly home and we've got Lizzie's parents staying over.'

'Rob, we have to talk.'

'What about?'

'The money you gave Susan Porter, for one thing. What was that about?'

'It wasn't about anything. Simon felt sorry for the girl and bad about Paul, that's all. It was his way of helping her out. Look, I'm home now. We can talk about this tomorrow if you want. Give my love to Mum. Tell her Lizzie will drop round in the morning to see her.'

Sometimes, Harry thought – feeling thoroughly hacked off – life seemed to conspire against you. And tonight was one of those nights. He'd spoken to nine people in The Crown pub, all of them regulars, and most of whom had been there last Monday night – yet none of them had been able to confirm the exact length of time Ken Lazard had been at the pub. Some said they'd seen him at the beginning of the evening, some said at the end, but not one had said a definite *yes*, they'd seen him there all evening and given exact timings. Was there some sort of conspiracy going on that he definitely wasn't a party to?

He was about to give up and leave when another man walked into the pub. 'Evening, Derek,' he said to the landlord. 'A pint of bitter, when you've got a moment – that one you recommended last week, if you remember which one it was.'

The man smiled at Harry. 'Sorry. Hope I'm not pushing in?'

Harry held up his empty glass before putting it down on the counter. 'I'm leaving.'

The man looked around him. 'A bit quieter in here tonight, eh?' he said to the landlord. 'Not like that ruckus last week.'

'Yeah.' The barman threw a quick look at Harry and shuffled uncomfortably. 'Happens sometimes when you run a pub.'

'What was that?' Harry asked, more out of politeness than anything.

'Oh, nothing.'

'*Nothing?* I wouldn't say that. You're being modest, Derek. It could have turned nasty if you hadn't stepped in and calmed things down.'

Harry flicked a glance at Derek, picking up on the man's uneasy body language, then looked back at the man next to him. 'What night was that?' he asked casually.

'A week ago. Last Sunday wasn't it, Derek, when those two blokes had that fight?'

'Hmm …' Derek responded, turning away and reaching for a glass. His obvious reluctance to engage in conversation heightened Harry's interest. He pulled out his card. 'I wouldn't mind hearing about that if you've got a moment? Can we sit and have a chat? You may be able to help us with our enquiries.'

Ten minutes later he was back at the bar. 'I think you and I need to talk, Derek,' he said to the barman. 'I'd say you've been deliberately withholding evidence from the police.'

The man looked at him for a long, hard moment, then turned his back on him. 'Jackie!' he yelled. 'Come out front for a bit, can you?'

He turned back to Harry and sighed. 'We didn't tell you because we know what you lot are like. And we know Ken. He's had a rough time – what with all the terrible stuff with his wife – and he doesn't deserve you lot sniffing around. He might have a temper, but he's not a murderer.'

'You know that for a fact, do you? Wish I could be so confident of everyone I knew. Who was his argument with?'

There was the slightest of hesitations before Derek told him, as if it was being dragged out of him. 'The guy who was murdered.'

Harry's mouth became grim. 'Right. I think you'd better start at the beginning, don't you?'

When Harry let himself into his grandmother's house an hour later, he was surprised to hear laughter coming from the sitting room. He looked at his watch. It was nearly half past nine. He smiled to himself. Who was she entertaining at this time of night?

'Ah, Harry. Come in, come in. Claire and I were just having a little tipple to celebrate her birthday.'

Claire looked up at him and laughed. 'Your grandmother …' she said, shaking her head. 'She's a wicked, wicked woman. She'd corrupt the Devil himself, given half a chance.'

'Don't I know it,' Harry grinned, walking further into the room and giving his grandmother a kiss. He looked at the half-finished glass of whisky by her side. 'Is it alright for you drinking alcohol at this time of night?'

'Of course it is, boy. If I'm going to go, I might as well go in good spirits, eh?' She laughed at her own joke and gave him a poke. 'Get yourself a glass of something and come and join us. We can't let the poor girl go home without celebrating her birthday, can we?'

'There's no need,' Claire said. 'Really … I should be off anyway.'

'Nonsense. Harry looks as if he could do with a drink. Let's party.'

It sounded so ridiculous coming from an eighty-nine-year-old woman that both Harry and Claire laughed. Harry went off to get himself a beer, marvelling at the change in his grand-mother since she'd come off the last of her meds. It was like she'd been given a new lease of life now she wasn't feeling sick all the time, and, although he knew it was only temporary, he vowed they'd make the most of it. If she wanted to party – they'd party.

CHAPTER FOURTEEN

Kirsty peered at the alarm clock by her bed and flung the bedclothes back in horror. Eight-thirty. How had she slept that late? – as if she didn't know. She'd spent half the night worrying about the conversation she'd had with Susan, playing it over in her mind, angry with herself for not pressing harder for information. That was always something she'd been teased for, wasn't it? – her tenacity and refusal to let go of things. So where were those traits when she most needed them? She was pathetic. And now it was too late. She'd probably never see the woman again and she was none the wiser about anything.

No … that wasn't strictly true. She *had* learnt something. Susan had told her father about Paul's suspicions and Kirsty suspected there was more to that than she'd let on. It was *possible* that was the reason for her father's death. And if that was the case, then it was huge.

In the kitchen her mother frowned when she saw Kirsty was dressed for work. 'Are you going into the office again?'

'Yes.'

She needed to talk to Robbie. And maybe the police.

'You should leave things to Robbie. It would be nice if you stayed here to support me.'

'Oh, I'm sorry, Mum. I thought Anne was coming round this morning and the two of you were going out?'

'She is, but – maybe it's best if you don't go into the office today.'

Kirsty looked at her mother suspiciously. She had her full attention now.

'Has Rob been talking to you?'

Her mother looked awkward. 'He's just not sure it's a good idea for the two of you to run the business together.'

'*What*? Why not? It's what Dad always intended – you know it is.'

'Yes, well Dad's not here now and the situation's different. It's a lot of responsibility for Robbie – and he's clearly feeling the burden. We don't want to add to that.'

Kirsty couldn't help wondering what else her brother had been saying. 'Mum, I'm trying to ease his burden, not add to it. What do you think I've been doing the last nine months at Jean-Pierre's? I've been learning the business. I know what I'm doing and I can help Robbie.'

'I'm sure you think you can, love, but if he's not convinced … maybe now's not the time to push it? You've not been around the last year to see the pressure having the children has added to his life. He's really not been himself, and if on top of that he's got to train you up–'

'He'd have to do that to anyone he got in. And I know more about the business than most. I've been helping out since I was sixteen.'

'Yes, but I don't think any of us really expected you to make a career out of it. It was only ever meant to be a stopgap until you and Luke had a family.'

'Well, that's not going to happen now, is it?' Kirsty snapped. 'Are you saying it's more important for Robbie to have a career than me? I can't believe we're having this conversation.'

'You know how I feel. A career's fine until you marry and have children, but after that your duty should be to your husband and family – like Lizzie. You may not realise it now but having a family is very fulfilling for a woman–'

'But that's not relevant to me at the moment, is it?'

'Oh, darling … you'll meet someone else.'

'That's not the point. And what has any of this got to do with whether Rob and I work together or not?' She couldn't keep the impatience out of her tone and then felt awful as she saw her mother's eyes well up. 'I'm sorry,' she said quickly, reaching out to touch her arm. 'I don't mean to sound aggressive.'

Her mother shook her head and reached for a tissue from the table. 'No, I'm the one who should be sorry … I just want to feel my family close around me. I hate to think of you and Rob falling out.'

Kirsty gave her a hug, breathing in her perfume – letting the familiarity of it calm her.

'We're not falling out, Mum. We're just grieving, all of us, in our different ways. It'll get easier.'

They stood like that for a shared moment before Kirsty drew back. 'Though I'd better get going if I don't want Rob to fire me before I've even started working there. I promise I'll tread easily with him. Will you be okay until Aunty Anne comes?'

Her mother nodded. 'She'll be here soon. Aren't you putting some make-up on before you go?'

Kirsty tried to hide her frustration. 'No.'

'I don't know what's got into you these days. You've changed since you've been out in France. You even *look* different with your hair long like that and not styled. You mustn't let yourself go, it's not a good thing – and there's no need to smirk like that.'

'I'm not smirking. I know you think those things are important, but–'

'Yes, I do. Look at me, I'm in a terrible state but I still find time to do my make-up. It helps me face the day.'

'And if it helps, that's great, Mum. I'm just not as bothered about it as you are.'

She glanced at her watch. 'I must go.'

'You've not had any breakfast.'

'I'll buy something from the shop near the office.' She gave her mother a peck on the cheek. She looked genuinely bemused and Kirsty's heart went out to her. 'Look, call me if you need me later and I'll come home, okay? Rob and I will be fine. You'll see.'

She wished she felt as sure as she sounded. She was floundering in this new world that seemed to be opening up to her. And she felt desperately short of people she could turn to for advice.

Harry put his elbows on the desk and buried his head in his hands. His wild decision to party with his grandmother and Claire didn't feel quite such a good idea this morning. He couldn't believe they'd stayed up until the early hours. Well … he and Claire had … His grandmother had finally retired very ungracefully at eleven o'clock, needing more than a little assistance to get her up the stairs.

'Haven't enjoyed myself so much in years,' she'd mumbled, as they helped her into her bedroom. We should do this more often … we really should.'

'She's blossomed since you've been here,' Claire said, once they were back downstairs again. 'She's a different woman.'

Harry shrugged, embarrassed. Then he smiled. 'It's not very cool having to admit I'm living with my grandmother.'

'She told me about your parents travelling around a lot. That must have been hard for you as a little boy.'

'You get used to it.' He leant back in his chair and looked around his grandmother's lounge. Every inch of it was familiar – the photos of him dotted around the room, the china tea set in the display cabinet; the small Marie Antoinette clock sitting on the mantelpiece above the fire – and all of it was home. In this room he'd learnt to read, played games, done puzzles (there'd always been one on the go), snogged his first girlfriend and decided on his career. Unremarkable memories along with a thousand others, but every one of them part of the fabric that made up who he was today. He couldn't imagine this house not being a part of his life, but knew he'd have to get used to the idea soon enough when his grandmother was gone. He'd never be able to afford to buy it, that was for sure.

Now, as he returned his gaze to Claire, he said, 'They were good to me, my grandparents, and I've been lucky to know them. Not everyone gets that.'

'Where were your parents?'

'My father's an archaeologist – very well respected. Unfortunately you don't get many Egyptian remains in the UK – which is his speciality now.'

His smile was rueful.

'You could have travelled with them as a child?'

'Yes.'

'But you didn't?'

'No.'

It was clear she was waiting for more and he shrugged. 'When I was quite young they took me, but once I started school they felt it was better for me to be brought up in the UK. It was fine.'

'Right.'

There was a wealth of meaning in that response, which touched on a nerve. He jumped up to top up her glass.

'More wine? Or something soft?'

'Have you got some sort of juice, or elderflower? I've had enough wine if I'm driving.'

Harry disappeared off into the kitchen and came back into the room with an orange juice for her and another beer for himself.

'What about you? Where do you live?' he asked, sitting back down in his chair.

'Cuffley. I've got a small flat there – ground-floor house conversion with a garden. It does me alright.'

'And family?'

'Both parents, sister, brother, niece and nephew. They're all local so we see quite a lot of each other. Bit of a madhouse when we get together, but it's fun. I couldn't imagine growing up without them around me.'

'Boyfriend?' His tone was casual.

Hers was equally flippant. 'Nah … I'm off men at the moment. You?'

'Not a boyfriend,' he smiled. 'Or girlfriend for that matter. Don't seem to have the time.'

'I know what you mean.'

'So you're off men – is that a permanent state of affairs?'

She laughed, tossing her head cheerily. 'No. Just taking a sabbatical.'

'Sounds like there's a story there somewhere?'

'There is, but I don't intend boring you with it tonight. Let's just say I get a bit fed up with the games you blokes sometimes play.'

'Surely not?'

'Surely yes, and something tells me, Harry, you could be one of them.'

He held up a hand and laughed. 'Not guilty.'

But even as he said it, he knew that some women might indeed charge him with that offence. He was pretty good at playing the non-commitment game, for example.

'I'll reserve judgment until I know you better,' she said airily, flashing him a grin. And that grin got to him, pushing him to test the ground.

'You think we might get to know each other a bit better, then?'

He liked the small stain of colour that warmed her cheeks, but her reply was nonchalant. 'Who knows – though, as I say, I'm off men at the moment.'

'Maybe we'll have to see what we can do about that.'

It was the drink talking – or maybe it was just the effect she had on him. He wasn't usually as direct around women.

'Hmm...' The look she threw him was doubtful but he took some comfort from the fact she hadn't rejected the idea outright.

She twiddled her glass in her fingers and looked at him over the rim, surprising him by changing the subject.

'Your grandmother's doing well, but … you do realise it's probably not going to be long now, before–'

'I know. I talked to her doctor a couple of weeks ago.'

'Are you okay with that?'

'Nothing I can do about it, is there? I just want to make sure she's as comfortable as she can be when the time comes.'

'She worries about that.'

'I know she does.' Drink loosened his tongue. 'I can't do what she wants, though. She doesn't seem to understand that.'

'What do you mean?'

He shook his head. Much as he longed to open up to someone – get another point of view – he knew he couldn't.

'This conversation's getting morbid and it's your birthday. Tell me a bit about yourself … How old are you today? If it's not too rude a question?'

She laughed. 'Not rude at all. I'm thirty-one. How about you?'

'Two years older – but you don't look anywhere near that, whereas I suspect I do.'

'Probably the company you keep adds a few grey hairs.'

'Hey – that's one thing I don't have.'

'Oh, fishing, are you?' She made a pretence of studying his hair and he laughed. He felt comfortable talking to her here, in his grandmother's sitting room … liked that they could be relaxed with each other.

The next couple of hours had passed quickly … and as he drank his way through another half-pint of beer, followed by a rare indulgence of a glass of whisky, he'd found himself becoming hypnotised by her soft, mellow voice and the mobility of her face – the way it suddenly lit up when she recounted some amusing tale of her childhood and family. When he'd finally seen her out at quarter to one in the morning, they'd very nearly kissed. But somehow it had ended up as an awkward bumping of noses and they'd both laughed embarrassed. As he shut the door behind her, he'd groaned out loud and banged his head on the door. *Prat.*

But it hadn't detracted from the frisson of pleasure he'd experienced.

'What have you got?' Beth asked, plumping herself down on the corner of his desk and relieving him of this embarrassing memory. 'Because you look like the cat that got the cream.'

He shuffled some papers around on his desk, then remembered that he had another reason for looking pleased with himself.

'I revisited The Crown last night.'

'And?'

'I've got witnesses who saw Ken Lazard attack Paul

Copeland the night before he was killed. Seems he really lost it.'

Beth's jaw dropped. 'No! You said his girlfriend mentioned he'd been in a fight. What happened?'

'Apparently Copeland walked into the pub and Ken recognised him. Told him to get out while he still could. Paul got bolshie and refused. The next thing Ken went for him and the landlord had to split them up. Paul apparently left with Ken's shouts ringing in his ears about how he was going to get him.'

'Jesus. That sounds damning for our Ken.'

'Yup. Definitely means another visit. In fact, come on, we'll go now.'

At the day care centre they were let in by an attractive, forty-something woman with a bright smile and dark, shoulder-length hair.

'What can I do for you?' she asked pleasantly, ushering them in. Harry showed her his card.

'Is Ken Lazard around?'

'Yes. In his office probably.' Her manner altered slightly, becoming almost protective. 'He's a good man, you know. He does wonderful work with our clients here.'

'And you are?'

She smiled. 'Kathy Wilkins. I'm a volunteer. My husband's over there – the one in the bright red wheelchair.' She rolled her eyes. 'He was never one for understatements. Come with me. I'll take you to Ken.'

Ken's expression became irritable when he looked up and saw Harry and Beth – and yup, there was a glint of fear in those eyes, too, Harry thought.

'I'm really busy,' he greeted them, shuffling some papers around on his desk and not standing up.

'We won't keep you long,' Harry said easily. 'But there are one or two things we need to clear up with you. I'm thinking that yet again you haven't been entirely straight with us, Mr Lazard –

123

is there anything else you feel you might like to tell us relating to Paul Copeland that you might have forgotten to mention?'

Ken looked at him briefly, then looked away again. 'Don't think so.'

'Like, for example, your fight with him the night before he was killed?'

It looked for a moment as if Ken was going to deny it, then perhaps realising the futility of it, he pursed his lips and shrugged.

'Oh, come on,' Harry said. 'I think you can do better than the silent treatment. Why didn't you tell us?'

'I don't think I want to answer any more questions without my solicitor.'

'Your *solicitor*? Sounds like you've been preparing yourself for this moment, but I don't think we need to go down that route quite yet, do you?'

'My solicitor's also my mate. He advised me to call him if you found out about the fight – so that's what I'd like to do.'

Harry tried to hide his frustration. A solicitor meant more delays, more time-wasting, and he needed to get on and find out some facts.

'Well, that's your prerogative–'

'Yeah, it is. Whatever that means.'

'In that case I'm afraid I'll have to ask you to accompany me to the police station.'

'Are you arresting me?'

'All I want is to ask you a few questions at this stage. But if you want your solicitor present, then it needs to be done on a more formal basis and you'll have to come back with us to the police station. It's up to you.'

'Right. If you wouldn't mind waiting outside, then, while I make the call and phone my wife?'

In the interview room a couple of hours later, Harry sat

across from Ken and his solicitor – a large, balding man in his forties who was built like a tank. His expression was more belligerent than Ken's.

'Okay,' Harry said, after the preliminaries were done with the recording procedures. 'Let's get down to business, shall we? When was the last time you visited The Crown pub, Mr Lazard?'

There was the slightest of hesitations. 'Last night.'

His response took Harry by surprise.

'What time?'

'I got there about seven-forty-five.'

'Well – that's interesting. I was there last night. I didn't see you.'

Ken shrugged. 'Maybe I arrived after you'd gone.'

'Nope. Don't think so. I got there just after eight.'

How come no one in the pub had told him?

Ken hesitated. 'There's a quiet room at the back of the pub. I asked Derek if I could use it. Thanks to you, I've become a bit of a focus of attention to everyone – I wanted some peace and quiet.'

Harry let it go for the time being. 'Can you tell me about the fight you had with Paul Copeland on the evening of Sunday, 13th November 2016?'

Ken shrugged. 'There's not much to tell. I don't usually go in there on a Sunday, but Magz had a friend drop by and I nipped up for a quick one. The man walked into the pub and I recognised him straight away. There was no way I was drinking in the same pub as him, so I approached him and asked him to leave.'

'I was told it was a bit more aggressive than that.'

'Well, what do you think? Wouldn't you be aggressive in my place? The man put my wife in a bloody wheelchair, for Christ's sake, and didn't even have the decency to feel ashamed about it. Anyway, he wasn't having any of it. Told me to piss off, and refused to leave.'

'So you went for him?'

'I'll admit I saw red – and I went for him. We had a tussle but were pulled apart by Derek pretty quickly. Said he'd call the police if there was any more trouble. And that's when the useless piece of shit got his jacket and left.'

'I have a witness who says you left, too, straight after.'

'Yeah, well he'd ruined my day, hadn't he? I downed my drink and went. I just wanted to get home to my wife.'

'So what time was that when you left?'

'I don't know exactly. I was in a state. About six, I reckon.'

Outside the interview room, Beth and a couple of others were watching through the glass. Turning away, she headed for the door.

'If Harry asks where I am, tell him I've gone to get the pub's CCTV coverage for the Sunday. We never asked for that.'

CHAPTER FIFTEEN

I n the act of collecting her jacket, Beth looked over to where
the phone was ringing on Harry's desk. Coming to a decision, she walked over and picked it up.

'DC Macaskill…'

'Hi. Is DS Briscombe there?'

'Not at the moment. Can I help?'

'Are you working on the Paul Copeland case?'

'Yes.'

She straightened some papers on Harry's desk. Not that she
needed to, really. He was so tidy.

'My name's Joshua Wells. I'm a reporter with the *Barnet
News*. I think I might have some interesting information
for you.'

'Oh?' Beth stopped her tidying and kept her voice neutral.
'What sort of information?'

The man laughed. 'Now that would be telling. I don't want
to overplay my hand. I'm hoping we can come to some sort of
deal here, where if I help you a little, you might feel inclined to
help me.'

Beth sighed. They'd wondered when the press would start moving up to the next level, and it was always a gamble knowing how much to involve them.

'We're not into playing games, Mr Wells. If you've got information, you should tell us.'

'I believe you've just picked Ken Lazard up for formal questioning?'

How the hell did he know that? 'Are you following us or something?'

'Actually, I've been keeping my eye on him. It might interest you to know that I met up with Paul Copeland on the day he was killed. He had some interesting stuff to say about Ken Lazard.'

He had Beth's full attention now but she tried not to sound too keen as she responded coolly.

'What sort of stuff? How come you haven't come forward before now? This is a murder investigation.'

She could hear the smile in the man's voice. 'I've been holidaying in Spain with my girlfriend – had other things on my mind. Do you guys want to meet up with me or not? I ought to warn you that I intend running a story either way.'

Beth grabbed a pen, coming to a decision. She needed to go out anyway. She could kill two birds with one stone.

'Okay. I'm on my way out now, as it happens. Could you get to The Crown pub in Barnet for, say, midday? I'll meet you there.'

'Okay, you can't miss me – I've got shoulder-length hair, tied back in a ponytail.'

He was poring over some handwritten notes when Beth walked into the pub. He was in his early thirties and not bad-looking, if ponytails were your thing.

'Drink?' he asked, standing up and offering his hand.

'No thanks. Lots to get on with. So if we could just get on…?'

'Sure thing.'

He sat back down and gave her a laconic stare. 'How's the investigation coming on?'

'These things take time.' She pulled out her notebook. 'You say you saw Paul Copeland on the day of his death?'

'That's right. But before I give you any more, what's the deal here?'

'There's no deal, Mr Wells. You're duty-bound to tell us anything you know, or we can bring you in for withholding information.'

'Josh, please. And don't give me that. I've been around long enough to know what I can or can't do. All I'm asking is that if you charge anyone, you let me know before it hits the mainstream press. I don't think that's unreasonable. In return I'll tell you what I know now and keep you posted on anything new I might find out. I'd say that's a good deal from where I'm sitting.'

His eyes twinkled engagingly at her, charming her despite herself. She sighed. 'Okay, tell me what you've got and I'll run it past my boss.'

She looked at him, waiting expectantly, and after a few moments he spoke.

'I had a phone call from Paul Copeland the day he was killed. He told me he had a story for me and wanted to know if he could make some money out of it. I told him it depended how good it was, and stressed that it had to be true. We met up at his flat that morning and he filled me in on his background – how he'd accidentally hit Mr Lazard's wife with his car and been imprisoned for it, but had now been released. He told me that the previous night he'd gone to a pub in Barnet and Ken Lazard had been there. Apparently Ken went for him and a fight broke out. They were separated by the landlord, who told Paul to leave.'

'You're not telling us anything we don't know, so far,' Beth said, shaking her head.

'Right. So did you know that after that fight, Ken Lazard followed Paul home?'

Beth's gaze sharpened. 'How do you know that?'

'Paul told me. He said he didn't live far away from the pub and walked home. As he opened his front door he apparently heard a noise at his gate and there was Ken Lazard. Paul said he made some weird gesticulation with his hands and told him that he'd better watch his back, because now Ken knew where he lived, he'd be back – and maybe Paul should start getting used to the idea of being in a wheelchair himself.'

Josh Wells leant back in his chair, looking pleased with himself. 'I can see you didn't know that bit,' he said.

'No, we didn't. Did Copeland say anything else?'

'Just that the guy had put the fear of God into him. He was quite agitated – wanted me to run the story so that it would be out there in the public domain. Seemed to think that would put the brakes on Ken Lazard not to act on his threats. He also wanted money for the story but I had to tell him that even if we paid something, it wouldn't be life-changing. He wasn't very impressed by that – told me that there *could* be more significant stuff, but in that case he wouldn't bother coming to the likes of me, he'd go straight to the national press.'

'What time of day was this?'

'Ten-forty-five. My girlfriend and I were leaving for Spain later that day. I didn't have time to check stuff out so I thought I'd get onto it when I got back. Only, of course, events overtook me. It was only when we got home last night that I read about Copeland being murdered. Do you think Ken Lazard did it?'

'We're keeping an open mind at the moment. Did Paul say if he was meeting anyone else that day?'

'No, but I know he was frightened of Ken Lazard and definitely worried by the fact that he knew where he lived.'

Beth dropped her notebook into her bag and rose from the table. 'Thanks for that. Can you come down to the station as soon as possible to make a formal statement?'

'Sure. Anything to help my local bobby – especially when she looks like you. Cool hair, by the way.'

His grin was flirtatious and a reluctant smile escaped her lips. Despite the ponytail look, which wasn't great, he had a certain charm about him – and he probably thought they were a sympathetic match.

'Should you be saying that sort of thing if you've got a girlfriend?'

He shrugged. 'We don't go around with our eyes shut just because we've got partners, do we?'

He rummaged in his pocket and pulled out his card. 'My numbers are on here if you get anything new you can pass on, and if you tell me where to go, I'll call in at the station to give that statement – show you what a law-abiding citizen I am.'

As they took their leave she waved Josh on, while she stopped to speak to the landlord.

'You gotta minute, Derek?'

'Sure. What's bugging you now?'

'My partner, DS Briscombe, was in here Monday night, asking a few more questions about Ken Lazard?'

'Yeah.'

'We were just wondering why you didn't tell him that Ken Lazard was here at the same time?'

'He didn't ask.'

'Well, I'm asking now. I understand he was in a back room?'

The man hesitated; he was definitely looking uncomfortable now but he gestured her to follow as he led the way to a small room off the main bar. Inside were a couple of tables and chairs and a leather sofa by the fire.

'Who told you?' Derek asked.

Beth ignored the question. 'Is this where Ken was? Was he alone?'

'I don't know. I was too busy talking to your mate. You'll have to ask Ken.'

'You know, we wouldn't like to think you were somehow involved in all this, Derek, but it's beginning to look like it's possible, the way you seem to be covering up for him the whole time.'

'Now, hang on. I've not lied about anything, and I've known Ken for years. I'm not saying he's not above throwing a few punches every now and then, but I can't believe he'd murder anyone.'

'Even if that someone put his wife in a wheelchair? Maybe things got out of hand?'

Silence.

'Do you have CCTV footage of the fight?'

'Yeah. I told your mate I'd dig it out.'

'And have you?'

He nodded.

'I'd like to take it back to the station so my bosses can take a look. Do you have a problem with that?'

Derek sighed. 'No.' He walked back into the main bar and rummaged around under the counter, pulling out a plastic carrier bag.

'And what about outside? Have you got footage for that?'

'It's all there.'

'Thanks,' Beth said, taking it from him. She gave him a straight look. 'I still get the feeling you're holding something back from us, and that's not a great idea. We might need to bring you in for further questioning. Think on that.'

Back at the police station, she was disappointed to see

that Harry wasn't around. Should she go to DCI Murray with what she'd learnt from Joshua Wells? She looked through into his office and saw that he was on the phone – and not in the best of moods by the look of him. She saw him pull out a packet of something from his drawer and watched as he unwrapped a piece of gum, popped it into his mouth and started to chew on it energetically. Someone had told her that although he'd quit smoking two years ago, he freely admitted that he was now hooked on the NiQuitin gum instead.

She chickened out and decided to tackle the CCTV first.

When Harry loped into the incident room an hour later, she could barely contain her excitement at how the day's events were turning out, but first things first.

'How did the rest of the interview go?' she asked, squinting up at him from her seat at the desk.

He scraped his fingers through his hair. 'I've let him go for now. But he's definitely holding something back from us.'

She grinned. 'And I think I know what it is. I've been quite busy, mate, while you were doing the fun stuff.'

She told him about her meeting with Josh Wells and her subsequent conversation with the landlord of the pub. 'I've watched the video footage of the fight and wow, was Ken angry – he'd really have done Copeland some damage, I reckon, if Derek and a couple of others hadn't stepped in. Mind you, Copeland's attitude was pretty provocative. I think I'd have been boiling mad in Ken's shoes, too.'

And you wouldn't want to witness that, she thought, remembering the times when she'd completely lost her rag with her brothers when she was younger. Her elder brother in particular had known just which buttons to press and boy, had he enjoyed pressing them.

'Want to take a look?' she asked, tilting the screen towards him. 'It's an old system he's got and I was able to bring the tapes back with me. He's got cameras both inside and outside the pub, which has turned out to be very useful.'

'Just let me get a coffee. I'll be back in a minute.'

He disappeared off, and she found her thoughts drifting reluctantly back to her brothers again as she gazed absently out of the window. She wished she could rewrite her family history, but she knew that wasn't an option – you were dealt the cards you were dealt in life, and you had to get on with it. Her father was a bully, lording it over the family with his vicious remarks and even more vicious temper, and as a consequence, her mother had spent her life creeping around on eggshells, terrified of upsetting him. Her two brothers – one older than her, the other younger – had never found the balls to stand up to him either. Now both of them were following in his path of petty crime, and she was so glad to have got out before she, too, had become a no-hoper. She had Andy to thank for that … and inadvertently, Briony. Poor, vulnerable Briony, who'd been as much a victim of circumstances as she had.

'Right … what have you got?'

Harry was back, clasping a mug of hot coffee in his hands as he peered down at the screen in front of her.

She brought her attention back to the screen. 'Well, you know about this bit …'

Flicking the switch, she played back the fight scene between Ken Lazard and Paul Copeland. Even though there was no sound, there was no mistaking the taunting expression and actions of Paul Copeland, nor the absolute fury of Ken's response as he went for him.

'But that's not all,' Beth said, when they came to the end of the scene. 'Take a look at this. It's the video footage from outside the pub when Paul Copeland left after the fight. I think you'll find it interesting.'

Harry leant forward over her shoulder to study the grainy image.

'There,' Beth said, pointing at a lone figure exiting the pub. 'That's Paul Copeland … and this …' she fast-forwarded the footage, '…is our mate, Ken, leaving the pub forty-five seconds later. And look … recognise that red car?'

Harry nodded. It was the same adapted Volkswagen he'd seen parked outside the Lazards' house.

'This is where it gets interesting,' Beth said, 'because Ken doesn't stop at his car and get in. He carries on along the road – walking in Paul Copeland's footsteps – just like Josh said. And definitely looking furtive, if you ask me…'

She looked up at him, clearly pleased with herself.

He nodded his head slowly. 'Good stuff. Do you get to see where they go?'

Beth shook her head. 'No. But we've requested more CCTV footage to analyse from the council for further along the High Street, which might include the roads leading to Paul's flat. By the way …' She looked at him. 'The landlord at The Crown confirmed that Ken Lazard was at his pub last night when you were there.'

'Well, why the bloody hell didn't he mention it?'

'Because you never asked, apparently.'

Harry shook his head. 'That man's beginning to seriously piss me off. There's got to be more to it than that.'

'I agree. If it's any consolation, he was looking a bit worried when I left – especially after I told him we might need to bring him down to the station for further questioning.'

'Well, let's hope he takes the threat seriously.'

He straightened up and knocked back the rest of his coffee in one go. 'Does Murray know about these developments?'

She shook her head. 'He was on the phone when I came in and didn't look to be in the best of moods. I thought I'd leave it to you.'

'Thanks – can't say I blame you, though. He can be a cantankerous bugger sometimes. Catch you later.'

At the door he turned back to face her. 'Well done for all that, by the way. You've done a good job.'

She felt a little glow at his approval, though she did her best to look nonchalant. It was one of the things she was beginning to love about working here – the effort she put in seemed to be appreciated. And she wasn't used to that. It was a nice feeling.

CHAPTER SIXTEEN

K irsty leafed her way through her father's diary, linking his appointments with the relevant files, her mind not really on the job. She'd woken up that morning so convinced she'd got a lead to follow after her conversation with Susan, but now it felt like she'd come to a dead end. She'd spent half the day going through his diary and correspondence but had found nothing linking him to Paul Copeland. It had been Robbie who'd handled the tenancy details and odd bits of correspondence, not her father. Maybe Rob was right and she was barking up the wrong tree. Coincidences did happen after all – and how likely was it really, that their father would be caught up in some criminal activity? It seemed ludicrous even for her overactive imagination. And yet…

On impulse she jumped up from her desk and opened the archived filing cabinet, pulling out a folder marked Land Bordering Dip Farm. This had been the start of her troubles – the sale of her grandmother's land. She'd been doing work experience at Jordan's to give her an insight into the legal side of their transactions, when she'd come across the details of the deal they'd done. She'd been shocked – and ashamed – of what her father had done.

'What have you got there?'

Rob's voice from the doorway made her jump and she instinctively slammed the file shut, replacing it in the cabinet.

'Nothing in particular. I'm just familiarising myself with Dad's filing system. How was your lunch with Simon?'

'Okay. He asked after you – sent his love, for what it's worth.'

'I hope you threw it back in his face?'

Her brother sighed. 'No, Kirsty, I didn't. Whatever went on between you two, I'm not getting involved. We do a lot of business with Jordan's and we shouldn't let personal stuff cloud our relationship with them. Dad and Tony were friends for over fifty years – we've known Simon all our lives.'

'And I've never liked him.'

'That's not exactly true. I remember a time ...'

'Oh, for God's sake, I was fifteen – it was a schoolgirl crush.'

'But it wasn't a schoolgirl crush in February, was it?'

'Thanks, Rob.'

'I'm just saying. He's going to be at the funeral on Thursday. I hope you're not going to make things difficult?'

'Oh, get lost. As if I would. Anyway, I'll have more than enough on my plate dealing with Luke.'

'Luke's way too much of a gentleman to make a scene at a funeral.'

'Well, for all our sakes let's hope you're right.'

He turned away from her and headed for his office. She hesitated, but knew she had to clear the air with him. 'Have you got a moment?' she asked, following him through.

He chucked his coat on the back of a chair and turned to look at her. 'A quick one. I've got an appointment in Totteridge. What's up?'

She took a deep breath. 'Is there anything going on that I should know about?'

'What do you mean?'

When she just looked at him, he frowned irritably. 'There's nothing going on, Kirsty.'

'What about the money you gave to Susan Porter? You know Simon as well as I do. He's not the type to give someone like her money because he feels sorry for her.'

'Yeah, well maybe there was a bit more to it than that, I don't know. He said he wants to do the flat up – maybe even sell it. It's not illegal. He wants the flat back and is prepared to buy the tenant out. We've done it loads of times and Susan was over the moon with the offer. One minute the poor girl's sick with worry about not being able to afford the rent, and the next she's walking away with a couple of grand in her pocket. You tell me the negative in that.'

Kirsty didn't want this … didn't want to be hearing that it all made sense when her instincts told her that it didn't. She took a breath.

'Did Susan also tell you that she thought Paul might be mixed up in something suspicious? That she told Dad about it?'

'No. Mixed up in what?'

'She wouldn't say. She was terrified, Rob. There's something going on, I know there is.'

'Maybe there *is* – or was – with Paul. But don't confuse it with what happened to Dad.'

'But don't you see? Maybe what she told Dad is the reason he was killed, too. It's too much of a coincidence.'

Her brother sighed. 'Kirsty, coincidences happen … look how we bumped into the Campbells on a walking safari in the middle of Africa. Who'd have expected that? Honestly, I don't know what's got into you. This obsession you seem to have that Dad was murdered … it's not helping things. Shit happens. He was hit by a car and the driver drove off – probably because he was pissed. Of course we want the bastard caught, but I can't believe it's got anything to do with Paul Copeland.'

She so wanted to believe him – so wanted to be able to leave it to the police to handle – but there was a niggling anxiety that just wouldn't let go, and she knew she needed to do some sorting in her head. Was it possible that Rob knew more than he was letting on? She hated herself for even thinking it, but there was a dark side to Rob that she'd never understood – his villain moments he'd jokingly call them ... saying she'd be shocked if she knew the thoughts that ran through his head sometimes. Even Lizzie had confided there were times she felt she didn't know her husband. 'And then if I get upset with him about something ... you know – a bit teary as you do, he gets all angry with me ... tells me not to be such a girl. He says he can't deal with women when they're like that. He doesn't get that we're wired differently to men, and that for us, tears are often just a release mechanism.'

Kirsty watched as her brother gathered some papers together. 'I've got to go,' he said. 'Will you be okay here on your own?'

She shrugged moodily. 'I've managed alright so far today. I can do it, Rob. I resent that you went to Mum behind my back and made out that I'd be more of a hindrance than a help.'

'That's not how it was.' His expression eased a little as he circled his desk to place a hand on her shoulder. 'Of course you can help, but what I don't need is you stirring everything up at a difficult time. I'm sorry to say this, but you're not always the most relaxing of people to have around. You know that.'

His words got to her, but she didn't rise.

'What time are you leaving today?' he asked.

She shrugged. 'I'll go through some more of Dad's stuff – get myself up to speed with what's going on, and then head off home to Mum. I spoke to her earlier – she's in a stew over the funeral arrangements.'

'Well, just don't go feeding her all this stuff about Dad's death being more than an accident. She doesn't need that on top of everything else.'

'Maybe we need to prepare her–'

'No, Kirsty – she's got enough on her plate. In the unlikely event the police do turn something up, we'll handle it then.'

'So you admit it's possible?'

'Of course it's *possible*; I just don't think it's likely. So until we hear to the contrary …'

'Fine.'

'Don't be like that …' He squeezed her shoulder. 'I know it's hard for you to let things lie, but it's only been a few days since Dad's accident. Let the police get on with their job and gather what information they can. Once we know what we're dealing with, we can take it from there. If there's anything suspicious, you'll have my full support. I promise you.'

His eyes were genuinely sympathetic and for the first time she got the impression that he was taking her concerns seriously. She felt her muscles relax a little.

'Okay. I'll hold you to that. Will you be coming over later?'

'I'll try to. I've got a lot to get on with here, and I want to get over to the flat to do some work there, but if I can drop by on my way home, I will. Call me if you need me for anything.'

Five minutes later he was on his way out again, throwing her a careless wave as he went. She watched as he crossed the road, brushing aside the hurt she felt. It was natural now he was married, that as little sister, her nose had been put out of joint. She needed to toughen up, get a life of her own.

And as soon as the funeral was over, she would.

As Kirsty entered the house a couple of hours later, she could hear low voices coming from the lounge. She took a breath, hanging her keys on the hook, before following the sound of those voices.

'Kirsty.' Her mother looked pleased to see her. 'You remember Dan?'

'Of course.'

Kirsty looked over at the white-haired man. It had always been something of a family joke that Daniel Curtis hadn't married because he'd never got over his first love for her mother – but now that her father was no longer there, it suddenly didn't seem quite so funny anymore. She was sure he'd only come to offer his condolences, but she couldn't help it, she found her hackles rising at the sight of him sitting in her father's chair.

'Have you had a good day at the office?' her mother asked.

'It was okay, busy. Do you want me to get supper on? What have we got?'

'It's all sorted and ready to go but that would be helpful – I'm going to run Dan home. His car's at the garage being repaired and he got a cab over here, bless him. It just needs putting in the oven if you don't mind? It's the chicken casserole on the hob.'

'I'll see to it, then I'll nip up for a shower after that.' She was glad of an excuse to leave them. 'Drive carefully.'

Later, as they sat down to supper together in the kitchen, her mother looked at her over the table.

'I could sense there was a bit of a chill with Dan. You've no need to worry, you know. He was just being nice popping over to see how I was, and it was the least I could do to drop him home, seeing as he didn't have a car.'

'I know. I'm sorry. It just took me by surprise, seeing him there. Maybe don't mention to Rob that he dropped by? You know what he can be like.'

'Kirsty, I'm not going to start treading on eggshells just to pander to Rob's sensitivities. Were things any easier with him today? I did have a quiet word with him about things when he rang.'

'We're getting there.'

'Good. I can't bear to see the two of you at loggerheads. And he's got a lot on his plate at the moment with a young family, the business and trying to get that wretched flat they bought ready for letting.'

'I don't understand what's taking him so long. Anyone would think he didn't want to get it let. They bought it a year ago. It should have been well finished by now.'

'Kirsty you have no idea what pressure a new baby puts on a family – let alone when it's twins.'

Kirsty shrugged. 'It just seems to be taking forever. Anyway … You said on the phone you were worrying about the arrangements for Thursday?'

'Yes, I hardly got any sleep last night. Can we just go through it all? Make sure we've got everything covered…?'

CHAPTER SEVENTEEN

'Good morning.'

Harry looked up from his desk as Beth breezed over, looking chirpy as a baby bird in spring.

'Is it?' he asked wearily.

It didn't feel like a good morning to him. It had been a long night where he hadn't got a wink of sleep for worry, and it hadn't been the Paul Copeland case that had kept him awake either. It had been the sound of his grandmother throwing up into her bowl in the room next door to him, which had happened several times during the course of the night.

'Yup, it's definitely a good morning,' Beth said, perching on the edge of his desk. 'And I think you'll agree with me when you hear what I've got to say.'

Harry waited.

'I was here till nearly ten o'clock last night.'

'I'll make sure you get a medal.'

Beth pulled a face.

'It turned out to be fascinating stuff going through those CCTVs. Want to come and see?'

Now she did have his attention.

'I don't share your fascination with CCTV. Just tell me.'

'It shows our Ken following Paul Copeland as far as the road where he lived. There's no coverage after that. But – and this is where it gets good – it also shows Ken driving in his car along the same route the next morning, and turning into Myton Road – where again we lose him.'

'The day of the murder?' Harry mused. 'What time?'

'Nine-fifteen.'

'Maybe he was casing the place?'

'Maybe – we know Copeland met up with the reporter after that so Ken couldn't have done anything then. But he could have called back later and got Paul into his car under some pretext or other and … bingo. Opportunity to murder.'

Harry gave it some thought. 'It's a possibility. Good work.'

'But that's not all. I was checking out the CCTV in the area where Dominic Cartwright got run over and guess what I saw there?'

Harry couldn't help smiling at the way she was looking so pleased with herself. It transformed her face when she smiled like that, softening the severe effect of the short hair, which he was beginning to suspect was a bit of a front. He remembered how she'd clammed up when he'd asked about her family, and realised that she gave very little away about herself at all. Even though he suspected that was a deliberate ploy on her part, he resolved to at least show a bit of interest when the time was right. He knew how difficult it could be moving to a new area.

'Don't tell me,' he responded to her question. 'The car that ran him over?'

'Yeah … in your dreams. That would be too easy. There isn't any CCTV on that residential road. But the main road is different. This one I think you'll be interested to see … come on.'

A few minutes later, looking over Beth's shoulder in the airy incident room, Harry gave a start of surprise at the sight of the man walking into the main entrance of the pub near where Dominic Cartwright had been run over. He frowned, peering closer at the grainy image as Beth froze it.

'I know him ... but where from? It's a crap picture.'

'Jordan's Solicitors, remember? He's the son, Simon Jordan.'

'Of course.' Harry peered closer. 'Now that is interesting. What's he doing there? De Souza did say Dominic Cartwright was meeting someone for a drink. Could it have been him?'

'He didn't mention it, did he? Do you want me to call him? Arrange to see him?'

But on phoning Simon's office, Beth was informed that he was in Manchester for the day on business, and not back until later that evening.

'No worries,' Harry told her. 'He'll be at the funeral tomorrow, I'm sure. I'll have a word with him then.'

It was as difficult as she'd known it was going to be, but however hard it was for her, Kirsty knew it was worse for her mother – who'd been tearful all morning, and now sat with a miniature picture of her husband clasped tightly in one hand. They stood, arms linked, in the first pew as two of her father's closest friends gave moving eulogies to the man Dominic Cartwright had been. They stood through the short memorial service conducted by the vicar and then they moved as if in a trance back to the cars for the silent drive to the crematorium. Kirsty's head was full of memories of the complexities that made up her father: his extrovert, sometimes brash personality that could have her cringing with embarrassment or roaring with laughter in the same breath; the way he'd spread his arms wide, even now she was an adult, to envelop her in that enormous bear-hug; his tenacious, protective love for all his family; his impatience and irritable withdrawal from them all when something was on his mind. Life had been never been easy with Dominic Cartwright around, but nor had it been dull.

And now he was gone, leaving an enormous void where once he'd reigned supreme ... and no one seemed any nearer to bringing the person guilty for his death to justice.

She thought about the phone call she'd had from Susan Porter last night and shook her head in wonder. She'd never have believed it – that she would hear from her again – but the woman had been drinking, she could tell, and was tearful.

'I'll meet you,' she'd sobbed. 'Tell you what I know. I saw Paul's parents today – it was awful. It made me realise that we need to know who killed him. They need to be punished. When can we meet?'

And because Kirsty didn't want her changing her mind when she'd sobered up and had time to think, they'd agreed to meet tonight, after the funeral proceedings.

At the golf club the welcome line seemed to go on forever. It felt wrong. Wasn't this something you did at weddings rather than funerals? Yet Kirsty went along with it and supposed it made sense – it might be the only chance some people got to pay their respects to her mother.

He was there, standing in front of her, before she had time to prepare herself, and she felt the jolt of shock right down to her toes. She found herself absorbing his features ... the dark, almost black hair, sprinkled with the odd dash of grey, the brown eyes, sombre now rather than twinkling. She searched his face for some sign that ... what? He might have forgiven her for doing the worst possible thing someone could do to their partner?

'I'm sorry for your loss,' Luke said, stooping to kiss her briefly on the cheek.

Unprepared as she was for seeing him, her immediate impulse was to slide her arms around his firm, familiar body and cling on tight – drawing from the pool of strength only he could offer. The feel of his skin on hers as his lips brushed her cheek, the familiar scent of him, got to her before she could erect the barriers. Her heart contracted with physical pain. *Oh Luke,* she thought. *How could I have been so stupid?*

She cleared her throat, hoping that none of these emotions showed. 'Thanks.'

He squeezed her hand. 'I'll catch up with you later.' But she doubted he would. He'd come to pay his respects to her father, someone who, despite the fact that they were so different, he'd liked and got on with – and she suspected he'd leave as soon as it was polite to do so.

She watched him move off into the room and then someone else was taking her hand, kissing her cheek, saying how sorry they were.

The next hour passed in a blur and she almost forgot about Luke in the sea of well-wishers who queued up to pass on their own personal memories and stories of Dominic Cartwright.

Tony Jordan and Bob Grose, her father's two closest friends who'd spoken at the memorial service, were standing protectively around her mother, she noticed, and her heart went out to them. They'd been a part of her mother's life for so long and now they anchored her, steadying her when she might have faltered. Over in one corner she could see DS Briscombe trying to look unobtrusive as he took stock of the people there. Was it a sign that he thought there was more to her father's death than an accident that he'd come? She'd give anything to know.

'Hello, Kirsty.'

She froze. She didn't need to look around to recognise that voice. She turned slowly.

'Simon.'

His dark good looks were even more striking in the sombre black suit he was wearing, the vivid pale blue of his eyes even more arresting as he looked at her warily.

'I know you probably don't want to talk to me, but we go back a long way, your family and mine. I couldn't not come. Terrible shock – your poor mother. I thought Dad's address was very moving.'

'Yes.' Her response was terse.

'You're still upset with me.'

'What do you expect?'

He shrugged. 'I don't know why you and Luke made such a big deal of it. It was one night and we were pissed. Lots of people do stupid things when they've been drinking – I bet Luke's no saint.'

She cast a quick glance round to make sure they were out of earshot. 'I don't want to have this conversation with you now, Simon, but you just don't get it, do you? You know exactly why Luke could never forgive that. I would have told him in my own time. The fact that you had to go blabbing about it to everyone, knowing the harm it would do…'

'I'm sorry. I'd had a few pints. I was chuffed I'd pulled you – you know I've always liked you.'

'And you knew I didn't feel the same.'

'I know that's what you said, but I'd say that's debatable after what happened, wouldn't you?'

'No,' she said shortly. But she was confused. She'd known him all her life, for God's sake … had never thought of him in that way apart from that brief crush when she was fifteen, and he'd soon put paid to that.

As always, the memory of that night made her uncomfortable. It had so nearly become more than just a crush. If she hadn't stopped him when she had…

'Come on, Kirsty, there's always been a connection between us. Why won't you just admit it?'

'Because I love Luke, and any connection there may have been is long gone.'

He shrugged. 'I know that's what you want to believe … but I have very enjoyable memories of our night together.' The glint in his eye challenged her to deny it. '– As I'm sure you do if you were being honest about it.'

'I don't even remember it,' she said cuttingly. 'And that's the truth of it.'

She could see she'd hit her mark, and she knew him well enough to know that whatever was coming next it would be biting. He didn't disappoint her.

'Well, for your information, it was a memorable lay – one of the best. I think you'd remember that if you let yourself.'

One up to him. She saw red. Had to physically prevent herself from hitting him. But she remembered where she was – the occasion.

'This isn't an appropriate conversation, Simon.'

His expression lightened. 'You're right. I'm sorry. I didn't come here to argue with you. And for our parents' sake we shouldn't let this come between years of friendship. Maybe we can go out for a drink sometime, you, me and Robbie? Like the old days?'

He was unsettling her, tapping into her confusion so that for a moment she even found herself considering it. But she could never do it – it would feel like a double betrayal to Luke even if he no longer gave a damn.

'That's not going to happen. Now if you'll excuse me, I need to make sure Mum's alright.'

She stalked off, head held high, but inside she was mortified.

She hadn't thought it was possible to feel any worse than she already did, but she'd been kidding herself. Coming back had opened up a host of wounds that still needed to be dealt with.

'Hey … you okay?' It was Rachael, slipping an arm around her shoulders and guiding her towards a quiet spot in the corner.

She nodded.

'I saw you talking to Simon.'

Kirsty looked over to where he was now locked in serious conversation with her brother. Just briefly, they both looked her way.

'He's a bastard.'

'What did he say?'

'Just trying to defend himself over what he did.'

Rachael's eyes were sympathetic, but there was also a deep understanding in her gaze. 'You know, honey, it happened – whether or not he let the cat out of the bag. Maybe you need to ask yourself why?'

Kirsty looked at her in frustration, but she knew her cousin's words were well intended – spoken out of a desire to help rather than to criticise. She'd always been the more sensible one, and Kirsty respected her opinions.

'You're not going to start saying that I secretly fancy him as well, are you? Because that's what he's implying.'

'I wouldn't dare, only you can know that–'

'Yeah, and I absolutely know that I don't. I'm disgusted with myself.'

'Then end of story – put it behind you and move on.'

'Without Luke…' It was more a statement than a question.

Her cousin's expression was wry. 'We both know Luke's not easily going to forgive something like that, given his history.'

And that was the truth of it. If nothing else, it made her feel better about the decision she'd taken to go to France. Staying would only have added to her misery.

'It's so good of your mum to have the funeral before my wedding,' Rachael said, changing the subject. 'Thank her for me, will you? I know it will be really sad that Uncle Dom's not there, but …'

'Of course I will. She was a man on a mission, I can tell you. I don't know how we managed to pull it together so quickly, but I don't think it was just about you. You know what she's like … Needs to tick the boxes as quickly as she can.'

Rachael smiled. 'I do know, but I'm grateful all the same.'

'Kirsty?'

Robbie was at her shoulder. 'Can I have a word?'

'I'll leave you to it,' Rachael said, giving her arm a quick squeeze. 'Catch you later.'

Her brother was looking irritated. 'I was just talking to Simon.'

'I saw.'

'Can't you cut him some slack? You have to accept that what happened was as much your fault as his and move on. We have to work with him. It could make things very awkward if you keep up the hostilities the whole time.'

'He acted like an arse.'

'I know he did. But maybe it's about time you acknowledged that you didn't act much better. You're the one who was engaged, not him.'

'Thanks, Rob.'

Her brother shrugged. 'I'm simply pointing out that you were both at fault. We all need to move on from it.'

'And maybe we should think about using another firm of solicitors to do our stuff? Don't you sometimes think it's a bit incestuous, the relationship we have with Jordan's?'

Rob looked like he was about to have an apoplexy.

'*Kirsty*, we've worked with Jordan's for the last forty years. You can't come marching in, staking a claim to the business and demanding that we change everything, just because you slept with a guy and now regret it.'

He wasn't pulling any punches – and put like that it made her look unprofessional, which was the last thing she needed when she was trying to convince everyone she was a credible partner for the firm.

'I'm sorry. I just think–'

'Well, don't – leave that to me for the time being and you concentrate on learning the business and helping Mum. And if you're serious about wanting to be part of Cartwrights, then the first thing you have to realise is that sometimes you have to compromise – and that includes keeping personal feelings out of business dealings. Think on it.'

She watched bleakly as, without another word, he turned and strode away from her. Had he always been that arrogant? She felt disloyal thinking it. He'd always had that dominant streak – like their father – but these days she was finding him increasingly difficult to deal with. Hot tears welled up. She felt useless. Useless. She needed a drink. She looked around and saw someone with a tray.

'Thanks,' she said, moving over and helping herself to a glass of white wine. She took a large gulp, felt it hit her bloodstream. That was better. She took some more.

'You okay?'

It was Luke this time, his brown eyes concerned.

He looked so debonair, she thought, in his dark jacket and tie. His hair was longer, and he seemed to be growing a beard. She liked it. She was glad that she'd taken some care over choosing what she was going to wear today. Mostly she'd chosen the black and grey, fitted dress and chic, silver-grey scarf because it was appropriately sombre without looking too gloomy, which her father would never have approved of. Now she was pleased that with the black heels she was wearing, she felt suitably confident to hold her head high.

'I'm fine.'

'Stupid question. I know how much you loved your dad. You must be feeling dreadful.'

The lump in her throat was so tight she thought it might choke her. She took another swig of her wine and felt it swish through her system. She needed to slow down, not fall into the trap of drowning her sorrows. She put her glass carefully down onto a table next to them.

'It's just not knowing what happened,' she said into the silence that had developed. She hesitated before adding. 'There's a chance he could have been murdered.'

It was the first time she'd said the word out loud and it sounded shocking even to her own ears. Had she said it as a genuine cry for help or as a way of getting his attention? She wasn't sure, but she had his attention now alright, and it was an exquisite feeling.

'*What?* What are you talking about? I thought it was an accident.'

'That's what everyone seems to want us to believe – but I'm not so sure.'

'Why not?'

She shouldn't be talking about this now. Rob would kill her if he knew. But she needed to offload to someone. She glanced quickly around before bringing her eyes back to his face.

'Did you read about that guy who was murdered in Brookmans Park last week?'

Luke nodded.

'He was one of our tenants. Dad went to see his girlfriend a couple of days later to offer his condolences. The same day he was killed.'

'And?'

She shrugged. 'There's not a lot to go on, but she told me that her boyfriend knew something and that she'd told Dad that.'

She could see the doubt in Luke's eyes. 'That doesn't mean there's a link necessarily. What do the police say?'

She shrugged. 'Oh, they won't commit to anything, and Robbie thinks I'm being paranoid, but ...' She looked around, then lowered her voice. 'I'm meeting up with the guy's girlfriend tonight. She says she's got something to tell me.'

He frowned. 'Is that a good idea? Shouldn't she just go to the police and tell them?'

'Of course she should, but she's too frightened to.'

'Christ, Kirsty, don't put yourself in danger.'

He ran a hand through his hair. She remembered how he always did that when he was frustrated by stuff – or worried. 'You shouldn't–'

'If you're going to start sounding off like Robbie and telling me what I should or shouldn't be doing, I'm out of here. Don't you realise this is my father we're talking about? I need to know what happened to him, Luke.'

'Okay, okay, I get it – just be careful, okay?'

She straightened her back. 'Don't worry. I'm not your problem anymore and I'll be fine.' Her voice was flippant, as if she didn't give a damn. 'I'd better get on and mingle. It's nice to see you, Luke.'

'You, too. Look ... You know you can always call me? Promise me you'll be careful tonight?'

'Of course I will.'

'Where are you meeting this woman?'

'The Curry Buffet.'

'Does anyone else know you're meeting up?'

'No.'

He hesitated. 'Would you like me to come with you?'

Of course she would, but she had some pride. 'Thanks for offering, but I'll be fine – and she'll probably be happier if it's just me.'

Was that relief in his eyes? 'Okay. But do me a favour? Text me when you get home, so I know you're okay?'

She nodded and that stupid heart did a flip. At least he cared enough to worry about her getting home safely.

'I take it you're all still going to Rachael's wedding?' he said.

'I think so. As long as Mum's up to it. You?' She didn't look at him as she asked the question.

'Yes. I guess I'll see you there, then.'

He didn't look overjoyed at the prospect and she found herself saying waspishly, 'You needn't worry. I won't embarrass you.'

He shrugged. 'You can do what you like, Kirsty. As you said, you're not my problem anymore.'

Harry looked around him, taking it all in as unobtrusively as he could. He never felt comfortable at these events, especially when he was there as part of an investigation. The thought came to him and was instantly dismissed, that it might not be too long before he was attending a funeral service that wasn't business. He'd had another sleepless night last night and knew his grandmother had also been awake for most of it. He'd heard her radio, even though it was running on quiet.

'DS Briscombe?'

It was Kirsty Cartwright standing in front of him. Her blonde hair sat stylishly on her shoulders, and she looked self-possessed and elegant as she offered him a sandwich from a plate.

'You might as well,' she said, when he hesitated. 'We've ordered far too much food. We weren't sure how many people would be coming back for this part of the proceedings.'

'Thanks.' He took a couple of sandwiches.

'Have you found out anything new about Dad's accident?'

'Nothing, I'm afraid. We always hope for CCTV footage in

these circumstances, but unfortunately your father's accident happened in a quiet residential road that isn't covered. Although–'

He broke off, wondering how much to say. He didn't want to start feeding unwarranted suspicion. On the other hand … things weren't progressing as quickly as he'd like.

'The CCTV on the main road did happen to show Simon Jordan walking into a pub on the corner of the main road and Buxton Road, where the accident happened. Is there any chance he could have been meeting your father, do you think?'

Kirsty's brow furrowed as she shook her head. 'He's not said anything. Have you asked him?'

'Yes, just now.' Harry shrugged and took a bite from his sandwich. 'He said he was nipping in for a quick pint before meeting a client at the golf club, and had no idea your father was nearby.'

'But you don't believe him?'

'I'm not saying that at all. He sounded genuine. Said he heard the sirens and felt terrible later, when he realised that they were probably for your father.'

'Our families have known each other forever…'

She looked at him probingly, and he felt uncomfortable, realising that something significant was about to be asked.

'My brother thinks I'm being paranoid, wondering if it wasn't an accident. Am I?'

He hesitated, giving her question fair consideration. 'I wouldn't say that. The most likely scenario is that it *was* an accident. But there are a couple of factors that we need to check out before we can categorically state that.'

'Such as?'

'Mostly just making sure there's nothing to link the two deaths apart from the obvious fact that Paul Copeland and your father knew each other. We've not found anything so far.'

She nodded – looked for a moment as if she was about to

say something more – then pursed her lips firmly and gave a thin smile. 'If you'll excuse me, I'd better get on and mingle. You will keep us posted?'

'Of course.'

He watched her go, and wondered what it was that she'd decided not to share with him.

CHAPTER EIGHTEEN

A
t eight o'clock that evening, Kirsty buried her chin in her scarf as she hurried along Barnet High Street. This was the last thing she felt like doing after the funeral, but she accepted she wasn't in a position to negotiate times and places. She peered through the large window of the Curry Buffet and saw Susan Porter sitting at a small table for two in the far corner. She had her head buried in a menu, and to Kirsty it was obvious she was trying to keep a low profile.

'Hi,' she said, dropping down into the chair opposite. 'Sorry I'm a bit late.'

The other girl shrugged and threw a quick look round. 'Shall we get some food and then talk?'

Five minutes later they were back at their table.

'How was today?' Susan asked her.

'Grim.'

'Yeah. I'm not looking forward to Paul's funeral either. Sorry I broke down on the phone.'

'It's perfectly understandable.'

'Paul's parents are the ones I really feel sorry for. He was their only child and they're real upset.' She looked a bit embarrassed. 'Kept telling me they didn't want to lose touch … I was their only link with Paul now. It was sweet …'

They were both silent for a minute and Kirsty could almost sense Susan weighing up in her mind what to say next.

'You were going to tell me about your conversation with my father?' she prompted.

The other girl nodded. 'It's probably nothing – and you must promise me you won't say nothing to the police? I don't want them coming back to see me.'

Kirsty nodded.

'Paul was onto something but he wouldn't tell me what. I can't get it out my head that it might have been something to do with the guy in the upstairs flat.'

Kirsty's eyes locked on the other woman's in shock. '*Simon Jordan*?'

'Nah, not Simon. He don't live there anymore. He's let it out to a bloke called Tim Burman, an old friend from way back, he said, but there's been some unsavoury types going in and out. We started off being friendly, like you do, and Tim's okay, but when we realised what some of his friends was like, we kept out of it. They're not like Simon.'

'So what did Paul think was going on?'

'That's what he wouldn't say.' She looked suddenly edgy. 'I've been trying to put it together in my head. The night before he got killed, he was in a fight. He wouldn't tell me what it was about, but he came in with a cut lip and a bruised eye. The next morning, we had a row 'cos he said he was meeting up with someone and there could be some money in it for us – a nice little earner, he said. He wouldn't tell me any more and I told him I didn't like the sound of it, but he just laughed … said I'd be skipping all the way to the bank if it came off.'

'So what did you say to my father?'

'I feel so bad about that now, but I couldn't get it out my head that maybe it was one of the guys upstairs he was meeting, and I wanted your dad to know 'cause he was the managing agent.'

'What did he say?'

'That I should tell the police.'

'And did you?'

She shook her head. 'No, 'cause that same day a note was pushed through the front door addressed to me.' She broke off, casting an anxious look around the restaurant before bringing her gaze back to Kirsty and lowering her voice. 'It said for me to keep my mouth shut unless I wanted to end up like Paul.'

'Susan! That's serious.'

'You think I don't know that? That's why you mustn't say nothing to anyone else.'

'But the police might be able to track something from the note.'

'It were just a piece of paper shoved inside a scruffy envelope with my name on it. Who's going to be able to track that?'

'But fingerprints ...'

'I ain't gonna risk it. Whoever they are, they're not people you mess with. I seen what they done to Paul.'

Her eyes were terrified and Kirsty backed off. 'Okay. Did my dad say or do anything else?'

'No.'

'Did you get the impression ...' She broke off, disgusted with herself for even considering the possibility. But some little demon pushed her on. '...That he knew anything about any of it?'

'*No.*'

Relief surged through her at the look of shock on Susan's face.

'I'm sure not. He was telling me to go to the police. He was really kind. As I was telling him all this, there was suddenly a lot of noise come from upstairs, people arguing. He said he'd use that as an excuse to go and suss 'em out. After he left here,

I heard him knock on their door, saying he was the landlord and wanted to inspect the flat. I could hear some woman obviously weren't happy about it, but then I heard him going up the stairs. Five minutes later, he left.'

'Did you mention your conversation with my father to the police?'

The girl's look became defensive. 'No. I told you. I was frightened and I didn't want to open up a can of worms. I didn't know for sure any of it was to do with them upstairs – or how involved Paul was. And if it *was* to do with them, I've still got to live there. Or thought I did 'til your brother gave me that money.'

'But don't you see? This could put a completely different slant on everything. It makes it possible that Dad's death wasn't an accident. Maybe someone knew he'd been to see you and was worried you'd said something, or maybe he saw something and they threatened him – and my dad wasn't the sort of man to back down in a confrontation.'

Kirsty's brain was whirring. She should go to the police with this, but something was holding her back. It wasn't something she wanted to think about … but Robbie had given Susan that money to go … What if there was more to all this than she realised? What if Robbie was somehow involved?

She couldn't even go there.

'What time on that Thursday did my father visit you?'

'I don't remember exactly. It were early – about nine-thirty?'

'Was he going on anywhere after that?'

'He didn't say. Look … I told you all I know. There's nothing more. And it might have nothing to do with any of it anyway.' She looked at her watch. 'I've got to go. Is this on you?'

Kirsty nodded distractedly.

'Thanks,' Susan said, standing up. She hesitated. 'You got my number now. You'll let me know if you find anything out?'

'Yes.'

'Thanks … good luck. And be careful.'

After she'd gone, Kirsty ordered another coffee and went over it all in her head. There was nothing concrete … nothing she could go to the police with, really. Not yet. As usual, the next step seemed to involve talking to Rob.

And that was something that was beginning to worry her.

Kirsty's mobile rang, waking her up. The alarm clock by her bed told her it was two o'clock in the morning, and she groped clumsily for her phone and put it to her ear.

'For God's sake, are you okay? Where are you? You were going to text me.'

She groaned, hauling herself up on her pillows at the sound of Luke's worried voice. Damn, she'd forgotten she said she'd text him when she got home. She'd got back, her head buzzing with her conversation with Susan, only to find the Jordans and Groses still there, which had put paid to her having a quiet conversation with Rob, or texting Luke. Now she saw that she'd slept through three texts and a missed call from him.

'Oh God, sorry … I'm fine,' she mumbled sleepily. 'I got back and there were still people here with Mum. I forgot.' She hesitated before adding, 'Thanks for checking up, though. Hope you weren't too worried?'

'Christ, Kirsty. You feed me all these conspiracy theories and then expect me not to worry when I can't get in touch with you?'

'Sorry,' she said again.

He let out a breath. 'How did it go?'

She hesitated, but really Luke was the only person she felt she could talk to.

'It was interesting. I think she believes there's a connection between Dad's death and her boyfriend's. I just don't know where to go with it.'

'Sounds like it should be the police. It's what they're there for.'

Again she hesitated. 'I'm not sure. I need to speak to Rob first.'

'Why? What's he got to do with any of it?'

'Nothing, I hope. Look, I don't want to go into it now. Thanks for calling, I do appreciate it, but it's been a long day and I'm exhausted—'

'Do you want to meet up? Talk about it?'

Just for a moment, she was tempted. Maybe he'd help her make some sense of all this. But then sanity kicked in. If there was one thing she'd learnt that day, it was that to see him was detrimental to her resolve to move on.

'I appreciate the offer, but I'm okay, thanks. I just need to speak to Robbie and then I'll have a better idea of what to do.'

'Okay, but you know where I am if you change your mind.'

'Thanks.'

'And Kirsty?'

'Yes?'

'Don't do anything stupid?'

She smiled to herself in the dark.

'I won't.'

'Good. Well … sleep tight.'

'You too …'

She clicked her phone off and turned on her side, pulling the duvet over her. She felt suddenly lonely in the big bed. If Luke was here, she'd be snuggling up to him, laughing at his groan of resignation as she wriggled her cold feet between his warm legs. She felt a self-pitying tear seep out of the corner of her eye. Why had she done it? She loved Luke. She never would have believed she could betray him like that for the cheap thrill of the moment. But she had. It was the hardest thing to come to terms with – that she could do the one thing that, in his eyes, made her no better than the mother who'd deserted him. They'd talked about it often enough for goodness' sake – she'd always known that infidelity of any sort would be a deal-breaker for him.

She allowed the tears to run freely, something she'd not done in at least three months. She'd seen that as a sign she was getting over him, but seeing him at the funeral had made her realise she was a long way off getting over him and it was possible she never fully would. He'd been her first love and maybe that was what first loves were all about – she needed to accept that a part of him would remain a part of her, forever.

When she'd done with her crying, she went into the bathroom to splash her face, and as she stared at her blotchy eyes in the mirror there was a new calm about her. What was done was done. She'd made a huge mistake and she was paying the price. She just had to make sure she learnt from it and stuck to her resolution that never again would she drink so much that she lost control of her inhibitions.

CHAPTER NINETEEN

When Kirsty walked into the office the next morning, the first thing she did was collar Robbie.

'Have you got a moment?'

He looked up from where he was reading the paper on his desk, saw the determination on her face and sighed as she sat down opposite him.

'What's up?'

'What makes you think anything's up?'

'I haven't been your brother all these years without recognising the signs.'

'Oh. Well, you're right, as it happens.' She took a breath. 'I learnt some interesting stuff yesterday – about Dad's death.'

She saw the resignation in his face before he said, 'Right. I saw you talking to DS Briscombe. Did he have anything new to say?'

'He asked me if Dad could have been meeting Simon – apparently they've got CCTV footage showing Simon walking into a pub very near where Dad was killed.'

Rob looked surprised. 'He never mentioned anything about meeting up.'

'That's what I said. Apparently he said he'd just dropped in for a beer on his way to the golf club. He had no idea Dad was nearby.'

'Well, there you are, then, I'm sure that's true.'

Yes, but… I learnt something else yesterday. I met up with Paul Copeland's girlfriend last night, Susan? She told me that Paul was onto something. She didn't know what, but he'd said it could earn them some money and she wondered if it might be something to do with the tenant upstairs – who just happens to be an old friend of Simon's. Don't you think it's rather odd how Simon's name keeps popping up?'

Her brother raised his eyes. '*No*, Kirsty, I *don't*. Are you seriously suggesting Simon's the sort to be involved in murder? That he'd murder his father's best friend? We've known the Jordans all our lives, for God's sake.'

'I know, and of course I'm not saying that. I'm just trying to make sense of it all.'

'I think you're clutching at straws. I told you before … coincidences happen. You'll be accusing me of being involved next because I was the one to pay Susan off. And before you dig yourself in any deeper …'

Her brother pushed the paper he was reading across the desk to her. 'Perhaps you should take a look at this.'

Man Held for Questioning over Brookmans Park Murder.

She stared at the headline in shock, then looked at her brother.

He nodded. 'Read it. Some unnamed source says he witnessed Paul Copeland and another guy having a fight in a pub the night before he was murdered. He reckons they had history and this guy threatened to do Paul in. Paul hadn't long been out of jail, so it could well be a revenge killing.'

She remembered Susan saying how Paul had come back with a bruised eye and cut lip and her face fell. 'Did you know Paul had been in prison?'

'Yeah – he was quite upfront about it when he applied for the tenancy. He was done for dangerous driving and had served his time. That was how he put it and I told Simon as much. He didn't have a problem with it. Read the article. It doesn't look like they're looking for anyone else now, so I don't see any way Paul's death can be linked to Dad's.'

Kirsty read the article in silence. It wasn't very long and didn't really add much to what Rob had told her. Witnesses to the fight in a pub had come forward and further evidence, not specified, apparently strongly linked the suspect to the murder of Paul Copeland. Police now had up to 36 hours to question him before either charging or releasing him.

When she'd finished reading, she looked up. 'That still doesn't prove that Dad's death was an accident,' she said. 'And he definitely spoke to the upstairs tenant in Myton Road the day he died – so I'm at least going to speak to Simon about it and find out who this guy is.'

'Kirsty, I haven't got time for this. What's the *matter* with you? Just let it go. Why are you so convinced it wasn't an accident?'

Kirsty wasn't really sure herself. She just knew she had to do it. 'We owe it to Dad to find out,' she said stubbornly. 'And I've got a gut feeling that something isn't right.'

'Yeah, well, a great place the world would be if everyone acted on their gut feelings. You should leave it to the people who know what they're doing. I don't know why I bother saying anything, though – you'll just do your own thing as usual. Meanwhile, some of us have to get on with keeping the business going.'

Kirsty stood up. 'Well, I won't keep you from your *work* any longer,' she said, pushing the newspaper back to him and eyeing his coffee pointedly. 'But I do intend speaking to Simon later. Just so you know.'

Simon Jordan viewed Kirsty with a certain amount of suspicion as she walked into his office that lunchtime. Through the glass window she could see his father, and she gave an awkward little wave. She was beginning to run out of steam and for the first time questioned if Robbie might not be right and she should be leaving all this to the police. But whatever little demon it was pushing her on to find out more about her father's death, it wasn't letting go of her quite yet. And she was here now.

She sat down in the chair Simon indicated.

'What can I do for you, Kirsty? I'd like to think it's a social call but after our conversation yesterday, I think that's unlikely.'

She hesitated, remembering Robbie's words about mending fences. 'I'm sorry about that. It was a difficult day.'

He looked surprised, but his expression eased as he acknowledged her apology with a nod of the head. 'So…?'

'It's awkward, but I need to ask you something about Dad.'

'Dom? Okay … if I can help at all?'

She took a breath. 'I just need to know for sure that his death was an accident. There are a couple of things niggling me that I thought maybe you might be able to help me with.'

She wasn't really surprised that his expression became more wary. 'I can't think what, but fire away.'

He waited patiently while she struggled to come up with a diplomatic way of putting it.

'How well do you know the tenant in the upstairs flat at Myton Road?'

'Tim?' He frowned. 'I know him from years back. We were at primary school together. We didn't particularly stay in touch, but when he was looking for somewhere to live, someone told him I was moving out of my flat and he emailed me. It worked for both of us, so I moved out and he moved in.'

'What's he like?'

He smiled. 'Good-looking chap. I can fix you up with a date if you like. You can decide for yourself.'

She hoped her expression revealed that she wasn't impressed with that answer. He shrugged. 'I don't really know what he's like in any depth. Seems nice enough, he's an antiques dealer – pays his rent every month and that's as much as I have to do with him.'

'Well, apparently Paul Copeland and his girlfriend had their doubts about him and some of his friends, and I know Dad went up to inspect the flat on the day he died, because they were being noisy. He may have been one of the last people to see Dad alive.'

Simon gave an astonished laugh. 'You're not suggesting he may have had something to do with Dom's death?'

When he saw that she clearly was, he shook his head firmly. 'No. I'm sorry, I can't believe that.'

'It seems strange that Paul Copeland suspected him of something and ends up dead, and then Dad goes to see him and …' She broke off, unable to finish.

'Look, Kirsty.' Simon came round the desk and hesitated before putting an arm around her shoulder. She should have shaken it off – would have done in any other circumstances – except that it was nice to have a bit of contact with another human being, even if it was him. She felt so confused at the moment. Rob was right, she was bumbling around like a pathetic amateur sleuth, and it was getting her nowhere.

Why was she putting herself through this?

'I can't imagine how difficult it must be for you – especially when you and your father fell out so spectacularly,' Simon said. 'I'm not rubbishing what you're doing but, you know, the last thing Dom would want now is for you to drive yourself to distraction over an imaginary crime that in all probability doesn't exist outside your head. I may not know Tim well, but to suggest he might be involved in one, if not two, murders is inconceivable. Anyway, they've arrested someone over Paul Copeland's death now. Didn't you hear the news?'

'I know.' She bit her lip, then ploughed on determinedly. 'Sergeant Briscombe mentioned that you were in a pub very close to where Dad had his accident?'

She felt his withdrawal as he stepped back to look down at her. 'You're not suspecting *me* now?'

'Of course not. I just wondered if you might have seen anything either before you went into the pub or after you came out?'

'No, I didn't. Yes, I was there, but I literally dropped in for a quick pint and a sandwich before heading up the road to the golf club. I could see something was going on, but I was in a hurry and didn't have time to hang around.'

'Everything alright?'

Kirsty swung round at the sound of Tony Jordan's voice coming from the doorway.

He walked into the room and gave her a hug as he kissed her cheek. She hugged him back, clinging onto the familiarity of him.

'How are you doing, chicken?'

'Not too bad.'

'Good. I thought your mother bore up well yesterday and I know how glad she is to have you back in the fold. I'm heading off to lunch. Do you two want to join me?'

'Sorry, I'm in a bit of a rush,' Kirsty said quickly.

'And I've got Peter Mercer coming in half an hour,' Simon said.

'Ah yes. Give him my regards. See you soon, Kirsty. Tell Mum Margot and I will pop over sometime at the weekend to see her.' And with a little pat on her shoulder, he was gone.

'Where were we?' Simon said.

Kirsty sighed. 'We're done. I just wanted to speak to you before I went to the police.'

'With what exactly?'

174

'I'm not sure. I don't want to drop Susan in it, but I think they should know about her suspicions.'

'But it doesn't sound like they need to now if they've got the guy.'

'We don't know they have for sure, and maybe there's more to it all than they realise. I want them to know about Paul's suspicions about the tenant, and the fact that Dad also spoke to him. At the very least I think they should question him.'

'Wouldn't they already have done that?'

'I don't know. That's what I want to check out.'

Simon ran a hand through his hair. 'I'm not sure it's a good idea going to the police about anything.'

She looked at him sharply. 'Why not?'

He hesitated, then shrugged. 'Think about it. If you tell them about him, they're going to want to know who gave you the information. Then in all probability they'll interview the girlfriend again, and I don't know if you know that we paid her some cash to erm … leave? It could be awkward if that came to light.'

'Rob told me that wasn't illegal.'

'It's not exactly illegal …'

'Then what are you worried about?'

It was obvious from his expression that he was getting frustrated with her. 'Because it's not exactly good practice either and I'm sure we'd all rather not draw attention to cash deals and stuff that we don't need to.'

She was catching up with him fast but she needed to hear him say it. 'What sort of stuff? What are you saying, Simon?'

He held her gaze. 'I'm saying that Robbie wouldn't want attention being drawn to the company's books. And neither would we, because we're the ones who do the legal bits for you.'

He hesitated, obviously wondering how much more to say, then shrugged. 'There have been other cash deals over the years and some purchases done in Lizzie's maiden name, for example, to make it less obvious that it's a turn – with the proceeds being paid into her account in the Isle of Man. That wouldn't go down well with the taxman. And the deal on your grandmother's land wouldn't be the only discrepancy they'd find if they really chose to investigate Cartwrights books, though it would be one of the more serious because it was defrauding your aunt out of part of her inheritance.'

Kirsty was looking at him in horror. It felt like the mire was getting so deep she'd soon be drowning in it.

'There's no need to look like that. Cartwrights isn't the only company in the country bending the rules a bit to make a decent living, and neither are we. But it's imperative that both sides trust each other not to drop the other side in it. It's a relationship that's worked well for forty-odd years – ever since our parents first started out and needed those deals to survive. To be blunt, Kirsty, we don't need you coming in here and messing everything up. And it doesn't take much these days to have the tax inspectors crawling all over you.'

'But you're a solicitor – you're meant to be above that sort of thing.'

There was an indifference to his expression that made her realise just how unaffected he was by the immorality of what they did. He shrugged.

'It's small fry. So the odd property gets turned. Who cares? No one's getting hurt and everyone's making money out of it.'

'Except for the people being swindled *out* of money that's rightfully theirs – like my aunt.'

'I told Robbie and your father that your grandmother's land deal was too close to home for comfort.' He shrugged. 'Your dad gave me a rough time over it – that I hadn't been more careful about what you saw while you were doing your work experience here.'

'So you knew why I left?'

'Of course I did.'

Kirsty felt flattened. She needed to be alone. She got up to go.

'What are you going to do?'

'I don't know. I need to think. But I do know one thing. There's no way I can work in that sort of set-up.'

Simon, too, rose from his desk, his expression set. 'Then maybe you should go back to France or find a job in another company. You need to get real, Kirsty. You've been very happy to take what your father provided for you all your life – but now's the time of reckoning. Are you really going to stand against us all – tear not only Dom's reputation to shreds, but also Robbie's, your mother's, the company's – risk ruining them all financially just to salve your conscience? I don't think it's in you to do that.'

Without another word she turned and left. But as she headed out onto the street, her anger burned at the fact he knew her so well. He was right. How could she even think of exposing her family like that?

The whole business left a nasty taste that wouldn't go away as she headed back to Cartwrights. None of what she'd learnt today had lessened her gut instinct that there was more to her father's death than met the eye, nor had it lessened her determination to find out the truth. If there was a link between Paul Copeland's death and her father's, then she wanted to know about it. And there was one more thing she needed to do before she even considered giving up and leaving it to the police.

The prospect didn't fill her with any enthusiasm whatsoever. After all, if her father *had* been murdered, his murderer was still out there. And who was to say he wouldn't kill again?

CHAPTER TWENTY

'Right, Harry.' Murray fixed his sharp eyes on Harry's face and leant back in his chair, his fingers steepled together in familiar fashion. 'I've got five minutes for you to bring me up to speed on the Copeland case before I need to scoff some lunch down and head off to the Met. How's the interview with Ken Lazard going?'

It was funny how, despite having worked with Murray for over two years, he still had the power to unnerve Harry when he looked at him in that particular way, his thick, bushy eyebrows set in a severe frown.

'Well, as you know, we pulled him in yesterday after Beth spoke to the *Barnet News* reporter. We're due for another session this afternoon. He's not saying anything at the moment, apart from *no comment* or trying to make us feel guilty at forcing him to leave his invalid wife home alone.'

'You need to be careful how you handle that one or you'll have the media swarming over us like ants – we don't need that at the moment.'

'No, sir.'

'What did he say about the CCTV showing him following Copeland?'

'That he wasn't following anyone. He was walking to the off-licence to buy some beer to take home.'

'Do you believe him?'

'No, but it's difficult to prove because the CCTV doesn't stretch to the off-licence. He's not being straight with us, though, and I could see he was unsettled once he knew he'd been caught on film the following morning. He said he was just taking a roundabout route to work to avoid the traffic, but that's bollocks. It's completely the opposite direction.'

'Well, keep working on him or you'll have to let him go.'

'I'm aware of that, believe me.'

Murray looked at him and half-smiled. 'I'm sure you are. So what have you got so far on Copeland's movements that day?'

'Not a lot. It seems he wasn't working but his girlfriend was. All she knew was that he was meeting up with someone at some point but he wouldn't say who or where. That could have been Joshua Wells – the reporter Beth spoke to – or someone unknown. Ken Lazard's car was picked up on the CCTV turning into his road at around 08.30. He could therefore potentially have followed him to a rendezvous if he left early, although according to Ken's work, he arrived at his usual time of around nine-thirty. We have a statement from the reporter – Joshua Wells – confirming that he met up with Paul at his flat at ten-forty-five. Paul filled him in on the background of his story and told him that he was fearful for his life after Ken Lazard had attacked him the previous night in the pub. He said that Ken had followed him home and threatened to put him in a wheelchair so he'd know what it was like. He wanted Wells to run the story as a form of protection for himself, and also wanted payment for it. Wells apparently said he'd look into it and get back to him. Of course he never did because Paul was killed later on that day and Joshua Wells didn't learn about it until a week or so later when he got back from his holiday.

'So not looking very good for Ken Lazard.'

'No.'

'What about the other chap who died? The estate agent. Any connections coming through?'

Harry shook his head. 'Not really, although …'

Murray looked at him and waited.

'I know how you feel about coincidences, which must be beginning to rub off on me,' Harry said with a rueful smile. 'There is one loose connection – a firm of solicitors in Whetstone. They're friends of the Cartwrights and the son also happens to own the house where Paul Copeland lived. He was seen on CCTV entering a pub at the top of the road where Dominic Cartwright was run over. Says he nipped in for a pint before meeting a client up at the golf club, and had no idea Cartwright was in the vicinity. Apart from that, no links.'

'Have you spoken to the client he was meeting?'

'Not yet. I only tackled him about it yesterday and didn't feel a funeral was the right place to start taking statements. Beth's chasing it up today.'

'What's he like?'

'Early thirties, pretty average. No that's a lie. Better-looking than average, educated – clearly not short of a bob or two. Not the sort you'd naturally have earmarked as a criminal.'

'So what are your thoughts?'

'I wish I had some. Paul Copeland was clearly no saint. When his girlfriend told him he was kidding himself thinking he could afford a better flat, he told her she didn't know everything. Maybe – it's possible – he was mixed up in something illegal that was going to bring some money in, and it went wrong? Or maybe he was blackmailing someone. Or maybe he was just hoping his story about Ken Lazard might bring in some cash. Against that, Ken Lazard's clearly got a temper and there doesn't seem to be much doubt he followed Paul home and threatened him. He had both motive and opportunity – and he's clearly not telling us the truth. We need a bit of a breakthrough, to be honest.'

Murray reached for a file on his desk, signalling an end to their conversation. He looked up at Harry, the expression on his well-worn face reflecting an unusual level of empathy for him.

'I know how frustrating it is. But as my old boss used say, keep digging, it'll come – just be sure to recognise the signs when it does.'

Ken Lazard stared Harry out across the table in the unimpressive, grey-walled interview room. His attitude was belligerent. He was clearly getting fed up with all the questions.

'I told you, I went to the off-licence to get some beer and then I went home.'

'And the following morning – when we have you on video turning into Paul Copeland's street?'

'There was a lot of traffic. I didn't fancy sitting in it. I took a roundabout route.'

'A very roundabout route,' Harry said. 'In fact, one that was completely the opposite direction to the way you needed to go to get to work.'

Silence.

'Come on, Ken. Do you think I'm stupid? You're not being straight with me.'

'I've got nothing else to say, except either charge me or let me go. I have a disabled wife at home who needs me.'

'Then the sooner you answer my questions, the better. I'll ask you again. Why did you go to Paul Copeland's house that Monday morning?'

'For a cup of coffee?'

Harry glared at him.

'No comment,' Ken said.

'Did you see Paul Copeland that morning?'

'No comment.'

'Did you follow Paul Copeland that morning?'

'No comment.'

'We can sit here all day if you like, Ken: I'm not going anywhere. I want the truth and I'll sit here until I get it.'

'You wouldn't know the truth if it kicked you in the arse. You've already got me nailed for that bastard's murder.'

'Try me. If you're innocent you've got more chance of proving it if you help me find the real killer. Can't you see that?'

Ken glanced at his solicitor, who simply shrugged his shoulders.

He looked back at Harry, clearly considering his options.

'Alright ... So maybe I did go to Paul's house that day,' he said finally. 'I wanted to see him. Let him know I was watching him. He put my wife in a wheelchair, for Christ's sake, and he didn't give a shit.'

Harry leant forward. 'What happened?'

'Nothing. I sat there till about nine and he never came out. I needed to be in work by nine-thirty, so I left. I knew there'd be plenty of other opportunities to collar him.'

'Was anyone else around? Did anyone see you drive off?'

'What do you think? That's why I didn't own up to it. Nobody notices shit these days.'

'You realise things aren't looking good for you?'

''Course I do, but not much I can do about it, is there?'

He looked genuinely despondent, as if finally the bravado was deserting him and the reality of his situation was beginning to sink in. He reached for the glass of water in front of him with a hand that wasn't quite steady.

'You could try telling me your exact movements the night Paul died. The timings you give aren't great as an alibi. We have one person at the pub puts you leaving around ten-fifteen, and your wife says you didn't get home until nearly an hour later. It doesn't take you an hour to drive from Barnet to Potters Bar.'

A knock on the door interrupted them and Harry paused the tape as Beth walked into the room.

'Can I have a word?'

Harry frowned, frustrated at the interruption just when he felt he was beginning to get somewhere. He turned towards the tape. 'DC Macaskill has just entered the room. I'm pausing the tape and will resume this interview after conferring with her in a separate office.'

He pushed his chair back and rose from his seat. 'Excuse me a minute, will you, Ken? And while I'm gone you might like to think about your situation. If you're innocent you should have nothing to hide. And the sooner we know exactly what we're dealing with, the better it'll be for all of us.'

'What's up?' he asked Beth out in the corridor.

'Sorry, but there's someone I thought you'd want to know about in Interview Room One. She reckons she's got information for us that will prove Ken Lazard couldn't have murdered Paul Copeland.'

When Harry walked back into Interview Room Two to carry on with his interrogation of Ken Lazard, there was a lightness to his step that hadn't been there before. Finally they were getting somewhere. He switched the tape back on, entered the necessary details, then turned his attention back to the man sitting opposite him on the other side of the table.

'Right, Ken. You'll never guess who I've just been talking to? Or maybe you can?'

He waited for a moment and when Ken made no response,

said, 'I've been having a chat with your colleague at the day centre, Kathy Wilkins. Can you guess what we've been talking about?'

He watched as the other man's face paled but his expression was stubborn as he waited for Harry to say more.

Harry leant back in his chair. 'So … in your own time … perhaps you'd like to fill me in on what you and Mrs Wilkins were doing the night Paul Copeland was murdered?'

Harry savoured the last bit of his iced bun, wiped his mouth with a napkin and then rose from the table in the canteen, prepared for business. He hoped the break would have given Ken Lazard time to consider his options and realise that further prevarication wasn't helpful to either of them.

'Ready for this?' he asked Beth.

'You bet,' she responded with a grin.

Five minutes later he was back in his familiar spot, facing Ken over the pale grey table. He tried to gauge the other man's mood from his body language, but whatever he was feeling, he was hiding it well.

'Okay, Ken, you've had some time to think about things now. Are you ready to tell me about Kathy Wilkins?'

The man stared at him steadily. 'I could be, but it depends how confidential it will be. I'm sure you get where I'm coming from?'

'I think I do. But I need to hear it from you.'

'If I tell you, can you keep it from Magz?'

'I can't promise. That'll depend on how relevant it is to solving Paul Copeland's murder.'

'And if it's not relevant?'

'Then we may be able to keep it quiet. But I can't guarantee that.'

Ken sighed, shaking his head and staring off into the

distance. After a few moments when no one said anything, he turned back to look at Harry.

'I love Maggie – and Kathy loves her husband, you need to know that. But – it's difficult, you know? Dealing with stuff … going without sex. We got to talking about it one night and it just came to us that it would be the ideal situation. Neither of us is looking to leave our partners and this way, no one gets hurt, see. Me and Kathy have got an outlet not only for the sex, but also we talk about stuff that no one else would understand unless they were in the same boat as us. That's how it started really: we both felt such anger against the people who fucked up our lives and it was just good to be able to talk it through with someone. The sex bit came later. It's a release, that's all. Don't get me wrong. We know it's worse for Maggie and Phil – but it's difficult for us, too, in a different way.'

'So where were you the night Paul Copeland was killed?'

'In the pub, like I said. Kath and I meet there when we can, and Derek lets us use one of the rooms upstairs for a bit of private time and then we usually go back downstairs, have a drink with the punters, and go home.'

'And that Monday night?'

'Was no different. Look, most of our mates know the set-up. It's why they were so cagey when you spoke to them. They didn't want to drop us in it.'

'So you're saying that you were with Mrs Wilkins from what time?'

'We met at the pub at about quarter to nine. We were upstairs for about an hour and then came down for a quick drink before leaving around ten-fifteen, I reckon.'

'It still leaves a gap of approximately half an hour before you met up and an hour between leaving the pub and getting home.'

'That's because I checked the tyres and put petrol in the car on my way to the pub, and I dropped Kath home afterwards and we talked in the car outside her house.'

'What petrol station was it?'

'Tesco's.'

'Have you got the receipt?'

'I doubt it. I could look, I suppose. I put twenty quid in and paid cash.'

'You say you dropped Mrs Wilkins home. How did she get to the pub?'

'She got a lift with a friend and I said I'd drop her back.'

Harry finished scribbling the notes he was writing and looked across the table at Ken. He hesitated, but really, was there any point making the bloke's home life more difficult than it already was?

'Is there anything else you want to say that you think might be relevant or helpful to the investigation?'

Ken shook his head. His eyes shifted away from Harry's, whether because he wasn't being straight or because he was embarrassed by these revelations, Harry didn't know. He switched off the tape.

'Okay. That'll do for now. For the time being you're free to go.'

Ken looked at his solicitor, who nodded. They both rose.

'You won't say anything to Maggie?'

'Not at this stage. I'll let you know if that situation changes.'

'Thanks.' He looked awkward, as if he was about to say something else, then he shrugged and the shutters came down again as he followed his solicitor from the room.

'Does that let him off the hook?' Beth asked, gathering up the empty coffee cups.

Harry sighed. 'Not entirely. There's still that window of opportunity both before and after his time at the pub. He could have done Paul in, shoved him in the boot of his car, kept his rendezvous with Kath Wilkins and then dumped him in the early hours. Or he could have done him in after he and Kath Wilkins parted, and still dumped him.'

'He'd have to be a pretty cool customer to have a dead body in the boot and meet up with Kath as if nothing's happened.'

Harry remembered how Ken had spent the first interview sessions being completely uncooperative. 'Yeah, he would – but then I'd say he is a pretty cool customer … wouldn't you?' He rose from the table. 'What are you up to this afternoon?'

'Not a lot.'

'Did you check out Simon Jordan's client? The one he said he was meeting at the golf club?'

'Yup. John Harper. They met up for nine holes, apparently. He reckoned several people saw them.'

'Golf on a Thursday morning. We're in the wrong job, aren't we?'

He held the door open so she could pass through. 'Do you fancy nipping round to our friend Derek in the pub again to see if he'll now verify Ken's story?'

'Sure. What are you going to do?'

'Think I'm going to pay another visit to Paul Copeland's girlfriend, Susan – see if she knew Ken was harassing Paul. She said he'd been in a fight but reckoned she didn't know who it was with. I can't see it myself.'

'Maybe Paul felt more guilty about it than he let on, so didn't tell her?'

'Not if that reporter's anything to go by. He said Paul was out to make it all as public as he could.'

Back in the open-plan office, Beth took her jacket off the hook. 'I'll head off, then, shall I, to interview Derek?'

'Yeah, let's get it done. And maybe while you're at it you could gather some more CCTV footage – from Tesco's petrol station? We might be able to back up Ken's story that way.'

'Sure.'

'What are your plans after that?'

'Thought I'd come back here and go through the witness statements. See if there's anything we could've missed. I want to get away on time tonight, though.'

'Doing something interesting?'

Beth didn't do looking nonchalant well.

'Visiting my grandparents.'

'What, the ones you were talking about that you've never met? I thought you didn't want to see them?'

She shrugged. 'Maybe I've been swayed by seeing the relationship you've got with your gran,' she said diffidently. 'My own family are a waste of space – that's why I moved away – but that could be why my grandparents cut them off, in which case I might find I get on with them quite nicely.'

'Well, I hope it goes well.'

'Thanks.' Beth's expression, though Harry didn't think she realised it, was wistful, as if she was secretly hoping for good things to come from this meeting.

'I'll see you Monday, then, if nothing comes up before?' Harry said.

'Yup. Have a good one.'

Outside Susan Porter's front door, Harry rang the bell and waited. But when the door opened, it wasn't Susan Porter who came out but a short, stocky fellow with a recycling bag in his hands, who looked as taken aback to see Harry as Harry was to see him. The man pushed past him, exiting the building, and Harry took advantage of the door being open to slip in. The first thing he noticed was the pile of post sitting on the shelf in the hall. Ignoring it, he crossed the short distance to Susan's internal door and knocked smartly. There was no response.

'You'll be 'aving a long wait, mate. No one lives there anymore.'

It was the stocky man, back from emptying his bin. He had a rough, cockney accent.

'Oh? I thought Susan Porter lived here?'

'Moved out a couple of days ago.'

'Any idea where to?'

'Nope.'

'And you are?'

'Who wants to know?'

'Detective Sergeant Briscombe.' Harry pulled out his card, and immediately the man's eyes narrowed.

'Alan Flint,' he responded briefly.

'You live here?'

'No. I'm visiting.'

'Is the upstairs tenant in? Tim Burman? We've been trying to contact him about an incident that happened last week. He's not got back to us yet.'

'That's because he's out the country on business, in France. It's why I'm flat sitting.'

'When's he back?'

'Dunno. Soon. Your message is on the answerphone. I'm sure he'll get back to you.'

'Make sure he does, please. Tell him it's urgent.'

Harry picked up the pile of post addressed to Paul Copeland and Susan Porter. 'I'll drop this down to the agents. They should have a forwarding address for Miss Porter.'

CHAPTER TWENTY-ONE

Kirsty ended her call to a prospective vendor, scribbled a note and then looked through the glass partition to where Robbie was packing up for the day.

'You heading off early?' she asked, popping her head round the door.

He nodded. 'Lizzie says she needs a break. She's had a couple of bad nights so I'm on bath duty tonight. When I've dealt with them, I'll go over to the flat. We need to get it finished so I can get it let.'

'I could babysit for you one night if you like? Give you both a break?'

Rob ran his hand through his hair. 'That would be great. We haven't had a night out, just the two of us, in ages.'

He sounded tired and Kirsty felt for him. 'Well, my social calendar's hardly overflowing. Just choose a night that suits you and let me know.' She hesitated. 'I spoke to Simon today.'

'I know. He phoned me.'

'Oh. Right.'

'Of course he was going to phone me, Kirsty. He's worried about what you're going to do. And so am I, to be honest.'

It seemed that at almost every meeting, she and Rob were arguing these days. She wanted to tackle him about the things Simon had said – about how he could be happy blurring the lines between legal and illegal, about doing deals in Lizzie's name, which had come as a real shock to her … But she realised there was only so much she could absorb in one day.

'All I want is to tell the police what Susan said about Dad seeing Simon's tenant on the day he died, so that they can question him about it. If you agree to that, then I'll agree to take a step back and let them get on with it.'

'*For Christ's sake*, Kirsty, that could lead to them interviewing Susan again and I've told you, we just want to keep a low profile – we don't want them poking around in our business.'

'You're worrying me, Rob.'

Her brother took a breath. 'There's nothing to worry about. Whatever happened to Paul Copeland had nothing to do with Dad; I'm convinced of that. It's an unfortunate coincidence. But if Cartwrights get sucked into this and the police start delving into things too deeply it could become a bloody nightmare at a time when we really don't need it.'

'*I don't believe you.*' Kirsty's previous intention not to say too much, flew out of the window. 'I was *shocked* by some of the things Simon told me today about your business practices. I don't know how you can work like that.'

'It's a case of necessity.'

'*Bollocks.* I get that years back when Dad and Tony first started with no money, *maybe* they felt justified doing the odd cash deal to help make ends meet. But there's no excuse now. I thought you took pride in what you did.'

'I do. We offer a bloody good service to our clients – and we're *not* crooked. So we bend a few rules with trusted contacts we've built up over the years … You show me any small business that doesn't do that.'

'Rob, what planet are you on?'

'Not the same one as you, clearly.'

'Cartwrights is a successful business now. You don't need to risk your reputation, or worse. It can't be right that you're doing deals in Lizzie's name – why do you do that? Is she happy about it? Does she even know?'

She could see she'd hit a nerve and, knowing Lizzie as she did, she wasn't surprised. She bet there would have been some heated arguments over that.

'I've only done that a couple of times. She's from the Isle of Man. It's a good tax move.'

'Tax *dodge*, you mean.'

'This isn't getting us anywhere. Okay, you want this tenant of Simon's interviewing? I'll see him. Hear what he has to say and report back to you. Will that do?'

He was changing the subject, but she was sick of it, too – sick to the stomach at the thought of the wider implications of all that was coming out.

'I'll come with you,' she said flatly.

'If you do, then you stay outside. In the unlikely event he's dangerous I don't want you in there. It'll seem more like a routine visit if it's just me.'

'But you've got Lizzie and the girls to think about. If anything goes wrong–'

'Kirsty, you may not like the way I do things, but I'm not the sort of brother who lets his little sister do the dirty work. I'll be the one to go in and see him.' He looked at his watch. 'And if we're going to do this, let's do it. I'll have Lizzie on my back if I'm not home when I said I'd be – and believe me, she's far more scary than any bloody tenant.'

Fifteen minutes later, Kirsty sat in her car outside 28 Myton Road and watched as her brother walked up to the front door and rang the bell. When no one answered, he rang again, then turned to her with a shrug before retracing his steps back up the path.

'No one's in,' he said through her open window. 'I'll try again tomorrow on my way into work.'

Kirsty sighed, but nodded. 'Okay. Thanks for trying. I'll see you tomorrow at Mum's. And don't overdo it tonight with the decorating. The amount of time it's taken you to decorate that flat … It should be looking like a showpiece by now.'

She watched as he climbed into his own car and was about to pull out after him, when a movement in an upstairs window caught her eye. Was someone up there, watching them? And if so, why hadn't they answered the door?

She frowned as her eyes dropped to the front door again. Something was niggling at the back of her mind. Something to do with when she'd come to visit Susan here, that first time.

Then she realised what it was.

Robbie had driven off and it looked like the person at the window had also disappeared. Kirsty left it a couple more minutes before opening her car door and getting out. She walked down the path to the front door and realised she was right.

Tim Burman's bell was on the right-hand side of the front door and Paul Copeland's was on the left.

So why had Robbie been ringing Paul Copeland's doorbell instead of Tim Burman's – knowing the flat was empty?

The anger that flared through her was matched in equal parts by fear. What was going on? Why would Robbie deceive her like that? They'd always been so close – partners in crime with a small 'c' – but these days she was beginning to feel she didn't know her brother at all. It felt as, if step by step, her faith in her family was being shattered, and she wasn't sure how to handle it.

But there was no question of backing out now. Without

giving herself time to think, she pushed the bell marked *Tim Burman.*

Holy shit! What was she doing?

'Yeah … what do you want?'

The voice coming from above her head was impatient and made her jump. She looked up at the aggressive, bulldoggish features of the man glaring down at her, and tried a smile.

'Hi. I was just wondering if Tim was around?'

'No, he ain't.'

She took a step back so she could see him better. 'I need to speak to him, I'm–'

'Oh, I know who you are.'

She blinked at him. 'I don't think you do…'

'Oh, yeah. You're from the agents.'

Her brow creased. How did he know that? 'Oh, well … yes, I am … and I need to speak to Tim.'

'As I said, he's not here.'

'When's he back?'

'Don't know …'

He broke off at the same time as Kirsty heard the sound of the gate opening behind her. She turned around to see another man and a young woman walking down the path towards her. A quick assessment of the man told her that it wasn't Tim Burman. This man was much younger than he'd be if he'd been a school friend of Simon's.

'I'm coming down,' the Bulldog guy called out to them, disappearing from the window.

Kirsty stood to one side as the couple approached the front door. Just briefly, her eyes met the blank gaze of the girl, before the door was flung open and both she and the man disappeared through it.

'Look, there's no point you hanging around. Tim's away – won't be back for a couple of days.'

The man didn't look any more attractive close up than he

had done from a distance. He was only an inch or two taller than her but he was stockily built and quite intimidating close up. She held her ground bravely.

'Look … I'm not trying to be difficult. I just want to speak to Tim for a couple of minutes, that's all.'

'He'll be busy when he gets back. Better off emailing him.'

'Okay, I'll do that, but also …' She rummaged around in her bag and pulled out a business card, glad she didn't have to give him her mobile number. 'He can call me at the office anytime.'

The man snatched the card from her fingers and without another word, shut the door in her face.

Her expression was uneasy as she walked back to the car. How had he known who she was?

She tried to think it through logically, and came up with two possibilities – neither of which afforded her any comfort. One was that he knew she'd been asking questions about Tim Burman, and for some reason had her pegged. And the other was that he'd been aware of her all along – perhaps because he had some sort of connection to her father or Robbie. The thought of them being involved with someone like him was inconceivable – yet why had Rob deceived her just now?

As she pulled out of her parking space, she looked in her rear-view mirror uneasily. Could someone even be following her?

She suddenly felt very alone – and it wasn't a pleasant sensation.

It was eight o'clock when Harry let himself into his grand-mother's house. He noticed Claire's car parked out on the road and felt an uplift in his spirits, but it died swiftly when she met him at the bottom of the stairs and he saw her expression.

'What's the matter?' he asked.

'Your gran's had a fall. She's okay now. I've got her to bed. But she was upset and disorientated when I arrived. I don't know how long she'd been lying there, but I think she may have twisted her ankle which might limit her mobility.'

Harry took the stairs two at a time, stopping only to knock briefly on his grandmother's bedroom door before entering.

'Are you alright?' he asked, hurrying to her bedside.

'I'm fine, boy.' She sounded irritable, her voice weaker than it had been. 'No need for you to worry your head. Stupid thing. I don't know how it happened. That damned coffee table I expect – always knocking myself on it.'

'I'll move it. Are you sure you're okay?'

He heard Claire at the doorway and turned. 'Should we call the doctor?'

She shook her head and shared a look with him. 'She won't let me.'

'I'm fine now, I tell you. It was just uncomfortable lying there on the floor but I knew one of you would be here soon enough – good thing Claire knows where the spare key's hidden.'

'Well, I'll be off, then, and see you tomorrow,' Claire said. 'Call me if there's a problem: I can always nip over during the day if you want me to.'

'Thank you, my lovely.'

'I'll see you out,' Harry said.

At the front door he watched as she put her coat on. 'Do you think she'll be okay now?'

'I think so. I checked her over: nothing broken, I'm sure of that, but she'll probably have some bruising. Call the doctor if you're at all worried.'

Harry nodded. 'Luckily I'm around now for the next couple of days, barring anything urgent coming in that I get called out for. What are you up to this weekend? Anything interesting?'

She pulled a face. 'Family lunch on Sunday at my place. I don't know what made me do it. It seemed like a good idea at the time – a sort of belated house-warming – but it'll be manic. You?'

He shrugged. 'Nothing much. I'm meeting some mates for a drink tomorrow night, but other than that it'll be a quiet one.'

He could have added *again,* but didn't.

'Want to come along to mine on Sunday?'

He sensed the offer was out before she'd given it any consideration … probably on the back of feeling sorry for him.

'You don't have to,' she added quickly, when she noticed his hesitation. 'I'm just being selfish, because I'd make you work hard for your lunch, helping me get stuff ready before they arrive. I stupidly turned down my mum's offer of help.'

'What's on the menu?' he prevaricated, a teasing light in his eye.

'Roast beef and Yorkshire, with all the trimmings.'

He gave a low whistle. 'You're on. As long as everything's fine with Gran by then.'

'Great. Shall we say about eleven? I'll text you my address.'

He watched as she made her way up the path to her car. He liked everything about her, he thought. From the way she walked – with her back straight and that easy confidence that seemed to reflect her personality, right down to the swishing chestnut-coloured ponytail and slim figure that would catch the eye of any man.

'Harry?'

Upstairs in his grandmother's room, his expression softened as he took in the pale features. Despite her words to the contrary, he could see the fall had shaken her. She looked frail and ill sitting there propped up in her bed.

'Anything I can get you?'

'Yes, a bottle of pills and a decent glass of brandy, so I can finish off what God's started.'

'*Gran*–'

'Don't tell me not to talk like that. I've had enough; you know I have. And you know what I want to do about it. Time's running out, boy – I need to know there's a plan in place.'

'*Jesus, Gran,* please don't start this again. You know I can't do it even if I wanted to. I'm a policeman.'

Her face lost some of its belligerence as she smiled at him. 'I know you are, love – but you're also my grandson. I know you love me and I'm asking you to help me have a peaceful end when things get bad. I don't want to die like your grandfather did. I'll admit it to you and no one else, I'm terrified of that happening.'

'It doesn't have to be like that. There are all sorts of things they can do to make sure it's peaceful when the time comes.'

'That's what they said to John.'

'And that was ten years ago. Things have come on enormously since then. I'll contact the Macmillan team, get them to come over and talk to you.'

'You can do what you like. But if you won't help me, I'll find a way of doing it myself so that I don't need to rely on you.'

Her voice was resolute and he felt useless. All these years of being a policeman, dealing with all sorts of complicated issues, and he didn't know how to handle his own grandmother. And it didn't make matters any easier that he completely got where she was coming from. He'd probably feel the same in her shoes: he wouldn't want to suffer the lingering, painful death his grandfather had, that was for sure, and he wouldn't hesitate to speed things up if he got the chance. But the fact remained that assisted suicide was still illegal – and he was meant to uphold the law, not bend it to suit his own requirements. If he got found out, it wouldn't only mean the end of his career, it could see him put in prison for a good, long stretch. And he probably would be. He could see it now – they'd feel the need to make an example of him.

He loved his grandmother more than anyone else, but was he really prepared to risk all that and throw his life down the pan?

He shook his head. 'I can't listen, Gran.'

'Please at least think about it?'

As if he thought of anything else. He tried to sound convincing. 'I don't believe in euthanasia, you know that.'

'But I do, and it's my life. You've got to do this for me, Harry. There's no one else I can ask.'

CHAPTER TWENTY-TWO

K irsty had a quick glance around before turning into her parents' drive, but it was difficult to tell if anyone might be trailing her. After her confrontation with *Bulldog* she hadn't felt like going home, so she'd gone back to the office and caught up on some paperwork. She'd also Googled Tim Burman, but hadn't found out much about him, apart from the fact that he was an antiques dealer specialising in 19th-century furniture and paintings. She'd seen a picture of him, though, and was forced to admit he looked perfectly normal and, as Simon had said, not bad-looking.

Now, hanging her jacket on the stand in the hall, she went in search of her mother in the lounge.

'Oh Kirsty.' Her mother jumped up agitatedly from her chair. 'Thank God you're back.'

'What's the matter?'

Her mother shook her head, tears forming in her eyes. 'Robbie and I have had a huge row. He stormed out of here in such a temper. I've never seen him like that.'

Oh, God ... Was that because she'd put him in a bad mood?

'Mum, calm down. I'm sure it can't be that bad. Tell me what happened.'

'He left work early because he'd told Lizzie he'd help with the kids tonight, but he dropped in on me first to check I was okay.'

'And ...?'

'He hadn't told me he was coming. I wasn't expecting either of you that early. Dan was here...'

'*What!? Daniel Curtis?*'

Kirsty felt her own blood shoot straight to boiling point. Hadn't her mother taken on-board *anything* she'd said?

'For God's sake, Mum. What was *he* doing here again?'

'It's been hard for me. Dan called to see how I was getting on, and I broke down on the phone. He was worried about me.'

'He has no *right* to be worried about you, that's our job. No wonder Rob was annoyed. Why didn't you call one of us? We'd have come straight back.'

'I wasn't expecting anyone to come. He just turned up. It was kind of him.'

'I warned you Robbie wouldn't like it.'

'I know you did. But he's being unreasonable. I've known Dan most of my life – he's an old friend.'

'Who we all know would like to be more than friends!'

Her mother tossed her head. 'Maybe he would, I don't know. But I'm not interested in that and never have been. If you think that's why I let him come over...'

She seemed to shrink inside herself, and immediately Kirsty felt remorse. She moved swiftly over to give her a hug.

'I'm sorry, of course I don't. ... I just know what Rob's like at the moment. It's exhausting having to tread on eggshells around him the whole time and this'll make him ten times worse.'

'I know. I haven't seen him in such a rage in a long time. I hope he doesn't take it out on Lizzie.'

'What makes you say that? Why would he do that?'

Her mother shrugged. 'I don't mean in a physical way. I know he wouldn't do that. He was just in such a strop.'

'I'll give it a while and then I'll call them. He'll calm down.'

But when she made the call an hour later, Lizzie informed her that he was out.

'He said he was going to the gym and then the flat to do some decorating. I've tried to call him a couple of times, but he's not picking up.'

'Was he alright?' Kirsty asked. 'Did he tell you what happened?'

'No and yes,' Lizzie replied. 'No, he wasn't alright, and yes, he did tell me. He saw red apparently, that Dan was sitting in Dom's chair. I did try to point out that there are only two chairs in that room, so if he wasn't going to sit on the settee, there probably wasn't much choice. But he wasn't having it.'

'Can you ask him to call me when he gets back?'

'I can try, but you don't seem to be his favourite person either at the moment _ though I wouldn't take that too personally. He's a nightmare these days, if you want the truth. I just mentioned tonight that the flat seems to be taking forever to be finished, and he exploded. Stormed out of here and told me he'd see me when he sees me.' She sighed. 'I guess it'll all calm down. At least he managed to hide his mood from the kids while he was bathing them. We could just do with a bit of a break.'

Kirsty hesitated, wondering whether now would be a good time to bring up the property deals that had been done in Lizzie's name, but she couldn't do it. At the end of the day, it was between Lizzie and Rob what they did, and she didn't really want to get involved. But it was another thing she filed away for the future. If she did get involved in the business, things would have to change.

'I said to Rob I'd babysit if you want some time together?'

'Oh, Kirsty, that would be great. We're fine, just tired with everything that's going on. To be honest, I'm glad he's out of my hair tonight. He's not the only one who needs a bit of space.'

After showering and going downstairs to fix a sandwich that she didn't really want, Kirsty looked at the time. It was quarter to ten, and from the silence in the house she gathered her mother had already gone up to bed. Up on the landing, she hovered uncertainly outside her door. Part of her wanted to knock and see if she was okay – but she felt so low herself she knew she didn't have the strength at the moment to give her mother the support she needed. She could hear quiet sobs coming from within, and felt the tears spring hotly to her own eyes as she continued on her way. *She was crap.* A crap daughter, a crap sister, a crap fiancée …

Shutting the door to her own bedroom quietly behind her, she automatically went about the normal preparations for bed – getting undressed, putting her dirty clothes in the wash basket, brushing her teeth – but none of her anxieties would go away. Not her father's death; the business inconsistencies that seemed to be unravelling at a rate of knots; her issues with Rob; her run-in with Bulldog. She desperately needed someone to talk to – and she knew there was only one person who'd fit the bill. Sitting on the edge of her bed, she grabbed her mobile before she could change her mind and texted Luke.

He wasn't someone who'd stand out in a crowd – he made sure of that. But when you got up close and personal, it was a different matter. He had a knack of charming the most truculent of characters with his blond, floppy hair and unusually dark brown eyes that twinkled engagingly as he turned on the charm. Amazing what a decent disguise could do. His clothes were casual – the usual jeans and T-shirt – but chosen with care so that they showed off his muscular physique without making it look too obvious.

He'd been eyeing up the girl in the red dress for over an hour, bracing himself to make the move as she twisted and gyrated on the dance floor with her friends. They were having a good time but now, as the evening wore on, other watchers were moving in and already a couple of her friends had paired off. He'd miss the boat if he didn't act soon.

He manoeuvred himself closer to the group, dancing slightly to her left, his eye catching hers then sliding away a few times, until he realised she'd taken the bait and was now dancing so that she was facing him. Result.

He flashed her a grin and narrowed the gap between them. He was a good dancer and so was she. It added an extra level of appreciation for them both as they moved in harmony to the music, and when, ten minutes later, the tempo changed, slowing down, she made no objection when he drifted in, closing the gap to take her in his arms.

He felt the tingle in his groin straight away. It was certainly good stuff, that GHB, and he'd taken just enough to heighten his sexual appetite without overdoing it. You had to be very careful about that, because too much …

'How about a drink?' the girl murmured in his ear. 'My name's Patsy, by the way.'

'Sure thing. Unusual name – what's it short for?'

The girl laughed and pulled back to look at him. 'Patricia – dreadful, isn't it? Don't know what my parents were thinking. What's yours?'

'Ben,' he lied easily.

He guided her over to one of the small tables against the wall, which were filling up fast. 'If you don't mind saving this for us, I'll get the drinks. What's yours?'

'Screwdriver, please.'

It felt like a bit of an omen really.

Up at the bar he ordered the drinks, and made sure no one was watching before deftly slipping a small amount of the liquid he was carrying in his pocket, into her drink. He gave a little smile. With any luck it would pep her up enough to give them both a good time tonight. And boy, did he need to do something to get his mind off everything.

An hour later on the dance floor, it seemed to be working. His tongue was down her throat and she was kissing him back as if her little life depended on it.

'Hey, steady,' she protested, her hand pushing his away from where it had strayed between her legs.

'Sorry,' he muttered.

'You're moving too quickly,' she said in an aggressively inebriated voice. 'I think we should finish our drinks and go.' She shrugged. 'But I'll give you my number if you want and you can call me?'

Stupid cow. Did she really think he was interested in dating her?

'Okay, sorry. I'm getting ahead of myself, I know. Had a bit too much to drink, I think. Anyone told you you're gorgeous?'

She grinned at him coyly, her manner relaxing again. 'I just need to pop to the Ladies. I'll be back in a minute.'

He watched her trip unsteadily on her high heels across the dance floor, stopping to chat to a couple of girl friends on her way.

He had a few minutes, he reckoned, until she got back. He leant back in his chair and looked around him. It amused him to see one of his mates on the dance floor who didn't give him a second glance with his expensive wig on. It was surprising what a sense of liberty and power that gave him. Looking like a completely different person made him feel like one, too. He'd felt enormously stressed all day, feeling that his life was spiralling out of control, but look at him now – he felt completely back in charge again with his disguise in place. And it enabled him to do things he'd never be able to get away with in his normal life. It was a release for him and everyone needed a release, didn't they?

Sometimes he worried that maybe his pastime was becoming too much of a need for him, but he was still in control, wasn't he? He could get up and walk out of this sweatbox if he chose to without a backward glance – but the truth of the matter was, he didn't want to. He needed an outlet for the anger and frustration that had been building up, to stop it from festering and spilling over into his normal life – and he knew from past experience that this was the best way of dealing with that … even if it was only a temporary relief.

He took advantage of Patsy's absence to slip a bit more liquid into her drink. That should do it.

Half an hour later they were leaving the nightclub, his arm around her as he guided and supported her out into the fresh air. She was flopping around like a wet fish, and any attraction he'd felt for her disappeared, lessening his excitement. He already knew this wouldn't be one of his better experiences. No point wasting too much time taking her back to the flat. There was a tiny alley a short distance away with a few houses backing onto it. He already knew one was empty and for sale. Easy to unhinge the back gate – he'd checked it earlier and left it unbolted. It would be perfect.

'Don't feel good,' she mumbled, clutching onto his arm tightly.

'You'll be better in a minute with the fresh air. I think that last cocktail was one too many for you. Come on, this way. I'll get you a cab.'

The stupid woman barely put up any resistance at all. She was out of it, making only a half-hearted attempt to push him off when he pushed her down on the ground in the back garden. His gratification was brief and disappointing, lessened by the fact that he hadn't been able to indulge in his usual games and activities.

He stood up and left her there – returning to the flat with a sense of dissatisfaction that did nothing to suppress the frustrations that were already beginning to resurface.

He knew it wouldn't be long before he did it again.

CHAPTER TWENTY-THREE

'What's up?' Luke asked Kirsty in Costa's the following morning. His manner was brusque, as if he didn't want to be there.

Well, neither did she, but he was the only person she felt she could turn to.

'Thanks for coming. I'm sorry to eat into your Saturday. I'll try to be quick.' She hesitated. 'You remember I told you I was worried that Dad's accident wasn't an accident?'

He nodded.

'I need to talk to someone I can trust to see if I'm being paranoid or not. Robbie tells me I am – but then I'm beginning to suspect that he's got a vested interest in saying that.'

'What do you mean?'

His voice was impatient and she frowned. 'Please bear with me, Luke. This isn't easy and you'll understand why in a minute.'

She stirred her coffee, trying to marshal her thoughts. 'I told you about meeting up with Paul Copeland's girlfriend and how she was suspicious of the upstairs tenant? And that Dad called on him, the same day he died?'

'Yes.'

'Well, I know it's all circumstantial, but I told Robbie about it because the tenant upstairs is a friend of Simon's and I thought he might know him. I also tackled Simon about it. Both of them tried to fob me off, saying I was being paranoid thinking he might be involved in any way – and that I should leave it to the police. But the thing is, I've come to realise that neither of them want me poking around because basically they don't want the police, or more accurately, the taxman, looking into *them* too closely.'

She eyed him anxiously, glad that he was hearing her out without interrupting. 'You will keep this next bit confidential? It's really difficult for me and I just can't get my head round it … but Cartwrights seem to have a thing going with Jordan's whereby they don't always do things by the book, if you know what I mean?'

'I think I can guess.'

'It's part of the reason why I went to France. Before that, while I was doing my stint at Jordan's, I came across some papers. They were sale papers on a piece of land – Grandma's land.'

'But you knew it had been sold.'

'Yes, but this was a second deal. When Gran died, Rob and Dad said the land wasn't worth much because it was agricultural and had no development potential. It was sold, and the proceeds went into Gran's estate to be divided up between Dad and Aunty Anne. This second deal was dated several months later, when it was sold with planning permission to Stantons Luxury Home Developments – you know them, they're the ones in Highgate. It sold for an extra quarter of a million pounds. I drove up there yesterday to take a look and there's a sign up saying they're building eight luxury houses there.'

Luke gave a low whistle. 'So basically, it was turned?'

'I'm learning to hate that expression, but yes. I don't

pretend to understand the ins and outs of it all, but the land was originally bought by a company called Hampton Estates, who then sold it on to Stantons after they got planning permission. Hampton Estates is owned by Dad and Tony Jordan – and that's not the only deal Cartwrights have done like that.'

'So what happened when you found the papers?'

'I didn't know what to do. I didn't want to believe it. I didn't say anything to Tony or Simon, but I copied the paperwork and tackled Dad about it that night. He told me I was naive if I didn't think that sort of thing went on all the time. I felt sick, Luke – that they could con Aunty Anne and Rachael out of money that was rightfully theirs. They'd never have done that if Uncle Pat were still alive. We had a huge row about it and then Dad must have told Tony and Simon that I knew, because that weekend was the weekend Simon asked me to meet him at the pub.'

She broke off, realising they were entering perilous territory.

'Why did he want to do that?'

'He said he needed to explain it to me, but he didn't come up with anything I didn't already know. I told him they were all shits for double-crossing Anne and Rachael like that, but at the end of the day, as he pointed out, my hands were tied unless I was prepared to expose my whole family and drop them in it.'

'And that was the night you and he–? It makes it all the more incredible that you could have done that.'

She didn't need him to tell her that. She shrugged, knowing that while she still felt sick with shame over that night, she'd done all the grovelling she intended doing. 'I don't understand it myself so why would you? I was so upset about everything I got really pissed, and you know what I can be like when I drink too much. And then suddenly, Simon was there, being really sympathetic. Do you think I wasn't disgusted with myself the next day – that I haven't regretted it every minute of every day since?'

'You should have told me straight away.'

'I know, and I wanted to, but I knew what a big deal it was going to be for you. I was just trying to pick the right moment, and then Simon let it out and it was too late.'

'We're straying off the point.'

'I know you don't want to talk about it.'

'You're right, I don't. We've talked it to death. You knew how important fidelity was to me. It may seem old-fashioned–'

'Of course it doesn't. It's just as important to me. If you knew how bad I feel …'

For a long moment they stared at each other. Couldn't he *see* how much she meant it? How could he not when they knew each other so well?

'Oh, Kirsty.' Just for a second, she sensed indecision in him, a slight easing in his attitude, and she waited – hope springing pathetically to the surface. But then he shook his head and she knew the moment had passed.

It brought her back on track, saving her from embarrassing herself by dissolving into tears that would achieve nothing. She straightened up in her seat, remembering why she was here.

'Anyway, after I tackled Rob and Simon about the tenant yesterday, Robbie told me he'd go and visit Tim Burman himself and ask him about Dad's visit – see if he could throw any light on anything. But …'

She paused, even now finding it hard to believe what Robbie had done – and even harder telling someone about it. 'For some reason – when we got there – I saw him deliberately ring the wrong doorbell. He rang Susan Porter's, knowing she no longer lives there, and then came back to the car and told me there was no reply from Tim Burman's flat.'

Luke frowned. 'Why would he do that? Maybe he made a mistake. Did you ask him?'

'It was no mistake. They're both clearly marked on separate sides of the front door – and no, I didn't ask him because I didn't realise what he'd done until after he'd gone. But that's what's worrying me, Luke. I'm getting the feeling more and more that Robbie's somehow caught up in all this, and how can I go to the police if my own brother's involved?'

'That's some accusation, Kirsty.'

'I know it is. I'm also sure he'd never do anything to hurt anyone, but …' She took a breath. 'After he'd driven off, I rang Tim Burman's bell myself. Some really rough type answered who told me he knew who I was, and basically, he tried to scare me off. That's how it felt anyway. It was horrible.'

'Who was this guy? Do you want me to speak to him?'

'No. He's not the sort you'd take on lightly.'

'Kirsty, I don't like the sound of all this. What are you going to do?'

It was one of the things she'd always loved about him – that he might advise her, but he never tried to *tell* her what to do, like Robbie would have done.

'I don't know. You're a solicitor, that's why I needed to talk to you. I mean … how bad is all this stuff for Rob and Mum, if it did come out?'

Luke's eyes were serious. 'The wheeler-dealer stuff is one side of the coin, and if that came out there could be repercussions with the taxman and maybe even the Fraud Squad, depending on what's gone on, but … You don't need me to tell you that if Robbie's connected to that tenant's death or your father's in any way, then it's a totally different matter.'

'I can't believe he is. You know him, he does get hot under the collar sometimes and stomps around, but I can't see him standing around while people are getting killed. Especially not his own father.'

But he could be weak. That was surely why he'd never stood up to their father over all this stuff. And if there were others who had a hold over him – not such nice people…?'

'Then go to the police and tell them about the guy in the flat and the fact your father spoke to him.'

'But what if Rob's been drawn in inadvertently?'

'Only you can answer that, Kirsty. It depends on how important it is to you to find out the truth about what happened to your dad versus the possible implications for Rob and your mother if all the business stuff comes out.'

She almost groaned out loud. He was only putting into words what she already knew.

'You won't say anything to anyone? I need to think it through before I decide anything. I'm sorry to drag you into it, but …' She gave a little smile. 'Old habits die hard, I guess.'

He didn't return her smile. In fact, if anything, his manner became cooler. 'Yes they do – but sometimes it just needs to be done. I won't say anything, but for God's sake be careful and don't take any risks. A lot of this could be supposition, but if it isn't …'

She nodded. She didn't need him to tell her it could be dangerous.

She sighed. Was she any the wiser about what she was going to do?

Much as she wanted to find out the truth about what had happened to her father, she knew the last thing he'd want was for her to risk exposing her brother and mother – she could almost hear his voice telling her that now.

So there was her answer. Let it go.

And perhaps she would – but only at a price. And she'd be speaking to Robbie about that.

Feeling that at least she'd made some small headway, she turned her gaze back to Luke.

'Thanks for listening. I'm sorry to dump this on you.'

He shrugged. 'Just don't do anything rash – or at least let me know before you do it.'

'Okay, I will.'

She took a sip from her coffee, then said on a diffident note. 'How have things been with you?'

He nodded, accepting the change of subject. 'Good. They've made me an associate. I'm going to specialise in family law.'

'It's what you wanted.'

'Yes.'

He hesitated, his expression a giveaway, and she waited, suddenly guessing what was coming and not wanting to hear it.

'I should probably tell you that I'm bringing a friend to Rachael's wedding. Her name's Eleanor Rothby. She's one of the secretaries at the office and she had reasons why she didn't want to be at home that day. We're only friends – but I thought you should know.'

So much for Rachael's confident assertion that he hadn't met anyone.

'Oh, right. Cool. I'm glad you've moved on so quickly.'

'It's been nine months, Kirsty – and she is only a friend.'

'That's fine.' Her voice was flippant, as if she didn't mind at all. 'Really. Thanks for telling me.'

'What about you? Anyone in your life?'

'No.'

She looked at her watch. She'd been going to tell him about the latest development about her mother and Rob and Daniel Curtis, but didn't have the heart for it now. Scraping back her chair, she rose from the table. 'I won't hold you up any longer. Thanks for coming. It's been helpful running things past you.'

'Remember what I said about being careful?'

'I will. See you at the wedding, then.'

And with a careless little wave she walked away from him, hoping he hadn't picked up on her utter sense of desolation.

CHAPTER TWENTY-FOUR

Harry looked at the empty plates on the table and made to jump up and help Claire clear them away, but before he could move, Claire's mother's arm stayed him.

'No, no love. You did your bit before we all arrived. You stay put and leave this to us. We'll be back in a minute with the coffee.'

She had the same blue eyes as Claire, and the same no-nonsense air about her that made him decide not to argue with her. But apart from the eyes, physically there was little similarity. Her hair was blonde instead of chestnut, her face rounder, and she was a couple of inches shorter than her daughter.

No sooner were the words out of her mouth than it seemed a whole army of people swept into action as Claire's two sisters-in-law also jumped up and started to clear the plates and glasses, amongst much laughter and chatter.

A small tug on his sleeve had him looking down at six-year-old Ben, who was staring up at him in awe.

'Have you got a gun in your pocket?'

Harry smiled. 'Not today.'

'Where's your uniform?'

'I don't wear one. I'm not that sort of policeman.'

'Why not?'

'Because I'm a detective and detectives don't wear uniforms.'

'I want to be a 'tective' when I grow up. I'm very good at 'membering' things. Aren't I, Daddy?'

Claire's oldest brother, Mike, ruffled his son's hair. 'You certainly are, sport. He knows the names of twenty-one different dinosaurs,' he added, not without some pride.

By the time Ben had finished rattling off all twenty-one names, Claire's mother, Helen, had returned to say that coffee was being taken through to the lounge.

'So where are your parents, Harry?' Helen asked. 'Are they local?'

'No. They've lived abroad for most of my life and they're currently living near Cairo. My father's an archaeologist.'

'What an interesting life, though I'm not sure I'd like to be living in Cairo at the moment. Did you travel much with them when you were younger?'

'Not really. I went to boarding school over here and lived with my grandparents in the holidays – although of course, I did visit Mum and Dad in some of the countries they were in.'

'Ah, right.'

Simple enough words, but he had the feeling that Helen was more astute than most and would pick up on the sense of disorientation that had brought to his life. He'd never given it much thought, finding it easier to park the issues he suspected could be lurking beneath the surface of his conscious mind. But seeing the easy camaraderie between Claire and her family, the way they chatted about mutual acquaintances and shared memories … For the first time it brought it home to him how devoid his life had been of people who mattered.

Apart from his grandparents, there'd not really been anyone.

He'd got friends of course. And they were good mates – most of them from his university days, a couple through his work. His old school friends he rarely saw, as they were dotted around the country and always had been, though they tried to meet up a couple of times a year. His job had seen to it, of course, that he didn't always make those reunions.

Claire, it seemed on the other hand, had a million friends going right back to her cradle. He liked the idea of that – envied the sense of roots it seemed to have given her.

'So how long have you and Claire been seeing each other?' Mike asked, topping up his coffee. Of her two brothers, he was the most like Claire – and her father – with the same brown hair. Her other brother, Tom, was blond like Helen.

Claire flicked a mischievous glance at Harry before moving her eyes back to her brother and answering for him. 'We're not dating, Mike. We're just mates. I roped Harry into giving me a hand for when you lot arrived in exchange for a decent meal.'

'And delicious it was, too,' Harry said. 'You can rope me in anytime.'

'Of course it was,' Helen said with a wink. 'She was taught by the best.'

Everyone laughed, including Claire, who shook her head. 'I'm not going to deny that, Mama. You are, without doubt, the best.'

An hour later, after they'd gone, Harry helped Claire clear away the final bits and pieces.

'You don't have to,' she protested. 'You've done more than your fair share today.'

'I'm happy to. I've enjoyed it. Your family are great. Your dad's very quiet, though, isn't he?'

'Yeah. Years of being shouted down by the rest of us, I think.' She looked at him ruefully. 'It wasn't too much for you? We can be a bit overwhelming at times when we're en masse, and while I'm used to it and enjoy it, I know others aren't always of the same mind.'

He wondered if there was more to that statement than met the eye. A previous partner perhaps, who'd found it an issue?

'I won't lie and say I didn't feel a bit overwhelmed when they all arrived together like that, but they were all so easy, I think anyone would be hard pushed not to like them.'

She smiled. 'Thanks. I don't know what I'd do without them, but my previous partner found it a bit of a struggle. It's why we finished.'

'Ah, I wondered.'

She shrugged. 'It wasn't just them. He didn't like most of my friends either, and towards the end, it became a game he played. Leaving it to the last minute before telling me he wasn't coming when we went out – or making it difficult fitting in with arrangements. He had two brothers himself but they weren't close, and, even though I tried to initiate stuff, he wasn't interested. It was never going to work.'

She put some boiling water into the teapot and poured out two cups of tea.

'When did it finish?'

'Six months ago.' She shrugged. 'It's life, isn't it? Come on. Let's take this through – you'll need to make a move soon: your grandmother will be wondering where you are. How was she this morning?'

Harry followed her through to the lounge and sat down opposite her. 'Not brilliant. She seems quite a lot weaker – though she insisted I come here for lunch. She's still bedridden. It's difficult knowing what I can do to make things more comfortable for her.'

'I don't think there's much you can do, except be there for her.' She hesitated. 'You realise … it may not be long now?'

He nodded. 'The doctor told us when she came off the

meds that things would speed up if she stopped them. But what can I do? It's what she wants.'

He thought about the other thing she wanted and immediately felt the full weight of burden on his shoulders again. It would be such a relief to share it with someone, but it wasn't exactly the sort of thing you could casually drop into conversation.

'What?' Claire said, seeing his expression.

Harry shook his head. 'Nothing.'

'I can see there is something, but if you don't want to talk about it, that's fine.'

'It's not that. Well, I suppose it is really. It's … sensitive.'

Their eyes held for a long moment and something in her patient expression gave him courage to plough on.

'Has she ever … discussed with you what she wants, when the time comes?'

'The euthanasia, you mean?'

It sounded shocking hearing it put in such blunt terms. But he felt relief at having it out in the open.

'Yes. I'll admit I can't handle it when she starts on about it. It's why I didn't want to move in with her.'

Claire hesitated. 'I deal with quite a few people in your gran's situation, Harry. There are more people than you realise wanting to end things themselves in the peace of their own homes, with their loved ones around them. I've tried to tell Jean that all that is possible without going to the lengths she wants to go to. The chances are you can keep her at home with palliative care and she'll slip away peacefully.'

'I know – but that's not what happened with my grandfather. And unfortunately that's what she remembers. It was a farce the way they dealt with him, and it wasn't pleasant. She's …' He broke off, remembering her words, that it was only him she was telling how scared she was of dying like that.

'I don't want her to have to go through that,' he finished lamely.

'Then when the time comes, we'll do our best to see she doesn't,' Claire said. 'I don't want to interfere – she's your grandmother and I'm only the carer – but I'm very fond of Jean and if I can help in any way?'

'Thanks, but she's not your responsibility and I shouldn't be putting this on you – shouldn't even be discussing it with you.'

'Whatever you say to me is in confidence. I mean that.' She smiled. 'And don't worry … We'll get her through this. And we'll do it right.'

Harry finished the dregs in his cup and stood up to go, thinking how quickly she seemed to have become a part of their lives. 'You're a godsend, you know that?'

She flashed him that mischievous smile as she, too, rose from her chair. 'I think that's the good meal talking.'

'What made you do this sort of work anyway?'

Claire shrugged. 'I like helping people, and older people in particular. I used to work for the local council, but the lack of continuity and organisation was so frustrating I decided I'd rather do my own thing privately. Then I saw Guiding Hands were starting up and looking for care workers, and thought I'd give them a try. It's working out well: they make a real effort to match carers to patients and do their best to give us 'regulars' whom we can form decent relationships with. One day I'd like to form my own company and really tailor my services to people's needs – but I've got a bit more learning to do yet.' She laughed self-consciously. 'We'll see if that one ever happens.'

Harry smiled at her as they moved into the hall. 'I get the impression you're very determined. If you want it to happen, it will.'

At the door, he turned to say goodbye. She was standing close, the top of her head just about level with his nose. It made it such a small move to tilt her chin with his finger so he could lower his lips to hers in a thank-you gesture. But the bolt of excitement that shot through him at the contact was spectacular. He found his other hand coming up so he could cup both her cheeks in his palms, his mouth deepening that kiss as he felt her own surprising response.

When finally they pulled apart, he gave her a lopsided smile and cleared his throat. 'Well, thanks for the lunch. I'll, uh, see you later, then, at Gran's?'

She smiled back. 'Yeah, okay. And thanks for all your help. Don't know how I'd have managed without you.'

He knew it was a load of bollocks, but he still found himself feeling pleased as Punch as he walked off down the path.

CHAPTER TWENTY-FIVE

Monday morning Kirsty parked her car and crossed the road to the office, feeling that every meeting with her brother these days seemed destined to be fraught with tension. She'd done a lot of thinking over the weekend after her talk with Luke, and whilst she'd decided she wasn't going to do anything that might cause problems for her mother and brother, she still wanted to know why Robbie wasn't being straight with her.

'How are you?' she asked ten minutes later, as they sat sipping coffee in his office.

He shrugged.

'I tried to call you Friday night after your row with Mum – and Saturday. Lizzie said you didn't come home.'

'I wasn't in the mood for company. I stayed over at the flat.'

He didn't meet her eyes.

'That's a bit hard on Liz, isn't it?'

'I didn't want another family domestic.'

'Rob ... Lizzie deserves better than that.'

'He was sitting there, Kirsty ... in Dad's chair ... as if he belonged there. I just saw red. I wanted to smash every single thing in that room.'

'I can imagine – I felt the same. But Mum's known him for years. You can't ban her from seeing him.'

'I know I can't. I just don't get how she can't see how that would upset us when we know the history. And you didn't overhear what I did.'

'What do you mean?'

I heard him telling her that Dad hadn't always appreciated her, that he'd taken her for granted sometimes.'

'Bloody hell. What did she say to that?'

'That she knew that. But that it was what long-term partners tended to do.'

'Well, that's true enough, isn't it?'

'I guess so. It just made me angry. She should have been more loyal to Dad.'

'She probably would have been if it was someone who didn't know them so well. She was really upset about your row, Rob–'

'Alright. I'll go round at some point. But when I've cooled down. Otherwise I'll just say the wrong thing and we'll be off again – and I've got enough on my own plate at the moment.'

She stared at him helplessly, wanting to ask him *What?* What was on his plate that was making him so difficult these days? But she knew her brother well enough to know there was no point pushing him when he was in this sort of mood. Shelving the problem of their mother, she tackled him about the other thing that had been bothering her.

'I've got something to ask you about Friday night – when we went to Paul Copeland's flat. Why did you ring the wrong doorbell?'

He blinked.

'What? What are you talking about?'

'You rang Paul Copeland's bell instead of Tim Burman's – and then you came back to the car and lied to me.'

She felt remarkably calm now it was out in the open. She saw the shock on his face – the embarrassment at being caught out – but he rallied quickly, his expression becoming defensive. 'Well, if you knew that, why didn't you say something at the time?'

'Because I didn't know what to think! My own brother deceiving me.'

'That's not how it was.'

'Then how was it? Because that's how it felt.'

He glared at her in frustration. 'I was trying to protect you. I know you're upset about Dad, but you're like a loose cannon at the moment. We can't just go stumbling into someone's flat accusing them of murder. I'm not a bloody policeman. What was I going to say after establishing the fact that Dad had been there? Ask him if he'd then followed Dad and run him over? We have no idea what we're dealing with. It could be something or nothing. But if there's any chance at all that it's *something*, we need to remember that these people may have killed once and might well do so again. Now Dad's gone it's my duty to look out for you.'

'And if he was involved in Dad's death?'

Robbie's look was stubborn. 'Then let the police handle it. Dad wouldn't want us to do anything that might affect Mum in any way. You know that, and I've already told you how things stand – we don't want the police poking around unless it becomes absolutely necessary.'

'So you're prepared to brush aside the fact that he might have murdered our father?'

'For God's sake, Kirsty, you haven't got a scrap of evidence that the man had anything to do with Dad's death. Just let it go. Leave it to the people who know what they're doing. We've got a business that needs sorting out–'

'Well, that's something else I want to talk to you about because, judging by what you've told me so far, I'm not happy with the way this business is run.'

'I think I've got that message.'

'Well, I'd like to take a look at the accounts to see exactly what's been going on. And I want to start with the sale of Grandma's land.'

'Why?'

'Because that's where it all began for me.' She lowered her voice so that Sharon couldn't hear. 'I can't work like this, Robbie – worrying about the taxman knocking on the door the whole time. I don't know how you can live like that.'

He shrugged. 'We know what we're doing, Kirsty – it's no big deal.'

'What *planet* are you living on? You can't get away with that sort of stuff these days. How would you feel having to explain yourself to Lizzie and the kids if you got banged up for fraud or tax evasion?'

'That's not going to happen unless *you* drop us in it. You don't get it, do you? We've got used to a certain standard of living. If we didn't do the occasional cash deal or turn the odd property when we got the chance, we wouldn't be able to maintain the lifestyle we've got.'

'Well, tough shit. There's such a thing as living within your means.'

She calmed her voice with an effort. 'Look, I don't want to cause trouble and this isn't how I pictured us being in the family business together. But don't you see, it's a chance to start over – in a business we can be proud of, rather than having to look over our shoulders the whole time. Would that really be such a bad thing?'

Rob glanced at his watch. 'I've got to go. I've got a viewing. We'll talk about this another time.'

'Okay. But just so you know ... I'm going to have a word

with that policeman that came to the funeral. Just to see if they've spoken to this Tim Burman, and if so, what he said. I'll be discreet, I promise.'

Rob's eyes were stony. 'I'd much rather you didn't, Kirsty, but when did anything I say ever stop you? Do what you want.'

After he'd gone, Kirsty forced their disagreement to the back of her mind and got on with checking appointments and tackling the post. She'd just taken a new valuation request and was hanging up the phone, when the outer office door opened and D.S. Briscombe walked in.

She had to smile when Sharon, never the most proactive of secretaries but always appreciative of a 'fit' bloke, leapt up from her desk with a beaming smile on her face and offered assistance.

Harry's eyes met Kirsty's through the glass pane as she heard him say, 'I was up at Paul Copeland's flat on Friday and saw there was quite a bit of post. I meant to bring it down to you then, but I'm afraid my day rather ran away with me. I thought you might want to forward it on to his girlfriend if you've got her address?'

Kirsty rose from her desk. 'Do you want to come through?' she called.

'Tea or coffee?' Sharon asked brightly.

'Neither, thanks, I've just had one.' Harry gave her the benefit of his best smile as he walked into Kirsty's office.

He sat down in the chair Kirsty indicated and handed Paul Copeland's post over to her. 'I called at the flat hoping to speak to Susan Porter, but according to the chap upstairs, she's moved out. Do you have a forwarding address?'

'We've probably got it on file. I think she's staying with her brother. I've got her mobile number, though, so I can give her a call and let her know her post is here.'

She said the words without thinking and Harry was quick to pick up on them.

'I didn't realise you knew each other?'

'Uh, we don't. Not really. I bumped into her the other night and we got talking. We ended up swapping numbers.'

'Ah, right … Would you mind giving it to me? I could do with asking her a few more questions about her boyfriend's death.'

'I'm not sure I feel comfortable handing over her number without her permission–'

'Don't worry. She doesn't need to know it was you. I can easily track her number down, you know – it's just quicker this way.'

Kirsty hesitated, but she could hardly refuse. She picked up her mobile from the desk, looked up the number and handed him the phone.

'How's the investigation coming on?' she asked, watching as he wrote it down.

'Slowly. We've got a couple of leads but nothing concrete yet.'

'Have you spoken to the guy in the upstairs flat, by any chance? Tim Burman?'

'No … but I'm on my way to interview him now, as it happens. Why do you ask?'

Kirsty shrugged. She had to be careful. She didn't want to betray Susan's confidence.

'I'm just interested. Susan mentioned that Dad visited him the day he was killed and I wondered–'

She broke off. It was beginning to sound ludicrous even to her.

'If there might be some connection?'

She nodded. 'Robbie says I'm being ridiculous and he's probably right, but the whole thing just feels so wrong. So unlikely that Dad should die like that.'

'It happens, you know. I'm afraid I see it all the time.'

There was genuine sympathy in Harry's voice, and to her horror Kirsty could feel her eyes welling up. 'I know.'

'I don't remember seeing anything in his statement about seeing your father, but I'll ask him and if there's anything relevant, I'll let you know.'

'Thanks.' Kirsty smiled. 'I know I've probably just got to let it go and accept that it was an accident, but it's hard to do that when you haven't got the facts.'

'We're doing our best to track the driver down. We've interviewed everyone in the road now, and put a sign up near where it joins the main road. We've had a couple of passers-by come forward, but all we've discovered so far is that it was a dark-coloured saloon car being driven by a dark-haired man. Not much to go on. We're also checking local garages for bodywork repairs, but in the absence of eyewitnesses, it's very difficult.'

He stood up to take his leave. 'Thanks for your time, Miss Cartwright.'

'Call me Kirsty, please.' She, too, rose. 'You will keep us posted?'

'Of course – and if anything should come to your attention?'

'I'll let you know.'

After he'd gone she deliberated over whether she should phone Susan Porter about the post and warn her that Sgt. Briscombe was likely to call. Deciding that could be awkward, she took the coward's way out by simply texting that the post was at the office if she wanted to pick it up – not for the first time grateful for the wonders of modern technology.

'Thanks for seeing me, Mr Burman.'

Harry smiled at the other man as he took the seat he was offered and pulled out his notebook. His quick glance took in the careless disorder of the flat, confirming evidence of someone who'd recently been away – passport and euros tipped out onto the coffee table, a discarded ferry crossing booking.

'I'm only sorry I wasn't around last week when you were trying to get hold of me.'

'You were away in France, I believe?'

'Yup, I'm an antiques dealer. Most of my stuff comes from France, or sometimes Italy.'

The man was fairish-haired, well spoken and mid-thirties. He looked towards a communicating door as it opened and a very attractive, dark-haired young woman walked in. She halted abruptly at the sight of Harry sitting in his chair.

'Ah, Tanya,' Tim Burman said. 'Just in time to make this gentleman and myself a cup of coffee. You don't mind, darling, do you?'

'Of course. How you like?' Her voice was low and heavily accented as she addressed Harry.

'White, no sugar, thanks.'

She nodded, returning Harry's look with a timid one of her own before turning round and heading back out of the room again.

'My girlfriend,' Tim said easily.

'Where's the accent from?'

'Turkey. She's studying English over here. We bumped into each other, literally, in Waitrose and that was it. Funny old thing, love.'

He looked a bit embarrassed and shrugged. 'Now, what can I do for you?'

'We're investigating Paul Copeland's murder, as you know. Obviously we've got the written statement you gave to my colleague, but I wondered if you'd mind answering a few more questions?'

'Sure. Fire away, though as I already said to the other guy, I don't think there's much I can say that will be of use to you.'

232

'Well, you've already answered some of what I was going to ask. You're an antiques dealer, you say? Do you have an office address I could make a note of?'

'No. I work from here. Sell most of my stuff through eBay. It's so simple these days. No need to pay out for an office.'

'What sort of car do you own?'

'A silver Mercedes-Benz 190 Coupé. And a van and larger truck for my imports.'

'And where do you keep those?'

'In a storage facility in Hatfield.'

'Did you know the tenant downstairs, Paul Copeland?'

'Only to say hello to.'

'And you didn't see him on the day he was murdered?'

'No. I said that in my statement. Shocking business.'

'We're trying to get a picture of where he went that day. You can't help us with that at all? You didn't see, or maybe hear, him leave the building that morning?'

The man shook his head. 'I'm sorry. Not much help, I know, but to be honest, we had very little to do with each other.'

'Any strange happenings that ever caught your attention?'

Tim Burman looked at him curiously. 'What sort of strange happenings?'

'I don't know. People hanging around outside? Stuff like that?' He was thinking of Ken Lazard, but again Burman shook his head.

'Not that I noticed. And I'm here at the flat a fair amount of the time, when I'm not abroad.'

'I believe you had a visit from Dominic Cartwright, the managing agent for this flat, a couple of days after Paul died?'

Tim looked surprised at the change of tack. 'Well, yes – apparently so, but I was out at the time. Personally, I'd have made him book an appointment to come back – he's meant to give us notice of anything like that, but …' He shrugged.

'Tanya wasn't to know that, of course, and her English isn't very good, so she let him in. A couple of my mates were here at the time. They said Cartwright carried out a quick check of the flat and then he left.'

'Were you aware that he's also dead now?'

'*No*. Christ, what happened?'

'Hit-and-run. We're trying to see if there could be any connection between the two deaths and obviously the family are keen to get some answers.'

'God, I'm sorry about that. It's surreal. I mean … I know it's stuff you probably deal with all the time, but …'

He shook his head, and Harry closed his notebook, standing up to take his leave. 'Could I have a quick word with your girlfriend about Mr Cartwright's visit?'

'Sure. Though as I said, her English isn't up to much yet. Sorry about the coffee … Don't know what's happened to that.'

Harry smiled. 'No worries.'

'*Tanya?*'

There was a small delay before the door opened again and the girl walked in, but five minutes later Harry was taking his leave, none the wiser. Her English had been appalling and most of her responses limited to a helpless look in Tim's direction, with nothing new to add at all. It was clear he was going to get little from that quarter.

'Well, if anything should come to mind,' Harry said, offering Tim Burman his card, 'just give me a call on one of these numbers and I'll get back to you.'

'Sure thing,' Tim said. 'Sorry I couldn't be more help. I hope you find whoever did it. It's all rather put the wind up Tanya and it would be good to be able to reassure her.'

'We'll do our best,' Harry said. 'And thanks for your time.'

CHAPTER TWENTY-SIX

Beth could hardly wait for Harry to come in. Her delving around that morning had borne results and she was eager to share them. She read the report on her desk again just to make sure she'd got all the relevant details firmly in her head, and checked her own notes. She was well aware it could all be coincidence and might not change anything, but it seemed to throw the door wide open again as far as suspects for Paul Copeland's murder were concerned and she couldn't help feeling chuffed that she was the one who'd spotted it.

'Morning, Beth, good weekend?' Harry's voice was casual and upbeat as he passed her desk and headed for his own. She wondered if he'd had a date yesterday to put that smile on his face and spring in his step.

'Fine, thanks.'

She made two coffees, giving him time to settle himself in, then took them over to him.

'Hey ... where's mine?' Geoff Peterson called out as she walked past his desk.

She grinned at him. She quite liked the dark-haired, lanky, bespectacled Geoff, even if he was a bit of a quiet one. He'd asked her out for a drink one night – just as friends, he'd quickly assured her – which she was still thinking about.

'Sorry – only got one pair of hands. Anyway, isn't it your turn to make me one?'

'I was definitely born in the wrong generation,' he said, shaking his head ruefully.

'Whereas I was definitely born in the right one.'

She moved on. 'Oh, thanks,' Harry said with an appreciative smile, taking the cup from her. 'You didn't need to do that.'

'No problem, I was making one anyway. Got a minute?'

'Sure. How are you getting on trawling through everything? Anything new?'

'I think I have, as it happens. An interesting coincidence, if nothing else.'

'What's that?'

She could see she had his full attention as he waited for her response.

'Well, everything was just coming up blank, so in the absence of anything else to look at, I took a quick look at Mrs Wilkins' background – Ken Lazard's bit on the side,' she added, seeing his blank look.

'Oh, right.'

'And guess what?'

'What?'

'You remember how her husband is also in a wheelchair and attends the day care centre? That happened because he was attacked by some drunken yob at a party, who pushed him off a first-floor balcony. The poor guy broke his back.'

'Jeez.'

'Yeah, but what was worse was that the guy got off with community service because he claimed Phil Wilkins attacked him first and it was self-defence – even though Phil had a slashed cheek where the other guy had gone for him with a

236

broken bottle. Kathy was the only witness and obviously was never going to be unbiased, and in the absence of any specific proof, he got off. Apparently he two fingered Kathy and her husband as he walked free from the court. She also claimed afterwards that he was harassing them – hanging around the house and jeering at the fact her husband was now in a wheelchair.'

'Charming.'

'I know. Anyway, that guy, Gary Lytton, is now dead. Fell under a tube at Covent Garden last year.'

'No kidding?'

'Yup. I've got the file here.'

She handed him a blue folder. 'It was an open verdict because no one saw exactly what happened – it was pre-Christmas with masses of people on the platform. They don't know if he fell, committed suicide – or was pushed. Either way, he ended up very dead, and by the time our lot arrived there weren't many witnesses still around. Odd, though, isn't it, that now the guy who put Maggie Lazard in a chair should also be dead?'

Harry took the file from her and, for only the second time since this investigation had started, experienced the surge in adrenalin that came from discovering a possible breakthrough.

'Quite a coincidence. Well done. Even if it comes to nothing that's a good piece of detective work – which definitely needs following up.'

She looked embarrassed, and said gruffly to cover it up, 'How did you get on with Burman?'

Harry shrugged. 'Didn't learn much. He didn't see or hear anything – confirmed what Paul Copeland's girlfriend said – that they hardly knew each other.'

'What was he like?'

'Pleasant enough. Antiques dealer. Well dressed and educated, drives a Merc.'

'Ah, a smoothie – I'm getting the picture.'

Harry laughed. He looked at her closely, suddenly remembering.

'How did your visit to the grandparents go over the weekend?'

'Alright,' she said carelessly. 'We got on okay and they seemed pleased to see me. I was right about the reasons they fell out. My grandparents don't live in a posh area, but you can see as soon as you walk into their house what sort of people they are. Everything neat and tidy, in its place, photos of their son and grandchildren dotted around. But none of me or my family – they've cut themselves off completely from my mum, and I can't say I blame them.'

'Maybe you'll be the catalyst that reunites them all?'

She shook her head vehemently. 'No chance. My family haven't spoken to me in four years, since I joined the police. They see me as a traitor. Both my brothers have been in trouble, and my father's been a chancer all his life.'

Harry was careful not to show his surprise. 'That's tough for you.'

She shrugged. 'I wasn't much better myself when I was younger, but fortunately I turned things around, with a lot of help from Andy – my boyfriend,' she clarified. She gave a thin smile. 'He made me realise I had to get out before it rubbed off on me, too. I decided maybe I could do more good being on the other side of the fence – working from the inside out, if you know what I mean? I know it makes me sound a bit of a do-gooder – but it's why I joined the force.'

'It's why most of us are here, isn't it? To try and make a difference.'

Her eyes sparkled their response. 'It doesn't sound so stupid coming from you. It was hard going against family pressure, though, and it can be pretty lonely at times. Not that my family ever did much for me – but they were all I had.'

Harry found himself thinking of his grandmother – how she was pressuring him to do something that would undermine the very foundations of the career he'd chosen. Beth was right, it *was* hard going against family pressure.

'Except that now you've discovered your grandparents,' he said.

She nodded and smiled. 'Yeah. They're going to arrange for me to meet my uncle and cousins next. It'll be weird but I'm sort of looking forward to it. Don't know what they'll make of me, though.'

'They'll see what I see – a committed young woman doing well for herself.'

Her lips twisted wryly. 'Thanks, Harry – nice to know someone's got confidence in me.'

'I'm not bullshitting you. I'm not the only one who recognises your qualities. You should have more confidence in yourself.'

'And here endeth the lesson for today?' she quipped.

'No – here *starteth* the lesson for today,' he grinned. 'Plenty more where that came from.'

She laughed. 'Don't think I can take it. By the way, I forgot to tell you, there was a call from someone called Claire. She said she was round at your gran's and asked if you could call her when you got in. Sorry, I should probably have told you that straight away.'

'No worries. I'll call her now.'

Harry picked up his phone. 'I'll hang onto this file and have a read. Then maybe we'll pay Mrs Wilkins a visit.'

He waited until Beth had moved away before dialling Claire's number. He wondered if she'd given as much thought to where they might be going after that kiss as he had. It had been awkward when she'd come round later last night to help his grandmother. Neither of them had referred to what had happened between them, and there'd certainly been no repetition of it. Maybe she felt the same as he did … that she needed a bit of time to assimilate things.

'Claire?'

'Oh, Harry, hi. Sorry to call you at work but … your gran called me about an hour ago and said she wasn't feeling too good, could I go round? I nipped over between calls and I'm sorry, but I've a feeling she's going downhill – and quite rapidly. She was adamant she didn't want me calling the doctor, though. I thought you should know.'

'Hell. Thanks. Are you there now?'

'No, I had another call to make and I'm in Whetstone at the moment. I could go back if you want but … there's an added complication.' He sensed her choosing her words with care. 'Your parents arrived just as I was leaving. Your mum seemed quite agitated at seeing your gran like that. She was talking about calling the doctor and maybe transferring her to the hospital.'

'*No.*'

Harry jumped up from his chair. 'I promised Gran I wouldn't let that happen. I need to get over there. Any chance you can meet me? It might carry more weight if there are two of us.'

'Sure. I'm just finishing up here and then it's my lunch hour. I can be there in about twenty minutes. I'll see you then.'

Harry strode over to Beth's desk. 'Something's come up with my grandmother,' he said. 'I need to get over there. Do you reckon you can handle the interview with Mrs Wilkins on your own?'

'I think so.'

'Don't be too nice. If she has got anything to hide we want to rattle her – let her know we're on her case. Where was Ken Lazard when this chap fell in front of the train? Do we know? Was he interviewed?'

'Yes, because the Wilkins were apparently at the Lazards'

house for lunch when it happened. Their alibis seemed to stack up at the time.'

'Well, press her on it. Check who else gave evidence that they were there. I'll call you when I've finished with my gran – see where you're at.'

As Harry opened the front door to his grandmother's house he heard heated voices coming from the sitting room. He listened as his father said.

'I just think maybe we should respect her wishes.'

'But look how ill she is. She should be in hospital. I don't know what Harry's been doing. He should have called us – told us how bad she was.'

'Maybe she didn't want him to. You know what she's like. And you know what she said about going into hospital.'

'Yes, I do know. But it has to be the best place for her. They can make her more comfortable there – make sure she gets the treatment she needs.'

Harry felt his heart sink. This wasn't going to be easy.

He made a point of closing the front door so they could hear it – grabbed himself some time as he hung his jacket over the banister – then braced himself to walk into the sitting room.

'Mum, Dad – great to see you! But why didn't you ring to say you were coming?'

His mother looked at him reproachfully. 'We thought we'd surprise you. But why didn't you call us? Mum's in a terrible state and if Dad hadn't had to come back for a seminar, we wouldn't know anything about it.'

'I'm sorry, it's only been the last couple of days that she's deteriorated so much. I was hoping it was a temporary setback.'

'She should be in hospital, Harry.'

'She doesn't want that.'

'Well, what she wants and what she needs aren't necessarily the same thing. They can look after her properly there.'

'We're looking after her properly here. We've put in a request to the hospice care people to come and assess her for home care.'

He could see how distressed his mother was and he softened his voice. 'Look, I know it's hard for you coming in and seeing her like this, but it has only been the last couple of days, really – and I was going to call you.' He hesitated. 'She's not going to get better, Mum. The doctors have told us that. So sending her off to hospital isn't going to change the outcome. She stopped the cancer medication at the beginning of the year because it was making her feel so ill, and she's been feeling so much better these last few months. But now ...'

'You should have called me.'

'She was adamant she didn't want everyone racing back making a fuss.'

'She didn't want me here, you mean.'

'No, that's not what I'm saying.'

'She's never approved of the fact that I followed your father around the world instead of staying here with you and her.'

'Mum, let's not go into all that. You're here now and I'm sure she'll be glad of that – and so am I. We need to make sure her last days are the best we can make them for her.'

'Which is why she should be in hospital. They can give her all the care she needs there.'

'I promised her I wouldn't let that happen unless it was absolutely necessary.'

'We can't look after a dying woman here.'

'Yes we can. People do it all the time. The hospice will support us.'

'No.' He could see the fear underlying the determination in his mother's eyes. 'I think we should call an ambulance now. We're not doctors. I wouldn't have a clue how to look after her.'

'You won't have to do a lot. We already have Claire who comes in twice a day – you met her earlier – and the district nurse is visiting tomorrow to assess Gran's needs and see what extra help they can put in place for her.'

As if on cue the doorbell rang and Harry heaved a quiet sigh of relief as he quickly turned to exit the room. 'That's probably Claire now. I asked her to pop over. I'll let her in.'

'Everything okay?' Claire's eyes were sharp as they took in Harry's expression. He shook his head. 'My mother wants to call an ambulance.'

'Oh no.'

'I'm doing my best to talk her out of it.'

'Let me just check on Jean quickly, then I'll come down.'

'I'll come with you. I haven't seen her myself yet.'

Even he was shocked at the deterioration in his grandmother over the day. The swelling in her body had become quite grotesque, and he found himself diverting his eyes from it as he fixed his gaze on her face, searching blue eyes that were no longer clear and bright but cloudy and unfocused. He sat down on the edge of the bed and took her hand in his.

'Hi, Gran. It's Harry.'

'Harry.' The clasp of the frail hand in his was surprisingly strong as she gripped him desperately. 'They're here,' she said weakly, through parched lips. 'And they'll send me to hospital. I know they will. I don't want to go.'

Her voice was no more than a thin whisper, forced out between rasping breaths, and Harry felt his throat tighten. She sounded so vulnerable and looked as if she was on the verge of tears – something he'd never witnessed in all his years of living with her.

'I won't let that happen. Try not to worry.'

'You know what I want…'

'Gran–'

'Please… Soon I won't be fit enough to even swallow them.'

Harry turned his gaze helplessly onto Claire. Despite the number of impossible situations he'd found himself in over his career, he'd never felt so out of his depth, or so lost and inadequate as he did now. But worse than that, was that for the first time ever, he found himself considering doing what she asked, and to hell with the consequences.

Recognising his distress, Claire shook her head at him imperceptibly, and stepped in. 'Jean, there'll be no need for that. We'll make sure we look after you properly. And as it happens, I'm on leave for the next couple of weeks and not doing much. I'm sure Harry and I can come to some sort of arrangement where I can come in a bit more often if you need me.'

Harry looked at her in surprise, feeling an immediate easing of his load.

'Is that true? That would be amazing.'

She shrugged. 'I spoke to my work today and told them a close relative was ill and I might need to take some time off. I haven't taken any holiday this year so there wasn't much they could say really. They were fine about it.'

'That's really kind of you, Claire. I can't thank you enough.'

'You don't need to Harry. I'm doing this for Jean. We've become close over the last few months I've been visiting. There are only a couple of my clients I can say that about. Now, Jean – is there anything I can get you or do for you before I head back downstairs to chat with your daughter?'

'Pills …' she croaked. 'Just give me the pills in my cupboard.'

'Jean, darling, you know we can't do that. It would be the end of both our careers – we could even go to prison. You wouldn't want that, would you?'

They both stared in horror as tears welled in the old lady's eyes. 'I just want to die,' she whimpered. 'Please help me to die.'

It took Harry a few moments to compose himself before he walked back into the lounge where his parents were still seated, but by the time he left, half an hour later, they'd reached a compromise of sorts.

'Okay,' his mother had capitulated finally. 'I'll wait and see what the doctor says. I've already phoned her surgery and asked for a visit later today. I'll want to know exactly what's going on and what we can expect to happen over the next couple of weeks. Dad and I were only meant to be back for two days, but it's clear we need to stay on now.'

'What time's Dr Roe coming?'

'About six o'clock, but they couldn't guarantee it would be him.'

'I hope it is because he knows her case. I'll try and get back.'

'You don't need to, Harry. I'm her daughter and I'm perfectly capable of speaking to him on my own.'

'Well, just promise me you won't let them pack her off to hospital. Call me if there's any talk of that.'

'Harry, love. I know you love your gran, but the professionals know best in these circumstances. We need to be guided by them.'

Panic gripped Harry's heart and his voice was unusually fierce as he faced his mother out. 'No they don't, Mum, not always. *Promise* me she'll still be here when I get back. You can't come marching in and take over after six months of not seeing her, or knowing what's been going on. I promised Gran I'd do my damnedest to keep her out of hospital and if you make me break that promise, I'll never forgive you. I mean that.'

His mother looked at him in shock, and for a moment it was a stand-off as they stood in the middle of the room glaring at each other. It was left to Harry's father to step in and say, 'Why don't we wait and see what the doctor says, before we come to any decisions, eh? We won't do anything hasty, Harry. We'll call you if there's anything we feel you'd want to know.

We can talk about it later tonight at supper. What time do you get back?'

Harry ran his hand through his hair. 'I don't know. It depends what's going on. I'll try to be back by six-thirty, but I'm in the middle of a murder investigation at the moment. I'll call you if it's going to be later than that.'

'Fine.' His mother's tone was clipped.

She turned to Claire. 'Thanks for stepping in and offering to come in more often: we appreciate it very much. Obviously we'll need to discuss terms if you're going to do extra hours.'

'I can do that,' Harry said. 'I've got power of attorney as you know for Gran's stuff. Claire and I can work it out.'

'Very well,' his mother said stiffly. 'It's obvious I'm not needed here. I'll go and see if *my mother* wants anything.'

Harry watched helplessly as she stalked out of the room, then looked at his father, who shrugged. 'Give her time. She was shocked at the change in Jean and I know she's been feeling guilty about not being here.'

But not guilty enough to do anything about it the last six months, Harry couldn't stop himself from thinking. God forbid she should come over on her own to see how things were. What was it about his mother that she didn't seem capable of doing anything without his father? It had been like that for as long as he could remember, and it amazed him that his father never had anything to say about it. She went everywhere with him and he knew it hadn't been the easiest of relationships with them living in each other's pockets like that. In his youth he'd consoled himself with the thought that it was because they were so in love they couldn't bear to be separated, but as he'd matured, that rather cosy image hadn't sat quite right somehow.

Harry sighed. 'Okay, we're all stressed, I know. I'll call you when I'm on my way home.'

'Rob not here?'

Kirsty was so immersed in reading the numerous emails that had been sent to her father before his death, checking to see if anything was still outstanding and needed to be dealt with, that she hadn't even heard the outer office door open, or registered Sharon's greeting of their visitor. She looked up as Simon Jordan walked into her office.

'No. He's out on appointments.'

'Pity. I was going to see if he wanted to come for lunch. Don't suppose you fancy a quick bite at the pub?'

Normally it was the last thing she'd have agreed to, but with some of her morning's readings firmly etched on her mind, she made a pretence of looking at her watch and then shrugged carelessly. 'Why not?'

He looked pleased, and if he was surprised he didn't show it.

'Great. We'll just go to the Rose and Thorn, shall we, so we don't need to drive?'

It was Monday and unsurprisingly the pub wasn't busy. After they'd chosen a small table by the window and ordered their food, Simon smiled at her.

'I must admit, it's a pleasant surprise that you agreed to come to lunch with me.'

'There's a reason,' she said coolly.

'Oh?' His smile was wry. 'I might have guessed.'

'I've been going through some of Dad's files and I don't like what I'm finding.'

'What's that got to do with me?'

'I'm not sure – because I'm not sure of the legality of every-thing. But I need to ask you something.' It was something that had been bothering her ever since he'd told her he knew why she'd gone to France. 'Did Rob know about me finding out about Grandma's land? That that's what I fell out with Dad about?'

'Of course he did. We work very closely together.'

And yet Rob had told her that he hadn't known the reason.

She eyed him deliberately. 'I know you work closely together. So close in fact, that you have a joint company that acts as some sort of holding company for properties you *turn*. Like my grandmother's land.'

'We've never hidden that fact.'

'You've never broadcast it either.'

'Look Kirsty, we can go round in circles like this forever. To be honest, what we need is to know that you're not going to do anything stupid that might drop us all in it.'

And I can't give you that reassurance. It may seem old-fashioned of me, but I don't like what you do, and if I find out anything that suggests a link between Dad's death and the company, then I'm telling you now my loyalty to the firm won't stop me from going to the police.'

Simon's lips tightened. 'That would be a mistake. There's no link, and you'd be causing serious embarrassment to your mother and brother, as well as me and Dad. Is that what you want?'

'Of course not, but my father's *dead*. You don't seem to realise the enormity of that. How would you feel if it was Tony?'

He stared her out for a long moment, his eyes boring into hers. Then finally, he seemed to come to some sort of a decision.

'It's your choice, of course, but before you even consider going to the police, there's something you should probably see that might change your mind.'

'What?'

'Not here. I've moved into Paul Copeland's flat for a while

to sort out what needs doing before I re-let it. Meet me there between seven and eight. I'll show you then.'

He looked up as the waiter arrived with their food. 'Ah, just in time,' he said, picking up his napkin.

But Kirsty had lost what little appetite she'd had. He'd worried her. What could he possibly have to show her that he believed would stop her from seeking out the truth? Whatever it was, it had to be big.

'You know what?' She pulled out her purse and put some money onto the table before scraping her chair back and standing up. 'I'll leave you to it. I find I'm not hungry after all.'

He looked up at her, a rueful expression in his eye. 'Well, I'm sorry about that, but I'll see you later? Make sure you come. You could regret it if you don't.'

'Is that a threat?'

He returned her look calmly. 'No, Kirsty. It's a statement of fact.'

Two minutes after she'd gone, Simon's phone rang. Two minutes after that he hung up and found that he, too, had suddenly lost his appetite. He wiped his brow. Things were in danger of spiralling and it wasn't a sensation he liked. He only hoped he could deliver on what he'd promised. Otherwise Kirsty could be in big trouble.

CHAPTER TWENTY-SEVEN

Beth stared at Kath Wilkins across the table in Ken Lazard's office and thought she looked nervous. She waited until Ken had left them alone before looking at her notebook and asking her first question.

'So, Mrs Wilkins, as you know we're investigating Paul Copeland's murder and something's come to light that means I have to ask you a couple more questions, I'm afraid.'

'Oh?'

Remembering Harry's words about not being too nice, Beth kept her manner serious.

'It's come to our knowledge that Gary Lytton – the man who attacked your husband – died under what could be described as suspicious circumstances last year. You and your husband were interviewed by the police at the time?'

Kath Wilkins' eyes hardened. 'Yeah, we were,' she said. 'We didn't have anything to do with it, but it would be hypocritical to say Phil and I were sorry to hear about it. The man was a thug – I should think there were at least a dozen people out there glad to see the back of him.'

'You and your husband reported him to the police for harassment on several occasions?'

'Yeah. Bastard knew where we lived and he'd hang around, shouting comments about cripples as I helped Phil in and out of the car. How cruel is that? He told us he hadn't finished with us yet – he'd make us pay for what we'd put him through with the police and court case. He even threatened me physically – asked Phil how it felt knowing he couldn't protect his own wife.'

'Sounds a nasty piece of work.'

'He was.'

'When the police interviewed you about the accident, you said you were at the Lazards' for lunch?'

'That's right. It was a Saturday – they'd invited us over.'

'But there were no other witnesses to that?'

'One of their neighbours saw me and Phil arrive. The police were happy with our alibis at the time.'

'The death of Paul Copeland means we need to revisit everything.'

'I don't see why.'

'Well, look at it from our point of view. Gary Lytton puts your husband in a wheelchair and dies. Paul Copeland puts Maggie Lazard in a wheelchair and gets murdered – we wouldn't be doing our job if we didn't look into the possibility of the two being connected.

'What – revenge killings, you mean?' She gave a short laugh. 'Bit of a long shot, isn't it?'

The smile disappeared from her face as quickly as it had appeared and she stood up. 'If you've got anything else to ask me, I want a lawyer.'

Beth closed her book and also stood up, feeling she hadn't achieved very much at all. 'That's your right and if we want to formally question you again we'll give you notice, so you can contact one. Please stay in the area for the time being and let us know if you're going away for any reason.'

She could tell from the other woman's expression that she was rattled. It was some small consolation from what had otherwise been a pretty dismal outcome from her interview, and she couldn't help thinking her meeting with Ken wasn't going to be up to much either. She wondered if Harry might not have done things a lot better.

'You did fine,' he told her, back in the office later. 'You were never going to get some riveting bit of new information, or an instant confession. But we need to keep the Lazards and Wilkins in the frame for the time being. What did Ken have to say?'

'Same as her. The four of them were together at their house and the neighbours had witnessed the Wilkins' arrival, and the fact that none of the cars had moved for the whole afternoon. I've checked the witness statements from Lytton's file and it all seems to tie up.'

'Could have had another car lined up, I suppose, or called a taxi – or maybe we're just scraping the barrel because we're getting desperate. Requestion the neighbours. Check no one remembers seeing Ken or Kath leaving the house at any point for any reason – anything else you've found out?'

'Only more background on Gary Lytton. He was a bad un. Twenty-two years old and already served time for GBH, with cautions going back to when he was fourteen. He even put a mask on a couple of years back and robbed his own grandfather – terrorised him apparently because he'd dared to threaten him with going to the police if he didn't mend his ways. Kath Wilkins told me he'd have at least a dozen people wanting to do away with him, and I reckon she was probably right. I've got a meeting with Dave Coleman – he was the investigating officer into Lytton's death. He might have something to add. I don't get the impression from what I've read that Ken or Kath were particularly under suspicion, so they might not have been looking too hard in that direction.'

'Okay, well, keep on it. I'm going to give Susan Porter a call. I got her number off Kirsty Cartwright. We'll meet back here and swap notes later. In the meantime I'd better go and update Murray before he starts shouting.'

'You look about as pissed off as I feel,' Murray said, looking up from his paperwork as Harry walked into his office. 'Take a seat.'

Harry sat down. Murray's office wasn't big but it was always the same – a complete mess, with papers strewn randomly all over his desk – despite the fact that Harry had labelled some trays in a fruitless attempt to organise him. It amazed Harry that he could ever put his fingers on anything, yet somehow he seemed to manage.

'It feels like we're going round in circles at the moment,' Harry said. 'I thought maybe we had a breakthrough this morning, but now I'm not so sure. I don't know how much you're up to speed on the case?'

Murray rummaged around in the papers to his left and pulled out a wad. 'These are the reports you've been emailing through to me. They've made an interesting diversion from this bloody statistic collecting I'm doing at the moment. So what was your breakthrough?'

'Not sure it is one now. But you recall the two people working at the day centre – Ken Lazard and Kathy Wilkins – who have a bit of a thing going with each other? Can't blame them I suppose, in the circumstances – but the interesting thing is that both the people responsible for putting their partners into wheelchairs are now dead.'

Murray raised an eyebrow. 'That is interesting. And goes against the law of averages I'd say, considering their ages.'

'That's what I thought. We're following it up, but initial enquiries aren't looking promising. The Lazards and Wilkins have all got alibis for the timing of the other man's death, although they were together and are relying on each other to a certain extent.'

'They could have involved a third party?'

'It's possible; we're digging deeper. But the victim, Gary Lytton, was a complete thug by the sound of it. Even if it wasn't an accident, there won't have been a shortage of candidates wanting to do him in.'

His gaze flicked to the stack of files on Murray's desk. 'How are you doing on the rape statistics?'

'Getting there. As it happens we've had quite a good clear-up rate over the last ten years compared to some areas. But you heard about the attack in Hatfield on Friday night? We could have done without that.'

'No. I didn't.'

'Some woman thinks she might have been raped in a back garden after a night out at that new nightclub, Le-Roy's.'

'*Thinks* she might have been?'

'Reckons she was drugged. Doesn't remember anything until coming round in the early hours of the morning in the back garden of an unoccupied house. But she says the arrangement of her clothing and the fact she was sore suggested she'd been sexually interfered with and she wouldn't have done that consentingly.'

'Do you think it's the same man who attacked her as carried out the other attacks this year?'

'It's beginning to look like it could be from her description of what little she remembers of him – taller than average, floppy blond hair. Forensics are doing their stuff and we should get the report back anytime now. If she was raped, we'll need to step up the investigation – split the team between the Copeland case and this. That would make five attacks in the last fourteen months, all with similar MOs, all within a few miles' vicinity. Two of them were under the Met in Barnet and the other three – including this one – come under us. At least it gives me an excuse to get off my backside and do a bit of proper police work. It looks like we could have a serial rapist here.'

'Do you want a hand looking into it?'

'Not at the moment. I'm heading off in a minute to see the victim myself. I'll keep you posted.'

'Well, let me know if Beth or I can help.'

'Don't worry, I will. Have you got enough manpower for your needs?'

JAM is how I'll answer that one.

Murray's returning stare was blank, and Harry grinned. 'It's the *in* word, haven't you heard? *Just About Managing*. Which sums up how we operate on a day-to-day basis very nicely. Don't worry, I'll shout if things become *un*manageable.'

'How's your grandmother?'

Harry shook his head. 'Not good. The doctors aren't hopeful.'

'I'm sorry to hear that. I know you're close. She's told me more than once how lucky she is to have you in her life and how she hopes I can see what a *good* boy you are.'

Harry knew his returning smile was bleak. He doubted she'd be saying that now.

He thought of the zillions of things she'd done for him lovingly and unquestioningly throughout his life; the number of times she'd been there for him when he'd otherwise been alone.

Yet he couldn't do this one thing for her…

CHAPTER TWENTY-EIGHT

Kirsty was too unsettled to concentrate on her work that afternoon. She found herself going over and over her conversation with Simon. Something wasn't right, but she didn't know what, or who was involved. Could she even trust her brother?

As if tuning into her thoughts he popped his head around her office door. 'Sharon says you had lunch with Simon? That's a turn-up for the books. It would be nice to see the two of you getting on better again.'

'I don't think that's going to happen.' She looked up at him wearily. 'I'm beginning to sound like a broken record, Rob, but with each day that goes by, it's becoming more obvious that there's some sort of cover-up going on, and it frightens me. And you're lying to me without batting an eyelid, which worries me even more.'

'What the hell are you talking about now?'

'You told me you didn't know what Dad and I had argued about but according to Simon, Dad told them and you at the time that it was because I'd found out about the deal on Grandma's land. Why lie about it?'

Her brother walked into her office and closed the door behind him. His expression had turned to that anxious, almost fearful one that made her feel sick in the pit of her stomach.

'Because I know what you're like, and I didn't want more preaching from you. Believe it or not, I felt uncomfortable about doing it and when Dad told me you'd found out and taken the moral high ground, I respected you for that, but he told me not to tell you I knew – probably because he didn't want us both ganging up against him. I'm sorry, maybe I'm weak – but I have a family to support and they have to be my first priority.'

And hadn't that always been her father's standard line of delivery whenever he'd been home late or missed a school function? And the confusing thing was she knew he'd meant it. She couldn't just write him off as a complete shark. He'd loved his family – as well as the standard of life they had – and if it had come to a choice he would always have put his family first. She had no doubt about that … *did she?*

'What else did Simon say?' Rob asked.

She shrugged. 'He warned me off saying anything to the police. He wants me to go around to his Barnet flat this evening. Says he's got something to show me.'

Robbie frowned. 'What sort of *something*?'

'He wouldn't say.'

'Do you want me to come with you?'

'No, it's okay. I can't think what it is he wants to show me, though. Can you?'

'No.' He saw her expression, and added. 'Genuinely, *no*.'

'Well – I'll find out soon enough, I suppose. I'm meeting him there between seven and eight. I can fill you in after that if you like?'

'Maybe leave it until tomorrow unless it's anything really significant. It's impossible to have a quiet conversation in our house at the moment. And even when the twins are in bed they're both up half the night, teething. I really don't need all this other stuff on top of it.'

'Rob … I don't want to cause trouble for everyone–'

'*Then don't.* Dad's death was an accident, Kirsty. I really believe that.'

'Well, I wish they'd catch the guy who did it, so we'd know for sure.'

He shook his head. 'You just have to be patient. These things take time.'

Now, as she rang on Simon's doorbell bang on seven o'clock, she waited nervously for him to answer it.

'Hi.' As he smiled and stood aside to let her pass, she sensed he was agitated and it added to her own sense of anxiety.

'I can't stay long,' she said. 'I'm meeting a friend in half an hour.'

'Oh? Anyone I know?'

She scratched frantically for a name, cursing herself for not thinking it through properly. 'No … just someone I did some temping with.'

Now that it was lacking Susan and Paul's knick-knacks, the flat looked bare and devoid of character as she entered it. She gave a little shiver, remembering only too well the time she'd visited this house with Simon – when she'd woken up in his bed upstairs, having thrown all common sense and loyalty to Luke out of the window. She didn't want to be reminded of that occasion, so she fixed her eyes firmly on a patch of torn wallpaper and waited.

'It needs a bit of tarting up,' Simon said, following her gaze. 'Once people remove their bits and bobs, every scuff mark and scrape shows. I've moved in for a week or two while the decorators come and sort it out. It'll look completely different when they've finished with it.'

'What did you want to show me, Simon?'

He looked suddenly uncomfortable. 'It's not something I want to show you at all, Kirsty. In fact, I'd much rather not. If you could just assure me that you won't do anything to stir up trouble with either of our businesses–'

'I can't do that and you know why.'

He hesitated and she waited for him to speak, determined to try and keep the upper hand. His voice when he spoke was goaded, as if she'd driven him to saying what he had to say.

'In that case you leave me no choice. Our business means a lot to Dad and me – just as yours does to you guys. We simply can't afford for you to come blundering in and cause havoc. I'm sure if you really stopped to think about it, you'd see where I'm coming from – and contrary to what you seem to think, there's nothing really bad gone on.'

'Enough that you don't want people to investigate you.'

'Kirsty, do you know anything about tax investigations? They're a bloody nightmare. They crawl over everything you've done, going back years. One little discrepancy and they're onto it like sharks, demanding backup proof of what went on, receipts, money trails. We've both got small businesses – not only would it be exhausting and time-consuming, it would also be really stressful. Dad doesn't need that at his age, I don't need it and neither does Rob or your mum.'

'Does Tony know I'm meeting you here?'

'No. He and Mum are round at your mum's tonight. They want to give her as much support as they can.'

Was that supposed to make her feel guilty? That his parents were putting themselves out for her mother while she was threatening to destroy their livelihoods?

'You were going to show me something?'

For a moment their eyes clashed.

'Looks like I have to.'

He turned to the laptop that was sitting on the coffee table and opened it up, angling it so she could see the screen quite clearly from where she sat in her chair.

'I'm sorry about this. I really am. But you leave me no choice.'

She looked at him, alarm bells screaming. What could he possibly be about to show her that was so serious?

'Just watch the screen,' he said.

She turned back to the screen and frowned as he pressed 'play' and a video started up. The scene looked familiar and it didn't take her many seconds to realise where it was set: in Simon's old bedroom upstairs. A few more seconds and the image focused on a man on the bed, naked and in the middle of having sex with a woman. She watched shocked for a moment, before averting her eyes from the screen in revulsion.

'What *is* this? Turn it off. I'm not into porn.'

'Watch it,' he said. Something in his voice made the dread curl in her chest as her eyes returned to their viewing, suddenly suspecting she knew what was coming – and she was right.

As things progressed, the man turned to look directly into the camera, clearing the view, and it took no time at all for her to realise that the man was Simon – and the woman lying beneath him – was her.

Her eyes swung to his in mortification.

'Turn it off.'

His expression was grim. 'In a minute – I need for you to see it all before I do, just so you know exactly what we're talking about here.'

'No, Simon.'

'Watch it.'

She didn't want to, but suddenly she had to – as much for herself as for him. She'd been so drunk that night she'd been unable to remember anything of what had happened. Had almost convinced herself that nothing *had* happened – that it had all been a figment of Simon's imagination, despite the fact she'd woken in his bed the next morning. But here it was in black and white – in colour even – and there was no getting away from the facts now.

She watched as Simon collapsed on top of her, his head nuzzling her neck, before sliding slowly to one side and softly caressing her cheek with his fingers. And there she was – her face caught on camera for all the world to see – head tilted back, eyes closed, in contented post-coital bliss.

'There is more – quite a bit more actually when we get our energy back,' Simon said, jumping up to turn the computer off. 'But I think you've probably seen enough to get the gist of it.'

He saw her trapped eyes fix on the laptop.

'And before you even think about hurling the laptop against the wall, you should know that I've got another copy of that video footage on my office computer – just as a safeguard.'

She stared at him in disbelief. 'What do you intend doing with it?'

'Nothing,' he said firmly, pushing the laptop to one side out of her reach. 'Not unless you make me.'

'Are you *blackmailing* me?'

His voice was goaded as he rounded on her. 'I didn't want to do this, Kirsty, but you left me no option. I never had any intention of using that video footage.'

'No? So, what? You go round having sex with people and filming it without their knowledge?'

He looked uncomfortable. 'No I don't. But I felt I needed something like that as a safeguard after you found out about your grandmother's land. I wasn't sure what else you might have seen while you were with us.'

She stared at him in horror as the implications of his words sank in. 'Are you saying that you planned it all from the start?

That you arranged for me to meet you that night, fully planning to ... do *that* and *film* it?'

'No, that's not what I'm saying – I didn't expect that to happen at all. I hoped you'd open up to me and we could talk the land thing through sensibly. But you know I've always liked you. When you turned to me because you were so upset, I wasn't going to turn you down. And yes, I admit it – you were drunk and I probably shouldn't have taken advantage of that – but I'd had a bit to drink myself. The video idea came to me while you were in the bathroom – I realised it would be an extra safeguard. I know how stubborn you can be.'

She'd thought she couldn't feel any more disgusted with herself than she already did, but she was wrong. Now she had the actual physical proof that she'd slept with Simon, she was distraught. She jumped up from her chair.

'Well, *fuck you*. Do you really think you're going to stop me doing the right thing by blackmailing me? You who think you know me so well?'

'But I do, Kirsty. And I think that while you could put up with a certain amount of embarrassment yourself, you'd be mortified to have that video going viral to all your Facebook and Twitter friends. Not to mention Luke and your family. And believe me, I'd do it.'

She paled. 'If you did that, I'd go straight to the police and sue you for everything you've got.'

He shrugged. 'It wouldn't matter, would it, if I was already facing ruin of my own reputation, or in jail for fraud? All I'm saying is that if I go down, I'm not doing it without a fight. But there's a very simple way of avoiding all that unnecessary unpleasantness and you know what it is.'

She stared at him. 'Do Rob and your father know about this video?'

'Of course not. And they don't need to.'

She felt sick – was visibly shaking. She needed air.

'I'm going.'

'Kirsty, I'm genuinely sorry that I've had to resort to this. I really am.' There was a sincerity to his expression that confused her. 'But there are other people involved who would also be sucked in if you stir things up. That's why I can't let it happen. Believe it or not, I'm doing this for your own good as much as mine.'

'What do you mean? What other people?'

But he already looked as if he'd said too much as he shook his head. 'Just think about what I've said tonight. We've known each other all our lives, and whether you believe it or not, I care about you. Don't force me to do this. But know that if I have to, I will.'

Once Kirsty was back outside, she took deep, cleansing breaths of the cold night air before heading for the relative comfort of her car. She didn't know what to think. Those images were spinning in her head, but he'd confused her pulling the friendship card like that. Was there more to all this than he was letting on? Was he really trying to keep her quiet for her own protection as much as his?

But he'd created that awful video. That wasn't the action of a friend.

As she climbed into her Mini and started the engine, she found herself turning the car in the direction of Highgate. She needed to talk to someone, and while she despised herself for her weakness, it could only be Luke.

Back in Simon's flat, a man had materialised from the bedroom as soon as she'd left.

'You said too much, Simon, but never mind that for now. Think she'll cooperate?'

Simon nodded, more fervently than he was feeling. 'Yes. I'm sure she will.'

'I'm not convinced. I think maybe she needs a bit more persuading.'

'Look, I know Kirsty. She's not an idiot. She won't want those pictures splashed all over the internet, and at the end of the day she won't do anything that hurts her family.'

'All the same – she's being very stubborn about all this. I'm thinking maybe we need to convince her just a little bit more that she needs to back off.'

CHAPTER TWENTY-NINE

Harry looked at his watch and swore under his breath. Seven-forty-five. Where had the time gone? He'd got caught up dealing with a domestic violence incident and now he'd missed getting back for his grandmother's appointment with the GP. *He was crap.* He hoped to God his parents had taken his words on-board and had tried to put stuff in place to keep Gran at home. His phone buzzed and he looked at the screen. It was a text from Claire.

If you want to meet up tonight after your talk with your parents, you're welcome to come over to mine later? Your mum asked me to go round a bit earlier tonight so I saw Jean at six. No change but she's very frail. No worries if you're busy and can't come.
C x

Thanks, he texted back. *Would like that.*

He hesitated over the sign-off. Kisses weren't his thing. In the end he just left it at *Harry.*

'Did you know that the average person checks their mobile over a hundred times a day?'

He looked up at the sound of the voice and grinned as Beth approached his desk.

'Surely not?'

'Yup – an interesting little statistic I read in the paper yesterday.'

'What an exciting, fact-filled life you lead – thought you'd want to be getting away from statistics, not adding irrelevant ones like that to the bag. How's your day gone?'

She sat herself on the edge of his neat and tidy desk. 'Mediocre. You?'

'Same. I'm now seeing Susan Porter tomorrow. She was at work when I rang and working this evening, too.'

'Well, I met up with Dave Coleman, the DI on the Lytton case – the guy who fell under the train? He said one witness had said there'd been a man in a hoody standing between him and Gary Lytton on the edge of the platform before he fell, and he said Lytton looked at the man and seemed to take a step backwards, like in fear, just as the train was coming in. But he said everything happened so quickly he never actually saw what happened. Apparently, Covent Garden was heaving – they'd had to close the station the previous day because it was so jam-packed – and he said it was just as crowded the day of the accident. He felt Gary Lytton step backwards and fell, but he couldn't swear to it. He was adamant he didn't actually see him being pushed, though. He said that by the time the police arrived, the chap in the hoody had gone. I also found out that Lytton went to Covent Garden every Saturday. His dad has a stall in the crafts market and he used to help out at weekends, so it wouldn't have been difficult for someone to track his moves if they wanted to.'

Harry scratched his chin, giving it some thought.

'One other thing,' Beth added. 'I revisited the neighbours like you said, and one lady who lives across the road and knows the Lazards confirmed what she said to the police – that she'd nipped over to borrow some milk from Ken and Maggie at around two-thirty and some woman she didn't know answered the door. When she'd asked to speak to Ken and explained why, the woman told her that he was in the middle of serving up lunch and couldn't come to the door, but that she knew for a fact they were short of milk themselves as Ken had used nearly all of it to make the custard. From the description the neighbour gave of the woman, it did sound very much like Kath Wilkins.'

'Okay, so we know she was there. But we still don't have proof that Ken was. I remembered something last night … There's an alleyway at the back of those gardens if I remember correctly. He could have slipped out if he wanted to.'

'Almost impossible to prove, though.'

Harry sighed. 'Yes it is, and I've had enough for one day.'

He scraped his chair back and reached for his jacket on the back of the door. 'Now I've got to go and sort my parents out. Try to stop them from banging my grandmother into hospital.'

'Are things that bad?'

'She's going downhill fast.'

'I'm sorry. If there's anything I can do?'

'Thanks, that's kind of you, Beth, but there's nothing. We've known for a while it's coming – but it's happening so quickly it's taken us by surprise.'

The first thing he did when he got home was to go and see his grandmother. She hadn't improved any – the swelling was still grotesque and worse than that, he got the distinct impression that she'd shut down. Given up.

'What did the doctor have to say?' he asked her gently.

'Hospital,' she whispered back. 'I don't want that, Harry.'

'I know you don't. They can't force you, Gran.'

'Won't need to.' Her voice was so weak. 'It's what Helen wants, too. It'll happen.' She closed her eyes and turned her head away from him on the pillow. She let out a wheezing breath and said in the same feeble voice. 'I'm tired and I hurt. Go.'

The rejection Harry felt in that one word was devastating. She couldn't have made it any plainer how much she felt he was letting her down. For a moment he sat there, looking at her familiar features so drawn with pain now, knowing he could simply lift the pillow and place it over her face and there'd be no struggle. She'd welcome it.

He couldn't do it.

He rose from the bed. 'I'm not giving up on you, Gran,' he said in a clear voice.

And then he completely shocked himself by putting into words what he knew, deep down, he'd never really doubted. 'And if I have to, I'll do what you want.'

Downstairs, his mother was dishing up the food. He was aware of her quick scrutiny before she declared. 'Roast lamb, your favourite. You must be hungry after your long day.'

It was the last thing he felt like, but they'd delayed eating until he'd got back.

'Thanks.'

'Busy day?' his father enquired. Harry knew the tactic well. His father had become very adept over the years at being the peacemaker in the family, sensing when situations needed diffusing – and Harry had mixed emotions about it, acknowledging that, although at times it had come in useful, it had also left numerous disagreements unresolved.

But it wasn't going to work tonight. He waited until they were all seated and had taken their first mouthfuls before broaching the subject of his grandmother.

'So what did Dr Roe have to say?'

'It wasn't Dr Roe who came in the end.' His mother's tone was defensive. 'He apparently had an emergency call to go to and then a meeting. It was a locum that came.'

'Oh great.'

'She was very nice and very efficient. But she did feel that Gran would be better off in hospital where they can monitor her properly and look after her. And I have to say I agree with her, Harry. There may even be something they can do to help her rally–'

'*No.*'

Harry slammed his knife and fork down with a clatter, then tempered his voice when he saw the look of shock on his mother's face. 'Jesus, Mum, just look at her. She's not *going* to rally – she's dying. Anyone can see that. And Dr Roe knows it, too. He wouldn't be saying she should go to hospital. She's already made it perfectly plain to him that she doesn't want that, and he made it quite clear to us that we could deal with things here.'

'Harry, there's a lot to organise if she stays at home, and she might not even live long enough for it all to be put in place. I'm sorry, darling, it's just too upsetting and too much to think about.'

'Then I'll take time off tomorrow and work from home, and I'll organise it.'

His mother's face set in an obstinate line. 'There's no need for that. I'm her daughter and I'm home now. I'll do whatever needs doing.'

'Fine, then I'll give you the number for the hospice team and between them and the surgery, they can get things organised.'

'Harry, I don't think you understand what I'm saying.' His mother's voice broke. 'I don't want to have her here at home – she's my mother, and it's tearing me up, the thought of sitting here watching her die. It's too upsetting.'

And that was the crux of it, he thought viciously. As always, it was about what *she* could deal with, what *she* wanted – nothing to do with what his grandmother needed in her last few days. Years of resentment came bubbling to the surface – resentment he hadn't even realised he harboured until this moment.

He pushed his plate away, all pretence of appetite gone, and stood up. 'No, Mum, it's you who doesn't understand what *I'm* saying. You don't get it, do you? It's not about you and how upset you are. It's about Gran and what *she* wants in her final days. Have you ever sat down and had that conversation with her? Have you ever sat down with her and had a *meaningful* conversation about anything?'

'Harry, that's enough.' It was his father's voice, but Harry was too angry to heed anyone. 'I shouldn't think you can even remember the last time you and Gran really talked,' he said. 'If you had, you'd know that she's terrified of dying in an over-crowded geriatric ward like Grandpa did – in pain with none of his family around him at the end. So terrified that she's been stashing pills so that she can take them when the time comes, rather than have to go into hospital. Well, I'm telling you this … I made a promise to her that we'd keep her at home, and I won't break my word just because you feel you can't deal with it. I'll really fight you on this if I have to. And if you go behind my back and arrange for her to be admitted to hospital, I'm telling you now, I'll never talk to you again.'

He scraped his chair back and turned to leave the room.

'Where are you going?'

He knew the answer to that but he wasn't about to tell his parents.

'Out. I need to clear my head. Don't wait up.'

CHAPTER THIRTY

Outside Luke's flat in a quiet residential road in Highgate, Kirsty sat in her car feeling suddenly panicky. The upstairs lights were on which meant he was probably in, but what if he didn't want to talk to her? What if he had someone with him?

She looked at her watch. Eight-fifteen. Her options were simple. She either gave up and went home, or she called him.

She couldn't go home, not without telling someone about her plan. It had come to her from nowhere as she was driving here in the car – and was so simple she knew it had a chance of working, if she was brave enough to do it.

Pulling out her phone, she dialled his number, surprised to realise her fingers were shaking.

'Kirsty? Is everything alright?'

'No. It's not. Are you alone?'

There was the most infinitesimal of pauses.

'Yes.'

'I'm outside in my car. Can I come up? There's something I need to talk to you about.'

He sounded weary. 'It's all been said, Kirsty.'

'It's not about us, Luke. Please. I won't keep you long but I need to talk to you.'

Another pause. 'Okay, come up.'

His look was wary as he let her in. She tried not to make too big a thing of it as she glanced around her. It was Luke's flat but they'd decorated it together and it lifted her spirits, just a little, that he hadn't changed anything.

'You look like you could do with a drink?'

'Yes please, but something non-alcoholic if you've got it?'

'Elderflower cordial, orange juice or cranberry.'

'Cranberry. Thanks.'

She followed him into the kitchen and watched as he poured the red liquid into a glass. He turned around and handed her the glass. 'So, what's up?'

He was looking at her expectantly and she tried to order her thoughts as they walked through to the lounge. She sat down and took a sip from her drink before she looked at him.

'There's no easy way of saying this, and it's pretty sordid – but I need to tell someone. And it does sort of involve you.'

She couldn't bring herself to meet his eyes as she finished. She felt degraded and it struck her that if she felt like this here, now, with Luke, how would she feel if that video was plastered all over the internet?

'The bastard.' She looked at him startled, as he jumped up from his chair, his expression explosive. 'I'm going round to see him.'

'No!'

Her eyes flew to his in panic. She'd never seen him so angry – not even when he'd found out about her and Simon.

'It won't do any good, Luke. Even if you made him delete the stuff off his laptop, he's got copies of it on his office computer. He told me. And then he probably really would release the images, just to spite us.'

Luke was pacing the room, his hands balled into fists. 'He wouldn't be in any fit state, after I'd finished with him. I'm going round there, Kirsty. I'm not letting him get away with it. It's blackmail, the sick bastard. I never liked him, but even I would never have thought he'd stoop to something like this.'

She'd never seen him so agitated, and she kept quiet, letting him vent – after all, didn't she feel exactly the same?

'He wouldn't dare put them out there,' he continued. 'It would be as incriminating for him as it would be for you…'

'He'd have nothing to lose, Luke. That's what he said. If I uncover what's gone on and they get investigated, his dad, him, the business … they'd be finished – their reputation ruined.'

She watched him pace a bit more, then took the plunge, knowing that what she was about to suggest was going to sound pretty outrageous.

'I have no right to ask you this, but … I thought of a plan on my way here in the car, and I can't get it out of my head that it might just work. I don't want to involve you in it – or anyone else for that matter – but I need for someone to know what I'm going to do in case it all goes wrong.'

He stared at her hard. 'Now you've got me really worried. What are you saying?'

'As landlords we have a spare key to Simon's flat – and not only that, I don't think he or his father realise it, but I've still got the key to their office from when I was working there. I left in such a flurry that I forgot to give it back. I doubt they'll have bothered changing the locks. I was thinking that if I did it in one hit, maybe I could nick the laptop from his flat and the computer from his office, and get the images wiped before he even realised anything was amiss.'

'Are you *serious*? You're going to break into their premises?'

'It's the only way.' She could hear the plea in her voice.

'Kirsty! What if they're alarmed?'

'The office is, I know, but I'd be surprised if they've changed the code for that. I can check our records about his flat. If there's an alarm, we'll have it on file and we should have the code, too.'

The more she thought about it, the more determined she was becoming. For the first time since seeing those awful images, she actually felt she had the ability to fight back. And she was bloody well going to do it.

'You can't do it, Kirsty.' Luke's initial outburst had tempered now, and he surveyed her more calmly. 'Apart from the fact that it would be illegal ... there's obviously more to all this than meets the eye. It could be dangerous for you to start interfering. You should go to the police.'

She glared at him in frustration. 'Of course I *should* – but how can I, when my own family might be involved? I can't go to the police until I know what I'm dealing with, but at least if I can get the videos wiped, I won't have that hanging over me. I'm sorry. I know telling you this puts you in an awkward position but I'm not asking you to help me. I just want someone else to be aware of what I'm doing in case anything goes wrong.'

Luke ran an exasperated hand through his hair. 'But it's not that simple, is it? How can I let you tackle something like that on your own? It's madness to even think you could get away with it...'

But his voice wasn't quite as vehement as it had been, and she could see his quick mind sifting through the information she'd given him, even as he spoke.

'It's not really mad,' she said quickly, taking advantage of what she perceived to be a chink in his armour. 'It's just quite cheeky. He won't be expecting it, that's for sure.'

Luke eyed her thoughtfully. 'No, he won't ...'

He was considering her suggestion, seemingly drawn in

despite himself. 'Say you did do it ... just for argument's sake ... you'd have to take both computers away – make sure they were wiped by someone who knew what they were doing. Otherwise he could probably retrieve the files.'

'Oh.'

'What sort of computer does he have at the office?'

'Not a Mac, but it's a laptop of some sort.'

'Not too heavy, then.'

Her eyes gleamed as they held his. 'You're seeing that it's not such a mad idea after all, aren't you?'

'I don't know ... there's no guarantee that he doesn't have other copies as well backed up. But maybe it could work, if you get the timing right.'

'I'm not sure he's savvy enough to do more complicated backups. I could be wrong, but he was always saying how he hates technology. I guess that's just a risk I'll have to take.'

'I suppose we could ask Mark to do the erasing ...'

A grim smile spread slowly over Luke's countenance. 'And you know what? I'd love to see the look on his face if we did get away with it. Not that it changes anything, but I'm not sure I believe him when he says he didn't deliberately set out that night to ... do what he did. How many of us have videos set up in our bedrooms?'

Kirsty's heart leapt at this first sign of softening in his attitude.

'But you still chose to leave with him in the first place,' he added, squashing her hope before it had time to take root.

'I know,' she said simply. 'We both know what I can be like when I overdo the alcohol, but up until tonight there was a part of me that just couldn't believe I'd ever have done that. But I can't kid myself now.' She looked him straight in the eye. She needed him to see how much she regretted what she'd done. 'I'm so sorry. I know how devastated I'd be if you'd done that to me. I don't blame you for losing your trust in me. For what it's worth – I'm really strict with myself now about how much I drink.'

There was a long silence as they looked at each other.

The sound of the doorbell broke the moment.

'That'll be Eleanor,' Luke said, rising from his chair. 'She's dropping some work off to me.'

'Oh … no worries.' She grabbed her bag and jumped up from her chair. 'I'll be off. Thanks for listening, Luke.'

'Don't do anything without telling me,' he said, as she reached for her jacket. 'I'll help you get those computers. I don't know how we'll wangle it, but I don't want you doing it on your own.'

'You don't need to–'

'Yes, I do. Give me a call tomorrow and we'll work on a plan.'

'Thanks.'

Kirsty tried not to stare too hard at Eleanor Rothby as they passed on the doorstep. She got a whiff of expensive perfume and a vague impression of Cleopatra-style, short, dark hair, and pale skin heavily obscured by a vivid pink scarf. Kirsty's murmured greeting was ignored, the tentative smile, that took all her efforts to produce, returned with a cool glare that informed her that Eleanor Rothby knew who she was and wasn't impressed to see her there.

With a little swish of her head, the other girl turned to Luke with an exaggerated shudder. 'Sorry I'm late: the traffic's terrible and I'm freezing. Let's get inside where it's nice and cosy.'

So this was the *friend* Luke was bringing to the wedding? Kirsty found herself experiencing a dose of good, old-fashioned jealousy as she hurried swiftly past her into the cold night air.

As she drove home from Luke's, her mind was in turmoil. The more she thought about Simon, the angrier she got. She knew that some people revelled in sending nude selfies to their partners or friends – some of her own friends had even done it – but it wasn't something she'd give a moment's consideration to, and to think that Simon had filmed her without her knowledge…

She frowned as a terrible thought struck her. How had he done it? Had there been a video set up somewhere, or could there have been someone else in the room filming them? It was a vile thought, but for some reason she couldn't get it out of her head. Was that because subconsciously she remembered something? Had that person maybe even taken part himself? She felt sick as she remembered what Simon had said. Something about there being a lot more action to come after they'd got their energy back.

Stop it. She was just tormenting herself.

But it convinced her more than ever that, though it might not be the first time she'd conveniently forgotten what she'd got up to when she was drunk, it would definitely be the last.

She so needed to get hold of those computers.

But first off, she needed to speak to Robbie, and to hell with his broken nights.

When Lizzie picked up the phone, however, she seemed surprised that Kirsty should think he was at home.

'He's out with a client tonight. Didn't he tell you?'

'Uh no,' she said, remembering how Rob had specifically told her he was going home because he was so tired. 'We didn't see much of each other in the office today. I assumed he'd be home with you.'

'Well, you can probably get him on his mobile if you really need to speak to him. Can I help? Or pass on a message?'

'No, don't worry. It's not urgent. I'll call him or catch up with him tomorrow in the office.'

'I was going to call you, actually. We've got Simon coming round for supper tomorrow night. Only casual, but I wondered if you'd come over and make up the numbers? I know he's not your favourite person – and to tell the truth he's not mine either – but apparently he and Robbie have *important* things to discuss, and I thought you and I could have a catch-up.'

Kirsty could hardly believe her good fortune as it hit her what that meant.

'Oh, that's a shame – I would have done but I'm meeting up with some friends tomorrow night. Maybe another time?'

'Sure. It was just a thought.' Lizzie laughed. 'With any luck they'll lock themselves away in the study after supper and I'll be left to my own devices.'

Kirsty disconnected the hands-free. Was it her they needed to talk about? It made her think twice about trying Rob's mobile now to find out where he was and tell him about what had gone on tonight. She looked at the clock on the dashboard. Nine-thirty. Half an hour since she'd left Luke's. What would he and Eleanor be doing? Eating? She hadn't smelt anything cooking when she'd been in the flat. But they could have ordered a takeaway or gone out – or maybe even now, they were limbs a-tangled in bed?

She couldn't go there. On impulse, she called her cousin. 'Hey, Rach, what are you up to?'

'A few last-minute wedding things – nothing major. Why?'

'Oh, just feeling at a bit of a loose end. I wondered if you fancy coming for a drink? I could pick you up?'

'Let's do it,' her cousin responded with flattering alacrity. 'I'm getting bogged down with all this stuff, I could do with a break.'

'Great, I'll see you in about twenty minutes. I'll buy you a drink and you can come prepared to work – I need a positive strategy for getting over Luke and who better to turn to than my cousin the therapist?'

She disconnected the phone, feeling more positive already.

If Luke had moved on, then so could she.

CHAPTER THIRTY-ONE

Harry ate the last forkful of spaghetti Bolognese in the small but cosy kitchen, and sat back with an appreciative sigh as he smiled at Claire across the table.

'Thanks for that. I *was* hungry after all. Sorry if I've eaten your rations for the week.'

Claire stood up and smiled as he grabbed a piece of garlic bread and did a quick final wipe of his pasta bowl.

'Couldn't afford to feed you too often, that's for sure,' she said, clearing the bowls away. 'How are you feeling now?'

He picked up his glass and side plate and followed her over to the dishwasher. 'Calmer. You're right. Mum's not a monster. I just need to stick to my guns. I'll take the morning off and make the necessary phone calls. I'm sure we can get things set up quite quickly.'

'She may have calmed down by the time you get back, and perhaps you've given her something to think about. Let's hope so anyway.'

'I don't think she'll change her mind readily: I think she's frightened of dealing with it. But if I can show her that we'll get support where we need it–'

'It could be quite drawn-out: you do realise that?'

'I know. I'm not looking forward to it.'

'Your gran wouldn't be the first, you know – to do what she's done.'

She turned to look at him as she said it.

'Stash the pills, you mean?'

Claire nodded.

Harry sucked in his breath. 'I'll be honest with you, if things get much worse and she still wants it–'

'Don't say anything.'

'Sorry. You're right. Again. You're the only person I've told about it. Apart from my parents now.'

'Well, I already knew because Jean's talked about it with me, too. I think she sees me as being tougher than you in that respect. I'm not sure whether that's a compliment or not.' She half-smiled, reaching out for the cafetière and throwing some coffee into it. Harry watched as she did it, wondering just how much he could say.

'What are your thoughts on euthanasia? Do you have a view?'

Claire considered the question.

'I probably think about it more than most, doing my job,' she said finally. 'And if I'm honest, more and more I'm coming round to the belief that where people are genuinely at the end of their lives and in pain, or suffering from some terrible disease, they should be entitled to have some say in how they want things to end. The difficulty is allowing it while still protecting the more vulnerable people from being manipulated.'

'Yes, and that's the problem, isn't it?'

'Only for some people, though. Take your gran, for example. She's made it perfectly clear what she wants and she's not being manipulated by anyone. In fact everyone's trying to *dissuade* her from doing it. But really, if she wants to end things a week or two early when her life is clearly over, why should anyone be forcing her to suffer unnecessarily? I've seen both sides of the argument in practice, and it's changed me from being very anti-euthanasia to being more understanding of the realities of it. We can't prevent death – we're not going to change anything by making people hang on in there – so why not help them accept it in the way they want? For most of the clients I've talked to over the years, it's about the quality of their lives and how they want to be remembered by those they leave behind. I can understand that.'

'And so can I. But I'm a policeman and it would be going against everything I stood for if I was to–'

'God, I'm not saying you should do it, Harry. I'm just saying that I'm coming round to the idea of the law being changed, to allow people to have more say in what they want – as long as factors are in place to protect the more vulnerable.'

'But that's the difficult part, isn't it? It's hard to know that.'

'Yes, it is. And if that proof isn't there, then it shouldn't be allowed.'

She looked at him steadily for a moment, then smiled and shrugged her shoulders. 'How did we get onto this? It's all too grim. Do you want milk in your coffee?'

He nodded and she turned her back on him to fill his mug.

He looked at her straight back and shapely figure, and realised that somewhere along the line she'd slipped under his skin without him even being aware of it. Without giving himself time to think about it, he moved over to the worktop, taking hold of her arms and gently turning her to face him.

'Thanks,' he said simply.

He loved how the pink tinged her cheeks. 'I haven't done much – just fed you, and given you some space to calm down in. You'll handle it fine, but you know if there's any way I can help…?'

She was looking up at him calmly and he suddenly wanted

to see her as she'd looked when they'd kissed the other night – a bit dishevelled, less calm and controlled than she was looking now. He slid his arms around her waist and drew her to him, and when she made no move to push him away, he lowered his mouth.

It was as good as it had been the first time, and they both enjoyed the moment as they tentatively explored each other's mouths. He eased her back against the worktop, enjoying the feel of her body pressing against his. Her skin beneath her jumper was soft and his hands were gentle as he caressed the warmth of it. When they slid round to cup her breast she murmured softly against his lips, but her hand came up to still his.

He stopped straight away. 'Sorry,' he muttered. Christ, he felt like a fifteen-year-old.

She drew back from him with a rueful smile. 'Don't apologise. There's nothing I'd like more than to whisk you upstairs and finish this, but ...' She shook her head. 'If we do that I want it to be for the right reasons, not because you're feeling grateful to me.'

He blinked at her, then shook his head, smiling. 'What I'm feeling at the moment's got nothing to do with gratitude!'

She gave him a little poke. 'You know what I mean. You're in a state at the moment, about your gran and everything and it's understandable – but I don't want it to be a quick fling because you're in need of comfort and a bit of emotional release.'

The fact that she could be right didn't make it any easier pulling back from her. He felt as if he wanted to hold onto her warmth forever. He buried his head in her shoulder and held her for a long moment. Then he planted a kiss on the side of her neck, breathed her in one more time, and pulled away.

'I'm not going to take you on now over it. But I do like

you, Claire, and I know I'd feel the same whatever the circumstances.'

She grinned. 'Well, that's good to know. You're not too bad yourself. Come on, let's see what's on TV – chill out for a bit before you head home.'

She led the way into the lounge, looking at him as she put the tray on the coffee table. 'You know, maybe you just need to reassure your mum that the pair of you really can organise things *together*, so that she doesn't feel overwhelmed by it all? It must have been quite a shock for her, coming back and finding Jean like that.'

Harry grimaced. 'Even a United Nations peacekeeper would have problems negotiating a settlement with my mother.' He grinned as she laughed. 'But just for you, I'll try.'

They tucked up together on the settee and for a while Harry was able to forget about work, forget about his grandmother and the problems at home. It felt good sitting here watching the television with Claire. She seemed to fit just right in the crook of his arm, her glossy head resting contentedly against his chest. He felt like he could have sat there all night, except that then his overactive imagination took over and he found himself wondering what her bedroom looked like – how it might feel to wake up in the morning with her beside him.

Rejecting the baser images that began to form in his mind at the prospect of that, he forced himself to concentrate on the programme they were watching, and within a very short space of time his fatigue took over and he was dead to the world.

Kirsty swung through the gate into the drive and parked her car. A smile curved her lips. Meeting up with Rachael had been just what the doctor ordered and had only confirmed what she already knew. That she'd missed her cousin more than anyone else, after Luke. She'd toyed with the idea of telling her about what was going on with Simon and Rob, but it was all a bit close to home and she realised it could get her into hot water over the land issue – which she still hadn't decided how to resolve yet. They'd had a good talk about Luke, though, and how Kirsty should best handle her "Lukexit", as Rachael had termed it, and they'd even managed to have a laugh about stuff. Kirsty felt in better spirits than she had in quite a while.

She looked at her watch: it was nearly eleven, not that late. Would Eleanor be gone? She needed to phone Luke about the new development.

Well, it was urgent, wasn't it?

In the middle of dialling his number, she chickened out and resorted to texting.

'Heard from Lizzie tonight that Simon's going round to theirs for supper tomorrow. That's got to be our chance, hasn't it? Are you free?'

His response came by return. Not too busily occupied, then.

'Okay. Where shall we meet and what time?'

'At his office, 7.45? Then we can go to his flat straight after.'

'Okay.'

She managed to stop herself from texting back that she hoped he'd had a nice evening with Eleanor. Instead, stuffing her phone in her pocket, she opened the car door.

It happened so quickly she didn't know what had hit her. One minute she was climbing out of the car and the next she'd been grabbed by the collar of her jacket and was being hauled by the scruff of her neck. The speed and efficiency with which a hand was clamped over her mouth and her arm was twisted up her back left her in no doubt that whoever it was had done this many times before, and meant business.

'Keep quiet or I'll break your arm,' a voice snarled as she

was hustled roughly towards the shrubbery that edged the path to the back garden.

Out of sight of the house, she was thrust against the trunk of a silver birch, one knee in her crutch, pinning her to the tree … a hard elbow ramming into her neck.

'This is a warning …' he jabbed the elbow viciously into her throat '… to keep your nose out of things and don't go poking it into what don't concern you. That's how people end up dead. You getting the message?'

Kirsty nodded, her terrified eyes probing the dark, to get a view of the man's face. But a hoody was drawn over his head, making it impossible to see him.

'*Who are you?'* she managed to gasp.

The elbow beneath her chin tightened into her neck. 'What did I just say, little girl? You really expect me to answer that? You just make sure you do as I say, or I'll be coming after you. And you won't like that.'

His voice was a menacing growl, his face so close to hers she could feel his breath warm on her cheek, smell his after-shave. *Aftershave!* Whoever wore aftershave when they were attacking someone?

She twisted her head, trying to break free of his grasp, her eyes bulging with the effort to draw breath. One final exertion of pressure to show he meant business and the grasp on her throat was released as he thrust her hard into the bushes. She clawed wildly for support as she went down but all she heard was the snapping of twigs and branches, feeling them scratch at her face and hands as she crashed to the ground.

'You mind your business – and no running to the cops. Otherwise – next time it's curtains for you. Just like it was for your father.'

And with that, he was gone, running silently back down the drive. She heard a door slam, an engine start up – and the sound of a car speeding off down the road. Then silence.

Kirsty was shaking so much that for a moment she just lay there in the undergrowth, feeling traumatised. Where had he come from? Had he been waiting for her when she got home? Had he followed her from the pub?

Just like it was for your father. The words spun in her head.

She was right in her suspicions. It had been no accident. Her father had been murdered.

She tried sitting up and within a short space of time was dragging herself to a standing position, glad to see that nothing seemed to be broken. Her hand moved to her neck where he'd grabbed her. It felt sore and swollen, as did most of her body, and she rubbed it agitatedly. She looked towards the house, instinctively seeking its warmth and comfort in the cold night. The light was on in the kitchen and through the window she could see her mother doing a last-minute clear-up before heading for bed, totally oblivious to what had just gone on outside in the garden.

Two minutes later she'd let herself quietly into the house and was upstairs in her shower room splashing warm water onto her face. She looked at herself in the mirror over the basin. Two haunted eyes stared back, but she was surprised to see that her face wasn't the mass of scratches and marks she'd assumed it would be. She had two quite marked scratches down one side of her cheek – which were lightly bleeding – but apart from that, once she'd washed the muck off and got the twigs out of her hair, she looked relatively normal. Her hands were another matter, though, the palms scratched and bleeding where she'd clawed at the bushes trying to get a hold.

After she'd washed and cleaned herself up as best she could, she sat on her bed and tried to calm herself. There was no doubt in her mind now that she'd stumbled into something big – and her instinctive response was to do as her attacker had said and back off. Not only for her own safety, but also for her family's. How could she knowingly expose any of them to this sort of danger?

Should she call Luke? But he'd tell her to phone the police straight away – and she needed to get hold of Simon's computers first. Once she'd got Mark to wipe them, she could put her mind to the other stuff – perhaps have a long and much-needed talk with Robbie. All the way through, it was the fear of his possible involvement that was holding her back from going to the police. She needed to find out to what extent he was involved – if indeed he even was. She knew her brother, didn't she? Could she really imagine him being involved in something as clearly dangerous as this – condoning the murder of his own father?

Once she'd spoken to him, come what may, she'd go to the police.

CHAPTER THIRTY-TWO

He ordered a whisky in the overcrowded nightclub and tossed it back in one, pushing the glass back at the barman and indicating at him to pour another. He'd been sitting here a while now and had picked out a couple of possibilities. The first woman was drunk and clearly in the middle of a massive argument with her boyfriend, who'd already made two abortive attempts to walk out on her. It was only a matter of time, he was sure, before he really did leave for good – and she was hot. The second was alone, lost in her own private world as she swayed on the dance floor – probably a drug-induced euphoria which somehow wasn't quite so appealing – but she'd be a relatively easy conquest, if it came to it.

It probably wasn't the best time to be considering this – it was too close to the last time. But he was majorly stressed, things were piling up – and that was always the trigger. He didn't like it, but he couldn't seem to help himself. When pressure reached boiling point it needed a release, didn't it? And better to release his frustration here on some stupid, pissed slag than on his family and friends.

So he sat.

And waited.

It wasn't long before the decision was made for him. He watched through hooded eyes as the boyfriend of girl number one stormed off. He left it another ten minutes, just to check he wasn't coming back, then wandered over to the table just as she seemed to be reaching for her bag to leave. He flashed her a charming smile.

'You look a bit hacked off. Can I buy you a drink? They do a great Snowball here.'

She stared up at him through unfocused eyes. 'What's that?'

'Don't ask me. All I know is that it's got advocaat in it and it tastes great. How brave are you feeling?'

He saw her eyes flash to the door, as if expecting the boyfriend to re-enter at any time, then she looked up at him, defiance in her eyes.

'Yeah. Why not? Thanks.'

He slipped a generous amount of the liquid from his phial into her drink and a dash into his own. He was getting good at this.

Quarter of an hour later, he was helping her into her coat. She was being loud and belligerent, slagging her boyfriend off, and he tried to keep his face averted from the bouncers as he shuffled her out into the night, wishing the stuff would hurry up and do its work. Normally, he'd have stayed longer in the club, making sure she was pretty docile before they left, but he was worried the boyfriend might come back. He needed to get her out of there.

As it turned out, it wasn't hard getting her back to his flat. She'd drifted off in the car and was completely out of it now as he opened the passenger door and hauled her out. In the flat she appeared disorientated, asking where she was as he shuffled her through to the bedroom. He threw her on the bed and looked around. Everything was ready, just as he'd left it.

He picked up the handcuffs and clicked them onto her wrists...

Later, as he locked the flat up and left, he was sweating profusely. It hadn't happened to him before that he'd been unable to wake his victims up when he'd finished with them. What the hell was he supposed to do now? He could leave her there for a while, but not forever. He clung onto what he'd found on Google – that some people took longer to come round than others. But he hadn't liked the look of her – or the other thing he'd read – that some people never came round. That they could fall into a deep coma and even die.

Shit. That would be a game-changer.

He turned the key in the lock and double-locked it. At least he didn't have to stay here all night. He'd gagged her and left her handcuffed and tied to the bed. She wouldn't be going anywhere. He'd check on her first thing in the morning.

He drew a breath, trying to calm himself. He needed time to think – but the most important thing was to carry on as normal; not do anything that might arouse suspicion – he was good at that, wasn't he?

CHAPTER THIRTY-THREE

K irsty woke the next morning, hurting. As she got stiffly out of bed and looked at herself in the mirror, she saw that her neck looked ugly now the bruising was coming out, and she had several scratches on her face. She covered it all with make-up and a scarf as best she could, and headed downstairs.

'I'd like that, Dan,' she heard her mother saying on the hall phone. 'I must say, it would be nice to get out. How about I come over to you, give you a lift to the garage so you can pick up your car, and then we can go on to The Bell from there? … Okay, I'll see you then.'

She started guiltily as she turned and saw Kirsty on the bottom step. 'Oh, I didn't hear you, love. I've got some porridge on if you want some?'

'Thanks.' Kirsty tried to keep the censure out of her voice. 'You're meeting Dan later?'

'Yes. I told you his car was in the garage being repaired. It's ready now, and when he was here I offered to give him a lift to pick it up. I couldn't just say I'd changed my mind because my children disapprove.'

'Right.'

'Kirsty–'

'It's probably best we don't talk about it, Mum.'

She brushed past her mother and walked into the kitchen.

'What have you done to your face?' Sylvia asked, following her in.

'It's nothing.' Kirsty kept her head averted as she moved over to put the kettle on. I got scratched in some shrubbery yesterday. It was stupid. Do you want tea or coffee?'

'Coffee please. I need the caffeine.'

At the breakfast table, Kirsty stirred her tea distractedly.

'How was Rob yesterday?' Sylvia asked.

Kirsty shrugged. 'Still mad with you – and not very happy with me either.'

Her mother sighed. 'Hopefully he'll get over it – he usually does if you give him time to calm down. Things are obviously fraught for him. It's a lot, taking over the business – especially now there's another baby on the way.'

Kirsty gaped at her mother.

'Oh … hasn't he told you? I'm sure he will – they're still adjusting, I think. It's come as something of a shock apparently.'

'Are they mad? The twins aren't even two yet.'

'As I say, I think it was a bit of a surprise. But the girls should be easier by the time the new one – and let's hope it is one – arrives.'

No wonder he was feeling stressed, Kirsty thought as she drove into the office after breakfast. But then, so must Lizzie be. And he wasn't exactly being supportive, going out for the night last night – and lying to his wife about it.

'If you must know, I was over at our flat, decorating,' Robbie snapped. 'I didn't want to tell Lizzie because she'd have had a go about wanting me at home and I needed some space.'

'You've had the flat for ages. It must be nearly done, surely?'

'Don't you start. It takes time when you're doing it yourself

– and that's something we don't have a lot of at the moment. To be honest, your attitude these days isn't helping either.'

'Oh, so that's my fault, too, now – the fact your flat isn't getting decorated?'

She caught herself up, knowing she wasn't helping the situation.

'No, it's not your fault,' her brother said tiredly, surprising her. 'It's mine. It's all mine. I just feel so trapped. I love Lizzie and the girls but …' He ran a hand through his hair. 'It's all so much more *domestic* than I ever imagined. And now we've got another baby on the way – and I feel as if I'm barely keeping my head above water. I look at mates of mine with no ties, no debts, and find myself hankering back to a life I left years ago.'

'You know what they say about the grass being greener.'

'And it's true, I know – I'm not saying I want to leave Lizzie or anything–'

'Rob–'

'I'm not. But sometimes – and I'm sure Lizzie feels the same – I can't help wondering where *I* am in all this.'

'You need a break. Both of you. Bring the kids to Mum's and let us look after them while you and Liz go somewhere nice. Mum and I will love having them.'

'It would be good…'

'Then *do* it. Your and Lizzie's relationship is the most important thing in your life, Rob. There are times when you need to put it first.'

'You're sounding very grown-up all of a sudden.'

'I know what it's like to have a relationship fall apart, and it's not nice.'

'I know. Sorry.' He sighed. 'It's getting to me, this row with Mum. Has she said any more to you?'

'Only that he's just a friend and she has no intention of it becoming anything more. She's not going to stop seeing him, though, Rob, and in fairness, it's not for us to interfere in her friendships – especially when she's known him for years.'

She conveniently omitted the fact that her mother and Daniel were picking his car up from the garage and then going out for lunch.

'It just got to me – seeing him in Dad's chair.'

'I know.'

He sighed. 'I'm not handling all this stuff well…'

'Nor am I.'

Rob shook his head wearily. 'You seem to be doing a lot better than me, but I can't think about it at the moment. I need to get off – I've got a viewing in half an hour.'

He peered at her more observantly. 'What have you done to your face?'

Her fingers went automatically to the cuts on her cheek. Should she tell him what had happened last night? What had happened with Simon? They might be getting on better this morning, but nothing had changed since yesterday. Much as it destroyed her to realise it, she still didn't know how much she could trust him. And if he *was* totally innocent, what would he do? Call the police in all likelihood. And she wasn't in the mood for more confrontation over that.'

'I fell in a bush. Don't ask!'

'Poor you. You look battered.'

'You know, I'd be happy to come and help you decorate the flat if you want a hand?'

'No – no, it's fine. Thanks for the offer, but I see that as my private space at the moment.' He softened the words with a smile. 'Anyway, what do you know about decorating?'

'Can't be that difficult if you can do it,' she quipped back. 'And I've not even seen the flat yet.'

He acknowledged that with a nod. 'I know – and if I get stuck maybe I will throw a paintbrush your way, but I've nearly finished now, so I think I can manage. You can come and see it when it's finished.'

She shrugged. 'Suit yourself: the offer's there if you want it. I hear you've got Simon coming over for dinner tonight?'

She tried to sound casual as she asked the question.

'Lizzie mentioned she'd invited you. I wasn't totally surprised you said no.'

'Yes, well, I'm busy myself tonight as it happens,' Kirsty said, avoiding his eyes. She looked up. 'Rob…'

'What?'

'We do need to talk. There's something I need to do first, but after that, can we sit down and have a good chat?'

Her brother looked at her dubiously. 'What about?'

'A couple of things. There are issues that need sorting.'

She half-expected him to launch into her again and she braced herself, but surprisingly no attack was forthcoming. Instead he gave a resigned little sigh.

'Okay. You're right, we do need to talk. How did it go with Simon last night? What was that all about?'

She hesitated. 'I'll tell you later, when we talk about the other stuff.'

He eyed her suspiciously. 'You're not about to do anything stupid – or dangerous?'

'No.' A tingle ran down her spine at the thought of what was to come.

'Good, because I don't need anything else to worry about at the moment.' He got up from his chair. 'I'd better crack on. I'll catch you later.'

CHAPTER THIRTY-FOUR

Harry stood outside the terraced house in Enfield and looked around him as he waited for someone to come to the door. The garden he was standing in was small with barely enough room to house the two wheelie bins squeezed in side by side. Cars were randomly parked on both sides of the busy street, and opposite there were various shops providing anything from DIY, to insurance services, to a steaming cup of coffee sitting out on the polluted pavement. Having spent half the morning trying to pacify his mother and sort social services out, he was glad to be back on the job getting on with what needed to be done.

The door was opened by Susan Porter herself.

'How are you doing?' he asked, as she led the way through to a small but airy lounge at the back of the house.

'Up and down. Trying to keep busy so I don't think about the funeral this afternoon.'

He'd forgotten about that. 'Sorry if this is a bad time.'

She shrugged. 'Doesn't matter. What d'you want to talk to me about?'

'Just a couple of things that have come to our attention, then

I'll leave you in peace. You mentioned in our last conversation that Paul had been in a fight the night before he was killed, but I remember you saying you didn't know who the fight was with?'

She looked puzzled. 'Yeah, that's right.'

'Well, it was with a bloke called Ken Lazard. Does that name mean anything to you?'

'Yeah, of course. That's the bloke whose wife he ran over.'

She flopped down into a chair, her brow clearing dramatically. 'Why didn't he *tell* me, the silly sod, instead of leaving me to suspect all sorts of horrible things? Was it him what killed Paul, then?'

'We have no evidence to support that. It's just a line of enquiry.'

'But it could've been?'

Harry didn't answer.

'Oh, shit … I feel bad now.'

'Why?'

'Cos of what I said to Mr Cartwright's daughter 'bout the tenants upstairs. I thought it might've been them – dunno why really, except that some of Tim's friends are a bit rough and we didn't take to 'em.'

Harry suppressed an irritated sigh. 'Why didn't you say anything to me about that when we talked?'

'Cos I was scared. I thought if it *was* them, they might come after me next. Someone pushed a note through the front door threatening me if I spoke out about anything.'

'*What!?*'

Harry took a breath and counted to five. 'Have you still got that note?'

She hesitated…

'Have you?'

She got up from her chair and moved over to where her bag was sitting on the floor.

'I told Kirsty Cartwright I'd got rid of it, but …'

She fished out an envelope and handed it to Harry. It was a very simply worded message.

If you don't want to end up like your boyfriend, keep your mouth shut.

Harry found it difficult to hide his exasperation. 'You should have shown me this when I first came to see you. It's hard enough for us trying to find Paul's killer without feeling you're keeping information back that could be useful.'

'I were frightened – so would you be if you got a note like that shoved through your letter box. I feel a bit better thinking it could be that Ken Lazard bloke. I mean … he's not so likely to want to take it out on me, is he? – I weren't in the car. It's like I said before – I knew Paul was up to something but he wouldn't tell me what. I got it into my head it was to do with the guy who lived in the flat above us, but I didn't know that for sure. That night, Paul had the fight: he wouldn't tell me what it was about but when he was killed the next day, I thought it must be linked. I didn't dare say anything in case they came after me, too. And then when Mr Cartwright was killed after visiting the flat…'

Harry decided not to mention that Kirsty had already told him about that.

'Why did *he* go up?'

'They were doing their usual thing of being noisy, and he could see it were getting to me. He went up to have words wiv 'em. It quietened down after that, but I was scared they'd think it was me what sent him up.'

'Why were you suspicious of them? I interviewed Tim Burman. He seemed alright.'

'Tim's okay, but there's rough types what hang around with him – and foreigners.' She looked defiant. 'Paul didn't like 'em. He reckoned they looked shifty.'

'You said you told Kirsty Cartwright about her father's visit?'

'Yeah. Poor cow doesn't believe his death was an accident; she's trying to get to the bottom of things.'

Harry groaned inwardly. That was all they needed. He stood up to go, aware that he'd probably outstayed his welcome on today of all days. 'Well, thanks for filling me in on that. Are you planning on staying here with your brother for a while?'

'He says I can stay for as long as I like. The travelling ain't easy for my work, but until you find out who killed Paul I feel safer being away from Barnet.'

'I can understand that. As soon as we know anything, we'll tell you.'

'Thanks.' Susan's smile was wobbly as she escorted him to the door. 'I still can't believe any of this. It feels unreal – you know? I keep expecting Paul to walk through that door or call me on my mobile. Only it don't happen. I'm dreading this afternoon.'

'What time's the funeral?'

'Three o'clock.'

'Is someone taking you?'

'My brother. He'll be back anytime now. Will you be going?'

'Someone will be there. It might be me.'

She nodded. 'Okay.'

The office was buzzing when he got back, every desk occupied and teeming with activity as phones rang and conversations hummed in the background.

'Everything okay?' he called to Beth as he made his way over to the coffee station.

She gave him a thumbs-up – he hadn't realised she was on the phone.

'Catch you in a minute,' he mouthed, and she nodded.

Next stop was Murray's office, over in the far corner. Balancing two cups of coffee in his hand, he started to weave his way towards it.

'Harry?'

He looked over to where Geoff Peterson was sitting at his desk, waving a piece of paper at him.

He veered right. 'Yeah?'

'This report's just come in about a missing girl. If you're heading into the boss, you might want to take it in and show him.'

Harry put the drinks down on his desk and took the piece of paper from the other man's hand, scanning it briefly before tucking it under his arm and picking up the cups again.

'Thanks. When did it come in?'

'I've only just typed it up. Fresh off the block! How's your grandmother?'

'She's doing okay. Thanks.'

Through the glass, Harry could see Murray staring thoughtfully out of the window, his back to the door.

'Ah, Harry,' he said, turning round as Harry knocked and entered.

'Thanks for giving me time off this morning.'

'Did you get things sorted?'

'Not fully, but we're getting there.' He put the cups carefully down on the desk as they both sat down. 'The GP's trying to organise twenty-four-hour cover with a carer, but with the cutbacks they're saying that may not be possible, so we're trying for day care only to start with – we can cope with the nights ourselves. What with that and the hospice team coming later this afternoon, it's a bit of a waiting game. The trouble is my parents think she'd be better off in hospital, which is the one thing she's adamant she doesn't want.'

He ran his hand through his hair. 'It's doing my head in, to be honest.'

His thoughts flew back to that final conversation with his mother before he'd left for his meeting with Susan Porter that morning.

'Harry, believe it or not, I did take on-board what you said last night. And I know some of it was true – I don't know my mother. I don't know you. Not as much as I should. That doesn't mean I don't love you both, though. I'm going to talk to Mum today, but you need to know that if the surgery can't get things organised quickly for proper care here, then hospital's still my preference. She's going downhill fast, we can all see that.'

'There's no point going over it all again, Mum. You know what I want. If necessary, I'm happy to pay for any top-up care she needs myself. Just let me know the outcome and don't have her admitted behind my back.'

'I don't want to fight you on this.'

'Then don't.' He picked up his jacket and pinned her with his gaze. 'You know how strongly I feel about it. I don't want to end up doing something I shouldn't.'

And let her ponder that one, he thought, as he strode out of the house.

Now, as he looked at Murray, he sighed. 'There's so much red tape. And as usual, it all boils down to money. Hopefully we'll have an answer later today.'

'These things are never easy, you can only do your best. Now … How did you get on with Paul Copeland's girlfriend this morning?'

'Nothing much, apart from the fact that she omitted to tell us she'd had an anonymous note pushed through her door warning her to keep her mouth shut if she didn't want to end up the same way as Paul. No wonder she was edgy. I'll send it off to Forensics. You never know, we might get something off it. She also mentioned she didn't trust some of the friends of the chap who lives in the flat above theirs, Tim Burman. He seemed normal enough to me, but I'll get Beth to run a check on him. Have you heard about this?' He handed Murray the piece of paper Geoff had given him. 'It's a missing persons report on a twenty-one-year-old woman called Katrina Midwood: last seen last night at that new nightclub in Hatfield. She had a row with her boyfriend who apparently walked out of the club in a temper, and she hasn't been seen since. Didn't make it into work today and both the mother and the boyfriend say it's not like her. They're convinced something's happened to her – Mum was very insistent that she was coming home and we should look into it, even though she's only been missing since last night.'

Murray took the file from him, read the notes and looked up at Harry, his blunt features thoughtful. 'That's the same area the woman on Friday was attacked. It could be interesting bearing in mind what I've been looking into. And two attacks in less than a week–' He drummed his fingers on the desk, his thoughts clearly switching to this new line of enquiry. 'I know it's early days, but leave it with me. Perhaps I'll drop by on the mother on my way home.'

Out in the main office, Harry looked around.

'She's up in the incident room, if you're looking for Beth,' Geoff said.

'Cheers. I left your report with Murray – he's going to call on the mother tonight. I think he's wondering if there's a link with the attack last Friday.'

Upstairs in the incident room he found Beth studying the scraps of paper on the wall.

'Anything new?' he asked.

'Nah. I've been going over the sequence of events, trying to see if we've missed anything. But the frustrating thing is, I don't think we have.' She sighed. 'We need something new. Some sightings at least of Paul Copeland would help.'

'Anything show up on his bank statements?'

'Nothing unusual. And he was overdrawn – so if he was hoping to be paid for something, it never happened.'

'I saw Susan Porter today. She seems to have got it in her head that the chap in the upstairs flat is dodgy.'

'Burman?'

Harry nodded. 'Him or some of his mates. Run a check on him and the girlfriend, will you? – and the other chap I bumped into while I was there. What was his name...? Alan Flint, I think.'

'Okay.'

'*Harry...?*'

Harry turned as Murray came striding into the room.

'I just spoke to the girl's mother and she's still heard nothing. Not surprisingly, she's worried sick. I'm hacked off sitting in that office all day and I'm not liking the feel of this. I'm going round to see her now. What are you up to at the moment? Can you do the boyfriend, do you think? See what he's got to say for himself?'

'Sure, I'll give him a call. Then after that I'll probably head off to Paul Copeland's funeral.'

He turned to Beth. 'Let me know if you come up with anything interesting on Burman – I'll catch you later.'

Fraser Conway was in his mid-twenties and agitated.

'Christ,' he said, letting Harry into his flat. 'You've taken your time getting here.'

'I'm sorry,' Harry said. 'Busy day. I understand you're worried about your girlfriend ... Katrina Midwood?'

'Yeah. Like I said on the phone, she's been missing since last night. It's not like her. Her mum and I are really worried.'

'Maybe she stayed over with a friend last night?'

Fraser shook his head. 'I've spoken to all our friends. No one's seen her.'

'Can you just tell me what you know about her movements last night? You said you were both at the new nightclub in Hatfield, Le-Roy's?'

'Yeah, we went with some friends but they left before us.'

'There was mention of an argument?'

The man looked nervous. 'Look, I know what you're thinking. I stormed off because I was angry. I needed to cool down. When I went back, Kat was gone. I tried texting her, but I thought she was ignoring me because she was still pissed off. I only found out this morning when her mum rang, that she hadn't gone home last night.'

'What did you row about?'

'Her drinking. She doesn't know when to stop sometimes, and then she gets aggressive about stuff.'

'What sort of stuff?'

He looked uncomfortable. 'Oh, you know – usually stuff about us. Am I serious about her? Where we're going in our relationship … all that sort of crap.' He shook his head. 'She knows I'm serious about her.'

'And that's what you rowed about last night?'

He nodded.

'Did you ask anyone in the nightclub if they saw her leave?'

He shook his head. 'I just assumed she'd left after me and I went home. I should have gone to her house, I know, but then I'd have had her parents to answer to – and I wasn't in the mood.'

Harry closed his notebook and stood up.

Fraser looked up at him. 'What are you going to do? You are taking this seriously? I swear to God, it's not like her to disappear like this. Something's happened to her. I know it has.'

'We're looking into it, Mr Conway, and we'll keep you informed. I'll get down to Le-Roy's and take a look at their CCTV. Have you got a photo of her? Maybe that way we can see if anyone remembers what time she left and if she was alone.'

Harry walked into Le-Roy's and looked about him. Nothing much going on – not that he'd expect there to be much activity at five o'clock in the afternoon. He'd just about managed to squeeze Paul Copeland's funeral in before coming here, but disappointingly it had given him no new leads. Susan Porter had sat in the front pew with his parents, and had acknowledged him with a little nod, but there'd been no one else there that he'd recognised. After introducing himself to the parents and assuring them they were doing their best to get his killers, he'd taken his leave.

Maybe he'd have more luck here.

Loud music blared through the speakers and a handful of people were either sitting at the tables dotted around the dance floor, or propping up the enormous bar. He walked over to where the barman was drying glasses and chatting to a customer.

'Yeah, I remember her vaguely,' the barman said, studying the photo Harry showed him.

'You saw her last night?'

'Can't swear it was last night, but yeah, I think she was here.'

'Have you got CCTV for last night?'

'Should have.'

'Can I take a look at it?'

'You better speak to the boss about that. He's through there …'

Harry followed the direction he indicated, passing through a swanky black and white archway towards the back of the building, and coming to a halt outside a door with a brass placard displaying the sign, "The Boss". He rapped smartly on the door and pushed it open.

Inside, sitting behind a huge desk and chewing on a fat cigar, was a skinny stick of a man with straggly, thinning hair that was far too long for a man of his age.

'I rarely see the punters myself,' Ray Law said with a shrug, pushing the photo back across the table to Harry, 'but you're welcome to take the CCTV and have a look. It's what it's there for, after all.'

Back at the station he and Beth pored over the images.

'There she is,' Harry said. 'Freeze it. That's her, isn't it?'

'Yeah, it is.' Beth peered at the image of the couple standing at the counter waiting for their coats.

It was quite a clear picture and Harry frowned. 'Does he look familiar to you?'

She shook her head. 'Don't think so.'

Harry pushed "play" to let it run, and they watched as the man helped Katrina Midwood into her coat and supported her stumbling form out of the club.

'The boyfriend wasn't exaggerating when he said she was plastered,' Beth said.

'No.' Harry was still staring closely at the images. 'There's something about him …'

'You'd think you'd remember someone with hair as blond as that, wouldn't you?'

'Yeah, you would. Get a good still of him blown up so we can have a proper look.'

CHAPTER THIRTY-FIVE

'Where are you going?'

Kirsty stopped guiltily in her tracks at the front door and turned to face her mother. She hated lying, but she had no intention of telling her what she was really up to tonight.

'I'm meeting up with Sophie and a couple of the others.'

'Oh, right.'

Kirsty immediately felt guilty at leaving her mother on her own, but there was no way she could cancel tonight.

'I'm sorry, Mum, but you know Sophie and Tom have just got engaged. She wants to show off her ring, I think. Will you be alright on your own?'

Her mother shrugged. 'I'll have to be, won't I? Don't worry about me.'

Oh, God. But if she didn't do this tonight…

She closed the gap between them and gave her mother a hug. 'Oh Mum, I'm sorry … but I've said I'll go now. How about we go to the cinema tomorrow, just you and me? We could go for a meal beforehand?'

'I'm not sure about the cinema, but the meal would be

nice.' Her mother hugged her back, then drew away, forcing a smile. 'I'm sorry, too. I didn't mean to put you on a guilt trip. I'll be fine … really. I've got plenty of stuff to watch on the planner.'

Out in the car, Kirsty quickly texted her cousin. *'Huge favour to ask. If you're free, any chance you could pop round to Mum's tonight for a quick visit? She's feeling a bit low and I've had to go out. Sure she'd love to hear how the wedding plans are coming along. No worries if you're busy – I haven't mentioned it to her.'*

It was all she could do and the instant ping of a reply brought a smile to her face.

'Of course I can … no problem. Will's here and says he'll come with me. It'll be nice to see her. Xx'

With that sorted, Kirsty turned on the engine and exited the drive. As always, when she drove past Gobions these days, she felt a prickle of unease. That was where the body of the tenant had been found, and it was unsettling to think it had all happened so near to their house. She'd spent half her childhood playing there, and had great memories of it, but she wasn't sure she'd ever feel the same about the place again. She glanced apprehensively in her mirror, suddenly remembering the attack last night – but she couldn't see anyone following her, and gradually her tension eased.

Half an hour later she'd arrived at Jordan's Solicitors in Whetstone. She parked her car in a side road and pulled her hoody over her head, before making her way quickly over to where she could see Luke's car parked further down the road.

She slipped into the passenger seat and drew back the hood.

Luke smiled in the dim light. 'You're taking this seriously, I see. I must admit I didn't think to bring a hoody.'

'Don't worry, I brought you these.' She handed him an old hat and scarf of her father's. 'Not that you should need them. You're not coming in with me.'

'What? Of course I am. You can't do this on your own.'

'Luke, I wasn't thinking straight when I asked you. You're a lawyer. You can't be seen to be involved in anything illegal, and it would be irresponsible of me to expect it.'

Look, I get what you're saying, but ...'

'I mean it. I've thought it all through and I won't involve you in this. But you can still help. If you go to Costa's and choose a table by the window where you've got a view of the office, it will be a real security for me to know you're there. That way, if anything goes desperately wrong...'

'Kirsty–'

'How difficult is it–' she interrupted, '–unplugging a laptop and walking out with it? I can do this, Luke, and if anything *does* go wrong ... if the key doesn't work or the alarm goes off ... then I'll be out of there quicker than you can shout my name.'

It took a bit more persuasion but in the end Luke could see she wasn't going to budge. 'We'll meet back here after you see me come out,' Kirsty said, waiting until Luke had donned his cap and scarf before climbing out of the car.

'You head off to Costa's that way. I'm doing the roundabout route approaching the office from the other direction, to make it more difficult for anyone to link us together if there's any CCTV.'

He looked impressed. 'You have been thinking it through.'

'Yes, well, I may be daft in some ways but I'm nothing if not practical.'

Despite her brave words, her heart was pounding as she set off. Jordans' solicitors were situated towards the end of a block of shops on the High Street, and apart from a restaurant a few doors down, all the other shops and offices were closed. Kirsty breathed a sigh of relief. It made things easier. After a quick look round to make sure she hadn't acquired any unwanted interest, she inserted the key in the lock. Immediately the alarm started to bleep and using the torch on her phone, she closed the door behind her and hurried over to tap the code into the panel. The beeping stopped and she released her breath.

She wasted no time, heading straight for Simon's office on the far side, making sure to keep her head down. She didn't remember there being any security cameras, but they could have had one installed since she'd left. The laptop was sitting on his desk and she hurried over to unplug it. *Easy-peasy!* Her heart was still thumping but not quite so violently now.

Her phone buzzed in her pocket at the same time as she heard the key in the outer door.

Shit.

Her eyes flew in the direction of the sound, but the door opened inwards, blocking her view and she couldn't see who it was coming in from where she was standing.

She just had time to drop the computer back down on the desk and dive under it, before the reception area was flooded with light. Her heart was hammering so loudly she was afraid whoever it was would hear it. *Why hadn't she rung her brother, to make sure Simon had arrived? Stupid. Stupid! What if it was him?*

Footsteps approached Simon's desk and she shrank back as far as she could into the cramped space beneath it. Had he seen her? Would he notice the computer was unplugged? The chair was pulled backwards and she held her breath – expecting a face to peer in at her any minute, and yank her out. But it didn't happen. Instead, a pair of feet suddenly came into view as the owner of them sat down on the chair. Silence, then …

'Ah, Simon … Dad here … just got your message. So where is this file? What colour is it?

She heard the sound of Tony Jordan rummaging through various trays on Simon's desk above her, then a satisfied sigh as he obviously located it. *'Ah, think I've got it. Petrunesca. Is that the name? Okay … yes, this is it. What time are you seeing him in the*

316

morning? I'll drop it off to you at Rob's on my way home if you like ... Fine. By the way, who was the last person to leave tonight? It's a good thing I came back, the alarm wasn't on ... Are you sure? Well, it wasn't on when I came in – must have had a blip. I'll get Emily to book a service. Okay ... see you in about half an hour. Bye.'

The phone went down, the chair got pushed back and the legs straightened up. Thirty seconds later she heard the alarm keypad being pressed and the sound of the outer door being closed and locked. Then silence.

Kirsty found she was still holding her breath and she released it slowly, her heart still hammering frantically. Jeez, that was close – she needed to get out of there.

About to crawl out from under the desk, she stopped, as a new realisation hit her.

Shit! He'd reset the alarm. The minute she moved from under the desk, she'd trigger it – and then all hell would be let loose.

She sat for a full minute pondering her choices, before she dug out her phone and dialled Luke.

'Bloody hell, Kirsty, are you okay?' Just hearing his voice calmed her, worried though it sounded. 'I saw Tony coming in but I could only text you in case he heard your phone ring. I did walk past and saw him sitting at the desk, so I assumed you'd managed to hide?'

'Listen, I'm fine, but I've got a problem. He's reset the alarm, which means I'll trigger it the minute I move. I'm not sure what to do.'

Luke gave it some thought. 'If it's anything like ours it *will* trigger when you move, but if you put the code in quickly enough it should reset it – and hopefully no one will take much notice if it's only a short burst of activity.'

Kirsty didn't particularly like the hit-and-miss aspect of that, but she realised there was no other solution. 'Right. I'll leave it a while then, to let him get well away, then I'll just have to give it a try and see what happens.'

'I knew this wasn't a good idea. Whatever happens, don't hang around. Just get out of there. I'll wait until I see you come out and then I'll meet you back at the car.'

'Okay. But if I get caught, *promise* me you won't get involved? I don't want you getting into trouble. If the police come I'll just have to fess up to what I'm doing.'

'I must have been bloody mad letting you talk me into this. What on earth were we thinking?'

'Not now, Luke. You can preach to me when it's over.'

She left it another ten minutes before she made her move and she felt stiff and cramped as she eased herself onto her hands and knees. She switched on her phone torch to light the way and copying something she'd seen on television, she wiggled out from under the desk on her stomach, trying to keep below the levels of any sensor as she made her way over to the keypad. *It was working.* She got all the way there before she was forced to stand up to enter the code.

The noise the alarm emitted was deafening, but within a few seconds she'd punched the number in and it had stopped. Switching on the light, she walked unhurriedly back to Simon's office and sat down as if she was working. That way if anyone was curious about the alarm being triggered it didn't look too suspicious, and she figured it would take at least a few minutes for the police or Tony Jordan to get here if they'd been alerted. It was the longest two minutes of her life as she forced herself to wait – then picking up the computer, she walked calmly out into the reception area. A minute later she'd reset the alarm and was outside again, locking the door as she left. A quick glance around reassured her there were no police sirens screaming their way towards her. She looked briefly up towards Costa's before taking off in the opposite direction.

On the corner of the little side road where they'd parked,

Luke was waiting for her and he gave her a quick, hard hug before relieving her of the burden of the computer.

'You had me worried.'

'I had myself worried,' she joked thinly. 'Thank God he didn't see me.'

They headed quickly back to their cars, and she couldn't help smiling at the sight of Luke with her father's scarf draped thickly around his neck and the flat cap pulled firmly down over his head.

They got to his car first and he put the laptop on the back seat. 'What now?' he asked, turning to her.

'His flat, I suppose. I just hope his laptop's there. He's going to know it's me, of course, and I don't know what he'll say to his father about the office break-in, but I guess that's his problem.'

'We could ask Mark if he can wipe them tonight. That way, you might even get the office one back before they know it's been taken. Simon's not going to want to get the police involved, but if his father was to get in early and realise they've been broken into…'

'Luke, you're a genius, that's a great idea.' She looked at her watch. Eight o'clock. 'We need to be quick, though. Let's try. Follow me to Simon's – it shouldn't take much more than fifteen minutes. Then we can go to Mark's from there. What time did you tell him we'd get there?'

'He said it didn't matter, he's in all evening. Are you sure Simon's other computer will be in the Barnet flat and not his Whetstone one?'

'No, I'm not. But it was there when he showed me the video and he said he was staying there for a few days. I'm stuffed if it isn't. I don't think he's got round to giving us a spare key for the new flat yet.'

'Well, come on, we'd better get a move on. We don't know how long it's going to take Mark to do the necessary.'

But ten minutes later, Kirsty let out a curse as she heard a crash behind her and looked in her mirror to see that someone had pulled out of a side turning and collided into Luke's car.

Pulling over, she threw her door open and scrambled out.

'Luke! Are you okay?'

She ran to driver's side of his car, where she could already see him manoeuvring to open the door. A woman had jumped out of the other vehicle and was shouting hysterically in the road.

'Bugger,' Luke muttered, slamming his car door shut behind him. He approached the woman, his manner calm.

'Why didn't you see me and let me in?' the woman shrieked at him. 'It was completely your fault.'

'Now hang on a minute. I was on the main road travelling straight, and you were turning right out of a side turning. I think you'll find I had right of way.'

Luke seemed to catch a whiff of something around the same time as Kirsty did.

'Have you been drinking?' he said, his eyes drifting to the two children sitting in the back of her car.

'What fucking business is that of yours? I'm not hanging around here to be insulted.'

Before she'd barely had time to turn around, Luke had covered the distance to her car and removed her keys from the ignition.

'What are you doing?' she shrieked.

'You're drunk and you've got children in the car. I'm sorry, but I'm not letting you get in and drive off. I'm calling the police and I suggest you phone someone to come and pick your kids up.' A small crowd was gathering on the kerbside, but Luke ignored them as he pulled out his phone – turning to Kirsty at the same time.

'I'm really sorry about this, but we can't let her drive.'

'I know. I need to press on, though. God knows how long all this will take.'

'No, wait. Let's see how long it takes the police to get here.'

'Luke, it won't be quick, we both know that and if I want to get the computers returned tonight we need to get them to Mark as soon as possible. I'll be fine. You get the office computer to Mark as quickly as you can when you've finished here, and I'll meet you there when I've got his laptop.'

Luke didn't look happy and Kirsty pressed her point. 'We've got no choice, Luke. I'll call Robbie if you like – check that Simon's there – and if he isn't, then I won't go in.'

'You promise me that?'

'Yes.'

'Okay.' His manner eased a little. 'But make sure you call me as soon as you've got it.'

'I will. Good luck here.'

'Let's hope it doesn't take hours. I'll see you at Mark's, then.' He hesitated. 'Be careful.'

'I will.'

She drove off feeling apprehensive but happier than she'd felt in a long time. It was good having Luke back on-board, even if it was only temporary.

Harry opened the front door and let himself in. The house felt warm and cosy with good cooking smells coming from the kitchen.

'How's Gran?' he asked, as his mother came out into the hall to greet him.

'Not good. She's not eaten anything today. It's horrible seeing her like this. But she seems a little more contented in herself, and Claire came in earlier and made her as comfortable as she could – she's a godsend. Gran asked if you'd go up and see her when you got in. Your dinner's keeping warm in the oven. I'll dish it up for you.'

His grandmother's breath was rattling in her chest as he sat gently down on the edge of her bed. Her eyes were closed but flickered open when she felt his weight beside her.

'Is that you, Harry?'

'Yes, I'm here, Gran.' He dropped a kiss on her cheek.

She gave a weak smile. 'Good boy.' The words were eked out between breaths. 'Will you ... sit with me ... tonight ... after supper?'

'Of course. I can stay now if you like?'

'No, no. As long ... as I know you're ... coming back. Promise me?'

'Promise. I'll be about twenty minutes, then we can carry on with the book if you like. We might even get it finished tonight.'

'We both ... know what the ... ending will be,' she said, her lips curving just ever so slightly. Her voice faded away and her eyes flickered shut again.

'I'll see you in a little while,' Harry said, getting up. 'Grab some rest while you can.'

As he sat down at the table and ate his supper, his mother surprised him by pouring herself a glass of wine and sitting down opposite him. She seemed agitated and he waited patiently. They'd avoided talking about their argument last night, apart from her brief reference to it earlier, and he suspected there was more to come.

Now she took a breath and said, 'Harry ... about last night.'

'Leave it, Mum. I'm sorry I lost it, but–'

'There are reasons why I did what I did – following your father around the world for most of our married life – and one day if you ever get married, maybe you'll understand.'

'What reasons?' He shook his head. 'I get that you wanted

to be together. I get that you put me into boarding school because you felt it was the best thing to do in the circumstances. What I don't get is why you didn't come back for holiday breaks? Even if Dad wasn't able to come, you could have. It's not as if money was an issue.'

'I can't tell you the reasons, but you seemed happy enough coming out with Gran when you were younger. It was your choice to stop that as you got older.'

'Because I got fed up with always being the one making the effort. It started out as an experiment the first time I did it. I wanted to go to that kids' rugby camp, if you remember, and it clashed with when you wanted me to visit. I thought you'd come over here instead but you didn't. After that I thought if you couldn't be bothered to come and see me, why should I make the effort to go to some godforsaken dig to see you.' He sighed. 'It was childish of me, but once I'd done it once …'

'I don't want to go over everything again either, but just so you know, I did manage to have a chat with Grandma today – it was a bit one-sided because she seems to be struggling so to speak, but I think we came to a degree of understanding.'

'Does that mean you'll agree to her dying in the peace of her own home?'

He knew the words sounded brutal but there was no sugar-coating it.

His mother looked discomfited as she rose from the table. 'As that seems to be what you both want.'

'Thanks, Mum.' Harry finished his meal and then he, too, rose. 'I'll make myself a cup of tea and take it up. She asked me to sit with her tonight.'

'She'll like that. Give her a kiss from me.'

Jean's room had an aura of peace about it when he walked in. He smiled at the little bouquet of flowers and card that Claire had placed on her bedside table. The room smelt fresh and clean and he was quite sure that would have been Claire's touch that evening when she'd prepared his grandmother for the night. She was a natural carer, anyone could see that, but it touched him that she obviously had a special fondness for his grandmother.

'Shall I read to you, Gran?' he asked, as he took his seat in the chair beside her.

She was very drowsy but somehow she managed to half-open her eyes and turn them in his direction.

'Yes,' she whispered. 'Stay with me tonight, Harry. Till I've gone?'

Something in the way she said it made him focus on her sharply. 'Gran? Are you alright?'

'I'm fine, boy.'

Her hand twitched on the bed as if to feel for his, and as he reached for it, his eyes fixed in shock on the two empty pill bottles nestling on the sheet next to her.

What the–

'Gran – what are these pill bottles doing here?'

She didn't answer and he jumped up from the chair, his voice urgent.

'Gran, answer me. Have you taken these pills?'

Her cheeks relaxed into the semblance of a smile. 'It's alright. Just stay with me.'

He stared at her in horror. 'How many have you taken? Who *gave* them to you?'

But already she was closing her eyes. 'Don't … spoil it, Harry,' she whispered. 'I beg you. No one needs to … know.'

His first instinct was to rush downstairs and call an ambulance … the doctor … anyone.

But he knew what would happen if he did that – everything he'd been fighting so hard to prevent. She'd be rushed off to hospital, have her stomach pumped, and there'd be no getting her home after that.

He sat down again, forcing himself to think it through, and

afterwards he couldn't remember how long he sat there before coming to a decision. But there came a time when he accepted that he wasn't going to call the ambulance or the doctor – or even his mother, who'd insist on calling them both. He'd do this one final thing for his gran, and live with the consequences if he had to.

But someone had helped her – had moved the pills from the cupboard to the bed so she could reach them. And that disturbed him. Who would have done that? Claire? His parents? The GP? One of the Macmillan team? None of them seemed likely candidates, and yet – if he had to choose one …

The stark reality hit him that the most likely person was Claire.

He didn't want to believe it, but he thought back to their discussion last night and the suspicion wouldn't be crushed. Might she see it as a way of helping them both out – him and his grandmother? She knew he didn't have the strength to do it, so she'd done it for him. Was that why she'd stopped things from going too far last night? Because she'd known what she was thinking of doing?

He sat there for a long time holding his grandmother's limp hand, trying to come up with the answers, but in the end he gave up.

It didn't matter who'd started this. It would be him who finished it.

Her breathing was still rattling on her chest but it was less harsh now, and she looked relaxed. He squeezed her hand. Now that the decision had been taken off him, he was glad to be here at her side, seeing her through this to the end. She'd loved him, parented him – had given of herself unstintingly. Now it was his turn.

He leant forward so his lips were close to her ear.

'Love you, Gran.'

He picked up the novel in one hand, held her fingers in the other, and quietly began to read.

It didn't take Kirsty long to get to Simon's flat in Barnet, and once there she parked up and sat in her car for a couple of minutes surveying the house. One small light shone from the downstairs flat, but the upstairs was shining like a beacon. She watched as a medium-sized van pulled up outside the house, double-parking while the driver jumped out and opened the rear doors. From inside the van, several people clambered out and made their way up the path to the front door. She watched as the door was opened by *Bulldog*, and slid quickly down in her seat as his sharp gaze raked the street before he closed the door again.

About to climb out of the car herself, she remembered her promise to Luke and dialled her brother's number.

'Oh, sorry,' she said when he picked up. 'I just remembered, you've probably got Simon there. I was just ringing for a chat.'

'Anything important?'

'Nothing that can't wait til tomorrow.'

'Okay, well yes, he's here. He came early, actually, and we're just serving up pudding because he wants an early night.'

'Fine, no worries. I'll see you in the morning.'

She let out a breath, unaware she'd even been holding it. That made things a lot simpler. Even if for some reason Simon got suspicious and dashed back, it would take him at least twenty minutes to get here and she'd be well gone by then.

She climbed out of the car, and making sure her hoody was still raised, walked swiftly up the path. She inserted the key in the front door and opened it quietly. No one in the hall. Good. Moving as quietly as she could to Simon's door, she inserted the second key. She held her breath as she edged the door open, waiting for the dreaded bleeps that would precede the screeching sound of an alarm. Nothing. She took a deep breath. She wanted to turn around and run – forget about the computer, forget about Simon or Bulldog upstairs – and just get the hell out of there. Well, she would … in just a minute, when she'd got his laptop.

Closing the door quietly behind her, she switched on the overhead light. A quick glance around the room confirmed she was alone, and yes … there was his laptop still sitting on the table.

There didn't appear to be signs of much decorating going on as of yet, and the place looked tired and scruffy. Not the sort of place she could imagine Simon being happy in for long.

Moving quickly over to the table, she unplugged the computer and was just picking it up in her arms when, for the second time that night, the sound of a key in the lock had her freezing in her tracks.

No time to move or dive under a table this time, the door was flung open and a tall, fair-haired man stood in the doorway, his sharp eyes doing a quick scan of the room to make sure she was alone, before coming back to pin her in his gaze. In spite of the cold night, he was wearing a thin, black T-shirt and jeans, with running shoes. He looked fit and she gave her chances a big fat zero if it came to a dash for it. The smile on his face was no smile at all.

'Hello…' he said softly. 'What have we got here?'

The menace in his tone sent volts of electricity shooting through her. She stared back at him like a trapped rabbit, Simon's laptop weighing incriminatingly in her hands.

'I uh …'

More chills swept up her spine as he shut the door quietly behind him and began to advance slowly towards her.

'It better be good, sweetheart. I'm not the most patient of

men. I'll ask you again. What are you doing here?'

'I'm a friend of Simon's,' she said nervously. 'I dropped by to borrow his laptop. He's out at a friend's for dinner tonight but he gave me the key and said to let myself in.'

Her voice grew in strength as she trotted out her prepared lines. She'd considered that it might go wrong – of course she had – but she couldn't have predicted how vulnerable she'd feel now it had. He stopped a couple of feet in front of her, blocking her escape. He seemed to fill the whole room, but she held her ground, trying not to panic.

'A friend, you say? And how long have you known him?'

'Oh, forever,' she returned, confident in that fact at least.

'So I'm guessing you're Kirsty?'

That unseated her. Her eyes widened. 'Uh, yes … that's right. How do you know that? Who are you?'

The man's eyes bore into hers. 'I'm Tim Burman. I keep an eye on things for Simon when he's not around. If I'm not mistaken, you've been trying to get in touch with me?'

Oh crap.

'Ah, right. Yes … I have.'

He pulled a phone from his pocket and speed-dialled a number. Then he said in a low voice, 'I'm in your flat and Kirsty Cartwright's here. She had a key and let herself in. Says you know about it and said she could borrow your laptop.'

Kirsty's heart sank. Now she was in deep shit. Tim Burman's eyes fixed on her as he listened to the reply.

'Well, get back here as soon as you can. We'll be up in the flat.'

He ended the call and looked at her. 'Looks like you haven't been telling me the truth, Kirsty. Simon didn't sound at all happy that you were here.'

The sound of her phone bleeping in her pocket made her jump. Her eyes locked with Tim Burman's.

'Aren't you going to answer that?' he asked conversationally.

'See who's trying to contact you?'

'It's probably just my mum seeing what time I'll be home.'

'Why don't you look at it and see?'

She didn't want to give up her only contact with the outside world. She cursed that she hadn't put it on silent. *Stupid.*

'Really ... it won't be urgent.'

'*Look* at it.' There was no mistaking the threat in his voice, and pulling the phone from her pocket with shaky fingers, Kirsty entered her code. He snatched the phone from her hand and looked at the screen.

'It's from Luke.' He smiled. 'He says all's well now and he'll meet you at Mark's.'

'Oh, right.'

'Who's Luke?'

'A friend.'

'Why's he texting you?'

She thought quickly. 'Because we're meeting up at Mark's for a takeaway and a film. They're expecting me.'

'So you're going to text him back saying something's come up and you won't be able to make it. Tell him you'll catch up with him tomorrow.'

Tim Burman thrust the phone at her, removing the laptop from her arms at the same time and putting it back down on the table. 'Do it. And don't try anything clever.'

She had the terrifying sensation of being totally out of control and she tried to claw back some authority. 'Now look here ... I don't know what all this is about, but Simon wouldn't be happy about you treating me like this–'

'You'd be very stupid to take me for a fool, Kirsty.' He pulled a knife from his pocket. 'I'd hate to have to use this and make an even bigger mess of Simon's décor, but I'm not playing games here. Now text your Luke. Dictate it, so I can hear exactly what you're saying.'

Kirsty looked at the text Luke had sent. Her fingers were shaking so much she could barely make out the words. *'All finished here now. On my way to Mark's, I'll see you there. ETA?'*

She tried to think clearly. What could she say to alert him without also alerting Tim Burman?

'Unfortunately something's come up and I can't meet up with you and Mark tonight. Enjoy the film and I'll call you tomorrow.'

Tim Burman grabbed the phone, checked the message and then pressed Send, before putting it in his pocket.

'Right, we're going upstairs now.' He flicked the knife in the direction of the door. 'Move.'

Kirsty didn't budge. 'I'm not going anywhere with you, you're crazy. You can't go around pulling knives on people and kidnapping them.'

'Can't I?'

His cruel smile looked out of place on the deceptively handsome face. 'I've got away with it a few times in the past. Don't see why this should be any different. Now do as you're told and move – and don't try anything silly. There's nowhere for you to run and no one to hear if you scream. That's the beauty of these old houses – thick walls. It's unlikely the neighbours would even hear.'

Even so, her instinct for self-preservation kicked in with surprising force as she went for it – uttering such a loud, piercing scream that it made him recoil with shock for just a second, before he lunged out and grabbed her, swinging her round so that one hand was rammed over her mouth to silence her, while the other brought the knife up to her throat.

'Do that again and you're dead,' he spat. 'And you better know I mean it.'

She felt the shocking prick of the blade as he deliberately pierced the skin, the warmth of her own blood as it trickled down her neck. She let out a terrified gasp.

'Next time it will go deeper. Now *do as I say, and move.*

We're going out of the flat and upstairs to mine – and no more tricks. Do you understand me?'

She nodded, still reeling from the shock of that knife slicing her skin. She offered no resistance as he twisted her left arm up her back and shoved her towards the door and out into the hall.

Upstairs in his flat she wasn't surprised to see Bulldog, and he didn't seem surprised to see her. Around the table by the window sat the half dozen or so people she'd seen entering the house earlier. They were all looking at her fixedly.

'Told you it was her,' Bulldog muttered. 'Recognised the car. Nosy bitch ain't the sort to give up.'

'To her cost now,' Tim replied, throwing her roughly down onto the settee. 'It was a good thing you saw her, but we could have done without this tonight.'

'What are you going to do with her?'

Kirsty couldn't believe what was happening. She stared up at them in silence, knowing that whatever they decided it wasn't going to be good news. She looked from one to the other, then at the people around the table. The atmosphere was fraught with tension.

'I don't know yet. We need to sort this lot out first. But she's seen too much.'

'Just like her father did,' Bulldog said, looking directly at her as he said it.

She jumped on his words. 'What do you mean? What did he see?'

'Never you mind.'

But she was catching on now, the images she'd seen coming together, as she filtered and processed them. The two people she'd observed arriving that first time she'd come here, when Bulldog had peered out of the window; the people sitting round the table – their faces, now she studied them more closely, filled with confusion and apprehension. They looked foreign and you didn't need to be an expert in body language to see the tension and vulnerability emanating from them as their eyes flicked to each other, frightened and disorientated. She recalled how they'd almost seemed to tumble out of the white van, exhausted and dishevelled as they'd walk up the path to the house. Comprehension dawned.

'You're people smugglers…' she said, her eyes turning back to Tim in shock.

'Aren't you the clever one? Take her into the bedroom and tie her up,' he said to Bulldog. 'We'll decide what we're doing with her when Simon gets here.'

'Simon's involved in all this? I don't believe it.'

She felt herself being hauled roughly up from the settee.

'Then don't.' He was already turning away from her, his mind clearly on more important things as she was dragged off into one of the bedrooms.

'Now we can do this the easy way or the hard way,' Bulldog said to her grimly, throwing her down onto the bed and pulling a length of rope from one of the drawers. 'Which is it gonna be?'

Common sense told her there was no point fighting him: she'd learnt that lesson if nothing else tonight. She lay quietly as he pulled her hands together behind her back, trying to keep just a chink between her fingers in the vain hope that at some point it might make it a little easier to work them free. He worked swiftly and deftly, and five minutes later, she was trussed neatly as a chicken, hands and legs – with a gag between her lips for good measure.

'Don't try to be clever,' was Bulldog's parting shot as he left her on the bed. 'Otherwise we might just have to chuck you out the window head first and be done with you.'

She didn't doubt for one moment that he'd do it.

CHAPTER THIRTY-SIX

Luke sat at the traffic lights, waiting for them to turn green, and heard his mobile ping. Kirsty – thank God for that. He grabbed the phone and looked at the screen. But as he read the message he frowned. Her reply made no sense at all.

He stared at the message and his blood chilled. Had something gone wrong? Was she trying to tell him something?

His first instinct was to turn around and head straight back to Barnet, but he was only two minutes from Mark's now, and forcing himself to think rationally, he decided to offload the computer first so that Mark could at least get to work on that.

He took a minute to think about a carefully worded reply. Her message had been deliberately neutral and if she was in any sort of trouble then his needed to be the same, but he also needed to know if she was okay.

'That's a shame. What's up? Hope it's nothing serious?'

As he pulled into Mark's driveway a few minutes later, he still hadn't received a reply.

'Are you kidding me?' Mark asked in horrified tones. 'You never told me the computer was *stolen*.'

'It's not,' Luke said tersely. 'It's borrowed. The plan is to return it tonight before he even realises it's gone.'

'Luke—'

'I know.'

'You're a *solicitor*.'

'I know that, too.'

And it worried him. He'd acted illegally tonight; there was no escaping it. He could be struck off by the SDT if it came out. But the realisation was no more than a fleeting notion in his head before it was instantly dismissed. He realised now what he should always have realised … that without Kirsty his life was meaningless anyway.

'I get that Kirsty means a lot to you—'

'I'd do the same for any friend,' Luke interrupted impatiently, 'wouldn't you? All we're asking is that you delete any video footage of her and Simon Jordan. No one should be able to get away with doing that sort of thing, Mark – not unless it's by mutual consent.'

'I realise that, but I don't like the sound of it.'

'And you think I do? How would you feel if it was Linda someone had done that to? Look, I haven't got time to argue about this now. I'm worried Kirsty might be in trouble and I need to go and find her. I'm asking you as a mate to do this. Just find any compromising stuff that's got Kirsty on it and wipe it. I'll hope to be back in an hour or so to pick it up again.' He looked at his watch and hesitated. It was nine-thirty.

'I can't believe I'm saying this, but … if you haven't heard from me in the next hour – call the police and report us missing. If everything's alright, I'll definitely call you before then to let you know.' He racked his brains, trying to remember the name of the detective Kirsty had said was handling her father's case. Hiskin? Hascombe? The name eluded him and he swore under his breath. 'If you don't hear from me and you call them, just mention that there may be a connection to the death of Dominic Cartwright. And here …'

He pulled a pen out and scribbled something on a scrap of paper that was lying on the coffee table. 'This is Simon Jordan's address. It's where Kirsty was heading and where I'm off to now.'

'I don't like the sound of this. Maybe I should come with you?'

'No. The best thing you can do is get to work on that computer – please. I'll be fine. But, as I say … if I haven't rung you within the next hour, then call the police.'

'Okay … if you say so, but for God's sake be careful.'

'Don't worry,' Luke said grimly. 'I will.'

Outside Simon Jordan's flat, Luke looked about him. His heart missed a beat as he spotted Kirsty's Mini parked on the other side of the road. He moved quickly over to it. It was empty.

Where the hell was she? He'd tried to call her from his car but she hadn't picked up – and she hadn't responded to his text. He looked back in the direction of Simon's flat, noting the dim lighting. It didn't look like anyone was there, but he needed to make sure and there was only one way to find out. Taking a deep breath, he crossed the road, walked up to the front door and rang the bell.

No response.

He looked at his phone for the hundredth time. His anxiety was getting the better of him. In fact it was getting to manic proportions. Why wasn't she answering? The fear that something might have happened to her was all-consuming, making him realise he didn't give a toss about what had gone on in the past – he just needed to know she was going to be with him in the future.

He punched out her number and waited. Again, no answer; it rang six times then went to voicemail.

'Hi, it's Luke. Mark and I are wondering what the problem is and if we can help at all? Give me a call.'

He returned the phone to his jacket pocket and, for want of anything better to do, headed back to his car. He'd wait until Simon got back. It was all he could do.

He'd only been sitting there for five minutes when his phone rang. He grabbed it from his pocket, but it was only Mark.

'What's happening?' his friend asked.

'Not a lot. Kirsty's car's here but it doesn't look like either she or Simon are. I don't know what's going on.'

'Well, I don't want to worry you more, but I think you should call the police now.'

'*What!? Why?*'

'There's some serious shit on this guy's computer, man. And I mean serious. Kirsty's not the only one he's videoed. There's footage of eight other women and it's not pretty. Looks to me like he drugs them or something, then likes to film himself doing all sorts of things to them. It's highly incriminating stuff – and he's going to be pissed when he finds out you've got hold of it.'

'Shit.'

Out of the corner of his eye, Luke saw Simon Jordan's car pull into his driveway. He sat bolt upright in his seat.

'Simon's just got back,' he said into the phone. 'And Kirsty's not with him. I need to speak to him.'

'I don't think you should do that, man. Call the police and wait for them to come.'

Luke watched as Simon climbed hurriedly out of his car.

'It'll take too long.'

Luke was already opening his own door. 'I need to find out what's happened to Kirsty. I've got to go.' He hesitated, but in view of what Mark had told him, he knew he had no other option. Now wasn't the time to be worrying about the fact that he, a solicitor, had aided and abetted a crime. 'Give me fifteen minutes. If I haven't called you back by then, call the police – get them over here as soon as you can. I'll call you later.'

He hung up and was out of his own car in an instant, but by the time he'd crossed the road, Simon had already entered the house and had shut the door behind him. He rang the doorbell.

'Who is it?' Simon's voice sounded jumpy on the other side of the door.

'It's Luke Talbot. I'm looking for Kirsty. Is she with you?'

There was a moment's pause. 'No. Why would she be?'

'Open the door, can you?'

'Luke, just go home. I'm telling you she's not here.'

'Let me see for myself. Then I'll go.'

There was noise going on in the hallway, more people maybe? Then the door was flung open – and he found himself looking down the barrel of a gun.

He reeled back in shock. *'What the...'* His eyes spun from the weapon, to the man holding it.

'If you want to see Kirsty, you'd better come in,' the man said smoothly. 'And no false moves or you'll be history. There's a silencer attached to this gun.'

Luke looked in horror at Simon, noting the other man's discomfort as his gaze shifted away. 'You better do as he says,' he muttered.

'Where is she, Simon?'

'Come on. Move it ... upstairs,' the man ordered, slamming the door behind him with a resounding thud. 'Who else knows you're here?'

'The police, everyone,' Luke said, wishing he hadn't put the fifteen-minute deadline on that call.

The other man glared at Simon. 'See what you've done? You better hope he's bluffing.'

Luke heard Simon's voice, scared and bleating behind him.

'I haven't done anything. I don't know what this is about any more than you do.'

They were upstairs in the flat now, and Luke just about had time to take in his surroundings and the number of people there, before a sharp blow to the back of his head had him crashing to the floor.

It was nearly eleven when Harry's phone rang, bursting into the silence of the night and rousing him from the unreal state he'd drifted into, thinking about his grandmother. She'd been dead a while now and as he sat there still holding her hand, he could only be glad. He thanked God that his mother hadn't popped in to say goodnight. He wouldn't have relished hiding the truth from her – but if he'd told her what Jean had done, he wouldn't have put it past her to call an ambulance.

Her end, when it came, had been the death she'd wanted – a peaceful passing where the length between breaths had simply got longer until they'd finally ceased altogether.

Now, he lifted her hand and kissed it, gently replacing it on the cover before looking at his mobile to see who was calling.

Beth.

He frowned. It had to be urgent for her to be calling at this time of night.

Rising from his grandmother's side, his eyes were caught by the two incriminating pill containers sitting on her bedside table. He hesitated for only a moment, before picking them up and slipping them into his pocket.

'Beth,' he said, walking out of the room and closing the door behind him. 'What's up?'

'I've just been talking to a friend of Kirsty Cartwright's. He thinks she's gone missing and wants us to check it out.'

'*What?* Where are you?'

'In the car, heading over to Barnet. The guy who's reported her missing, a Mark Berryman, had an address where she was last known to be going. And guess where it was? 28 Myton Road – Paul Copeland's address. It's complicated but if you meet me there, I'll wait for you and fill you in. Peterson's heading over to Berryman's as we speak.'

Harry hesitated, thinking of his grandmother lying in her bed on the other side of the door. But he could almost hear her voice in his head. *Don't mind me, boy, you go and do what needs to be done. I'm not going anywhere now.*

And that was the truth of it, he thought, as he shut off his phone and headed quietly down the stairs. The lights were out; his parents had gone up for the night. Nothing to be gained by alerting them tonight to the fact that she was dead. Probably better all round if they simply found her like that in the morning.

The shaft of guilt that pierced him at the thought made him realise his agonising wasn't over with yet. But he'd have plenty of time to ponder that one. For now, he had a job to do.

CHAPTER THIRTY-SEVEN

Luke came to with a groan. He felt stiff and cramped, every muscle in his legs and arms screaming for release. He was lying on the floor, hands and legs tied securely together. His head was pounding and the effort it took to even open his eyes was tremendous – but once he'd managed it, all of that paled into insignificance as he gradually became aware of his surroundings and found his gaze resting on Kirsty's anxious face. She was lying on her side on a bed above him, trussed up as efficiently as he was, her green eyes enormous in her face.

Kirsty.

He thought he'd spoken her name out loud and was surprised that no sound was forthcoming. It was then he realised that on top of everything else, he was gagged. And so was she.

He hadn't a clue what was going on, but it was obvious they needed to get out of there fast – something that was obviously easier said than done.

He tried a reassuring smile aware that it probably just came out as a slight twisting of his facial muscles. But it seemed to have the desired effect as Kirsty's face did a similar muscle-contorting exercise. For a moment it was enough that she was safe.

But for how much longer was another matter. As the fog in his mind cleared and his memory returned, he had no doubt that the man with the gun, whoever he was, meant business.

He tried to wiggle his hands, to get some purchase, but they'd done a good job of tying him up. He cursed himself for not being more prepared. He had a penknife in the boot of his car, but what good was it there? He needed it here to cut through the rope. He frowned, trying to clear his head. It was obvious that wiggling his hands wasn't going to achieve anything but he observed his fingers were free. If Kirsty's were, too, maybe they could work on each other's knots. He caught her eye again and jerked his head towards the floor. He saw her eyebrows crease in puzzlement. He did the gesture again, this time nodding his head at her before gesticulating to the ground. He saw that she'd got it as she began to edge herself slowly to the side of the bed, heaving herself up to a sitting position and dangling her legs to the floor. Within a few seconds she was standing, frowning down at him as she tried to work out the simplest and possibly least painful way of joining him on the floor. It clearly wasn't as easy as it looked with her feet tied firmly together. Eventually, she bent her knees as low as she could and toppled over with a soft thud, her head landing on his stomach, and knocking the breath out of him. It grounded him having her close to him like that and he savoured the moment briefly, before edging out from underneath her.

She turned to face him and started to move closer but he shook his head at her. She stopped. He considered for a moment then made a big movement of twisting his head to the side. She wasn't getting it. He thought some more, then repeated the action, nodding at her, then turning his head in a semicircular motion to the side. Her expression cleared and she turned so that her back was presented to him. Immediately, he did the same, turning his back to her and edging closer until he could feel their hands touching. He stroked her fingers for just a moment, then slowly, clumsily, he got to work on her ropes.

'Shit...' Harry said in a drawn-out breath when Beth had finished filling him in. They were sitting in his car outside Simon Jordan's house, and his mind worked frantically over what she'd just told him.

'So in a nutshell,' Beth said, 'Kirsty Cartwright broke into Simon Jordan's office to get hold of his computer to remove some dirty images he held of her, and now she's gone missing. And this guy Mark reckons there's other stuff on the computer he's got that's extremely incriminating for Simon if we should get hold of it. That's why Geoff's gone over there to take a look.'

Her phone rang and she answered it. 'Hi, Geoff. *What ... are you sure? Bloody hell* – we're outside his house now. We're about to go in and question him about Kirsty Cartwright ... okay ... that sounds like a plan. I'll tell Harry ... No, I think we'll be fine but if Harry says different I'll call you back ... Who, the boyfriend? No ... not that I can see.' Her eyes did a quick sweep of the other cars in the road. 'You'd have thought he'd have made his presence known when my police car turned up if he was here. Maybe he's gone missing, too. Okay, we'll catch up later.'

She ended the call and looked at Harry. 'You probably guessed that was Geoff. He reckons there's loads of shit on that computer that spells big trouble for Simon Jordan – he also says that Kirsty's ex-boyfriend, Luke Talbot, still hasn't turned up. Apparently, he told Mark he was going to tackle Simon about Kirsty's disappearance and he hasn't heard from him since.'

'So where the hell are they all?'

Beth shrugged, but there was a gleam in her eye. 'You'll never guess what he said about the computer? He reckons this guy could be going around drugging women and then taking them back to his place to film himself doing dodgy stuff with them. He said rape's just the beginning of it and he's getting the computer back to the station now to let Forensics at it.'

Harry's eyes narrowed. 'Are we sure? Sure it's Jordan, I mean?'

'No doubt, apparently. He clearly gets off seeing himself in movies, according to Geoff.'

'Right. Well, we've got specific grounds for questioning him now. Let's go get him.'

'You know what I'm thinking?'

Harry turned back to her. 'What?'

'I'm wondering if Simon Jordan could be the rapist that DCI Murray's been digging into? Is that possible, do you think? And if so, should we be calling him? Murray, I mean?'

Harry was already out of the car. 'Time enough for that later. First off, we need to see if he's got Kirsty Cartwright in there.'

He rang the doorbell and waited. When there was no immediate response he knocked heavily on the door.

Upstairs in the flat, Bulldog peered cautiously out of the window. The first thing he saw was the police car parked on the other side of the road.

'It's the cops,' he said, turning to face the room.

'How many?' Tim Burman rasped.

'Looks like just the one car that I can see.'

Tim Burman swung round to Simon. 'Get down there and get rid of them,' he growled, pushing him to the door.

'What shall I say?'

'I don't care. Just get rid of them. And if they won't go, take them into your flat and make sure you shut the door behind you. That way it'll give us a bit of time to clear this place. The last thing we want is them traipsing up here. Call me when they've gone.'

At the bottom of the stairs in the hall, Simon hesitated. He was sweating profusely and he took a moment to steady himself. 'I'm coming,' he called out, quickly opening his front door before moving over to let them in. On the doorstep were the same two police officers he'd seen previously.

'Mr Jordan – you may remember me, Harry Briscombe from Hertfordshire Police?'

'Yeah, sure. What's going on?'

'We're looking for Kirsty Cartwright.'

'Kirsty?'

'Yes, it seems she's gone missing.'

'You're kidding. Well, I'm sorry to hear that but I don't understand. How can I help?'

'You've not seen her tonight? We have reason to believe she was coming here to see you.'

'No, I haven't. I've been out all evening – having dinner with her brother, as it happens. I've only just got in.'

'Would you mind if we came in to verify that? Took a look round your flat?'

'Yes, I would, actually. Do you have a warrant?'

'No, but I might think you've got something to hide if you don't let us in, and I can pick one up pretty quickly.'

Simon appeared torn and Harry waited, giving him time.

'Well, you can come into the flat if you want but if you want to do any more than that you'll need a warrant.'

'Fair enough, sir.'

Once inside the flat, he closed the door and threw his keys onto the side table. His face glistened with sweat and he pulled a handkerchief from his pocket as he turned to face them. Clearly nervous, Harry thought, not without some satisfaction. In fact, shit-scared.

'Do you mind telling me when you last saw Kirsty?' he asked.

'Yesterday evening. She dropped round here for a coffee. You can ask her brother Robbie. He can verify that – plus the fact that I've been with him all evening tonight. I mean … I don't get why you think she'd be here. And what gives you the right to start questioning me as if I'm a bloody criminal? It may have escaped your memory but I'm a solicitor.'

'We have it on good authority that Kirsty Cartwright's last known movements this evening were that she was heading over to this flat, to relieve you of your laptop. Which I understand has some rather incriminating pictures of her on it?'

Harry kept the full extent of his knowledge regarding Simon's computer to himself for the time being, but he observed how the colour drained from Simon's face as his eyes shot to where his tablet sat nestled on some folders on his desk.

'Why would she do that?' he blustered. 'And who told you that anyway? I'd say that whatever happened in private between me and Kirsty is our concern. If we choose to film ourselves it's not against the law, and it's no one else's business but our own.'

'Except that Kirsty didn't choose to film anything. You filmed her without her knowledge and she was upset about that, wasn't she? She told her boyfriend Luke Talbot about it. Have you seen Mr Talbot this evening?'

'No.'

'Well, apparently he, too, was on his way here – and he,

too, it seems, has suddenly gone missing. Bit of a coincidence, wouldn't you agree?'

'I haven't the faintest idea what you're talking about. I told you, I've been out all night. If they've both disappeared, maybe they've gone off together. Maybe they're over at Luke's place.'

'Both their cars are outside.'

Simon pulled out his mobile and punched in a number. 'Here, I'm calling Robbie Cartwright now. He'll tell you. I only left theirs about half an hour ago. How that can have given me time to dispose of two full-grown adults, I have no idea.'

Harry took the phone from him as a sleepy voice answered the call. 'Mrs Cartwright? This is Sergeant Briscombe from Hertfordshire Police …I'm sorry to be calling you so late …'

By the time Harry had finished the call, he was forced to admit he was thrown. The Cartwrights had confirmed everything Simon had said. On top of that, he now had Robert Cartwright worried sick about his sister.

'What do you mean she's missing? Who told you that?'

'We don't know any more than you do at the moment, Mr Cartwright, but she's been reported missing by a friend of hers, a guy called Mark Berryman. Do you know him?'

'Yes, I do.'

'Well, I can only suggest you give him a call if you want to know any more. We've found no evidence so far to suggest that anything untoward has happened to your sister, but obviously we're taking the report seriously and want to check it out. We'll get back to you as soon as we know anything.'

He ended the call, handing the phone back to Simon Jordan, and considered the options. Jordan was right … he wouldn't have had the time to do anything as major as disposing of two adults on his own between getting back here, and Harry and Beth arriving.

But maybe he hadn't done it on his own?

Harry's thoughts switched to the other person whose name had a habit of cropping up in their investigation. Tim Burman.

And they shared the same address.

'Is Tim Burman in?'

'I don't know,' Simon said in an exaggeratedly patient voice, more confident now his alibi had been backed up. 'As I keep telling you, I've not been back long. I've not heard any noise, though, so I think he may be out.'

'Let's go see, shall we?'

A muffled sound from what was probably a bedroom had Harry and Beth stopping in their stride.

'What was that?' Harry asked.

'What?'

'That noise. It sounded like it was coming from behind that door.'

'It's probably upstairs. The noise really carries through the floorboards. Maybe Tim is in, after all.'

Harry was already striding towards the door.

'Don't go any further,' Simon said sharply. 'I've just about had enough of all this. If you want to search my flat you'll do it the proper way … with a warrant.'

Another sound, more of a moan this time, and Harry's steps quickened. Totally disregarding Simon's order he threw the door open, stopping dead in his tracks at the sight that confronted him. A woman gagged and handcuffed to the bedposts stared back at him in absolute terror.

But it wasn't Kirsty Cartwright.

As he rushed towards the bed to free her, he remembered the picture of Katrina Midwood, the woman who'd been reported missing that morning. There was no doubt in his mind that this was her.

'Beth, call an ambulance and request urgent backup!' he shouted, as he fumbled to untie the woman's gag.

'Oh no you don't.'

He swung round at the sound of Beth's voice, just in time to see her launch herself at Simon Jordan and headbutt him in the stomach, bringing him crashing down to the ground.

'Jeez ...' Harry abandoned what he was doing and sprinted into the other room where Beth and Simon were now tussling on the floor. Throwing himself at the other man, Harry hauled him up off Beth and sent a fist crashing into his jaw that sent him flying back down onto the ground again. He made no further move to resist them as he lay there, nursing his jaw in his hands, looking at them aggressively.

'He was trying to escape,' Beth said breathlessly, her eyes shining with exhilaration. 'I can't believe I brought him down.'

'That was some tackle,' Harry said admiringly. 'Are you okay?'

'I'm fine. I knew my self-defence classes would come in useful one day.'

'Don't move,' Harry barked at Simon when he would have sat up. He pulled out his phone. 'Beth, can you see to the girl in there? I'll get some backup and a couple of warrants for here and Burman's flat.'

Outside in the street, Bulldog loaded the last of the upstairs flat's inhabitants into the van parked out in the road. At their feet, Kirsty and Luke, hands still tied, bounced helplessly on the hard floor as it was driven swiftly away into the night.

Back in the incident room an hour later, Beth yawned and took a sip from her coffee as she and Harry watched the video footage Geoff Peterson had isolated for them.

'Got him,' Harry said with quiet satisfaction, as he viewed a full facial image of Simon Jordan having sex with an unconscious woman.

'Yeah, but … that's not his flat, is it? Look at the decor in the bedroom – it's much too posh.'

Harry frowned. She was right.

Then his brow cleared. 'It must be his other flat … the one in Whetstone. We'll need to check that out as well. Get Geoff to arrange for another warrant, will you? In the meantime …' His face was grim. 'Time could be running out for Kirsty Cartwright and Luke Talbot. We need to seriously put the wind up Simon Jordan and get him to tell us where they are. I don't believe him when he says he doesn't know. Has his solicitor arrived yet?'

'He's in there with him now.'

'Right. Let's get on, then.'

In the interview room, Simon was looking haggard as Harry switched on the interview tape and went through the usual procedure.

'Just to confirm for the records that you've requested the presence of your solicitor, Mr Raymond Edmondson, for the duration of this interview. Now, I will ask you again, Mr Jordan, do you have any information concerning the whereabouts of either Kirsty Cartwright or Luke Talbot?'

'No. I've already told you that. How many more times do I need to say it?'

'As many times as it takes for you to tell us the truth. But maybe we need to be a bit franker about what we already know, to encourage you to be more open and honest with us.'

Simon looked at him warily. 'What do you mean?'

'Were you aware, for example, that Kirsty had already carried out the first part of her plan tonight? Namely, to break into your office in Whetstone and relieve you of your office computer?'

'*What?* No way. You're lying.'

'I've got no reason to lie. We've taken a look at that computer and I think you know what we've found on it.'

Silence.

'For the sake of the tape, I'll clarify that. We found a number of images on your computer that would seem to suggest you're a serial sex offender. It's obvious that most, if not all, the women you're filmed having sex with have been drugged. Interestingly, my boss has been working on unsolved sex attacks in the area. As we speak, my colleagues are seeing what they can do to match the pictures we have on your computer to some of the victims on our files. I think we both know what the results of that will be.'

'That's an office computer. There are several of us there. Anyone could have copied those images onto it.'

'But it's your face we see on the screen, abusing those women. We see it as clear as day. And of course there's your latest victim, Katrina Midwood – currently in Barnet Hospital. How do you explain her away?'

'She was there of her own free will. She was quite happy to leave with me last night and take part in a bit of bondage.' He smirked at Harry over the desk. 'You should try it sometime. It might take on an added dimension with the job you do – the handcuffs and all that.'

'Which might have worked as a defence if we hadn't also got video footage of our own from the nightclub last night where, despite the wig you were wearing, you can clearly be identified, and are seen slipping some liquid into Katerina Midwood's drink as well as your own. What was that?'

Simon made no response and Harry let him stew on it for a while before leaning forward in a conciliatory fashion.

'Look, Simon. You're shot, we both know it. And you can go one of two ways. You either stick it out and give us the silent treatment over Kirsty's whereabouts, or you decide to be cooperative and help us out. If you do the latter, I'll make sure your cooperation goes on record. If you had anything to do with Kirsty's disappearance, now's the time to tell us. It can't do any good prolonging things. We've got enough to hold you in custody until we either find Kirsty and Luke, or charge you. I'm going to give you ten minutes to think about it and talk to your solicitor. I hope when I get back, you'll have had time to realise that the best thing you can do now is cooperate with us.'

CHAPTER THIRTY-EIGHT

Kirsty lay on the floor of the van and wondered how much more she could take of the stink of petrol and chemicals clogging her nose, threatening to make her spew. It was cramped and dark in the back of the van and she was grateful for the reassuring solidness of Luke's form behind her. She wished more than anything that she didn't have the gag on her mouth; that she could talk to him, tell him how sorry she was for dragging him into all this – how much she loved him. On a scale of one to ten, pride didn't rate highly now that her life was in danger. She wanted him to know there could never be anyone else for her.

She felt the pressure of a stinking shoe pressed close to her face and tried not to gag. Not a word was being spoken in the van by its other occupants and it felt spooky knowing there were at least half a dozen people seated around them, none of them saying a word. What if one of them suddenly leapt up and cut her throat? She tried not to let her imagination run riot and pressed closer to Luke. She felt him shuffle at her side, realised he was turning over, and then once again she felt the slow, inexorable movements of his fingers as they went back to work on her ropes in the dark. She wasn't at all hopeful that even if he freed her she'd be capable of doing anything, but she was grateful for the sense of hope it gave her.

It felt like an age, but probably wasn't actually that long, before they came to an abrupt stop. She heard the sound of doors being opened outside and then the van lurched briefly forward again before coming to a final halt. The engine switched off. Wherever they'd been heading they'd clearly arrived. She blinked hard as the van doors were flung open and bright lights shone into the back of the van. Luke had managed to loosen off her ropes quite considerably, she realised, but for now she held the threads firmly in her grip not wanting to give anything away.

Rough hands hauled her forward as Bulldog slung her effortlessly over a hefty shoulder. Luke, she noticed, was dragged to the edge of the van and made to stand on the ground.

They were in a large warehouse, pretty empty apart from a dozen or so beds and chairs lined up against the walls. It looked like a poor man's dormitory, but right now Kirsty would have given anything to lie down on one of those beds, close her eyes and wake up to find that all this was a horrific dream. It didn't look like her wish would be granted, as she was dumped unceremoniously onto the floor then pushed down into a sitting position against the wall. Luke was shoved into place next to her.

'Everyone out,' Tim Burman barked inside the van. He turned to Bulldog as, one by one, the other occupants jumped out. His face was tight and it was clear he was battling to control his anger and not making a good job of it. 'We don't need this. I'll kill that bastard Simon when I get my hands on him.'

'I don't understand what's going on,' Bulldog said. 'What was she doing in his flat in the first place?'

'Don't ask me. We shouldn't have got involved. If you hadn't spotted her in her car we wouldn't even have known she was there.'

'I thought she was spying on us. I didn't think we could just leave her there after she'd seen this lot.'

Tim walked over to where Kirsty and Luke were sitting. Kneeling on one knee, he reached round and tugged at the knot, ripping Kirsty's gag off.

'So how about you tell us now what you were doing in Simon's flat tonight?'

He had the manner of a man not about to put up with any bullshit, and Kirsty tried not to be too intimidated. She stretched her jaw, trying to ease the discomfort from her mouth.

'I told you. I was borrowing his laptop.'

'Without his knowledge.'

Kirsty hesitated but decided she had nothing to gain by not telling the truth – and a lot to lose.

'He's got stuff on there – personal stuff that I wanted off. I knew he was round at my brother's tonight so I–'

'Broke in.'

'*Let* myself in – I had a key. I didn't cause any damage and I was going to give him the computer back once I'd wiped it.'

'And what about him?' He jerked his head at Luke. His whole manner was wired, his eyes shifting back and forth to the warehouse doors as if expecting the police to rush in at any minute.

'Luke knew what I was doing and he got worried when I didn't pick up on his messages. He was coming round to check I was okay. That's all. Look, I don't know what all this is about, but my problem isn't with you–'

'It is now, babe.' His tone was uncompromising. 'You've seen too much.'

Kirsty shook her head vehemently. 'We haven't seen

anything – we're not interested in what you're doing. Whatever it is, it's your business–'

He gave her a pitying smile. 'Are you trying to tell me that if I release you now, you'd forget all about what's gone on tonight and not go straight to the police and tell them everything you know? Because if you are, we both know you're lying.'

'Did you kill my father?'

The words were out before she could stop them and she immediately wished them unsaid, knowing she was only digging herself a deeper hole. She saw straight away from the cruel twist to his lips that he had done – and that knowledge alone was enough to seal her fate.

He hesitated, as if wondering how much to tell her, but then, clearly deciding it would all be irrelevant soon enough anyway, he gave a shrug. 'Both of you are too nosy for your own good. Yes, I had him killed – I didn't do it personally, but he had to be got rid of. He insisted on inspecting the flat that day when I was out and Tanya didn't realise not to let him in. Unfortunately, like you, he witnessed the visitors we had – rather a lot of them that day – and it seems he clicked straight away as to who they were. He didn't let on, though, not then. Luckily for me, he thought Simon might be involved and chose to confront him before doing anything about it. He went straight over to see him and when he wasn't there, he called him. Told him that the only reason he wasn't going straight to the police was because of his friendship with Simon's father. They arranged to meet at a pub after your dad's next appointment, only sadly, of course, your father never made that meeting.'

'*Simon* was involved in his death?' She couldn't believe it.

'Indirectly. He panicked. He does a lot of the legal – or perhaps I should say *illegal* – stuff for me. He called me to ask what he should do, how he should handle things. He's a bit naive like that – didn't realise that there was only ever going to be one option. What we do is serious shit, with serious people. We can't afford to leave loose ends lying around.'

And she and Luke had just become loose ends, she realised bleakly.

Her eyes flashed to Luke's and she could see he was thinking the same thing.

'What are you going to do with us?'

Some little demon pushed her to ask the question, even though she didn't want to hear the answer.

'You know what? I'm really pissed off with you for putting me in this position. It's not like I take pleasure in killing people. Usually I'm Mr Nice Guy. I fix these poor sods up with a new home, get them fresh identities and give them a break. I make a lot of money out of it, but I work fucking hard, and it was all going well until you and your father – and that bloody Paul Copeland – stuck your oars in. This isn't a business where you can let that sort of thing happen – one chink in the armour and the whole chain collapses. I'm sorry, I really am … but I'm sure you can see I have no choice. I have to get rid of you.'

He looked so *normal* … yet here he was talking about killing them as if it was a regrettable inconvenience.

'How can you sleep with people's deaths on your conscience?'

He gave a thin smile. 'I've always had a bit of a bypass on the compassionate gene. I see it as a strength, not a weakness.'

At her side, Luke made a noise. Tim looked at him, then shrugged and untied his gag, too. 'Got something to say?'

Luke's glance flicked to Kirsty before moving back to the other man's face. 'Look – as Kirsty said, we're not out to make trouble for you. And we're certainly not prepared to die for a cause that's got nothing to do with us. I'm a solicitor – I could even be useful to you–'

'Do you take me for a fool? I've been doing this job for three years now and the only reason I get away with it is because I never take chances. Someone even blinks in my direction for too long and I take them out. Some might say I'm paranoid about it, but it's kept me out of trouble so far. You won't be changing my mind.'

Again, Kirsty was shocked by the detached, almost rational way he said it. As if it wasn't people's lives he was talking about, just a practical solution to an irritating problem. His phone rang and he straightened up to answer it. He listened for a while, his mouth tightening into an ominous line.

'How long ago?' he barked. 'Why didn't you phone me sooner? Thank God we got them out. No. Don't do anything. Just stay where you are and watch the house. Make sure you're not seen. And put someone on to watch his flat in Whetstone in case they release him and he goes back there. Let me know if anything happens – and I mean *anything*. No one goes near that flat until I give the all-clear. We may need to move our base.'

He clicked off the phone, his expression ugly. 'See what you've started?'

He kicked Luke viciously in the ribs, making him crease up in pain. 'They've arrested Simon and knowing that slimy little toad, he'll do anything to save his own skin. Alan, make sure none of that lot go anywhere out of this building – not even for a piss. As for these two …' He turned back to look at them. 'Call Monty. Get him to bring the car over. Tell him we've got another job for him.'

CHAPTER THIRTY-NINE

'Any news on Tim Burman returning to the flat?' Harry asked Geoff Peterson, grabbing himself a coffee from the machine and stirring two teaspoons of sugar into it. He'd been disappointed but not really surprised that there'd been no one at home when they'd broken into Burman's flat.

'Nope. No sign of anyone. We've left a uniform on guard at the house and he'll call if anyone comes back.'

'Why are you so interested in him?' Beth asked.

'Because if Simon is responsible for Kirsty and Luke's disappearance, he couldn't have dealt with them on his own in the time-span he had. Geographically, Burman's the logical one to have helped him out.'

'But we don't even know the guy's involved in anything.'

'Susan Porter and Kirsty Cartwright seemed to believe he was. And now Kirsty's gone missing, I'm inclined to give their suspicions more credence.'

He downed his drink and chucked the cup in the bin. It was well past midnight and beginning to feel like it.

'Okay. Let's see what Simon Jordan's got to say for himself now he's had some time to think.'

Back in the interview room, Harry carefully laid out photographs of four women on the table. Then he looked at Simon Jordan.

'For the benefit of the tape, I've placed four photographs onto the table. Do you recognise any of these women, Mr Jordan?'

'No.'

Harry pushed them closer to him. 'Look harder.'

Simon cast them a cursory glance and shrugged. 'They don't look familiar.'

'You must have a very short memory. These pictures have been extracted from videos we found on your computer – all filmed within the last year. All four of these women were victims of sex attacks, with the same pattern of attack identified – and the dates of those reported attacks coincide with the dates on these videos. Do you have an explanation for that?'

Simon glanced uneasily at his solicitor before saying, 'As I said, it's an office computer – anyone could have put those films on it.'

'My colleagues are looking at your home laptop as we speak. If the same or similar images are on there...'

The solicitor leant closer to Simon and whispered something in his ear. Simon hesitated for a moment, then nodded.

'If my client tells you everything he knows, we'll expect some sort of a deal–'

Harry shook his head. 'It doesn't work like that. He needs to realise the severity of his situation. The crimes he's likely to be charged with are serious. We have video evidence of him actively participating in what looks like serial rape and other sex offences. If he tells us now where Kirsty Cartwright, and possibly Luke Talbot are, it's not going to change any of that but it will at least show in his favour.

'I don't know where Kirsty or Luke are, I told you that.'

'Mr Jordan–'

'It's the truth. I don't.' He hesitated, his expression calculating. 'But I may know who does.'

'Who?'

'I'm not telling you anything unless you give me something in return.'

Harry kept his expression neutral with difficulty. 'That's not going to happen and the sooner you realise it, the better. Do I need to spell it out to you how serious the charges are that you're facing?' He leant forward, his face grim. 'You're already facing serious charges of rape and physical assault. If anything happens to Kirsty Cartwright that we discover at a later date you could have prevented, it'll make things a lot worse for you. I think you need to think on that. We need you to tell us the truth – not only regarding the whereabouts of Kirsty and Luke, but also anything else you may know about Paul Copeland and possibly Dominic Cartwright. At the moment you're the common link between them – and that's not looking good for you.'

For a long moment, Simon Jordan held Harry's gaze, his expression stubborn, but just as Harry was resigning himself to the fact that they were set for a stand-off, he took a deep breath and emitted a heavy sigh.

'Look, I'm shit-scared telling you this. It's big – bigger than I ever realised. I would never have got involved if I'd known – and once I'd got sucked in, there was no backing out. If I tell you what I know, I want your word you'll give me some sort of protection, because if not, when they find out I dumped them in it, it'll be curtains for me just like it was for Dom and Copeland.'

Harry eyes narrowed, but he nodded. 'If we feel your life's in danger because of information you give us, then we'll give you protection.'

'Have I got your word on that?'

'Yes.'

'Okay.' Simon visibly relaxed. 'Where do you want me to start?'

'At the beginning would be good.'

'Okay. So I'll start with Tim Burman.'

'The tenant in your flat?'

'Yes. The antique dealings are just a cover-up. It's not antiques he's importing. It's people.'

Harry let out a breath. 'People smuggling?'

Simon nodded. 'He picks them up in France mostly and brings them back to the flat for a day or two before dispersing them. I ... assist with some of the paperwork. But I have nothing to do with smuggling them in.'

'Is your father involved as well?'

'God, no. This'll gut him.'

'So where did Paul Copeland fit in?'

'He became suspicious – tried to blackmail Tim. I didn't know at the time, I swear it, but Tim's guys did him over as a warning, and then apparently picked him up outside your police station where he was on his way to dob them in it.'

'Then they killed him?'

Simon nodded.

'For the sake of the tape, could you say that out loud please?'

'Yes, they told me they'd killed him.'

'What about Dominic Cartwright's death? Was Tim Burman responsible for that, too?'

He watched what looked like a genuine expression of remorse cross Simon Jordan's face.

'Yes. I never meant for that to happen, but Dom carried out an inspection of the flat just after Tim had picked up a new load of illegals and dropped them off there while he sorted a few things out. Dom was suspicious. He phoned me and asked me what the hell was going on – demanded that we met. I was out on an appointment and arranged to meet him at a pub near his next viewing to talk about it. I panicked. I phoned Tim … asked him what I should say. He told me I'd done the right thing and he'd meet us at the pub. I could have talked Dom down, I know I could, but I hadn't realised up to then how dangerous Tim was. How big this whole thing is. Dom never made that meeting. Tim saw to that.'

Harry's expression was grim as he looked at Simon across the table. 'Just so we're clear here. Are you saying it was Tim Burman who killed Dominic Cartwright?'

'Yes. Him or one of his henchmen. He told me it was a necessary safeguard.'

'Right. We need to know where Kirsty is right now. The longer we leave it, the more danger she's in. Do you want her to become a necessary safeguard, too?'

Simon shook his head.

'Then think. Where could Tim have taken them?'

'I have been thinking. The only place I know of is his lock-up in Hatfield – well, it's more like a small warehouse, really. He keeps his vans and odd bits of furniture there to back up his antiques alibi. He also uses it as a safe house for his 'customers', as he calls them, when they first arrive.'

Harry turned to Beth.

'He mentioned that when I spoke to him. Do we have an address? Did anyone check it out?'

'I took a quick look. It was locked up but I got a restricted view through the window. It was like Simon says … There was a small lorry in there and a few bits and pieces.'

Harry jumped up from his chair. 'Get Geoff in to finish off this interview, will you? We need to get over there.'

CHAPTER FORTY

Kirsty and Luke sat on the floor in a corner of the warehouse listening to Tim Burman telling his plan to Bulldog.

'As soon as Monty arrives with the car, load everyone back into the van. I'll make my way to the safe haven. Your first priority is to get rid of those two.' A quick toss of the head in their direction. 'After that you can head to Leicester and disperse this lot earlier than planned. They won't have proper papers, but as long as we dump them far enough from here, they won't be able to give anyone any information that could lead back to us. I'll call Terry and tell him to open up the shop to receive you. That'll give you an alibi for making the journey if you need one – you can say you were dropping off some furniture. Then meet me back at the safe haven tomorrow.'

Bulldog cast a cursory glance in Kirsty's direction. 'Where shall we dump them?'

'Wherever you want as long as it's not too close to here. Somewhere like the Great Woods at Cuffley would probably do. Won't be anyone around this time of night.'

Kirsty looked at Luke. She couldn't hide her fear. 'I'm so

sorry,' she whispered brokenly. 'I should never have involved
you–'

'Do you think I'd rather you were going through
this alone?'

'I'm sure you would. I should have listened to Robbie and
kept out of it.'

Luke gave a small shake of his head. 'It's not in your make-
up, Kirsty. Once you get your teeth into something…'

'Well, I was right to be suspicious, wasn't I?' she retorted
with a flash of spirit. 'Not that I get any satisfaction from that
now. They're going to kill us, aren't they?'

'Not if I can help it.'

'Have you got a plan?' She could hear the desperation in
her voice and felt ashamed of it.

'No, but I'm working on it.' He turned to look at where the
men were still talking, then said in a low voice, 'Turn around so
we're back to back again. Lean your head on my shoulder so
that it looks like you're just using me as a pillow to get some
rest. I'm almost there with your ropes now.'

Bulldog turned away from the window where he'd been
standing on watch, and looked at Tim.

'Monty's here.'

'Right. Get everyone back in the van. You know what
to do.'

Kirsty tugged at the ropes still binding her wrists. She still
wasn't free.

She felt herself being hauled to her feet by Bulldog. His
hands were on her waist, not on her arms, as he shoved her
towards the van. She felt his fingers splay over her hips, his
touch intrusive. 'Come on, my lovely,' he whispered in her ear.
'It's not all over for you quite yet.'

She shrank from him, hoping he didn't mean what she
thought he might.

In the van, she and Luke were once again thrown onto the

floor, the other occupants picking their way gingerly over them as they made their own ways to the bench seats provided. Then a slam of the doors and they were once again surrounded by darkness.

'Does anyone in here speak English?'

It was Luke's voice, sounding reassuringly normal as he asked the question.

Silence. Only the sound of the engine being started.

'Come on. Someone must speak English, surely?'

'I do.'

The voice was low and guttural, the accent heavy.

Both their heads turned in the direction of it and Luke spoke up again. 'Do you have a phone with a torch on it?'

A moment later, a small shaft of light filtered through the van.

'Thank you.' Luke looked up at the man. 'So you know what's happening here? With us, I mean?'

'They are going to kill you.' The man's voice was matter-of-fact, squashing any hope Kirsty might have had that they could get these people onside.

'They're going to try,' Luke said, 'but maybe if you helped us – if you called the police on your mobile, for example?'

'I am sorry, but we cannot help you,' the man said flatly. 'We have come through much to get to your country and cannot risk becoming caught by the police now. My wife and children are here already – all I want is to be with them now. You understand we are not war refugees? Everyone in this van is the same. If we get caught they will deport us.'

Kirsty couldn't see his expression in the dark, but the tone of his voice said it all, his words delivered with a weighty weariness that indicated he had no energy left – certainly not to fight the battles of people they didn't even know.

'But you can't just stand by and let them kill us!' she burst out.

The man shrugged. 'I have seen many people die. Two more – who are strangers to me? My duty is to my family. And I am no good to them in prison or dead.'

'Where have you come from?' Luke asked.

The man hesitated, but then perhaps realising they wouldn't be around to cause trouble anyway, replied, 'Afghanistan. It has taken us nearly a year to get here. Through Iran, then to Turkey on foot through the mountains – then from there to Greece on a boat, then Italy and finally France. We have been waiting in Calais for over three months. When they decided to close the Jungle, we were desperate. But we were lucky that we found someone with a boat.

'Ssh …'

Luke held his finger to his mouth and the van fell silent. From the front came raised voices and Kirsty strained her ears to hear what was going on.

'It's the fucking police, I tell you. You don't get three cars pulling into the yard like that with their lights turned off. We should go back, help them out.'

'Don't be bloody stupid.' It was Monty's voice, raised in argument as he slammed his foot hard on the accelerator. 'It's lucky we got out when we did. Keep your wits about you and *think*. If we get caught with this lot in the back we're all done for. Call Tim. Warn him. It's the best we can do.'

In the lead car, Harry pulled to a halt outside the lock-up. There were lights on inside. Good sign. He flicked the speaker control.

'Tom, where are you?'

'I'm heading round the back.' There was silence before his voice came again. 'There's one small exit door they could use but the area's fenced off. The only way out is along the side passage to the front where you are.'

'So if they're in there, we've got them.'

'Looks like it.'

'How long before armed response get here?'

'Five minutes.'

'Right. We'll wait for backup unless it looks like they're making plans to move, in which case–'

Even as he spoke, the small door to the side of the up-and-over was flung open and a man belted hell for leather in the direction of the main road.

'Shit! Everybody on him.'

Harry flung open his car door and was out in a trice, heading after the man.

'Stop. Police.'

It rarely worked and this time was no different, as the man showed no sign of slowing his pace.

Two steps behind Harry, Beth seemed to be having no difficulty keeping up with him, and he found himself pushing himself to his limit, aware that, whilst this was no competition, he certainly didn't relish the image of his female DC outrunning him. They were gaining on the man. There was perhaps fifty yards between them when he suddenly halted, swung around and pointed a gun directly at them. It was Tim Burman.

'Stop!' he shouted. 'Or I'll fire.'

'Do that and you'll be in even bigger trouble than you're in at the moment,' Harry shouted back, nonetheless coming to an abrupt halt and stopping Beth with his hand. 'Killing a policeman, Mr Burman. Think about it before you do anything stupid.'

'I'm done for anyway if you lot get me. Now back off – I mean it.'

He was facing them full on, the gun steady in his hand. He didn't see Geoff Peterson and the other man creeping up on him from behind.

'Okay, okay, look … We'll raise our hands slowly. We're not armed.'

After that, it all seemed to happen in slow motion as the two policemen jumped Tim Burman and his gun went off simultaneously. He crashed to the ground, but not before Harry felt the lurch to his stomach as the bullet found its target. He drew in a shocked breath, doubling over, aware of Beth rushing to support him.

'*Harry.*'

'I hope I've killed the bastard!' Tim Burman yelled, as he struggled with his captors on the ground. 'Get me a solicitor.'

Harry looked up at Beth, then shook his head, his expression stunned as he drew a deep breath and then exhaled slowly.

'Shit, I've worn that vest on countless occasions, but that's the first time I've ever had to test it out. I feel like I've been hit in the stomach with a cricket bat.' A relieved grin formed on his face as he straightened slowly up. 'Good to know it works, though.'

He took another couple of breaths, before straightening up and looking over to where Tim Burman was struggling uselessly to prevent the handcuffs being snapped onto his wrists.

'Where are Kirsty Cartwright and Luke Talbot?'

'Never heard of them.'

'Don't give me that. We know Kirsty went to Simon's flat tonight and that you took her upstairs while you waited for him to return. He's been quite chatty, has our Mr Jordan. It would look a lot better for you in court if you volunteered information at this point, rather than be seen as obstructing the course of justice.'

'I don't know what you're talking about and I'm not saying another word until I see my solicitor.'

'If anything happens to them and we find out you're

involved, you realise it'll make things a hundred times worse for you?'

'I'm quaking in my boots.'

'Take him back to the station,' Harry ordered, striding back the way they'd come. 'I'll meet you back there after I've checked the warehouse out.'

'I want my solicitor!' Tim Burman shouted after him.

'Yeah, yeah. You'll get him, don't worry. Just put in the request when they bang you up.'

'Found anything?' he asked one of the uniform, walking into the lock-up and looking round.'

'Nothing much. Looks like it's used as some sort of dormitory – look at all the beds dotted around the walls.'

'That's exactly what it *is* used for. This is where they bring the illegals when they come up from Dover before dispersing them. It's going to be a mammoth job getting to the bottom of all this.'

'Will Interpol get involved?'

There was a light in the young policeman's eye that reminded Harry of himself as a rookie.

'Probably … the works, I reckon.'

He turned to Beth. 'We need this whole warehouse sealed off and Forensics down here asap. I want it gone through with a toothcomb for any evidence that Kirsty or Luke were here. Can you see to that?'

She nodded, already pulling her notebook out to make a list of all the people she'd need to speak to.

'Also track down what other vehicles Tim Burman owns apart from the Merc. Simon Jordan mentioned a van but it wasn't at the flat and it's not here. We need to find it, fast. Meanwhile, I'm going back to the station to see what I can squeeze out of Tim Burman. Things don't look good for Kirsty and Luke Talbot if we can't break him.'

CHAPTER FORTY-ONE

'There … I've done it,' Luke's whispered exclamation was triumphant as Kirsty's ropes fell apart, freeing her hands. She rubbed them hard together, grimacing as the sudden increase in circulation resulted in painful pins and needles in her fingers.

'Do mine,' Luke said. 'Quickly.'

She started working on his knots. 'They're so tight.'

'Just keep at it. We've been going a while and if they *are* heading for the Great Woods, it won't be long before we get there.'

Even as he said it, they felt the van swing sharply to the left and the terrain beneath the wheels changed, becoming crunchy as if they were travelling on the stones of a car park.

'Hurry,' Luke said.

Her fingers were fumbling, not helped by the fact that they were stiff and unwieldy from being restrained themselves. She hadn't quite finished the job when half a minute later the van stopped and they heard the driver and passenger doors opening and closing.

'I can't do it,' Kirsty said desperately, pulling her hands

quickly away as the back of the van was flung open. Monty stood there, gun in hand pointing menacingly at them, Bulldog at his side.

'Out,' Bulldog growled.

Luke stared him out. 'So what are you going to do if we refuse?'

'Shoot you where you are, and pull you out myself. The choice is yours, mate.'

He grabbed hold of Kirsty and dragged her to the edge of the van. She felt his rough hand on her breast, deliberately manhandling her as he hauled her out.

'Get your hands off me.'

'What? … You telling me you don't like it a bit rough every now and then, sweetheart?' He gave a little snigger. 'All the ladies like a bit of rough once in a while – even the lah-di-dah ones like you.'

He fondled her some more, pulling her hard against him as he did so. It took every ounce of strength she possessed not to whip her freed hands round to lash out at him. But that was a secret she needed to keep to herself if she had any chance at all of surviving this night. And hope of that was fading fast.

'You deal with him,' Bulldog said to the other man, tightening his grip on Kirsty's arm as he dragged her towards some trees. 'I won't be long. I'm going to have myself a bit of fun before I do this one – teach her a lesson, stuck-up bitch.'

'*No! Luke!*'

Kirsty's scream was muffled by the hard clamp of a hand over her mouth as she was dragged across the car park through an opening in some bushes, and thrown heavily down onto the ground. The full weight of Bulldog's body followed instantly, pinning her to the cold, wet undergrowth as his hands captured her head, holding it still.

So intent was he on his purpose that he didn't seem to realise that her hands were free. Her fingers scrabbled desper-

ately through the twigs and leaves, searching for something –
anything – that could act as a weapon as she struggled beneath
him.

They curled around a large, jagged rock.

'See, bitch … not so sure of yourself now, are you?' he
taunted, his fingers grappling with her shirt buttons.

With all her might, she crashed the rock into the side of
his head.

'Aagh …'

He lurched sideways, the weight of his head collapsing onto
her shoulder. She could feel the warm trickle of his blood on
her neck … in her hair …

She needed to get him off her so she could help Luke.

She pushed as hard as she could, but already he seemed to
be recovering from the blow, groaning groggily as he pulled
himself upwards. A sudden crack in the night air stilled them
both. Kirsty had never heard the sound before but knew
straight away what it was. A gun.

'Luke!' she screamed.

She scrabbled desperately to free herself from Bulldog's
grasp until the crash of his fist into her face sent her head flying
backwards onto the ground.

'There ain't nothing you can do for him now, girl,' he spat.
'But you'll be joining him soon enough. Don't you worry.'

She wasn't unconscious, but all the fight seemed to go out
of her, as she lay there dazed.

Luke was dead. That was all she could think. Nothing else
mattered.

She could feel blood trickling into her mouth – the whole
side of her face was throbbing from where he'd hit her. As his
hands yanked at her clothing, it was as if all this was happening
to someone else. *She was too late. Luke was dead.*

And soon she would be, too.

It took the disgusting feel of his mouth, wet and slimy,

slobbering over hers again to kick her survival instincts back into action.

Maybe he thought she was unconscious? She didn't know, but he'd let go of her hands and now she was fighting back, lunging out to claw at his eyes and bring her knee up into his groin with all the force she could muster. She heard his roar of pain, felt him momentarily double over with the shock of it – but he was still on top of her and she couldn't shift him. She saw him raise his fist again and swung her head to one side, closing her eyes as she waited for the punch.

It never came.

She heard a thud and for the second time in the space of five minutes, his head crashed onto her shoulder.

Then, miraculously, he was being hauled off her and thrown to one side, and Luke was bending over her, pulling her into his arms cradling her as if he'd never let her go.

'Oh God, Kirsty, are you okay?'

'*Luke?*' She clutched at him in disbelief, unable to accept this really was his solid form she was clinging onto. '*You're alive.* But … the *gun.* I thought you were dead.'

'So did I,' he muttered into her hair. He held her tightly for a brief moment longer, then drew back and pulled her carefully to her feet.

'You okay?'

She nodded.

Dragging some rope from his pocket, he turned his attention to the unconscious form of the man on the ground.

'Luckily, our man in the van wasn't quite the heartless brute he made himself out to be when it came to it,' he said, yanking Bulldog's arms behind his back and knotting the rope tightly. 'He didn't like it that this bastard had dragged you off like that. And when the other chap took me off to deal with, he followed us. I was staring down the barrel of a gun, literally – just waiting for him to stop messing with me and pull the trigger. Then I heard the shot. It must have taken me a full five seconds to realise that the bullet had whizzed past my head, not through it – and that I was still standing and the man with the gun wasn't. The guy in the van had hit him from behind with a thick piece of branch. It caused the gun to go off but luckily it missed me. He knocked the guy out cold.'

'Jesus, Luke.'

'I know. He freed my hands, then called to his mates to get the hell out of there.'

Luke hesitated. 'I stopped him … gave him two hundred quid to get him to Leicester. I reckoned it was the least I could do.'

On the ground, Bulldog gave a groan.

The glow from the moon gave just enough light that they could make out his bulky form as he shifted on the ground.

'What did you hit him with?' Kirsty asked, eyeing him warily.

Luke picked up a thick stump of branch that was lying on the ground. 'This. It's the same one our mate used on the other guy–'

He broke off, the realisation that Monty was still out there hitting them both at the same time. Luke pulled something from his pocket and, to her horror, Kirsty realised it was a gun.

'Luke, no!'

'Ssh.'

She suddenly became aware of how cold and dark it was and how exposed they still were. What if the man had more than one gun? What if even now he was pointing it in their direction ready to …?

But as Luke cautiously started to retrace his steps, they heard the sound of an engine roaring into life and the screech of tyres as a vehicle sped swiftly and noisily out of the car park.

Luke turned back to her and released a sigh. 'Thank God

for that. I don't know about you, but I've definitely had enough excitement for one night.'

He dug his foot into Bulldog's ribs and rolled him over so they could see his face. 'As for you, you'd better start praying that you get a heavy prison sentence out of all this, because if you don't, I'll have you for what you tried to do to my–'

He broke off, suddenly turning to her in concern. 'You are okay? He didn't...?'

She shuddered. 'I'm fine.' She put her hand to the side of her head, realising that she'd got a hell of a headache from where he'd hit her.

'We need to get you looked at.' Luke said.

He reached into Bulldog's pocket and pulled out his phone.

'Don't mind if I borrow this to call the cops, do you?'

CHAPTER FORTY-TWO

'It's good you're taking a couple of days off, Harry – you look like you could do with it.'

DCI Murray observed the torment on the other man's face and glanced at the letter in his hand, before pushing it across the desk. 'And take this back. For the time being let's pretend I haven't seen it.'

'I'm sorry, sir, but I'm not going to change my mind.'

'Harry, I don't know what's triggered this, but believe me, we all have second thoughts in this job.'

'It's more than that.' Harry hesitated, but knew it was absolutely something he couldn't share.

'I can't tell you the full reasons, but let's just say I've had a personal conflict that I can't reconcile with staying in the force. I've given it a lot of thought and it's how I feel.'

Murray's shake of the head was dismissive, his voice exasperated. 'And you think you're alone in that? I'm not going to pry but you're good at your job and you've got a great career ahead of you. Don't throw it away. We need people like you.'

'I appreciate you saying that–'

'I'm saying it because it's true, man. Take the damn letter away and at least think on it some more.'

Harry hated his weakness for taking the letter back, even though he knew he wouldn't be changing his mind. He'd condoned an illegal action of the most serious kind, had even concealed the evidence and protected the perpetrator. There was no reconciling that.

'Now – how are you getting on with the Burman case?'

'He's finally talked. I think when he realised he was the only one that wasn't singing like a canary he gave up the ghost. He's admitted to being involved in the deaths of Dominic Cartwright and Paul Copeland, although he says it wasn't him who killed them. Flint and his sidekick were apparently responsible for that, although they're claiming they were only doing it under his orders, which seems more than likely. That also corroborates what Kirsty Cartwright and Luke Talbot said – that it was Tim Burman who was in charge and gave the orders. He's still refusing to tell us the names of the people on the other side of the Channel, though – and I don't think he ever will. I reckon he's too scared. They all seem to believe they'll be safer in jail than they would be out on the streets now.'

'With reason, I suspect. It's an ugly business and it's getting worse. Interpol reckon it's a huge ring we've strayed into, with very dangerous people at the head of it. It's already been taken out of our hands and I'm not sorry about that.'

'The really interesting one is Simon Jordan. We've tracked his phone records and they show he did speak to Dominic Cartwright the morning he was killed. Shortly after that he rang Tim Burman and then called Cartwright back, presumably to arrange to meet up with him at the pub. His story is that Cartwright never turned up – Burman saw to that – but he claims to have no knowledge that Burman was going to have him killed. I tend to believe him on that – and when he says he didn't realise what he was getting into with the people smuggling stuff. We can also definitely put his name to five sex crimes in this area over the last eighteen months. We found a man's blond wig and brown contact lenses in his Whetstone flat, which tie in with the witness descriptions and the CCTV we've got. The evidence on his computer is damning. I gave him one concession in return for his information – that we'd try to make sure he didn't end up in the same prison as Burman. He jumped at it.'

'Well, I can tell you we're top of the favourites list at HQ at the moment with regard the study they've been conducting – one of the lower areas of sex-related crimes, apparently, and we've cleared up a biggie to boot. Another reason why you'd be an idiot to leave. Your name's been noted. I wouldn't be surprised if there was a promotion in line for you after all this.'

Harry stood up. That piece of information would have wowed him a few days ago. Now it fell on stony ground.

'I'll do what you say and think about it while I'm off – but I can't see me changing my mind.'

'What about Paul Copeland's girlfriend? Has anyone filled her in?'

'Beth went round to see her. She's confirmed something else Simon Jordan admitted to. Apparently they paid her off to move out of the flat, under Burman's orders, in case she said too much about Paul trying to blackmail them. She was probably lucky to get away with her life, at the rate Tim Burman seems to dispose of people.'

'Lucky escape, then. Well, make the most of your time off – and think carefully about what you're going to do next.'

Outside in the open-plan office, Harry looked around for Beth. She was sitting at her computer.

'Guess what?' she said as he walked over to her. 'Remember that partial footprint they got near Copeland's body? It's a match to Arthur Flint's trainer – another piece of the puzzle sorted.'

'Great. Fancy a coffee before I go?'

'Yeah, sure. I'll get them from the machine.'

'No, let's go to Nero's or somewhere and grab an early lunch. My treat before I head off home.'

They were early enough that the coffee bar wasn't too crowded, and once they were seated Harry looked at Beth over his panini.

'I keep meaning to ask how things are going with your grandparents? When are you meeting the other members of your family?'

'We're meant to be meeting up in a couple of weeks' time, except I've just realised–' She broke off.

'What?'

Beth was silent for a moment, then she shrugged. 'I usually go home on the 29th of November and visit the crematorium. It's the day my boyfriend and Briony died.'

Harry's eyebrow moved up in surprise, but he was careful to keep his expression fairly neutral. He knew Beth well enough by now to proceed warily. 'You told me about your boyfriend, but … who was Briony?'

'She was my best friend.'

'God, I'm sorry. Do you want to talk about it, or would you rather not?'

Beth hesitated. Then she said quietly, 'I never really knew the full story. She suffered from depression and one day I think it all just got too much for her. She phoned me to say her life was a mess. She was standing on the edge of Berwick Cliffs. I knew I couldn't get to her quickly, but Andy was working in North Berwick so I rang him. They think the cliff crumbled and they both fell while he was trying to talk her down. I should never have called him. It's my fault he died.'

'Hey.' Harry's voice was soft. 'That was shit luck, but you

can't blame yourself. Anyone would have done the same in your shoes.'

'Would they?'

'Yes – and how do you think you'd have lived with yourself if you *hadn't* called him, knowing he was nearby and could maybe have saved her? The fact that the cliff gave way …' He shook his head. 'That was just rotten luck, and we more than most see how randomly death can strike in this job.'

She sighed. 'It was seven years ago, but Andy's still as much in my head now as he was back then. He turned my life around. Showed me there was another way to the stupid, petty criminal life I was leading, running errands for my druggy family. You look shocked, but that's what I was like as a teenager. It would only have been a question of time before I was picked up by the police and got myself a record. Andy was honest and decent. I felt like I'd been given another chance when I met him. We were only together less than two years but we both knew straight away it was right. Does that sound stupid?'

'No.'

'Have you ever felt that way about someone?'

'Nope. Never.'

'So maybe it's not that unusual that I've not been interested in another man since then? I was beginning to think there was something wrong with me.' She gave a half-smile.

'Sounds like he'd be a hard act to follow.'

'Yeah. Maybe.' She shrugged. 'Anyway, that's enough about me. Are you okay? About your gran, I mean? I haven't really had the chance to say I was sorry to hear that.'

'It was expected.'

'I know. But it's still a shock.'

'Yes.'

'When's the funeral?'

383

'My parents are firming it up today. End of next week, hopefully.'

'Does it feel weird, them coming in and taking over?'

Harry shrugged. 'Not really. She was Mum's mother, after all.'

In truth he felt relieved, more distanced from it all. As if he could somehow forget that someone had helped end her life and he'd been complicit in it.

'Yeah, but you're the one she loved.'

Harry thought about the will that had been unearthed last night and guessed that was true. She'd left him her house and fifty thousand pounds, and only a small legacy to his parents. His mother had been hurt, he knew, but she'd been philosophical about it.

'It doesn't really surprise me,' she'd said. 'You always were the apple of her eye. I know she was more of a mother to you than I ever was.'

Beth seemed to be watching the emotions that were flitting across his face. 'Sure you're alright?'

'Yeah.'

'You were lucky to have the relationship you had with your gran, you know – take that from someone who's never had that with any of her family. You were always there for her and she died knowing that. She couldn't have asked for more.'

A smile crossed Harry's face and with it came a sense of peace. She was right. He'd helped fulfil his grandmother's wishes in the end, even if he hadn't actually been the one to instigate them. And she'd be nothing but grateful to him for that. He could almost hear her saying it. *You did good, boy.*

He was glad he hadn't let her down.

He put his cup down and looked at Beth. 'Thanks,' he said. 'Now … before I head off on leave, there are a couple of things I could do with you finishing up on? I promised the Lazards that someone would go and see them – tell them formally that they're off the hook and fill them in. I've also made a note of a few things I'd like you to follow in my absence. We need to pull as much information on Burman's activities as we can for the Border Force & Immigration people. So if you can get a file together?'

'Sure thing.' Beth grinned. 'I can grab myself some kudos riding on the back of Golden Balls. You know that's what they're calling you at the moment?'

Harry shook his head and grimaced. 'Really? Ugh – that's crass.'

Just for a moment, he was tempted to confide in her. Tell her what he was considering and why. He felt he could trust her, that she wouldn't judge him if he told all. But he kept his counsel. What would he achieve? And it wouldn't be right putting that on her – dragging her into it by association. This was a decision that he and he alone needed to make – arguably the biggest decision of his life. No one else could do it for him.

He looked at his watch.

'You know what? Maybe I'll come with you to see the Lazards – we could do it now. If you take your own car we can head off in opposite directions afterwards.'

It was just a delaying tactic. He was meeting up with Claire this afternoon. She'd phoned him three times over the last couple of days since his grandmother had died and he hadn't picked up. Finally he'd texted her and they'd agreed to meet at her house. He still didn't know what he was going to say – he knew he couldn't stay silent. He had feelings for Claire. He hoped – if it *had* been her – that she could convince him that what she'd done was justifiable … right even. But he couldn't see it. And how could he even think about entering a relationship that was starting off on a footing like that? It bothered him that she'd left the pill bottles where he'd find them – why hadn't she just left them in the cupboard? Or taken them with her? Was it because she wanted him to know what she'd done, because she'd done it for him – or maybe to implicate him through his inactivity? If so, she'd taken a risk. Who was he to say he wouldn't have reported her? Wouldn't still report her?

He almost laughed out loud at that thought. Who was he kidding? That was never going to happen, and they both knew it.

That was why he had no choice but to resign.

When Harry and Beth arrived at the day centre, having called first to warn Ken Lazard they were coming, they were surprised to see not only Ken, but his wife and both the Wilkins there as well.

'It sort of affects us all,' Ken offered by way of explanation as he spread out the chairs in his office.

'Well ...' Harry looked around at the assembled group. 'There's not a lot to report, except to say that you guys have been eliminated from our enquiries now. We've caught the people who killed Paul Copeland and his murder was part of a much bigger chain of events that I'm afraid I can't comment on at the moment. I'm sure you'll follow the story in the papers as it unravels.'

'You can bet on that,' Ken said with a relieved grin. 'I knew I hadn't done it, of course, but it's not a position I ever want to be in again, being under suspicion like that.'

'We can really forget about it all, now?' Maggie looked at Harry and he nodded. Tears welled in her eyes. 'It was a worry. I don't know how me and the kids would've managed if Ken had been arrested.'

'I'm sorry we had to put you through it.'

Harry stood up to take his leave and Beth followed suit.

'What about the other matter?' Kath Wilkins suddenly said. 'You know Gary Lytton?'

Her anxiety was palpable, despite her effort to conceal it

and Harry's eyes traced the small group. There was no doubt from what they'd uncovered that Gary Lytton had it coming from someone, but if there *had* been a plan afoot that day to do him in, he found it hard to believe that the Lazards or Wilkins were the instigators.

'As far as I'm aware that case will remain closed,' he said. 'It's not relevant to our investigation any longer and we didn't unearth anything new, so I doubt the Met will reopen it.'

He looked from one to the other – Ken with a protective hand on Maggie's shoulder, Kath sitting next to her husband in his wheelchair, her hand resting lightly on his knee – and noted the relief in their eyes.

There was no doubting the love and commitment displayed in this room – despite the fact that Ken and Kath were sleeping with each other. Did Maggie and Phil suspect anything? It wouldn't have surprised him if they did. Maybe they had their own private conversations … and maybe they'd decided it was easier keeping things 'in the family' – rather than risking their partners seeking consolation outside.

The complicated lives we lead, he thought, as he and Beth took their leave.

CHAPTER FORTY-THREE

'Oh darling, your poor face, but at least the bruising's coming out now.'

Kirsty looked in the hall mirror at her mauve cheek and blackening eye, adding to the miscellany of scratches and bruises she already had, and was just glad it wasn't any worse. She'd been kept under observation in hospital for twenty-four hours once the police and ambulance had arrived, but although she felt like she'd been used as a punchbag, she'd been assured that no permanent damage had been done and there were no broken bones.

She grimaced at her mother. 'Not a pretty sight, is it?'

'Well, I'm certainly not going to grumble about it when I think how you could have ended up. I feel sick at the thought. When Robbie rang to say you'd gone missing …'

'Don't go there, Mum. I'm trying not to think about it.'

But it was proving harder than she could have imagined. She prided herself on being tough – accepting that shit happened and you got on with it. It shook her to realise how nearly being killed had significantly derailed her.

'Did you and Robbie settle things last night?' Her mother's voice was hesitant.

'Sort of.'

'He didn't look very happy when he left. I wish you'd stayed up a bit longer and told me what was going on.'

Kirsty sighed. 'I'm sorry. I was knackered and just wanted to get to bed.' She hesitated. 'I told him we need to change the way things are done even if it means the business doesn't make so much money. There's a fine line between legal and illegal, and he and Dad overstepped it. They're lucky so far that our reputation hasn't been ruined as a result, but we can't carry on like that. It could make things awkward for you with Tony and Margot – though that's probably the least of their worries at the moment with all this stuff that's coming out about Simon.'

'Oh dear. I just can't believe that Simon could do those things…'

Kirsty kept her mouth firmly shut, realising that she could believe it only too well – and it put a completely different slant on what had happened all those years ago.

She hadn't filled her mother in on what he'd done to her – the videos and everything – but she would. It was all going to come out anyway. She thought back to her younger self – possessed by raging hormones and an all-consuming crush on her elder brother's friend. What had started out as a harmless, alcohol-fuelled, tentative flirtation, had suddenly turned into a situation she couldn't control, and she'd been shocked and frightened by the unleashed passion of Simon's response. She'd finally managed to stop him, but only after her desperate insistence that it was illegal for her to have sex. He hadn't liked it, and it had revealed a side to his personality that had cured her crush overnight. It was why she'd found it so utterly incomprehensible that she could have slept with him.

'Mum, don't think about that now, though I'm sure Tony and Margot will need you as much as you need them over the next few months. But you must realise that the business has to change. God knows what will come out in all this, but I don't want to spend the rest of my life looking over my shoulder because I'm worried about being investigated. I think all this business has shaken Rob. Now's the best time to get him onside.'

'I never really understood it all – you know your father, he never talked business with me. But I suppose you're right.'

'I know I am.' Kirsty grabbed her jacket off the banister. 'Just make sure you stick up for me if Rob starts having a go.'

'I'm the last one he's likely to talk to at the moment. He's still not happy about me having Dan here that day.'

'Give him some space. I know Dan's a friend, but maybe don't overmention him at the moment? Rob will come round in his own time.'

'Before you go … I saw the solicitor yesterday about Dad's will.'

'Oh?'

'I don't understand why, but he's left £125,000 to Anne. Why would he do that? You don't think…?'

Kirsty's jaw dropped. *He'd done the right thing … in the end, he'd done the right thing.* A smile spread slowly across her face. Looking at her mother's expression, though, she was quick to realise that Sylvia was suspecting a far less charitable reason for his actions.

'Mum, if you're about to suggest that there was something going on between Dad and Aunty Anne? Don't be ridiculous. Of course there wasn't.'

'Well, why else would he do it?'

Kirsty hesitated. Did her mother need to know the extent of her husband's dishonesty? On the other hand, there'd been far too many deceptions and untruths and her mother wasn't that naive. Better to start with a clean slate, and better that she heard it from the daughter who'd loved him.

'Because it's money he owed her. He got more for Grandma's land than he told us – it's the reason we argued. Obviously when he got to thinking about it, he felt guilty and decided to put things right – and I'm glad he did. Anne doesn't need to know that, though, does she? She'll just think he's being kind.'

Her mother shook her head. 'I sometimes feel I didn't know your father at all. He was such a complex man.'

Kirsty sighed. 'Yes he was – but I feel I've sort of come to terms with that now. He was also the best dad I could have had. That's how I'm going to remember him.'

She looked at her watch. 'I'd better be off, or I'll be late.'

'Where are you going?'

'Round to Luke's. He's got the morning off because he's seeing the police again later.'

'Ah.'

Her mother still looked anxious but she managed a drawn smile at that piece of news. 'Are you and he back on then?'

Kirsty's mind flew back to that moment two nights ago, when Luke had saved her from Bulldog, his words indelibly imprinted on her brain. *I'll have you for what you tried to do to my...*

Had he been going to say *fiancée*? Or even *girlfriend*? Was there a small chink of hope there?

'I don't know,' she said. 'We've got some talking to do. I'm not sure how it'll go.'

Outside his flat, she took a deep, steadying breath – it might not be the fresh, clean air of the countryside that was swishing its way through her system, but it was good enough for her. It grounded her, made her appreciate how good it was to be alive, even if she was breathing in toxic traffic fumes. A man belted past her, out of breath as he ran for the bus, cursing when it drew away before he got there; across the road a small child wailed incessantly as its mother pushed it along in its buggy. Small things that made up her normality. And she clung to them as she rang the doorbell.

'How are you?' he asked, leading the way into his flat.

She followed him in and sank onto his settee. 'Exhausted. How about you?'

He sat down next to her. 'The same. I was at the police station for two hours yesterday going through everything, and I've a horrible feeling that they'll question me more deeply about the immigrants today, before I give my formal statement.'

'What will you say?'

'The truth. That nothing was revealed about who they were or where they came from, and that one of them saved my life.'

'At least he didn't kill the guy.'

'Thank God.'

'Will you tell them about him heading off to Leicester?'

There was only the slightest of hesitations. 'No.'

'I'm sorry to have involved you in this, Luke.'

'You were only doing what anyone would have done for their father.'

'That's generous of you.'

Luke smiled. 'Well, I admit, some people might not have been quite so proactive about it as you were, but I'd want you batting for me if ever I was in trouble, that's for sure. Your dad would be proud of you.'

Kirsty swallowed the lump in her throat, and changed the subject quickly. 'Sorry I didn't call last night like I said I would. I wasn't in a very good place.'

He looked at her keenly. 'You're okay, though?'

She nodded. 'Yes, but I think we need to talk.'

'You realise from what the police are saying that Simon drugged you that night?' He was looking at her intently.

'That's the one good piece of information to come out of all this. And it would explain so much as to why I didn't remember anything.'

'I'm sorry, Kirsty. For some of the things I said.'

'They were totally justified. At the time I agreed with you. I was disgusted with myself.'

He took hold of her hand. 'Is it too late for us?'

She looked at him searchingly. 'I don't know. What are you thinking?'

'I'm thinking you've been through the mill and I haven't been much use to you. But when that guy dragged you off and I thought I'd lost you–'

Kirsty nodded. 'I know – me, too. When I heard that shot...'

Luke's grip on her hand tightened. 'How about we give things another try? Take it slowly – see if we can find our way back?'

She nodded. 'I'd like that,' she said simply.

CHAPTER FORTY-FOUR

Outside Claire's flat, Harry sat in his car for several minutes. The house wasn't as big as his grandmother's and it was a semi rather than detached, but the rural setting knocked the socks off where he lived in Enfield and it gave him a sense of space in which to gather himself.

'Come about four,' she'd told him. 'I'm not due out again until six.'

He hadn't given any thought as to how he was going to start this conversation, but he couldn't put it off any longer. He climbed out of his car and walked down her front path.

Her face was unsmiling as she opened the door, and neither of them said much as she made a couple of coffees and took them through to the lounge.

Once they were seated, him in a chair, her on the settee, she looked at him.

'How are the arrangements coming on?'

'Fine. We should have the date fixed by this afternoon. Mum's waiting to hear back from the crematorium. You're welcome to come if you'd like to?'

'Thanks. I haven't spoken to you since it happened. Was … everything alright at the end? Like she wanted?'

Harry nodded.

'Good. I'm glad I saw her that evening. Even though she was so weak, we had a lovely chat. It's a nice memory to hold.'

Harry took a deep breath. 'There's something I need to ask you…'

God, this was impossible. 'Did she ask you again to … you know … with the tablets?'

There – he'd said it.

She blinked. 'I thought we'd agreed not to talk about that again? What's the point?'

'The point is because I think … maybe … someone helped her … gave her the tablets to take. And I don't know how I feel about that.'

'I see, and it wasn't you?'

'No!'

'Not that I'd want you to admit it anyway.'

When he just continued staring at her, comprehension dawned in her eyes. 'You think it was me?'

'I don't know what to think.' He was aware his handle was beginning to slip.

'I see. Have you told the police?'

'No.'

'Will you?'

'How can I when it was what she wanted? And then there'd be the whole performance of a post-mortem, and upset for my parents.'

'Is that why you've been avoiding my calls?'

He didn't answer.

She was staring at him hard. 'So regardless of whether I did it or not, I've been tried, judged and found guilty?'

'I'm asking you, Claire, if you did it. Because if you did, I don't know how I feel about that.'

'I'd have thought part of you might be feeling pretty relieved, knowing that was what she wanted. And if it wasn't me, you're taking quite a risk sharing this information. What's to stop me going to the authorities and reporting it?'

Anger. He could see the glitter of it in her eyes despite the fact she was trying to keep a tap on it.

'I don't think you'd do that.'

A pause before she emitted a long sigh. 'As it happens, in these circumstances you're right, I wouldn't.'

'So?'

She continued staring at him for a long moment, before saying, 'I thought maybe we had something going between us, you and I, and I totally understood where your grandma was coming from. If you'd asked me to help you, I might even have considered it. But do you honestly think I'd have taken it on myself to do something like that without telling you?'

He was a policeman. Normally he had a good line on whether someone was telling the truth or not, but he found with Claire he just couldn't be sure. His feelings were compromised. He needed to hear the words from her mouth.

'I guess the sad thing is we don't know each other well enough for me to answer that question. I need to hear you say whether you did it or not.'

'You're right, we don't know each other at all.' Her eyes were calculating. 'This could all be a double bluff on your part to try and shift the blame from you onto me. I've only got your word for it that you didn't do it.'

She saw his shocked expression and shook her head as she rose from her seat. The expression on her face was set. 'I think you should go, Harry. Now.'

'Claire–'

She turned away from him and walked into the hall. 'Don't say any more. There's no point. I look at you and I know I can trust you. I know you didn't do it, because if you had you'd admit it. But the difference is, you can't see that in me. You don't trust me in the same way. And do you know how that makes me feel?'

On the doorstep, Harry turned for one more try. 'Look–'

But she was already closing the door in his face.

And as he walked down the path, though he hated himself for thinking it, it struck him that she still hadn't actually denied it.

CHAPTER FORTY-FIVE

When Harry put his head around his mother's bedroom door, she was sitting on the bed staring vacantly into space. She was dressed in black with her hair tucked neatly under the little black hat she wore, and she looked as if her mind was a million miles away.

'Are you okay?' he asked.

She nodded but didn't look at him. 'Just thinking about Mum.'

'The car's going to be here in ten minutes. They just rang to confirm it.'

'They're late,' she said, frowning.

'It'll be fine, we allowed a fifteen-minute window if you remember?'

She looked up to where he was hovering in the doorway, as if reluctant to take the final steps that would place him firmly in the room.

'Come in and shut the door, will you? There's something I need to say. I'm worried about you and this decision you've made to hand in your notice.'

Harry suppressed a sigh, anticipating one of her homilies.

'Mum—'

'What will you do? It doesn't feel right, us going back to Egypt and you here unemployed. Gran made me promise I'd be more involved in your life. I feel I'm already letting her down.'

'When did she say that?' Harry smiled at the thought of his grandmother issuing her last instructions.

'The day she died. I told you we talked. I like to think we laid some stuff to rest.' She took a deep breath. 'And I think you and I need to do the same.'

'Mum—'

'I've been a rubbish mother and daughter. I don't need anyone to tell me that. I thought I had good reason at the time to choose your father over you. I wanted to save our marriage. Now I'm not so sure.'

Harry looked at her, shocked. He wasn't sure he wanted to hear any more. 'Don't put yourself through it, Mum. Whatever happened, it's history. You don't need to explain.'

'I do. I need you to understand why I made the choices I made. I was twenty-seven and you were two months old when your father had the affair.'

Harry stared at her stunned, but straight away that simple sentence made sense of so many things.

'Don't get me wrong,' she said quickly. 'Your father was very apologetic – ashamed of himself afterwards … but he said it was difficult going on digs, sometimes for months on end … with no female company. I didn't want to lose him. So I decided there and then that I'd accompany him everywhere.' She shrugged. 'It hasn't always been the best of decisions – but he knew he'd brought it on himself so he had no choice but to put up with it. It was easy at first – when you were little. We could take you with us. But then we had to make choices about your education – boarding school seemed the best option.'

'And it was.'

'I'm not so sure. I'm proud of you, Harry – of the man

you've become, but I've watched you grow up over the years and, apart from Gran, there's no one else you're really close to. No one else you let into your life. You keep everyone at arm's distance.'

'I've got good mates.'

He thought of Phil and James from school. They'd all been close back then. But could you still call yourselves good mates with people you only caught up with once or twice a year? He had more local friends – either through work or from the hockey club where he played when he got the chance. But he was forced to accept that maybe his mother had a point. He wasn't particularly close to any of them. But how could he be, with the unsociable hours and job that he did?

'And this decision of yours to resign – I just don't understand it. You love your job. It's all you ever wanted to do.'

'Circumstances change.'

'So what's changed for you?'

'I'd rather not talk about it.'

'You know, fifty thousand pounds may sound like a lot of money …'

'Mum. I'm quite aware that it's not going to support me for the rest of my life. I'll get another job.'

'Just like that? When you've put so much of your life into the one you've got?'

She stared at him searchingly, until finally her gaze dropped, and she said. 'It's because you know, isn't it?'

'Know what?'

She looked back up at him, and as he stared into her distraught eyes, his own widened in dawning comprehension, even as the words fell from her mouth.

'That I killed Mum.'

A stunned silence filled the room. Harry tried to absorb her words, but he was reeling with shock, and all he could think was: *Claire hadn't done it.*

He was aware of his mother still talking – the words, fuzzy and indecipherable, coming in a rush from a long way off as she unburdened herself. But he couldn't focus on what she was saying. It was unimportant compared to the bigger picture of him and Claire, and how this tipped their situation on its head. How was he ever going to unravel it all? It struck him that his mother had been wrong when she'd said he was so alone. Claire was someone he knew instinctively he could turn to … talk to. At least, she *had* been.

'Harry? Did you hear what I just said? Say something, *please.*'

He dragged his attention back to his mother, conscious of the muscles working in his jaw as he spoke.

'Some of it. I'm sorry. I … It's come as a shock. I don't know what to say.'

'She was obsessed with ending things herself. You know she was. At first I wouldn't even listen. But then she told me she'd asked you … and that she knew if I didn't do it, you would. I couldn't let her put something like that on you. She was my mother, and if anyone was going to make that decision for her it had to be me.'

She was looking at him with the closest thing to tenderness he'd ever seen in her eyes. They were swimming with tears, begging his understanding. Then she dropped her head in her hands and began to sob quietly.

He moved over to the bed, sat down next to her and put his arm around her shoulder. It triggered an unexpected memory from long ago – his first day at boarding school, when at eight years old, despite his resolve to be strong, he'd crumbled at the last minute and clung to her tightly, not wanting to let go. And it hadn't been her who'd broken that embrace.

He savoured the memory, holding it in his mind.

After a minute or so, she wiped her eyes with a tissue. 'It was awful, Harry – even though I knew I was doing what she wanted. And you realised, didn't you? I've seen the anguish it's caused you. You're a policeman. I looked it up on the internet – it's still illegal to assist a person to die and you can't condone that sort of thing. So you have to either report me or resign. That's how you see it, isn't it? That's why you've handed in your notice.'

This last was said in such a low voice that it was difficult to catch the words.

Harry's arm tightened around her shoulder. 'No, I didn't know, Mum. But Gran was right. I was considering doing it.'

He took a breath. 'And I'm as guilty as you are. I knew someone had given her the pills. I saw the empty bottles when I went up to read to her. But I didn't do anything about it. Didn't call you, didn't call the hospital. Just carried on reading until she slipped away.'

His mother's grip on his hand tightened. 'You were with her when she died? You never said that.'

'I was called out late that night if you remember? Everyone assumed I'd been in bed. When I got in next morning, you'd already found her and the doctor had been and signed the death certificate. It was simpler not to say anything.'

'Oh, Harry, I'm so glad you were there. I couldn't bring myself to go back in after I'd done it. I was frightened of what I might find. I knew if I'd found her struggling I'd have had to call an ambulance. What are we going to do?'

'Nothing. I believe I made the right call in not interfering, but you're right – it's why I'm resigning. But because of *my* actions, not yours. As you said, it's still a crime to help someone to die and if I can bend the rules once…'

They were both silent for a while, before his mother blew her nose, straightened her back and looked at him.

'I'm sure a lot more rules than that get bent. And you did it coming from a place of compassion, not evil. We need that compassion in our police force. No one wants to deal with a rigid, red-tape bureaucrat.'

Harry half-smiled. 'I'd like to carry on as if nothing's happened but I just don't think I can. My boss once said to me that everyone in the job has dilemmas to reconcile at one time or another, but the fact of the matter is, I've broken the very law I'm charged with upholding.'

'And you think no one else in your department's done things they shouldn't?'

'They're not me,' Harry said simply. 'I've got to do what I think is right.'

The sound of the doorbell interrupted their conversation.

'The car,' Harry said unnecessarily. 'I'm glad we've had this talk, Mum. But now we pretend it's never happened.'

He stood up and offered her his arm.

'Ready?'

CHAPTER FORTY-SIX

The pub wasn't one Harry had been to before and wouldn't have been his normal choice of venue. It was large and noisy, making him feel more tense than he already felt. He suspected that DCI Murray wasn't a frequent visitor here either – which was probably why he'd chosen it. He looked up now as Murray wove his way back towards him with their drinks. He felt sick with apprehension. He could guess why Murray had requested this meeting prior to him resuming work on Monday, and he knew there was going to be a clash. His boss was no pushover and didn't give up lightly when he set his mind to something. Could he tell him the truth about what he'd done?

Probably … he somehow doubted Murray would report him – could even believe he'd understand. But he knew he wouldn't do it.

'This won't take long,' Murray said, placing a beer in front of Harry and settling himself down in the chair opposite him. 'I'm sure we've both got better things to do on a Saturday morning.'

He reached into his pocket and pulled out the white envelope, slapping it firmly down on the table.

'I'm fed up with seeing this bloody thing reappearing on my desk. But I want one more chance to talk you out of it before I pass it on. What on earth can you have done, Harry, that's so serious you feel the need to hand your notice in?'

Harry shook his head. 'I can't give you my reasons, sir.'

'*Won't*, you mean?' He scrutinised Harry with those sharp eyes, until Harry shifted uncomfortably in his seat. It made him realise how a suspect must feel when Murray got his teeth into him during an interrogation. Then he gave a loud sniff and exhaled deeply before saying in an exasperated tone, 'Harry, we've all done things in this job – and outside of it – that may have crossed a line or two. For God's sake, it's a fine line sometimes and *easy* to cross. And it's inevitable that sometimes we'll get it wrong. But I'll tell you something. Those are the things that make you a better cop if you choose to learn from them, rather than let them drag you down. I don't know what lies behind your decision to quit but I do know you're one of the best men I've got on my team and I don't want to lose you. You told me that time you got involved with a woman in the case we were working on, and I figure this time if you're not telling me, there must be a good reason. But Christ, man, do you think you're the only one ever to be in this position? I've made mistakes – dozens of 'em. Done things I shouldn't have because at the time they seemed like the right answer. But I haven't thrown the towel in – and you know why? Because I know at heart I'm a good cop – I believe in the job I do. It's the day I lose that, that I'll hand my badge in – and not a day earlier. It should be the same for you.'

Harry hesitated. 'But what if you'd been a party to something illegal?'

'Parking on double yellow lines is illegal and we've all done that. You use your judgment. Only you can know if what you've done compromises the work you do – the *bloody good* work you do. And knowing you the way I do, I'd be gobsmacked – to use your generation's terminology – if that was the case.'

He downed his drink, pushed the envelope irritably at Harry and stood up to go. 'I'm getting as sick of this yo-yo lark as you are. But I'm asking you just one more time to reconsider. Be a realist when you make your decision. Does what you did really outweigh all the good you can do in the future? Think about it over the weekend. We've got an interesting case just come in to get stuck into – but if that letter finds its way back on my desk again, I'll do what you want and pass the bloody thing on.'

Harry watched him go, despising himself for his own indecision. He'd made up his mind, hadn't he? Was already turning his thoughts to what he could do next. But the truth of the matter was he hated the thought of doing anything else. He loved his job, harrowing though it could be, and the thought of being a private detective or security officer – or God forbid, a bodyguard of some sort? It held about as much appeal as a cup of sour milk.

He tapped his heel repeatedly on and off the floor – *knee jigging* his grandmother used to call it. He needed to talk to someone. But his mother's words came back as if to taunt him. *No one you're really close to.*

With the possible exception of Claire – had their relationship progressed – and he'd cocked that up good and proper. After his conversation with his mother he'd hoped to catch her at the funeral last week to clear the air – and she'd been there, sitting near the back. But she'd avoided his gaze and as soon as the service was over she'd scurried away. He should have made a point of going to see her as soon as he'd found out the truth. Why the hell hadn't he?

He suspected he knew the answer to that. Even though

they hadn't known each other long, there was something about Claire that set her apart from any other woman he'd dated – and it held him back. His history with relationships wasn't great, but he knew instinctively that she wouldn't put up with any crap from him. If by some miracle they resolved things and got involved, she'd expect more than he was capable of giving.

But he'd thrown one of the worst possible accusations at her, and at the very least he owed her an apology. The cowardly temptation to do it by text was instantly dismissed. It needed to be done in person. If she slammed the door in his face, so be it, but the longer he left it, the more difficult it was going to be.

He felt physically sick as he stood on her doorstep an hour later, and he put it down to the lack of sleep he'd experienced this last week. He braced himself as he heard footsteps.

She looked surprised, then wary, as she half-opened her front door to him. She was wearing a grey, figure-hugging dress with grey tights and a wide, black belt, polished off with low-heeled black shoes. He'd only ever seen her in jeans or work clothes. She looked great.

'Harry!'

'I need to speak to you. Can I come in for a minute?'

She didn't budge. 'What about?'

'I want to apologise.'

He held her gaze steadily. Now he could see her more closely, he could see the strain in her eyes. Her expression was cool as she opened the door wider and stood aside to let him enter.

In the lounge he turned to her. 'Thanks for coming to the service.'

'I liked your gran. I wanted to say goodbye.'

'You didn't hang around, though.'

'No.'

'Claire – I'm sorry. I was wrong to suspect you of …'

'Killing her?'

Christ, it sounded bald, put like that.

He shook his head. 'It was a terrible accusation to make – and a stupid one. I wasn't thinking straight. I knew I hadn't done it and I couldn't think who else might have.'

'Apart from me, apparently?'

'You were the only one I'd talked to about it. I thought … maybe you'd done it for me.'

'That's rather flattering yourself, isn't it?'

His lips twisted. 'Probably.'

'But now you know I didn't do it?'

He nodded.

'Are you going to tell me who did?'

'I don't think so. Do you want me to?'

She sighed, then said a little less heatedly, 'No – probably best that I don't know.'

'I'm really sorry, Claire. I made a complete mess of that conversation with you. I wasn't accusing you–'

'It sounded like it.'

'I was just trying to get at the truth.'

The silence between them stretched. He took a breath, running his hand through his hair. He wanted to get through to her, pierce that defensive skin, but he just didn't know how. Every instinct warned him against drawing her into his arms and just holding her, even though he was vaguely aware it was the one thing he wanted to do.

In the end it was her who spoke, a deft change of subject to possibly give them both a breather. 'I saw you did well on that murder case – it's so weird to think that sort of stuff is going on all around us and we have no idea.'

'It's an ugly business, and growing.'

'I don't get how these people aren't picked up coming through Customs?'

Harry shrugged, grateful to be on safer ground. 'It can be a combination of things. Sometimes it's as simple as bribing a bent Customs official to turn a blind eye, or sometimes, as with these guys, they had a false partition in the rear of the van that enabled them to sandwich several people between there and the front. Then they packed the van full of furniture, so even if they were searched it was unlikely they'd have been discovered. It must have been horrendous being squashed into such a tiny space for so long but it's amazing what people will endure when they're desperate.'

Claire shuddered. 'I can't bear to think about it. Talk about claustrophobic – I remember reading about those refugees who died of suffocation in a lorry last year. It was horrific. I don't know how you do your job seeing some of the things you must see.'

'Actually, I'm thinking of resigning.'

The words were out before he was aware he'd spoken them. She stared at him as if he'd suddenly grown three heads.

'What? Why?'

He didn't answer and it took only a few moments for her brow to clear. 'Is it because of this business over your grandmother?'

He shrugged.

Claire shook her head but he knew she got it, from the way she was looking at him. It didn't surprise him that she did – she was emotionally intelligent in a way that few other women he'd gone out with were. And now it was probably too late to explore that.

'It's your decision, Harry, but if you want my opinion – which you probably don't – I think you'd be crazy to jack your job in over that. You didn't give her the pills – all you did was fulfil her wishes and let her die peacefully with you at her side. If it was me, I'd be taking comfort from that.'

'I'm a policeman and I was complicit.'

410

'You're a man and a grandson, too! You have feelings and you loved your gran. She was a hundred percent compos mentis and knew what she wanted. I think you should accept that and move on from it.'

He felt an internal caving in of his muscles. He didn't feel exonerated exactly, but for the first time since his grandmother's death he felt more accepting of the situation.

More thinking to do.

'So, how are things with you?' he asked.

She made herself busy, tidying some magazines on the coffee table. 'Good, thanks.'

The reserve was back, keeping him at arm's length.

'I've missed you.' He felt a slight tautening of those stomach muscles again, realising that if he pursued this conversation and she was receptive, it was a commitment of sorts.

'Have you?' She gave him a considering look and he wished he could read what was going on in her mind. 'That's good to know, but … how long have you known it wasn't me who gave your gran the tablets?'

Oh crap. He could see where this was going and there was no heading it off.

'The day of the funeral,' he said.

'So you've left it a week before coming to see me?'

'Things have been manic. I should have come sooner, I know.' Even he could hear how lame it sounded.

'Like as soon as you found out would have been nice.'

'I was hoping to catch you after the service but you dashed off.'

'What else was I going to do?' Her voice was indignant. 'You'd more or less accused me of murdering your grandmother! I was half-expecting to be removed from the crematorium and arrested. I certainly wasn't going to hang around afterwards.'

She was pissed off with him, and no wonder. It would have

taken nerve to come to the service thinking that. He was sure he'd blown it, but something spurred him on not to give up. 'Look, I know I've handled things badly but … can't we try to unravel things?'

'I'm not sure we can, Harry.'

'I don't blame you for thinking I'm a dick.'

'Quite a few names come to mind, actually, but that's not one of them.'

The look she gave him only confirmed what he already knew – that she wasn't someone to be messed with lightly. He could almost feel her weighing him up, trying to decide whether there was any mileage left in their relationship. He wanted to reassure her, convince her that there was, but the words wouldn't form.

'What do you mean when you say unravel things?' she asked him.

It felt as if she'd thrown him a lifeline and he grabbed it. 'Try to forget the massive cock-up I made and get to know each other better?'

'I'm still not sure what you're saying, Harry. Are you suggesting we start seeing each other?'

He hesitated. *Was* that what he was saying? Why did it always come back to the same old, pathetic problem – his reluctance to tie himself down?

She was gauging his reaction, a sad smile forming on her face. 'You don't need to answer that. I can see from your expression that something's holding you back – and that says it all, doesn't it? It sounds selfish, but I'm not sure you'd be able to give me what I need, Harry. I've been in a one-sided relationship before and I promised myself I wouldn't go there again.'

What the *hell* was the matter with him, he thought, that he couldn't bring himself to say the words that needed to be said? His grandmother would be calling him a fool right now, and she'd be right – he'd have only himself to blame if he let Claire slip through his fingers. That thought was enough to spur him on.

'I don't blame you for feeling like that and I won't bullshit you. I'm *not* good in relationships – and I doubt I'm going to change overnight. But that doesn't mean I can't try?'

She stared at him for what seemed like forever. He wondered if she could sense his desire to move things forward … and the inexplicable uncertainty that held him back. Or whether she was writing him off as a complete and utter tosser.

'What worries me most, Harry, is the lack of trust … that you could believe I'd do something like that off my own bat. Even when you left here, I could see you weren't convinced.'

And he hadn't been. No point pulling the policeman's card about it being second nature to be suspicious of everyone and everything – it wouldn't wash with her. He had nothing to say, so he said nothing.

'I need to think,' she said.

'Of course.' His short burst of optimism had dissipated like a flat balloon. Maybe too much water had gone under the bridge for them to come back from it. And yet … as he took his leave a few minutes later, her words of 'I'll call you,' ringing in his ears, he couldn't help clinging onto a little vestige of hope as he looked into her face. He saw the sadness, saw the regret, but saw also the other mix of feelings that were warring for supremacy. He reminded himself that good or bad, nothing lasted forever. This moment would pass, and maybe when it did, she'd be prepared to take a risk and give him a chance. Time would tell, and at least, hopefully, they both had plenty of that.

When he got to the gate, he turned. She was still there, raising her hand in a half-salute before closing the front door. It was enough for now.

On that slightly more optimistic note, he found himself

plucking his mobile from his pocket and dialling Murray's number.

'So what's this case you were talking about?' he said, picking up pace as he headed for his car. 'I've got some time on my hands this weekend if you want a fresh pair of eyes?'

THE END

If you enjoyed my book, I'd love it if you'd pop over to Amazon and leave a Review. Reviews are so helpful to authors.

My first book in the series, Cry From The Grave, also featured Harry Briscombe but it's a stand-alone story that can easily be read out of sequence. For a little Teaser, just flip to the next page! You can get it for FREE by signing up to my website below or you can buy on Amazon.

Alternatively, if you're into a bit of Romantic Suspense, my new novel Shadow Watcher has also just been released

If you'd like to contact me about any of my books, I'd love to hear from you, so do come and say 'Hello' on Facebook or Twitter, or you can email me direct. All details given below:

In the meantime, Happy Reading!

http://www.twitter.com/carolynmahony

http: www.facebook.com/carolyn.mahony.3

Email: carolyn@carolynmahony.com

Website: www.carolynmahony.com

CRY FROM THE GRAVE

The bright sunlight glistening through the leafy avenue gave promise of a beautiful day, but even though the warmth brushed her skin, Hannah Walker shivered as she walked up the path to her front door. She remembered the first time she'd walked up this path with Ben, full of excitement at the prospect of moving in with him. Was it really only seven months ago?

She opened the front door and pushed the pram over the threshold, her eyes skimming the pristine, luxuriously furnished flat conversion. It did nothing for her now; but then why should it? She'd had no input into the décor. Ben had chosen it all. Her glance fell on the telephone sitting on the hall table. One phone call - that was all it would take…

Hardly aware of what she was doing, she started to walk towards it.

'Is that you Hannah?'

She stopped in her tracks.

'Leave her out in the garden, the fresh air will do her good,' Ben said, coming into the hall and eyeing her steadily.

'Then you and I can make-up before I leave for my appointment.'

Was he serious? Hannah lifted her hand unconsciously to where clever makeup hid the bruise on her cheek – but she wasn't about to antagonise him further.

'It's okay,' she said, avoiding his gaze as she parked the pram in the hallway. 'She's due a feed soon.'

'I said put her outside - she'll be fine in the back. You and I need to talk and I don't want her interrupting things.'

He was testing her, showing her who was boss, and after their argument earlier she knew better than to aggravate him further. She despised herself as she backed wordlessly out of the flat and did as he said.

You're a coward, Hannah Walker, why don't you stand up to him?

She parked the pram beneath the apple tree and leaned in to kiss Sophie on the cheek, breathing in the soft warmth of peachy skin, the familiar sweet baby scent that never failed to soothe her.

'You have a nice little snooze out here,' she murmured, smiling at the droopy blue eyes, battling to stay open. 'Mummy will come and get you very soon.'

She retraced her steps slowly. She didn't want to make up. He'd gone too far this time.

Inside the flat Ben was standing by the lounge window staring at Sophie through the glass. He turned as Hannah came in and walked towards her. Without saying a word, he lifted his hand to her cheek and traced the bruise lightly with his thumb. 'I'm sorry for this, babe,' he said finally, his expressive blue eyes contrite. 'I didn't mean to hurt you. But I've got a lot on my plate at the moment and you did push me.'

She kept her own face expressionless as she tried to ease out of his hold, but his hands dropped to her shoulders, drawing her resisting body tighter into his arms. 'Let's go and make up,' he whispered, nuzzling her neck. 'It's all this lack of sex, it's getting to me.'

He began to edge her clumsily into the hall. She could feel his arousal and shrank from it.

'The doctor said I should give things time to heal,' she said quickly, 'I don't feel ready yet.'

'You'll be fine. Come on, I'll be careful.'

His grip tightened as he backed her into the bedroom and her panic rose.

'No, Ben, I don't want to.'

She managed to shove him off, something snapping as she faced him. 'I can't just forget what you did, even if you can. There was no excuse for it.'

'So, what…?' His expression was ugly. 'You're going to punish me now by withholding sex? Is that what this is all about Hannah? Well, like hell you will …'

Afterwards, she kept her eyes closed, imagining herself a million miles away. She wouldn't look at him. Wouldn't give him the satisfaction of knowing he'd hurt her.

'You're about as responsive as a bloody marble statue,' he grumbled, throwing off the bed sheets and getting up. 'I'd get more enjoyment from a blow-up doll.'

She didn't answer.

'Don't ignore me, Hannah.'

She opened her eyes. 'It hurts me,' she said coldly. 'You know what the doctor said …'

'Oh, spare me all that six weeks bullshit. Dave and Laura were back in business after a fortnight. You just don't want me touching you. Admit it. Well don't blame me if I do what your father did and start looking around!'

He picked up his clothes and stalked off to the bathroom, leaving Hannah staring bleakly after him.

After a while, she rose and went into the lounge to check

on Sophie through the window. She looked so peaceful and innocent sleeping there in her pram. It soothed Hannah's heart just looking at her.

She moved back into the bedroom and sat on the bed, waiting for Ben to finish in the shower. Across the room the mirror on the dresser wasn't kind to her. She stared hard at her reflection, comparing it to the smiling photo on the wall. She looked a mess. Her blond hair hung lankly around her shoulders and she had huge dark circles under her eyes. The slim figure she'd always taken for granted had been replaced by lumps and bumps that still hadn't diminished since giving birth. No wonder Ben had gone off her.

But there was more to it than that, she knew. Losing a bit of weight and glamming herself up wasn't going to make any difference. He was jealous of Sophie, resentful of the way she'd disrupted their life and come between them. It was becoming so obvious.

When he'd hit her that morning his anger had seemed to burst from nowhere, his hand lashing out before she'd even known what was happening.

'Don't defy me, Hannah. It's about time you realised who's running the show here - who's paying for the food on our table. I don't give a toss that she's only three weeks old. I need you at this client's dinner tonight - and my needs come first. Always. Is that clear?'

He'd hit her before but this was the first time he'd done it when he was sober. It was a shocking awakening - stripping away the pathetic excuses she'd previously clung to that he didn't know what he was doing until she couldn't deny the unpalatable truth any longer. She, who'd been so condemning of her own mother's weakness in taking her father back, was no better a judge of character herself.

Tears filled her eyes and she rubbed at them fiercely. She

was so tired; she didn't have the energy to cope with all this now.

But you need to cope with it, Hannah. You need to think of Sophie.

She looked up as Ben strode back into the room.

'So - I'll meet you at Green Park tube at seven-thirty,' he said, reaching for his tie and executing a perfect knot in the mirror.

Hannah's eyes met his reflection stormily. 'I don't know who you expect me to get to baby-sit at such short notice. Your mum's made it obvious that she's not interested and I haven't seen any of my friends in ages. I can't just randomly phone someone up and expect them to–'

'I'm not interested in how you do it. Just do it. Phone an agency if you have to.'

He picked up his jacket and eyed her coldly. 'You'd better be there or I'll be seriously pissed off, I'm warning you. I'll see you later.'

And he was gone, swinging away without a backward glance. The kitchen door slammed as he went out into the back garden, and she felt a slight easing of the tension in her stomach. Across the hall and through the lounge window she could see him stopping to bend over the pram. Not a single hair on his gleaming blond head was out of place and his lean face, still tanned from his recent business trip to Cannes, was eye-catchingly perfect. He looked every inch what he was – the suave, up and coming City stockbroker.

She looked at him in his impeccably cut Armani suit and realised how easily she'd been duped; how cleverly his outward perfection concealed the imperfections that lay beneath.

'That's fantastic Han,' he'd said when she'd broken down in shock and told him she was pregnant. 'No more talk about gap years with your friends after uni now, eh? You'll be too busy bringing up our child. You'd better move in with me so I can make sure you're looked after properly.'

But being looked after properly had somehow turned into, '*where I can control you*', and as his job had got more sociable, so his drinking had increased, until she realised she'd become trapped in a nightmare of her own making.

But not any more she resolved, jumping up from the bed and turning away from the sight of him in the garden. This time he really had gone too far - and it wasn't just about her any more.

She crossed to the wardrobe, hauled out her jeans and a tee-shirt and headed for the bathroom. Her heart raced at the enormity of what she was about to do. It wouldn't be easy. She hadn't seen her mother since her father's death five months ago and their parting had been bitter. But she'd understand – wouldn't she?

She hesitated, her glance falling on the phone again. Should she call her mother? Explain?

She rejected the idea. Easier to do it face to face. However upset her mother was, she wouldn't throw her back out on the street.

Ten minutes later she was dressed and headed for the garden. A quick look round confirmed that Ben's car had gone. Now she'd made up her mind, she just wanted to be gone. She'd feed Sophie and leave - by the time Ben got back that evening there'd be nothing he could do about it.

Slipping the brake off the pram she leaned in.

'Come on poppet, time to...'

She broke off, staring blankly at the little dent in the mattress where her daughter should have been. Her heart jolted.

'Sophie?'

She jerked her head up and looked around. The sunny garden with its flowering spring bulbs looked pretty as a picture but there was no sign of her daughter anywhere. And the peaceful silence felt suddenly hostile.

'*Sophie!*'

Panic gripped her. She felt disorientated, remembering with a rush of relief seeing Ben leaning over the pram, before realising in the next breath that he had a meeting in London and would never have taken Sophie with him.

Where was she? Her mind was muddled. Had she already taken her in?

Think...

But it seemed the more she tried to remember, the more jumbled up her thoughts became.

She started to run back towards the flat.

No, no ... the road.

She changed direction, her feet flying over the short tufts of grass, her breath coming in suffocating gasps as she raced out through the back gate onto the pavement.

The long, leafy street was deserted.

'*Sophie...* '

The scent of baby lotion clawed at her senses, squeezing her heart.

'Are you all right, Hannah?'

It was her neighbour's voice, coming from a million miles away.

Hannah spun round. 'Sophie's gone. She's gone.'

'What do you mean...?'

But already Hannah was swinging away, choking on the sobs as she raced down the path into the quiet, deserted flat. She knew it was pointless, knew she hadn't brought her in but still she checked every room, flinging open each door before rushing back out into the sunshine to check the pram one final time.

And it was only as her blurred vision locked on the little indentation in the mattress – the only proof her daughter had ever been there – that she finally she gave vent to the scream lodged in her throat, the shrill sound echoing through the quiet neighbourhood as the full horror of what had happened washed over her.

Someone had taken her baby...

To be continued /...

Buy it today!

Amazon UK: http://amzn.to/1eNtrLb
Amazon USA: http://amzn.to/KywQ78

Or get the book for free by joining my mailing list at
www.carolynmahony.com

Made in the USA
Coppell, TX
12 April 2022

76417449R00249